J.F. MURRAY
HITCHED

Also by J. F. Murray

Fling
Hitched

J.F. MURRAY
HITCHED

MACMILLAN

First published 2024 by Macmillan
an imprint of Pan Macmillan
The Smithson, 6 Briset Street, London EC1M 5NR
EU representative: Macmillan Publishers Ireland Ltd, 1st Floor,
The Liffey Trust Centre, 117–126 Sheriff Street Upper,
Dublin 1, D01 YC43
Associated companies throughout the world
www.panmacmillan.com

ISBN 978-1-5290-9871-6 HB
ISBN 978-1-5290-9872-3 TPB

1 3 5 7 9 8 6 4 2

A CIP catalogue record for this book is available from the British Library.

Typeset in Sabon by Jouve (UK), Milton Keynes
Printed and bound by CPI Group (UK) Ltd, Croydon, CR0 4YY

Visit **www.panmacmillan.com** to read more about all our books
and to buy them. You will also find features, author interviews and
news of any author events, and you can sign up for e-newsletters
so that you're always first to hear about our new releases.

For the Swifties

Chapter 1

The Perfect Plan

Kate's wedding was going to be the happiest day of her life.

She had always known this in her heart and soul ever since she was a little girl. She had dreamed about it for as long as she could remember and, in less than a week, that dream would finally come true. She could see herself now, smiling in her immaculate white dress with her veil resting elegantly upon her wavy auburn hair as her fiancé, Norman, became her husband.

But even though she was a keen believer in manifestation, Kate knew it wasn't enough to just envision her perfect wedding. She was the designer of her own destiny, and there was only one way to ensure the fourth of July would be absolutely seamless.

Kate was a planner.

She planned everything. She lived for to-do lists, timetables, vision boards, calendars, itineraries, goal journals, sticky notes – the works. 'Fail to prepare, prepare to fail,' her mother, Margaret, had engrained in her mind from an early age. So it came as no surprise to others that Kate had spent two years methodically organizing her big day, ensuring that not a single thing could possibly go wrong. Everything was planned to a tee, from the wedding ceremony in Donnybrook Church of the Sacred Heart to the reception in Fitzpatrick Castle Hotel.

What did surprise people, however, was that Kate went one step further.

Because not only had Kate planned the perfect wedding, she had also planned the perfect hen party with her three best friends, Siobhan, Natalie and Chloe. She was fully aware that it was traditionally the maid of honour's job to plan such an occasion, but Kate couldn't help herself. Leave something so important in another person's hands? Not a chance.

Now, after months of meticulous preparation, the hen party was finally here. She looked down in excitement at the itinerary she held in her hands.

Kate's Bachelorette Party in Fabulous Las Vegas, Nevada, the cover read in a glittery font.

It looked more like a girly scrapbook than an itinerary, but within its sparkling pages, the ideal girl's trip was mapped out. It was colour-coded and time-tabled with activities for every hour of every day. She had scheduled the entire trip, right down to the minute.

Though it had been a big undertaking, Kate worked as an event planner for a living, so she knew what she was doing. She was the best in the business, frankly. If a client wanted to ensure zero hiccups for a particular event, they turned to Kate. Years of experience had made her an expert in crisis management, and she always had a contingency plan for anything that might go wrong.

But nothing ever went wrong under Kate's watch.

As she put the itinerary away in her handbag, however, Kate found herself plagued by that frustrating feeling one gets just before a trip. She was convinced she had forgotten to pack one last thing, but she couldn't put her finger on it. It was driving her mad.

'What the hell am I forgetting?' Kate said, thinking out loud.

'Hmm, let's see . . .' Norman said, standing in the doorway. 'How about your sanity?'

'Normie, please don't start again.'

'I just don't understand why you'd bother going halfway around the world for a hen party. Especially when the wedding is in less than a week!'

Kate sighed. Norman had been against the hen party from day one. He had chosen not to have a stag party, claiming he was 'above that kind of thing', but a hen party was a rite of passage Kate didn't want to miss out on. He was constantly worrying about her. She loved him for it but there was no need to catastrophize.

'Normie, me and the girls always said we'd go to the States for the first of our hens. And it's common in lots of countries for the bride to have her hen party the weekend before the wedding. Some even have it the night before,' Kate explained.

'I'm just afraid something will go wrong. Like one of you will lose a passport and get stuck or something, and the wedding will have to be post—'

'Normie,' Kate said, interrupting his panicking. 'Have you met me? I have every minute of the trip planned. You know I'm way too organized to lose a passport abroad.'

'It's not *you* that I'm worried about. It's the other three. They can be . . . messy,' Norman said.

'Normie, they're my best friends and I hardly ever see them. It hurts me when you judge them like that.'

'Well, I'm sorry you feel that way, Kate, but it hurts *me* when they drag you down to their level.'

'Well, we're all in our thirties now. None of us are going to go too crazy.'

'Promise me you won't get too drunk? You know how you can get. Last time you forgot the entire night!'

Norman was actually right about that. Kate was prone to

blackouts. She wasn't an alcoholic or anything – far from it. She was just a complete lightweight. The last time she had blacked out was at the Irish Dentistry Awards, where Norman had been nominated for Dental Surgeon of the Year. Kate had been so utterly bored that she started knocking them back to try and liven things up.

But, being the lightweight that she was, she had zero memory of the rest of the night. Apparently, she had gotten up on one of the tables and started singing karaoke, when there wasn't even a karaoke stand at the event. Her actions were so embarrassing that she was glad to have lost the memory. Norman had spent his whole life trying to win a 'dental plaque' and even though he had won that night, he always made her feel guilty for ruining his big moment.

In fact, he never missed an opportunity to bring it up.

'Good thing you never let me forget,' Kate sighed.

'Well, it's easy to forget who you are in Vegas.'

'I know who I am, Norman. And I know who I'm supposed to be. I promise Mrs Norman Cox-to-be will be on her best behaviour,' Kate smiled. 'I'll meet you downstairs – I need a minute to finish packing.'

'Okay, okay,' Norman said, throwing his hands in the air as he left the room.

Kate felt a deep sense of relief now that she was alone again. She had this bizarre crushing feeling in her chest as the wedding grew closer and closer. Whenever Norman was around her, she felt completely smothered. She loved him, but she needed some space to breathe. Kate had looked up how she was feeling on several wedding forums, and it was supposedly natural to feel a bit overwhelmed the week before your wedding. Thousands of women felt the same in the run-up to the big day.

It was perfectly normal.

The only thing that worried her was the fact that she still hadn't written her vows. Literally every other aspect of the wedding was planned to perfection, but whenever she sat down to write her vows, she went completely blank. If only vows could be written in a list format, then she would have them written in a heartbeat. It was stringing the bullet points into heartfelt sentences that she was struggling with.

Still, it was surely all part of pre-wedding jitters. She just needed to blow off some steam, and Vegas was the perfect place to do it. There was nothing she loved more than the idea of making new memories with her three best friends.

Memories.

That was what she was forgetting.

Kate had told the girls she would bring some old Polaroids of them from their summer J-1 in New York City nine years prior. The J-1 visa allowed foreign students to work in the United States for a summer and had become a staple of the college experience in Ireland. The girls had all spent a summer working on Times Square in an Irish pub called Scallywag's. It was how they all first met. The four of them started working together on the same day, and a lifelong bond was forged.

Kate still kept a memory box from her J-1 in her closet, and she had some hilarious Polaroids from that summer. One of the bachelorette games she had scheduled was recreating old photos of themselves, and then sticking them side by side in a scrapbook. It was the kind of thing Kate loved. The same photos but recreated exactly nine years apart. It was like something right out of a Taylor Swift song. She had been a die-hard Swiftie since day one, and *1989* had been the sound-track of her J-1, with the opening track 'Welcome to New York' capturing the vibe to perfection.

Kate headed into her walk-in closet and began to root around for her old memory box. After a few minutes of rummaging through junk, she eventually found a box with the label 'J-1 Summer – New York'. When she opened the lid, her brain was immediately flooded with a rush of nostalgia. The first thing she saw was her old work uniform from Scallywag's. She smelled the worn T-shirt and was immediately transported back in time. She could still smell the cheap hot dogs, burnt coffee and spilled alcohol on the fabric. She couldn't believe it had been nine years since she'd worn it. Where had the time gone? It literally felt like yesterday. Underneath the T-shirt, Kate found what she was looking for. A bunch of Polaroids of her and the girls during their iconic summer in New York. She picked up one of the photos and began to smile uncontrollably.

There they all were: herself, Siobhan, Natalie and Chloe, standing in Central Park, the night they had first met. In the Polaroid, they each held a different flavour of the alcoholic energy drink Four Loko, every J-1er's drink of choice. She was sure every Irish person who had ever done a J-1 summer had a crazy memory concerning Four Loko, or a lack thereof. Almost every time the girls would drink it, they'd wake up with a total blackout of the night before. There was nothing quite like the laughter they shared trying to piece together what had happened after those wild nights. They had become so fond of the toxic elixir that they were nicknamed 'The Four Lokos' by their disapproving boss. To this day, the four of them still had a group chat by that name, which they chatted in daily.

In the Polaroid, the girls were laughing hysterically with smiles of pure joy. Kate missed that time more than anything. She had always been a good girl, but not that summer. That summer she had been her wildest, truest self; unhinged in the best possible way. She had gone to New York for a good time, not a long time, and she said yes to every bad idea in the book.

It was perhaps the only time in her life she truly felt free.

She laughed at the Polaroid one last time and put it to the side. That was one photo they were definitely not going to recreate. They were in their thirties now, and The Four Lokos would surely be sticking to the vino all weekend.

But as she flicked through the other Polaroids, Kate suddenly felt her heart stop. Time came to a complete standstill as she saw the one photo she was trying to avoid. A picture of the one person she never wanted to see again. She brought the Polaroid closer to see his face.

The man she had first loved.

The man who broke her heart.

The one and only.

Trevor Rush.

Kate felt a lump in her throat. She tried to pretend she had forgotten about the photo, but she knew that was a complete and utter lie. She hadn't forgotten about Trevor Rush, not for one single day over the past nine years. She looked closely at his sleek black hair, his tanned Italian-American skin and his piercing brown eyes that always seemed to be able to see right into her soul. In the photo, they were standing in front of the Statue of Liberty, on the night they had said goodbye to each other. Although, at the time, it had not been a goodbye.

It had been 'to be continued' . . .

Kate put down the photo and tried to shake off the memory that was clawing her back to the past. But that's when she saw it.

An atom bomb of emotion.

The locket.

Not just any old locket. The one Trevor had given her that night.

It was heart-shaped and golden, with a keyhole in the centre. Trevor had promised her that if she came back to him the following summer, he would give her the key to open it. It was a romantic gesture that had made her feel like the luckiest girl in the world. But for reasons too painful to dwell on, Kate had not returned to him that following summer.

And so, the locket had never been opened.

She had tried to pick the lock many times with the help of YouTube tutorials, but she could never get it to crack. And it was too ornate to smash open, even though she had often considered it.

Kate tried to snap herself out of her sentimental trance. It was for the best the locket was never opened.

It was Pandora's box. She didn't know what was inside and she didn't want to know.

Trevor Rush had caused her far too much pain in the past, and Kate was looking forward to her future with Norman. She didn't like the phrase 'to get over someone you need to get under someone new', as it was a little vulgar for her taste. But she did believe that dating someone new could mend a broken heart by showing it how to love again.

Norman had done just that.

And she had met him in a serendipitous, romantic kind of way. One day Kate woke up in excruciating agony from her wisdom teeth emerging. It was unlike any physical pain she had ever experienced before. Kate couldn't drive so her mother had taken her to a new clinic owned by a respectable – and single – dental surgeon. Norman immediately cleared his schedule for her, removing all four wisdom teeth in one sitting. When she woke up, Kate was a new woman. He asked for her number and the rest was history.

In retrospect, her mother was clearly playing Cupid, but Norman had made a good first impression, in fairness. He quite literally took her pain away. What more could a girl ask for? Sure, it wasn't necessarily love at first sight, but over time she began to realize that Norman ticked every box on her list.

Ambitious. *Check.*

Loyal. *Check.*

Intelligent. *Check.*

Honest. *Check.*

The list was far more extensive than that, of course, but he ticked the most important box of all.

A man that would never hurt her. *Check.*

Norman wouldn't break her heart in a million years. Trevor Rush, on the other hand, had broken it in just a few months. He was a hammer of a man; destruction in human form. But Norman was the glue that had put her back together.

Kate put the locket back in the box and gathered up the Polaroids of her and the girls. She closed the lid on the memory box and shoved it deep into the darkest pit of her closet.

Trevor Rush was her past. Norman Cox was her future.

She put the Polaroids in her handbag next to the itinerary and took out her phone to check the time. She was still on schedule, of course, and her mother was due to pick her up in five minutes. She would have preferred to have gotten a taxi, but Margaret insisted on taking her so she could go over some last-minute wedding details.

Kate opened the group chat to see if the girls were following the timetable she had laid out for them. She didn't want any delays. Kate had even given them a far earlier time to meet than necessary, to ensure they arrived at the airport on time.

It was Hen Party Planning 101.

The Four Lokos

Kate: Everyone on their way? x

> **Natalie:** yep, on the train. had 2 shots of vodka for breakfast

Chloe: Trying to get all my cases into the car lol

Siobhan: OMG I SLEPT IN

Kate: WHAT???

Siobhan: Joking ;) I'm already at the airport

So hurry up bitches!

Kate: See you all soon x

Kate put her phone in her bag and felt herself fill with excitement. Everything was on schedule, just how she liked it.

'All set?' Norman asked as she came down the stairs with her suitcase.

'Yep, Mam will be here any minute.'

'Promise to text me every hour so I know you're safe?'

'I'll try my best, Normie, but there's an eight-hour time difference, so it might not be every single hour. But you have nothing to worry about. Like I said, the itinerary has been planned to perfection.'

'Okay, okay. You know I just worry because I care so much,' Norman said. His face produced a wide grin that revealed his full set of veneers. Technically speaking, he had perfect teeth, but Kate secretly felt that his porcelain pearls were a few shades too white. 'At least this time next week we'll be having the time of our lives on our honeymoon in Limerick.'

'It's not too late to change the destination to Paris . . .' Kate pried, even though it had been a bone of contention between them. 'Kissing passionately on the Eiffel Tower . . .'

'You'd hate Paris, Kate. And the Eiffel Tower is such a tourist trap. Trust me, you're not missing anything.'

'Yeah . . . you're probably right.'

'Where's my hug?' Norman said, holding out his arms.

Kate felt smothered once again. As his arms wrapped around her, she tried to remind herself that lots of women felt this way before their wedding.

'We're just so perfect together,' he said, squeezing her tight. 'That's why I hate being apart.'

Kate heard the beep of a car outside.

'Oh, that's Mam!' she said, eager to get out of the hug.

She stepped out onto the driveway and saw her mother's car. Kate lived on a street called Ailesbury Grove in Donnybrook, an affluent suburb of Dublin, and she knew she was lucky to call such a picturesque neighbourhood her home. The house itself, however, belonged to Norman. He bought it before they had met, and had paid in full without a mortgage, a feat he often bragged about. But the truth was that his parents gave him half the amount.

'Hi, Mam,' Kate said as she wheeled her case towards the car.

Margaret stuck her head out of the window, revealing her sharp haircut and austere visage. 'How's my future son-in-law?' she said to Norman before even acknowledging her daughter.

'I'm not too bad, Margaret,' Norman said. 'A bit worried about this one heading off though.'

'Oh indeed – I'm worried myself. But she was raised to behave herself.'

'As long as the other three don't lead her astray.'

'Okay, I'm all set,' Kate said after putting her case in the boot.

'Alright then. Promise me you won't drink too much? And please no karaoke. And—'

Kate kissed him on the cheek to end his worrisome rambling. 'I'll be fine, Normie,' she said. 'I love you.'

'I love you more,' Norman smiled as Kate got into the car. 'Great to see you, Mrs O'Connor.'

'Next time you see me, I'll be wearing the hat,' Margaret said, beaming with pride.

※

As she sat in the passenger seat on the way to the airport, Kate realized that her smothering feeling hadn't fully gone away. Margaret was yapping on about all the last-minute details that were due to be finalized for the wedding, but it was falling on deaf ears. All Kate could think about was that stupid photo of Trevor Rush. She regretted opening the memory box. Even though it was nine years since she saw him, seeing his face was still somewhat triggering.

'. . . and then you'll need to confirm final numbers with the hotel . . . and then . . .' Margaret was blabbering on. 'Kate, are you even listening to me?'

'Yes . . . sorry,' Kate said, snapping out of her daze. 'Don't worry Mam, I have all the planning done. I've had it done for months. There's no need to panic.'

'But there are a hundred different things you need to do the week of your wedding. And it would be a lot easier to get them done if you weren't going off gallivanting in Vegas.'

'Mam, I've already had the guilt-trip routine from Norman, I don't need it from you too.'

'Good God, what has you in such a snarky mood?'

'I'm just feeling a little bit anxious, that's all,' Kate said, trying to relax. 'When you were marrying Dad, did you feel a bit overwhelmed the week before?'

'Oh for God's sake, what is it with your generation and your obsession with the word overwhelmed? The only time that word should be used is when you're overwhelmed with joy. And it's not anxiety you're feeling, it's excitement.'

'Maybe . . . it's just, I can't seem to write my vows for some reason. And I—'

'Kate,' Margaret interrupted. 'Norman is a great man, and he's from very good people. Frankly, you're lucky to have him. He's a doctor who owns his own house for heaven's sake. With no mortgage, I might add. When you're writing your vows just imagine how comfortable your future with him will be. You won't even have to work – you can spend all your time at home raising a family.'

'But I *want* to work, Mam,' Kate said. 'And I don't even know if I want kids.'

'Oh, give up with that kind of talk,' Margaret said, not even willing to entertain the thought of not having grand-children. 'You're thirty years old for God's sake. The clock is ticking.'

Kate rolled her eyes. Her mother wasn't much of a feminist role model. It didn't make much sense, however. Margaret wasn't born in the 1950s. Her views were incredibly anti-quated for her age. But she was a social climber by nature and social climbers tended to be traditionalists. Norman was 'good stock' from a well-to-do family, and Margaret was obsessed with him. They often talked about what was best for Kate, even when she was in the room with them. It was like she wasn't even there.

'Well, having children is something I'll have to decide for myself,' Kate said.

'Don't even think about saying that to Norman before the

wedding. If you do anything to rock the boat, it'll put your father in an early grave. He's been waiting his entire life to walk you down the aisle. Surely you're not going to rob him of that. Are you trying to make his cancer come back?'

Margaret wasn't exactly easing Kate's smothered feeling. If anything, she was making it ten times worse. But then again, Kate thought, you can't spell smother without mother. Her father, Tom, had battled prostate cancer several years prior, and even though Kate had been by her dad's side every step of the way, she still lived in fear of it coming back. And Margaret loved using that hypothetical scenario as a guilt-tripping tactic.

'Alright, sorry Mam,' Kate sighed. 'I'm just a bit distracted. I opened my J-1 memory box to get some Polaroids for the girls and . . . I saw a pic of me and Trevor.'

'Trevor Rush?' Margaret said with disgust. 'The sleazebag who ruined your life?'

'Yeah . . . it was just a bit triggering.'

'Lord have mercy, people your age need serious help. It's always trigger this, trigger that. You're marrying a doctor and you're suddenly nostalgic for a DJ? I have no words to describe how ridiculous that is.'

'I'm not nostalgic – I still hate him as much as I ever did. It was just a pang, that's all.'

'Good,' Margaret said, relieved. 'Because Trevor is the one who threw you in the gutter, and you're very lucky Norman came along and scraped you out of it. Don't ever forget that.'

There weren't many things that Kate and her mother agreed on, but hating Trevor Rush was a rare crossover in both of their Venn diagrams. Her mother was right, after all. He *was* a sleazebag who had ruined her life. And Kate refused to let the memory of him taint her hen party.

'I'm sorry I said anything, Mam,' Kate said. 'I feel stupid

for bringing it up. You're right. The feeling I have is excitement, not anxiety. Norman is the man for me, I know that.'

'There she is,' Margaret smiled. 'There's my girl.'

Margaret pulled up in front of Terminal 2 departures at Dublin Airport. Kate hopped out and grabbed her suitcase from the boot. 'Thanks for the lift, Mam,' she said.

'I hope you enjoy yourself – but more importantly, I hope you appreciate the perfect life you'll be coming home to. Perfect husband, perfect house, perfect neighbourhood. You have what everyone wishes they had.'

'I know, Mam,' Kate said, hugging her mother goodbye. 'See you soon.'

Kate felt her claustrophobia finally ease up as she breathed in the fresh open air. It was time to push down whatever feelings of anxiety she had and focus on having the bachelorette party of her dreams.

After all, that was the plan.

Chapter 2

The Reunion

As Kate walked through the automatic doors of Dublin Airport's Terminal 2, she heard the fabulous sound of Siobhan, Natalie and Chloe screaming with excitement.

'AHHHHH!' they screeched in one piercingly loud note that rippled through the airport.

'Hey, girlies!' Kate said as she ran towards them, dragging her suitcase behind her.

'Well, if it isn't the ride-to-be,' Siobhan smiled. 'Sorry, bride-to-be.'

Siobhan was by far the wildest of the gang. She was a plus-size girl from Derry who had confidence to sell. The curvy brunette had no filter whatsoever, and she was obsessed with sex, or as she called it: 'The Ride'. Siobhan had a higher sexual body count than the rest of the girls combined, a fact she was very proud of. Many people had tried to slut-shame her over the years. All of them had failed. Shame wasn't in her vocabulary and Kate respected her uninhibited nature. Lots of people said they didn't care what people thought of them, but Siobhan actually meant it. She was surely going to wreak havoc on Vegas. The men wouldn't know what had hit them.

'Are you old hags ready for the best weekend of our lives?' Natalie asked.

Natalie was the youngest of the group by almost a year,

16

something she loved reminding everyone of. She was a millennial just like the rest of them, but she 'identified' as Gen Z, due to things like her political activism and open bisexuality. Her short, black pixie cut and bony frame made her look like a long-lost member of the Addams Family, but she embraced this witchy aesthetic and dressed exclusively in black. She had a chronically online lifestyle, however, as a result of still living with her parents in the Midlands of Ireland. Despite the gorgeous scenery that surrounded her, she seldom touched grass. As someone who didn't spend too much time on the internet, Kate appreciated Natalie's heightened social consciousness and hot feminist takes.

'Girls, hold on, let's get a selfie,' Chloe said, holding up her phone.

'Natalie, you owe me €5,' Siobhan laughed. 'We had a bet to see how long it would take for Chloe to take a photo.'

'Oh come on, I need selfies to remember the trip. SMILE,' Chloe laughed, as she snapped the pic.

Chloe was the most self-obsessed of the group. If she didn't take a photo of an occasion, then it never happened. She was only five-foot-two, but she wouldn't be caught dead in anything less than a four-inch pair of designer heels. She was your typical South Dublin princess, but despite her wealthy background, her dream of becoming a social media influencer had yet to come true. She wasn't the sharpest tool in the shed, but Kate loved her for it because she could often be inadvertently hilarious.

What Chloe lacked academically, though, she more than made up for in other aptitudes. She was the Albert Einstein of emotional intelligence, and could often tell what someone was feeling even before they felt it. She had bouncy blonde hair, suspiciously large lips and was a little on the orange side with her fake tan. She had been called a bimbo by many a man but she had reclaimed the term, finding great empowerment in the unapologetic expression of her femininity, with Elle Woods being her greatest inspiration. She was currently surrounded by three Louis Vuitton suitcases, which was a little much, even for her.

'Oh come on, Chloe,' Kate laughed. 'Three designer suitcases for two nights?'

'Are you really surprised?' Natalie said. 'Even her emotional baggage is Louis Vuitton.'

'I can't believe the day is finally here, girls,' Siobhan said. 'The Four Lokos are heading back to the States!'

Kate felt her heart fill with genuine joy. She absolutely adored these girls, and she didn't get to see them nearly enough. It seemed as if adult friendships became harder and harder to maintain as one got older. This girls' trip was long overdue, and it was time to make up for lost time.

If anyone were to eavesdrop on any given conversation the girls were having, they would likely think they all hated each other. But nothing could be further from the truth. They lived to wind each other up and insulted each other non-stop, but always in the most playful of manners. Slagging each other was the best part of their friendship, and they never missed a zinger.

Sure, on any of their Instagram posts, they were always there for each other with the essential 'GORGEOUS' 'QUEEN' and 'STUNNING' comments. But in real life, it was no holds barred when it came to banter. They even had a motto that summarized their humour: Good friends *toast* each other but great friends *roast* each other.

The girls didn't actually have that much in common with one another, but Kate had read somewhere that friendships aren't actually formed by similar personality traits as one might think, but rather through shared experiences. They had made so many memories together that their radically different personalities just seemed to click. And the greatest of all those memories was the summer they shared in New York City.

Kate had gone on her J-1 by herself after her friends from Trinity College bailed at the last minute. A summer abroad was an experience Kate refused to miss out on, and so she got on the plane by herself. People told her she was mad to travel alone as a woman, with Margaret suggesting she was 'asking for trouble'. But Kate refused to let *what ifs* dictate her life. As terrifying as it was at the time, it turned out to be the best decision she ever made.

And she wasn't alone for long.

Kate, Siobhan, Natalie and Chloe all started on the same day at Scallywag's. None of them knew each other beforehand but they were all from Ireland, so it didn't take long for the banter to begin. Their boss had thrown them into the deep end despite the fact they had zero waitressing experience between them. There's nothing more bonding than starting a new job with people who are just as clueless as you are, Kate had learned. It was a miracle Scallywag's didn't go out of business that day with their antics. Orders were mixed up, food was delayed, drinks were spilled and complaints were filed. Were it not for their Irish charm, and a shortage of staff, they would have all been fired on the spot.

When the girls left work after their shift, they all decided the only way to de-stress after their horrific first day was to get absolutely hammered. They began hopping from bar to bar, getting to know each other better and better. And even though they were incredibly different people, they discovered one thing that united them all.

They were all Swifties.

When the bars closed, they began wandering the streets of New York singing songs from Taylor's *1989* album at the top of their lungs. They hit up the nearest convenience store and Siobhan bought them each a can of Four Loko. Kate had never heard of the drink before, but after a sip, she discovered the night was only just beginning. They snuck into Central Park after hours and, as they watched the sun come up, Kate knew their friendship would last for ever. They all decided to rent an apartment together in Brooklyn, marking the beginning of a legendary summer.

And so, The Four Lokos were born.

She always knew Siobhan, Natalie and Chloe would be her three bridesmaids. There was never any question about it.

Now, nine years later, it was time for the iconic hen party to begin.

'Girls, can you believe we haven't been abroad together since the J-1?' Siobhan said.

'I honestly can't believe that was nine years ago,' Natalie said.

'Stop, I already feel old enough,' Kate laughed. 'But that reminds me. I brought all our old Polaroids from that summer. Aaand I brought my Polaroid camera so we can recreate some of the pics!'

'OMG, that's the best idea you've ever had!' Chloe said, already thinking of a caption for Instagram.

'Okay, let's go check in,' Kate said, grabbing her suitcase.

'Hold on now, first things first. We have to look the part for the weekend!' Siobhan said, opening her carry-on handbag. She took out four pink bachelorette party sashes and started handing them out.

Kate's read 'I LOVE COX', and she began to howl in laughter. 'Siobhan, you got them customized for us?'

'Of course,' Siobhan said. 'Natalie, here's yours.'

Natalie's sash read 'ALL BI MYSELF', and she was not impressed. 'Oh for God's sake, mine is just a dig!' she moaned.

'No it's not! It's the perfect way to let people know you swing both ways but are also desperately alone,' Siobhan said.

'Gee, thanks,' Natalie said with a sarcastic grin.

Chloe's read 'SELFIE SKANK' – a fact she could not deny. 'Oh, I love mine!' she said, ecstatic. Predictably, she took out her phone to snap a photo of it.

Siobhan got hers out – one that read 'MAID OF DIS-HONOUR', and put it on with pride.

'A fitting title,' Kate laughed.

'Oh girls, it's so good to all be back together,' Chloe said, genuinely.

'I know. I missed you all more than men miss the point,' Natalie joked.

'I literally cannot WAIT for a proper catch-up!' Kate said. She was the mam of the group and the one who was always up to date with everyone's lives. If the girls had a problem, they called Kate. Planning the wedding had taken up so much of her time, however, that she hadn't heard the latest gossip and funny stories in ages.

But all of that was about to change.

She had planned a hen party they would never forget, and they would surely make enough new memories to last them a lifetime.

'One more thing, Mrs Cox-to-be. Your tiara,' Siobhan said. She took out a tiara decorated with fake penises that read 'Wife of the Party', and placed it on Kate's head. 'Let the weekend of debauchery begin.'

Chapter 3

Pre-Drinks

After checking in their bags and Siobhan begging to be strip-searched at US customs, the girls began walking towards their gate.

'I can't believe they didn't do a cavity search. I could have anything up there for all they know,' Siobhan said, disappointed.

'God knows there's enough room,' Natalie joked.

'Maybe I should go back for another scan.'

'Don't even think about it,' Kate laughed.

'Fine,' Siobhan sighed. 'Does anyone want McDonald's before we board?'

'Are you mad?' Chloe said. 'I'm not eating fast food before a holiday. I'll balloon!'

'The calories in an airport McDonald's don't count, everyone knows that.'

'Girls, we only have half an hour before we board, and I have cocktails scheduled in the itinerary,' Kate said.

'Good idea. Better to drink on an empty stomach anyway,' Siobhan conceded.

The four strutted towards the bar in their sashes, turning heads as they went, though this might have been because Siobhan was whistling at every man they walked past.

'Why is everyone always such a RIDE at the airport?' Siobhan asked.

'There's a scientific reason for it actually,' Natalie explained. 'It's because you know you'll probably never see them again, so they seem more desirable as a result. It's about scarcity. They could all be the one that got away.'

'Ugh, you're right. There's nothing hotter than a man you'll never see again,' Siobhan said, ogling the men as she looked around.

'Dear God, you're practically feral,' Kate laughed.

'Well, not all of us have been spayed, Mrs Cox-to-be,' Siobhan said. 'I'm still surprised Norman let you off your leash for the weekend.'

'He knows I'm in good hands with my bridesmaids.'

'Oh, that is such a lie,' Natalie laughed. 'Norman hates us.'

'NO HE DOESN'T!' Kate said, mortified.

'He called me a sexual maniac,' Siobhan said.

'Well, if the shoe fits,' Chloe teased.

'He's just easily shocked, that's all,' Kate said. 'He thinks we take it too far when we drink.'

'We do always take it too far, to be fair,' Natalie laughed.

'But we hardly ever see you any more. It's always "Norman wants to snuggle on the couch" or "Norman wants to binge-watch a new show",' Siobhan said, imitating Kate with a high-pitched voice.

'First of all, that's a terrible impression of me,' Kate laughed. 'And secondly, Norman is perfectly happy with me going away with my girls. I promised to text him every hour so he—'

'EVERY HOUR?' Natalie said, shocked.

'Well, it might not be every single hour. Anyway, he can track my location whenever he needs to.'

'HE GOT YOU CHIPPED?'

'Of course not!' Kate laughed. 'He can see my phone's location in real time.'

Siobhan, Natalie and Chloe all gave each other a concerned look as Kate walked in front of them.

'Look girls! There's the bar!' Kate said, spotting it.

The girls sat down at the bar and ordered a round of cocktails. After the bartender whipped up four espresso martinis, the girls toasted to what was sure to be the best weekend of their lives.

'Cheers girlies!' Kate said as they all clinked their glasses.

'CHEERS!' they all said, every bit as excited as the bride-to-be.

After tasting the delightful mixture of coffee and vodka, Kate reached into her handbag and produced the hen party itinerary.

'Here it is girls – the perfect hen party plan,' she said, her eyes lighting up.

'The unholy Bible,' Siobhan laughed. 'But I'm still annoyed you didn't let me plan anything.'

'Siobhan, did you really think you could convince Kate not to plan something?' Natalie said. 'Don't you remember when she planned her own surprise party?'

'What was I supposed to do? Not have my hair done for my birthday? And I looked very surprised in the photos, for the record,' Kate said.

'She probably has her own funeral planned too,' Chloe laughed.

'I have not! But I do want lavender on my coffin. And someone should read Psalm 23 at some point. And also—'

'Good God, you're too much,' Siobhan laughed.

'But my funeral won't be for another seventy years, touch wood,' Kate said. She knocked on the wooden bar top to seal it in. She was incredibly superstitious and didn't like leaving anything to chance. Better to be safe than sorry. 'Joke about my planning skills all you want girls, but you'll all thank me after we have the best weekend of our lives. It's jam-packed. Every single minute has been planned out.'

'But what if we take a notion and want to do something random?' Natalie asked.

'I have plenty of spontaneous things planned, don't worry.'

'Organized fun. My favourite,' Siobhan said sarcastically as she sipped her martini.

'I just hope there are lots of good photo opportunities in the plan,' Chloe said. 'We need to find a mural with angel wings and . . .'

'Oh no, we are not spending an hour at every landmark getting you the perfect pics. I want the photos to be so bad, we couldn't possibly post them. I'm getting ugly on this holiday,' Siobhan said.

'And you edit your photos into oblivion anyway, Chloe, so they don't have to even be good in the first place,' Natalie said, giving her a dig.

'I do not edit my pics!' Chloe said, offended.

'Oh please, you're always airbrushed within an inch of your life. And you're getting more orange by the minute with that fake tan.'

'That's supposed to happen. It's from this new brand I'm trying out.'

'What's the brand called? Orangutan?'

'Ha ha, very funny,' Chloe said, sarcastically. 'It's a developer tan from Bronze Beauty. It gets darker and darker and then you shower it off after sixteen hours. I'll be golden tonight and you'll all be green with envy.'

'Sure, we will,' Siobhan teased. 'So Kate, I know you're organizing everything but I went ahead and made us a Spotify hen party playlist. Is that okay with the bride?'

'Of course. Let's see it!' Kate said, excited. It was probably the only thing she hadn't thought of, and she was thrilled Siobhan had taken care of it.

'Okay, so here it is,' Siobhan said, showing them on her phone. 'So obviously I have loads of songs from Ms Swift. Taylor's Versions, obviously. I also have lots of Beyoncé. Shania Twain, of course. And my personal favourite artist . . . Kate O'Connor.'

Kate felt like the wind had been knocked out of her.

Siobhan had been on such a roll, but she just had to bring up Kate's failed music career. She had studied music at Trinity College in the hopes of one day becoming a singer-songwriter. Margaret had been completely against her choice of degree, claiming it wasn't a 'real course' and that she should have studied medicine, considering the high grades she received. But Kate had a dream to pursue. She got her degree, and after college she was ready to launch her career as a musician.

But she only ever released one single.

'Your Scar' by Kate O'Connor.

Written about the one and only Trevor Rush. It was a heartbreak song, of course, but she had hoped it would be a way to fix her broken heart. She and Trevor had dreamt of making music together as a duo that summer, but she wanted to prove she could do it solo. Some girls got a revenge bod after a breakup, but Kate wanted a revenge song. The song wasn't vengeful in nature, however; the revenge was supposed to be its success. She didn't believe in getting bitter. She believed in getting better. She thought she would turn her broken heart into art and have the last laugh over Trevor Rush. Karma would surely be on her side. She had planned it all, just as one would expect.

But the song was a complete flop.

Not even 1,000 streams.

Her attempt to fill the hole in her heart had only made

it bigger. And now anytime anyone mentioned it, she was reminded of the big embarrassing failure that it was. The big embarrassing failure that *she* was. She had inadvertently proved her mother right, something she hated doing. Then there was the hate comment that some internet troll left on the YouTube video of her song:

Another delusional hack going absolutely nowhere.

Although Kate knew the person behind the hate comment was some greasy-haired incel, the words still cut like a knife. And it was a fatal stabbing; the final nail in the coffin of Kate's singing career. She tried to tell herself that even Taylor Swift received negative comments, but Kate's self-esteem couldn't handle that kind of public criticism. As much as she wished otherwise, she just wasn't strong enough.

With her career down the drain, it was a miracle she had Norman by her side. He had made her feel good about herself when she was at her lowest. He had scraped her out of the gutter, as Margaret so eloquently put it. He encouraged her to apply for an advertised event management job where her planning skills could be leveraged. His advice had been exactly what she needed to hear, and she got the job. He had saved her from a life of rejection and despair, and she was not about to backtrack into those negative emotions she had long since said goodbye to.

'Girls, we're not listening to my song on this trip, no way!' Kate said firmly.

'What? Why?' Siobhan asked. 'It's a banger!'

'Yeah, it's literally one of my favourite songs,' Natalie said.

'"FOR YEARS NOW WE'VE BEEN APART BUT BABE YOU LEFT YOUR MARK",' Siobhan sang.

'Siobhan, please!' Kate said, mortified.

'"TIME HEALED MY BROKEN HEART BUT I'LL

ALWAYS HAVE YOUR SCAR"!' Siobhan, Chloe and Natalie sang at the top of their lungs.

'Please girls, I cringe every time I hear it!' Kate said, begging them to stop embarrassing her. 'Take it off the playlist right now.'

'Jesus, fine. Sorry for thinking our friend is talented,' Siobhan said, removing the song.

'If I was talented, it wouldn't have been a flop.'

'If Taylor only ever released one song, we never would have gotten *1989*. Just saying,' Chloe shrugged.

Kate was eager to change the subject to anything else. Thankfully, she had just the thing. 'Oh girls, let me show you the Polaroids! You're all going to die laughing,' she said, taking the photos out of her bag.

'OH MY GOD,' Siobhan shouted when she saw them. 'Look at our little baby faces.'

'Look how skinny I was!' Chloe said.

'And that's *without* Photoshop,' Natalie joked.

Siobhan picked up the photo of the girls drinking Four Lokos in Central Park. Kate thought she had left that one in the memory box, but she must have brought it by mistake.

'Okay, now this is a photo we NEED to recreate!' Siobhan insisted.

'Not a chance,' Kate said. 'There's no way in hell we're drinking Four Loko!'

'Kate, it's our signature drink! It's the whole reason the Americans called us The Four Lokos!'

'Girls, we're not twenty-one any more. We always blacked out whenever we drank it, and I want to remember every moment of this weekend.'

'Remembering a hen party is a sign of a bad hen party.'

'No, Kate's right,' Natalie said. 'I think I'd get sick if I drank it now.'

'Yeah, and it's probably riddled with calories,' Chloe added.

'Ugh, you're all a bunch of dryshites,' Siobhan sulked.

'I can't believe how much we've changed,' Kate said, looking at the Polaroid.

'Speak for yourself, Mrs Norman Cox-to-be,' Siobhan said, putting on a posh accent and lifting up her pinkie finger.

'What is that supposed to mean?'

'I don't know. I'm guessing Norman is the one who doesn't want you drinking Four Loko.'

'Oh, stop. He just doesn't want me making a complete fool of myself,' Kate said, brushing it off.

'Or doesn't want his future wife to remember she's a party girl at heart,' Natalie slagged her.

'I am not a party girl!'

'Oh pleeeease!' Chloe said. 'On the J-1, you were the craziest one of all of us! We were just followers – you were the leader.'

'Are you serious?' Kate asked, horrified. 'That's not how I remember it!'

'Don't you remember how we got that Polaroid in Central Park? You told a homeless man you'd show him your boobs if he'd take a photo of us!' Natalie wheezed.

'I did not! Did I? Are you sure that wasn't Siobhan?'

'Nope, all you baby.'

'The best time was when we were all hungover at work and Kate kept going behind the bar and pouring us tequila shots to keep us awake,' Chloe laughed.

'And then she threw up on that woman who was complaining about the service!' Siobhan roared, slamming her hand on the bar in hysterics.

'Oh my God, I was the worst back then!' Kate said, going puce.

'No, you were the best!' Natalie said. 'You made the entire summer. You're the reason we're all friends!'

'Yeah, and we want *that* Kate on this trip. Not Mrs Norman Cox-to-be,' Siobhan demanded. 'Norman has changed you. You've become such a people-pleaser. We want one last week with the real Kate O'Connor!'

'Well, based on what I'm hearing, Norman seems to have changed me for the better,' Kate said, mortified by what she had just heard.

'You see, this is what a relationship does to a woman. She's domesticated now. If I ever get married, someone please shoot me.'

'There'll come a point when the only word you want to hear is marriage.'

'Marriage isn't a word, it's a sentence,' Siobhan said. 'One man for the rest of my life? I can't even commit to one vibrator!'

Kate began to laugh at Siobhan's candour. 'You say that now, but everyone matures eventually.'

'Not me,' Siobhan said, adamantly. 'I can proudly say I was a fat skank then and I'm a fat skank now.'

'Don't say fat,' Natalie said. 'You're supposed to say curvy or plus size.'

'Are you actually telling me what to call myself when you're literally a size zero? I was fat before this whole 'body positivity' thing. I knew Burger King when he was still a Prince!'

The girls burst out laughing. 'Okay, fair enough,' Natalie conceded.

'Just call a spade a spade. I don't go around calling you a female dog. I call you a bitch because I love you.'

'How sweet,' Natalie said sarcastically.

'I was sweet enough to get that bi sash customized for you, wasn't I?' Siobhan said.

'Well . . . it's actually not accurate. I'm not bi any more.'

'Was it "just a phase"?' Chloe teased.

'Actually . . .' Natalie said, shooting Chloe a look. 'I'm pansexual now.'

'What's the difference?' Kate asked. She wasn't very tuned into the zeitgeist, and she was genuinely eager to learn.

'Well, for me, a person's gender or sex doesn't matter. It's really all about their personality.'

'But how do you have sex with a personality?' Siobhan said, confused.

'Um, by connecting with them on a deep emotional level?'

'You lost me.'

'Wait, why is there no P in LGBT?' Chloe asked, innocently.

'It's included in LGBTQ+.'

'LGBTQ+? What, is that like a premium subscription or something?'

'Yeah, it's €9.99 a month and you don't have to watch any ads,' Natalie said, sarcastically. The sarcasm was lost on poor Chloe.

'Well, I don't believe in labels,' Chloe said.

'You're wearing a Prada dress.'

'I obviously believe in *those* labels. But I think people should just love who they love.'

'That's literally what I just said,' Natalie said as she face-palmed herself.

'Wait Nat, when's the last time you've even had sex?' Siobhan pried.

'Not since my ex, Mark,' Natalie admitted. 'And that was well over a year ago.'

'Jesus, there must be cobwebs down there!' Chloe said, shocked.

'Yeah, but that's kinda on-brand for me. My aesthetic is spooky chic.'

'Oh, pack it up, Thursday Addams,' Siobhan said. 'Spooky chic isn't a thing. It's a vagina, not a haunted house!'

'Hold on,' Kate said. 'A few months ago in the group chat, you said you had sex daily.'

'I was trying to say I have dyslexia!' Natalie sighed.

'This is ridiculous,' Siobhan said. 'You literally have double the options we do! You should be getting some every night of the week!'

'Ugh, you're right,' Natalie groaned. 'The Olympics get held more than I do!'

'Maybe you should start seeing someone,' Kate suggested.

'You mean like a therapist?'

'No, I mean a person who you connect with. Someone who makes you feel good and wants to be with you.'

'Easier said than done, Kate. You can't just choose someone to have feelings for.'

'Yes you can! I chose Norman.'

'But we're living in hook-up culture. Nobody seems to want serious commitment these days.'

'Well, maybe you should stop going for the non-stick pans,' Siobhan joked.

'Bitch,' Natalie said, trying not to laugh.

'Nat, we support whatever way you identify. But I will not support you becoming a nun. You need to get some action on this trip. You need to put the sex back in your sexuality!'

'Okay fine. I'm open to the possibility. But only if I feel a connection.'

'Exactly,' Chloe said. 'Just see how it "pans out".'

'You're all impossible,' Natalie laughed.

'Okay, operation get Nat the ride is a GO!' Siobhan said, raising her glass. The girls all cheered.

'What about you, Chloe?' Kate asked. 'Anyone you like these days?'

'There's one person I like and one person who likes me. But they're not the same person,' Chloe sighed.

'Whatever happened to that cute Polish guy, Casper?'

'He ghosted me.'

'I saw it coming,' Natalie shrugged.

'It's okay though, because I keyed his car.'

'CHLOE! That's insane!' Kate said, appalled.

'What? He ghosted me so I haunted him. Fair is fair,' Chloe shrugged.

'You better pray he isn't the vengeful type,' Kate laughed. 'So there's really nobody?'

'No. I've tried the whole Tinder thing for so long. I've practically swiped my finger to the bone. But guys always say I look different in person.'

'Shocker,' Natalie muttered under her breath.

'And they always make assumptions about me based on nothing. I swear to God, if one more man calls me a drama queen, I'm going to set myself on fire.'

'Where do men get these crazy ideas?' Siobhan said, sarcastically.

'Aww Chloe, come on,' Kate said. 'There must be a million guys on Tinder who'd kill to go on a date with you.'

'But I just want to meet a guy in a real-life, romantic way, you know?' Chloe sighed. 'Like, I'm sitting in a coffee shop reading a book and a guy walks in and notices me.'

'Chloe, you don't read,' Siobhan said, calling her out.

'Well, he won't know that . . . until it's too late.'

'Don't get your hopes up, Chloe,' Natalie said. 'I told one guy I was looking for romance and he asked me if I wanted to give him a blow job in the rain.'

'OH MY GOD!' Kate said, horrified.

'Send me his number,' Siobhan smirked. 'He sounds like a keeper.'

'Well, not all of us have your one-night standards, Siobhan,' Natalie said, a little too judgementally.

'Slut shaming, Nat? Not very Gen Z of you.'

'I retract my statement . . . But honestly, though, whatever happened to the art of the cuddle?'

'Yeah, these days spooning always leads to forking,' Chloe sighed.

'Which makes me want to reach for a knife,' Natalie said. 'Men are only romantic until they get what they want out of you. Then BOOM, completely different person.'

'Yeah, men are always perfect at the start,' Siobhan said. 'That's why I keep getting new ones.'

'As for me, I'm sticking to men in literature . . . or fan fiction.'

'Nat, those are men written by women. They aren't real! A fictional man can't give you an orgasm!'

'Oh sweetie . . . you are so, so wrong,' Natalie said, shaking her head.

'I'm telling you girls, you all need to stop romanticizing men and see them for what they really are. At the end of the day, they're just toys. That's why Tinder is in my games folder.'

'But how do you not get emotionally attached afterwards?' Chloe asked Siobhan.

'I'm emotionally constipated. I haven't given a shit in years.'

'Lucky you,' Chloe said. 'I care way too much.'

Kate felt terrible for the girls having to navigate the world of singledom in the digital age. They were all amazing women with so much to offer, but it seemed like online dating made everything harder rather than easier. It was in times like this that she was glad of Norman. If she had to jump back into the dating pool she would surely drown.

'Don't worry, Chloe, the right guy will come along when you're least expecting it,' Kate said, reassuring her. 'Just date yourself for a while.'

'No, I deserve better,' Chloe said. 'I don't think I really want a boyfriend anyway. I think I just want a photographer. Once I hit 10K on Instagram, then I'll truly be happy.'

'Chloe, don't take this the wrong way, but you really need a niche if you want to be a proper influencer. You gotta have a gimmick,' Kate explained.

'Hmm . . . okay. Like what?'

'Well, that's up to you. It could be fashion advice, cooking tips, travel blogging . . .'

'Oh, travel blogging sounds fun! And I'm going backpacking through Southeast Asia in August!' Chloe said, excited at the idea.

'That's the perfect place to get good travel content,' Kate said, trying to encourage her. 'Which countries are you visiting?'

'Vietnam, Thailand and Colombia,' Chloe said, innocently.

'You mean Cambodia?'

'Oh yeah, that's the one!'

'Yeah . . . maybe travel blogging isn't the right fit,' Natalie laughed.

'But her heart's in the right place,' Siobhan said, finishing her espresso martini. 'Catch flights, not feelings.'

'Speaking of which,' Kate said. 'It's time to board!'

Chapter 4

Take Off

The girls arrived at the aeroplane door at the end of the tunnel walkway and stepped onto the Boeing 747 for their Aer Lingus flight bound to Vegas. The flight attendants and pilot were standing there smiling as they walked past.

'SIOBHAN?' the pilot gasped, out of nowhere.

'KYLE?' Siobhan replied.

'It's Karl,' he said, awkwardly.

Kate immediately knew from Karl's body language that Siobhan had slept with him before. He was a handsome fella with an attractive five o'clock shadow.

'I never knew you were a pilot,' Siobhan said, looking him up and down.

'I'm pretty sure I told you . . .' Karl said, slightly embarrassed.

'I've always loved a man in uniform,' Siobhan said, flirtatiously touching his pilot's hat.

Karl started blushing brighter than a beetroot. 'Enjoy the flight, ladies.'

The girls began to giggle as they walked down the aisle towards their seats.

'Siobhan, is there anyone you *haven't* had sex with?' Natalie asked, playfully.

'It's hardly my fault my vagina's a weapon of mass seduction,' she smirked.

'He was actually so hot though,' Chloe said, looking back over her shoulder.

'Don't act so surprised. I could pull anyone,' Siobhan bragged. 'He's packing too. I gave him five stars on Dick Advisor.'

'You really are something else,' Kate laughed.

The gals arrived at their seats and began to put their carry-on bags away. As they sat down and tried to get comfortable, a baby started crying two rows down and Natalie noticed the man in front of her had lowered his seat back all the way.

'Isn't there usually more legroom in economy?' Natalie asked, pushing against the man's seat.

'This isn't economy, this is bankruptcy,' Chloe whinged. She wasn't used to flying coach.

'It's just for a few hours,' Kate said. 'We can't all afford first-class.'

'But even for economy, this is bad. I'm surprised they didn't just Sellotape us to the wing.'

'I'm a very anxious flyer,' Natalie said. 'I can't sit like this for ten hours.'

The baby two rows behind them began to cry even louder.

'They better shut that baby up,' Siobhan said.

'Siobhan, please don't start a fight with an infant!' Kate said.

'But who even has babies any more? It's basically just keeping sperm as a pet!'

'Excuse me, sir, would you mind putting your seat forward?' Natalie politely asked the man in front of her.

The old man turned around and gave her a look of disdain. 'No, sorry, I have a bad back,' he said smugly.

Natalie's politeness clearly hadn't worked, so she decided to try a different approach. 'You're going to have a *broken* back if you don't put that seat up.'

The old man immediately put his seat forward in fear.

'You're going to hell for that, Nat,' Kate said.

'At least hell will have some legroom.'

'Maybe I should ask for an upgrade because I'm an influencer,' Chloe suggested.

'Chloe, you couldn't influence a fish into water,' Siobhan laughed.

A flight attendant suddenly approached the girls. 'Excuse me ladies, the captain asked if the four of you would like a complimentary upgrade to business class?' she said, smiling.

'THANK CHRIST!' Chloe said as she gunned it towards the front of the plane. The girls didn't question it and headed straight to their new seats in the business cabin. It wasn't quite first class, but it was still a tremendous upgrade.

'Okay, now this is more like it,' Natalie said as she looked around.

'These four seats are available, ladies,' the attendant said. 'Can I get any of you some champagne before take-off?'

'Four glasses, please,' Siobhan said. 'And the girls will have some too.'

'Certainly,' the flight attendant said before walking away.

The girls settled into their seats and were stunned by how fancy it was. Thankfully, they were sitting right next to each other, with two in front and two behind. Siobhan and Chloe sat in the front two while Kate and Natalie sat behind them.

'Did the plane crash and send us to heaven?' Kate asked, still shocked at the luxury of their seats.

'I manifested this, girls,' Chloe bragged. 'I said the word "upgrade" and it happened.'

'Oh, give me a break! Karl is clearly the one who got us the upgrade! So a little appreciation for my royal vajayjay would be nice,' Siobhan said.

'Yes, Your Vajesty,' Natalie said, bowing down.

'Well, I could have gotten us a free upgrade too if I tried,' Chloe said, defensively. 'Don't underestimate me.'

'We couldn't even if we tried,' Natalie muttered. 'At least Siobhan can't start an immature fight with a baby up here.'

'You're one to talk, Nat,' Siobhan said. 'Didn't you literally have a Twitter feud with Peppa Pig?'

'She knows what she did.'

The flight attendant returned with a fabulous tray of champagne.

'Thank you so much,' Kate said politely, as they all took their glasses. 'Girls, this trip is off to an amazing start already! Cheers.'

'To Karl the pilot and his magnificent COCK!' Siobhan yelled.

'SIOBHAN!' Kate said, mortified. They hadn't even taken off yet and the other people in business class were already staring at them.

'What? We're on a plane to Vegas, not Lourdes!'

'I just don't want people thinking we're too raunchy.'

'Oh no, don't you dare start with that shit, Kate,' Siobhan said. 'Men get to be loud and obnoxious twenty-four seven, 365 days a year and nobody bats an eye. Women are given one socially acceptable time to be their worst, most vulgar selves and nobody can say anything about it. Well, I for one intend to make the most of this rare and beautiful opportunity. This is a hen party, goddammit, and I'm allowed to talk about COCK!'

'Exactly!' Natalie said in support. 'Stick it to the man!'

'Nah, I much prefer when the man sticks it to me.'

'I'll never know if you're the best or worst feminist in the world, Siobhan.'

'I just think, instead of hopelessly expecting men to be better, it's time for women to be worse!'

'Hear, hear,' Chloe said.

'Women are way too well behaved these days. And as we know, well-behaved bitches seldom make history.'

'I don't think that's the exact quote . . . but yes! Fuck the patriarchy and all that,' Natalie said, raising her glass.

Kate realized Siobhan was right. There was nothing wrong with women being a little naughty on a hen party. She just wasn't used to letting her hair down. But so far, things were going even better than she had planned. After all, nobody could have planned a free upgrade to business class. And Siobhan's raunchiness was to thank for it.

'Oh, I better text Norman to tell him we're on the plane,' Kate said, taking out her phone.

Kate: Just got on plane with an upgrade to business class!!!

Norman: WHAT? That will cost thousands!!!

Kate: No, it was a free upgrade, don't worry!

Norman: You should have said. I almost had a heart attack!

Text me when you land.

Kate: Will do x

Kate put her phone on aeroplane mode and the girls relaxed into their luxurious seats. In just ten hours, they would be landing in the fabulous Las Vegas, Nevada.

Chapter 5

Turbulence

Five hours and ten glasses of champagne into the flight, the girls were having a whale of a time.

Siobhan and Chloe had turned around and were kneeling on their seats so they could chat to Kate and Natalie. The other members of the business class cabin seemed unimpressed by their seating arrangement and volume level, with one elderly woman in particular shushing them constantly.

But the girls didn't care.

It was a hen party, and they weren't going to dial it back for anyone. They were determined to play as many bachelorette party games on the flight as possible. So far they had played Would You Rather and Two Truths and a Lie, and they were trying to decide which game to play next.

'How about Never Have I Ever?' Chloe suggested.

'No way,' Kate said, ruling it out. 'Don't you remember we played that on the J-1? Siobhan had to get her stomach pumped.'

'Good times,' Siobhan said, thinking back. 'Oh, I have a game! Name the biggest ick a man has ever given you. GO!'

'Oh, I have one,' Chloe said. 'I once refused to have sex with a guy because he pushed a door that said pull.'

'Yes! That's a good one,' Siobhan laughed. 'Natalie, what's your biggest ick?'

'Dick.'

'Oh, come on,' Chloe laughed. 'It has to be more specific.'

'Fine, let me think,' Natalie pondered. 'Oh, I know! When a guy listens to those "alpha-male" podcasts.'

'YES!' Siobhan said. 'It's like, tell me you have a small dick without telling me you have a small dick.'

'And those Smegma male ones are even worse,' Chloe said.

'I think it's "Sigma", but totally agree,' Kate said. 'Podcasts are for one thing and one thing only. Listening to horrifically gruesome serial killer murders on your morning commute to work.'

'Oh, I just thought of a good one,' Siobhan said. 'When a man puts up an umbrella to try to be a gentleman, but the wind blows it inside out and he's just flailing all over the place!'

'No stop, that's the ugliest thing ever,' Natalie said, wheezing with laughter.

'I have another one,' Chloe said. 'When a guy is covered in tattoos.'

'NO WAY!' Siobhan said. 'Tattoos make a guy a million times hotter! Chloe, I thought you'd love to get inked!'

'I'd rather die than get a tattoo. It's like putting a bumper sticker on a Ferrari!' Chloe snapped.

'Oh sweetie, you're a Honda Civic at best,' Natalie teased.

'Kate, your turn! Biggest ick. GO,' Siobhan said.

'Hmm, I'm not sure,' Kate said. 'Norman doesn't have any icks.'

Siobhan, Natalie and Chloe all gave each other side-eye looks.

'Oh, come on Kate, Norman definitely has some icks,' Siobhan said, trying not to laugh.

'He does not! Norman is literally perfect,' Kate said, defensively.

There was an awkward silence and all that could be heard was the roaring of the plane's engine.

'Okay, what's with the deafening silence?' Kate said.

The three girls looked at each other suspiciously, as if they had been caught out.

'Someone needs to say it,' Siobhan said.

'Say what?' Kate asked, confused.

'NOT IT!' Chloe and Natalie said at the exact same time. 'SOMEBODY TELL ME!'

'Fine, I'll say it,' Siobhan sighed. 'Kate, don't take this the wrong way but don't you think Norman is a little . . . boring?'

'Boring? Norman isn't boring!'

'He just seems like the opposite of your type.'

'Oh please,' Kate laughed. 'He's a doctor for crying out loud!'

'Dentist,' Chloe muttered.

'He literally has no icks!'

'But what about those veneers . . .' Siobhan winced.

'Oh, so having perfect teeth is an ick now?'

'But they're *too* perfect,' Natalie said. 'He looks like Ross in that one episode of *Friends*!'

'Every woman wants to end up with a Ross,' Kate said, defending him.

'But, like . . . how do you moan the name Norman during sex? OHHH NORMAN!' Siobhan moaned loudly for all to hear. The elderly woman began shushing them again.

'Siobhan, please!'

'See! It's un-moanable!'

'Just as long as you're not marrying him for the sake of getting married,' Chloe teased.

Chloe's words made Kate feel a little worried. She had a deep understanding of human beings, and she often knew what people were feeling subconsciously. She was like an emotional psychic. But Kate was simply doing what everyone else did eventually. Choosing a life partner and getting married was part of most people's life journey.

'Well, everyone has to settle down eventually,' Kate shrugged.

'But to settle down, first you have to settle.'

'I am not settling for Norman. He literally ticks every box on my list.'

'Well, he icks my box,' Siobhan giggled into her glass of champagne.

'Love isn't a list, Kate,' Chloe said. 'It's about passion. And romance. I mean, I was a bit annoyed that he didn't even get you an engagement ring.'

'That's because Norman explained to me that engagement rings are just a marketing ploy invented by the De Beers Diamond company in the forties. They came up with this whole plan to make men spend three months' salary on a diamond ring. Norman told me he doesn't need a silly ring to show me how he feels about me,' Kate said.

The other girls looked at each other awkwardly once again.

'Kate, I'm not one for marriage or tradition or any of that shite. But you, of all people, deserve a ring,' Siobhan said.

'Yeah, and proposals are no time to be stingy,' Chloe said.

'Norman's not stingy!' Kate said. 'Frugal maybe, but not stingy.'

'Oh please. He probably still has his communion money. He could buy you a hundred rings if he wanted to.'

'If you girls knew Norman like I do, you'd understand why I'm marrying him. All that's wrong is that you need to spend more time with him. I'm going to arrange for us all to do some activities together after my honeymoon.'

'Ah yes . . . your honeymoon in Limerick,' Chloe muttered, unimpressed.

'I know! We should all do an escape room! It's the perfect way for you all to bond with Norman.'

'Forget we said anything,' Siobhan said, clearly having no desire to do an escape room with Norman. 'Alright, girls, new game! Truth or Dare?'

'No, that game triggers me!' Natalie said.

'Why?'

'I played it at a party once and someone dared me to go home.'

Kate, Siobhan and Chloe started howling laughing.

'It's not funny! It's trauma!' Natalie pouted.

'Oh God, that's too good,' Siobhan said. 'But we're playing it anyway. Kate. Truth or dare?'

'Hmm . . . dare,' Kate said.

'I dare you to go over and twerk on that woman who keeps shushing us.'

'Oh for God's sake! Fine, I choose truth then.'

'Alright . . .' Siobhan said, with a mischievous smile. 'Do you ever still think about Trevor Rush?'

Kate felt as if a lightning bolt had struck her in the heart.

She had only just forgotten about seeing the Polaroid of him that morning and now suddenly she was thinking about him once more. She had told the girls years ago that Trevor Rush was never to be mentioned again. And Siobhan had just dropped the T-Bomb. During her hen party, no less. It was classic Siobhan. She was a provocateur with absolutely no filter. And with the Dutch courage of the champagne, she was liable to say anything.

'Didn't we agree to never speak his name again?' Kate said, clearly irked.

'Oh come on, bitching about our exes is part of the hen party experience,' Siobhan said.

'Well, I won't even dignify your question with an answer. He was just some guy I had a fling with nine years ago.'

'Oh come on,' Chloe said, calling bullshit. 'He was a lot more than just some fling! Don't you ever stalk him on social media?'

'Nope. He's been blocked for nine years. Complete cold turkey.'

'I wish I had a Capricorn's willpower,' Natalie laughed.

'But you can't just block people out of your life,' Siobhan said.

'Yeah, that's not how you get closure,' Chloe said. 'You were head over heels in love with him. You were supposed to go back the following summer and start a life with him in New York.'

'Well, we all know what happened when I went to surprise Trevor for his birthday,' Kate said, trying not to remember the painful memory.

But it was already too late. Her mind was suddenly reaching back to that summer. Chloe was right. Trevor had asked her to stay in New York and start a life with him. But staying with him would have meant not finishing her final year at college. She had worked hard for her music degree and she was determined to finish it. So she promised Trevor she would return to him the following summer to be with him . . . for good.

They both agreed to do long distance for the year while she finished her final year. They talked on the phone every single day as they longed to be back together. The longing was so unbearable that Kate decided to book a flight to New York so that she could surprise Trevor for his birthday on the seventeenth of November. But when Kate approached his apartment building in Brooklyn, she saw the unthinkable.

She watched in horror as Trevor opened his apartment

door to a stunningly beautiful woman holding a bottle of wine. He kissed her on the cheek and led her inside.

At the time, it felt like the end of Kate's life. And in many ways, it was. But she had given him the benefit of the doubt, as any girlfriend would. She took out her phone to call him, certain he would have some kind of reasonable explanation. But he didn't answer.

All she got was a text that read: Can't talk, in a meeting.

Talk about a lie. Inviting a beautiful woman into his apartment for wine was not a meeting. It was an affair, plain and simple. Little did he know she had caught him red-handed. Crazy, party-girl Kate died that day. Certain types of painful moments have the power to change people for ever. And Trevor's betrayal was one of those moments. She flew back home with her heart in pieces and sent him a cold, vague Dear John message saying they weren't right for each other and she wouldn't be coming back to him the following summer. And then she blocked him before he could reply.

'I still think you overreacted,' Siobhan said.

'Siobhan, I saw him kissing a woman and bringing her into his apartment!' Kate said. 'While we were doing long distance!'

'It could have been his sister for all you know.'

'Trevor doesn't have any sisters! Why are you all making excuses for him?'

'Well, you could have marched over to him and demanded an explanation,' Chloe said.

'I called him to allow him to explain himself and he didn't answer. All he said was 'Can't talk, in a meeting.' That's why I sent him that break-up text. A taste of his own medicine.'

'But you blocked him on everything instead of fixing things. You even made *us* block him!' Chloe said.

'There was nothing to fix, Chloe. And I didn't want him reaching out to you three for answers either. I wanted the last word so I could hold my head up high.'

'I'm surprised you didn't confront him about cheating, though. Capricorns are usually very confrontational,' Natalie said.

'Yeah, it's almost as if the month someone's born in doesn't dictate their entire personality,' Siobhan said, sarcastically.

'Oh please. If astrology isn't real, then why is every man born between January and December a dickhead?'

'That's actually a good point,' Chloe nodded.

'Plus, Trevor was a Scorpio,' Natalie said. 'Sure, they're the best in bed but they always end up ruining your life.'

'Well, his days of ruining my life are over. He's a distant memory now. I haven't even thought about him in years,' Kate lied.

'Oh, so you threw away the locket?' Chloe asked.

'As a matter of fact, I did,' Kate said, lying once again.

'And the Academy Award for Worst Liar goes to . . .' Siobhan muttered.

'Well, I could never throw something like that away,' Chloe said. 'I'm too sentimental. It was like something out of a Taylor Swift song.'

'No, Taylor wouldn't tolerate a prick like Trevor. And I'm the same. If you break my heart, there are no second chances,' Kate said, sure of herself.

'Well, I do believe in once a cheater, always a cheater,' Natalie agreed. 'I think you did the right thing, Kate.'

'Thank you, Nat. Trevor was the biggest fuckboy in history. Don't you remember his stupid smirk? And the way he used to wink at everyone?'

'Yeah, that was hot,' Siobhan said, thinking back.

'It's not hot when you're his girlfriend and he's winking at other women! He was literally the world's biggest flirt. Certainly not the type of man you'd marry. He was a deadbeat DJ for God's sake!'

'Oh my God, remember his catchphrase every time he DJ'd?' Chloe said.

'ARE YOU READY TO . . .' the girls shouted at the top of their lungs.

'Please don't say it,' Kate said, mortified.

'. . . FEEL THE RUSH!'

Kate went scarlet. 'That is so cringey,' she said.

'He was such a ride though, so he could get away with it,' Siobhan said.

'Why are the trainwrecks always the most attractive?' Chloe said.

'It's because you're always trying to fix them.'

'Well, everyone loves a good fixer-upper,' Natalie laughed.

'Yes, but the problem is that you invest in him as a project and do all the repairs and then he puts himself back on the market with a higher value. And leaves you for someone better,' Kate said.

She felt a sense of sadness come over her as she said it.

One of the reasons seeing Trevor with that woman hurt so much was because Kate suffered with terrible 'ugly duckling syndrome'. In school she always felt as if she had fallen from the ugly tree and hit every branch on the way down. She had terrible acne that covered her entire face, horrifically crooked teeth that made it impossible to smile and a body full of freckles that gained her the nickname Crow's Egg. School hadn't been easy for Kate, mostly because teenage boys could be so cruel. A day hadn't gone by when she wasn't ridiculed.

But in her final year of secondary school, Kate decided enough was enough. It was time for a glow-up. It wasn't some idiotic ten-second makeover like in Hollywood movies where a girl simply takes off her glasses and ditches the pony tail, however. Kate had to get some serious dental and dermatology work done. She got tight braces with rubber bands and started Accutane in both pill and ointment form.

It took about eighteen months but by college, her glow-up was complete. Everyone told her constantly that she was a bombshell, but she still felt like the girl with acne and crooked teeth. Her freckles remained but she had learned to hide them. A lot of people found freckles beautiful, but the boys in her school had made her feel so insecure that she didn't like any attention being drawn to them, even if it was as a compliment. She even loved other people's freckles, but her own had been tainted by cruelty.

So, no matter how many times people told Kate she was a swan, she still couldn't get it into her head. And when she saw that beautiful woman step into Trevor's apartment, she felt everything she always believed about herself was true.

She was still that ugly duckling.

'Kate, that skank Trevor kissed was not better than you,' Chloe said.

'No, you should have seen her. She looked like a runway model. I had seen her at one of his DJ gigs too. She was determined to get him – I could see it in her eyes. He even winked at her. God, I was so blind back then. I couldn't see what was happening right in front of me.'

'But you couldn't have known that at the time, Kate.'

'Well, I should have seen the signs. He was toxic from the moment we met. Calling me Freckles when he knew I hated that nickname. Making constant empty promises, like telling me he was going to take me on a honeymoon around the world one day. And driving ninety miles per hour around Brooklyn in that death trap of a Mustang! But the worst thing was when he used to promise he would never hurt me. And that's exactly what he did.'

'That's not your fault, Kate. It's his,' Natalie said, comforting her.

'I know, but I was colourblind to all his red flags. And I ended up the fool. Trust me, ladies, find yourselves a man who doesn't need to be fixed. A doctor like Norman Cox,' Kate said, smugly.

'Dentist,' Chloe muttered once again.

'So, to answer your rather obnoxious question, Siobhan . . . No, I don't ever think about Trevor Rush. I am 100 per cent over the washed-up amateur DJ fuckboy and that's the end of it. Now, can we please go back to celebrating my hen party?' Kate said, eager to get the show back on the road.

'You're right Kate, I'm sorry for bringing it up,' Siobhan said, genuinely. 'You can dare me to do literally anything and I'll do it, no matter what!'

'Fine,' Kate said, trying to think of something juicy. 'Oh God, I can't think of anything!'

'I know,' Chloe said. 'We dare you to join the mile high club.'

'YES!' Siobhan said. 'Now we're talking! And Kyle has never been able to resist me.'

'It's Karl, and he's not just going to drop everything to have sex,' Natalie said.

'Have you never met a man before?'

'Well, you haven't a hope of getting into the cockpit.'

'True. But even pilots need a bathroom break. Watch and learn, skanks.'

The girls watched in shock as Siobhan walked down the aisle and began to speak to one of the male flight attendants. From where they were sitting, it was impossible to hear what she was saying but after a minute, the attendant knocked on the cockpit door. He whispered something to the captain, and then Karl stepped out into the front galley. Siobhan started batting her eyes and the flight attendant walked away towards the rear of the plane, knowing well where he wasn't wanted. Siobhan stepped backwards into the tiny lavatory and Karl pulled the galley curtains closed.

The girls were in stitches laughing. She had actually pulled it off. She'd definitely broken several laws, but Siobhan was never one for protocol.

'Fasten your seatbelts girls,' Kate laughed. 'I think we're about to encounter some turbulence.'

Chapter 6

Vegas Baby

When the girls finally touched down on American soil, they were already quite tipsy.

They each had their fair share of complimentary champagne, to the point where the flight attendant was getting a full workout just from tending to them. Eventually she gave up and started leaving the bottles. Kate had tried to get some sleep on the plane, but the girls kept waking her by reminiscing about their wild, younger days, with constant references to the old Kate.

It was something Kate found a little bit hurtful, although she dared not show it, for the sake of the trip. But wasn't it a little offensive for your friends to talk about your best self in the past tense? She was still fun. She had just matured. It was a natural part of going from your twenties to your thirties. The girls were still single and always up for partying and meeting new people. Kate just didn't need to do that any more.

She did miss having an active social life, however. Her nights with the girls were always iconic, but on the rare occasions they arranged a night on the town Norman always seemed to talk her out of it. As soon as she got dressed up, he would order a Chinese takeaway to be delivered or put on an episode of a show they were watching together and convince her to stay in. She loved Norman, but she was realizing that their relationship had become rather couch-based ever since he proposed to her. It was probably to be expected, she told herself. Kate had read somewhere that women love having a partner to go out with but that men love having a partner to come home to. She just wished those emotional needs weren't quite so one-sided.

However, her hen party was the perfect chance to make up for all the nights out she had missed with the girls, and she was determined to show them she was still the fun Kate they all remembered.

After collecting their luggage from the conveyor belt, Kate took her phone out and saw a text from Norman.

> **Norman:** Have you landed yet???

> **Kate:** Yep, just landed safe and got cases x

> Get some rest Normie, it's late there!

> **Norman:** I'll sleep when you get to hotel safe

> **Kate:** Okay, getting taxi now x

Kate put her phone away and the girls walked towards the airport exit, where their adventure was about to begin. She wasn't over the moon about carrying Chloe's unnecessary third suitcase but alas, someone had to.

'That flight flew,' Chloe said.

'Such a Chloe thing to say,' Natalie said, shaking her head.

'What's that supposed to mean?'

'Cut her some slack,' Siobhan laughed. 'She got her entire personality from a Bratz doll.'

The girls walked out through the automatic door and into the open air of Las Vegas. But they had somehow forgotten that Nevada in the summer was a far cry from the cold Irish weather they were used to back home. They were expecting the warm climate, of course, but nothing could have prepared them for the scorching heat they were currently experiencing.

'Oh sweet baby Jesus,' Siobhan said.

'Christ, how many degrees is it?' Natalie sighed.

'Let me check my phone,' Chloe said. 'OMG, it's 104 degrees Celsius!'

'That's Fahrenheit, you dope,' Natalie said. 'It's around 40 Celsius.'

'I think my body just entered menopause,' Kate said. Her auburn hair was already starting to look like red wool from frizz.

'Well, this is what global warming is doing to the planet, girls.'

'Look, it's 20 degrees Celsius in Ireland,' Chloe said, seeing it on her phone's weather app. 'That's the perfect temperature!'

'Yeah, but the sun only comes out in Ireland when you leave the country. If we stayed at home it would be lashing rain,' Siobhan said.

'True,' Chloe agreed. 'But my hair won't survive in this kind of heat!'

'Girls, don't worry,' Kate said, confidently. 'I did the research, and all the hotels and casinos are air-conditioned. We just need to get there and we'll be fine.'

'Well, we need to go NOW,' Siobhan said. 'It's only been ten seconds and I already have multiple sweat patches.'

'Those sweat patches are probably from joining the mile high club,' Chloe laughed.

'And it serves you right,' Natalie said. 'Sex on a plane? That's a new low for you.'

'I can go lower,' Siobhan shrugged. 'And we didn't have sex-sex, there wasn't enough room. We did everything but.'

'He put it in your butt?' Chloe said, horrified.

'NO!' Siobhan said. 'Although . . .'

'Well, I could never have sex on a plane,' Natalie said, prudishly. 'I happen to believe in a little thing called class.'

'I thought you were a Marxist?'

'Oh shut up!'

'Come on,' Siobhan laughed. 'Let's get a taxi before we faint.'

When they got to the taxi kiosk, the girls could see that there was a massive line of tourists trying to get to the Vegas Strip. Siobhan's jaw dropped when she saw the length of the queue. She immediately went straight up to the taxi marshal in charge of directing the cabs.

'Excuse me, sir,' she asked. 'How long is the wait time currently?'

'Ma'am, there's a line. You'll get a cab as soon as everyone in front of you gets a cab,' the marshal said.

'But you can't expect us to wait out in this heat?'

The taxi marshal looked at the girls and saw their bachelorette sashes, as well as Kate's penis tiara. 'Look, if you're here on a bachelorette party, there are party buses and limos down that way. It'll be quicker but it'll cost you.'

'You're a lifesaver! Thank you,' Siobhan said, running back to the girls, dripping with sweat.

'What did he say?' Kate asked.

'He said there are party buses and limos down this way. Let's go!'

'Wait, hold on. A party bus sounds expensive. There are only four of us. Maybe we should just wait.'

'Kate, our shoes are melting into the footpath.'

'Can we please just stick to the plan? A party bus is not on the itinerary,' Kate said, rigid as always.

'Neither is dying of dehydration, but that's what's going to happen if we stay here. Now come on!' Siobhan said, taking charge.

Kate felt anxious deviating into the unknown. Sure, it was roasting, but Siobhan was being a bit dramatic. They would have gotten a cab eventually and everything would have been fine. But the girls were already legging it down the lane and she had no choice but to follow them.

'How much longer?' Natalie whinged after about five minutes of walking.

'He said it was just down here,' Siobhan said.

'I can't walk for much longer in these heels,' Chloe whined. 'I'm going to end up with bunions!'

'We told you to bring flats for the flight,' Natalie said.

'I'd rather die in heels than live in flats.'

By now, Kate was really feeling the heat. She was practically dizzy. She had never experienced 40-degree heat before and the fumes from all the cars made it feel like so much more. She was severely sweltered. Not only was the heat destroying her hair but now it was starting to affect her makeup.

That's when they saw it.

They all stood in complete awe. The glory of it. The sublime majesty.

'You all see it too, right? It's not a mirage?' Siobhan asked.

'No, I see it too,' Chloe said. 'It's beautiful.'

Before them, in the distance, was a pink Hummer limo.

'Imagine the air conditioning in that thing,' Chloe said. 'I could blow it up my dress like Marilyn Monroe!'

'WE'LL TAKE IT!' Siobhan said, sprinting towards the chauffeur standing next to it.

'Excuse me?' the chauffeur asked.

'This beautiful pink oasis, how much for a ride?' she asked.

'To go to the Vegas Strip? It will be $1,000.'

'You must be joking,' Kate said, horrified.

'But Kate, that's only $200 each!' Chloe said.

'First of all, no, it's not. Second, it's a total rip-off. Norman will kill me!' Kate said. 'And isn't a pink Hummer limo a little tacky?'

'Kate, you're wearing a penis tiara on your head. I think we're past tacky,' Siobhan said.

'But the number plate says "Bridin' Dirty", for God's sake.' Kate suddenly heard her phone beep and saw that Norman had texted yet again.

> **Norman:** Why does your GPS say you're still at airport???

> **Kate:** Sorry Normie, the girls are trying to rent a pink Hummer limo

> **Norman:** Absolutely not! That will cost a fortune!!!

> It's only a 12 minute drive to your hotel

Norman was right. Not only was it extortionate, but it was also a little off-brand for Kate. It wasn't part of the itinerary, and she knew a successful hen party meant sticking to the plan. 'Girls, I've made up my mind,' she said. 'We're not paying $1,000 to drive a few minutes up the road.'

'But . . .' Chloe began.

'That's final,' Kate said, putting her foot down. 'Now come on, let's head back to the taxi rank.'

The girls began walking back to where they started, sulking like children who had just been told they weren't going to Disneyland.

'Jesus, girls, I'm sweating like a nun in a cucumber field,' Siobhan sighed in the unbearable heat. 'I don't think I can go on.'

'Look, we can see the line from here,' Kate said, squinting into the distance. 'And it's not as long as it was.'

After a thirty-minute wait, the girls finally reached the top of the line and jumped into a cab.

'Hey, sexy ladies,' the taxi driver said. 'Where are you heading?'

'The Fellatio,' Siobhan said as she sat in.

'It's the Bellagio!' Kate said, correcting her.

'Oops, Freudian slip.'

The driver started the car and pulled out of the driveway. 'No problem ladies. Would you like the air conditioning on?'

'YES!' they all roared at once.

'Alright, yikes, let's put it on full blast.'

The cool air filled the car immediately and it was like a breeze from heaven.

'Oh sweet Jesus, I thought we were going to die,' Siobhan said.

'But we're cool now and still on schedule,' Kate said. 'See girls, everything worked out and we're $1,000 better off.'

'Not used to the heat, ladies?' the taxi driver asked.

'No, we're from Ireland.'

'Oh, four sexy lucky charms!'

'Is that offensive?' Natalie muttered.

'Nat, shut up or he might turn off the AC!' Chloe said, elbowing her in the arm.

'Any Vegas recommendations?' Siobhan said. 'It's our first time.'

'Vegas virgins, eh? Hmm, let's see . . . well, it's Saturday night, so you have to go to Omnia in Caesar's Palace,' the taxi driver said. 'Best nightclub in Vegas.'

'That is exactly what I wanted to hear.'

'You're a bachelorette party, right?'

'What gave it away?' Kate laughed, pointing at her penis tiara.

'Then you have to get a champagne shower on stage at Omnia. They sometimes do it free for brides-to-be!'

'OMG, Kate, we have to!' Chloe said. 'Think of the boomerang!'

'We'll see,' Kate said, although she had no intention of enduring such torture. Having champagne poured all over her in a nightclub?

Absolutely not.

ॐ

When the taxi pulled up in front of the illustrious Bellagio Hotel, the girls stepped onto the pulsating heart of the Vegas Strip. Kate was completely mesmerized as she looked around. She had seen the pictures, of course, but they simply didn't do the place justice.

Everything was MASSIVE.

Kate was of average height, but she felt like a tiny ant that was about to be squashed by the sheer grandeur of the city-scape. The smell of alcohol lingered heavily in the air to the point where she could practically taste the sweet, sharp tang of liquor on her lips. She looked back towards the Strip and saw the neon playground waiting for them, an electric Eden calling them forth.

Chloe immediately began taking loads of photos. Even Natalie was speechless.

'Have a great trip, ladies,' the taxi driver said when he finished taking out their luggage. 'Be good now.'

'We won't,' Siobhan flirted back as she paid him the fare plus tip.

As they stood in awe of the Bellagio's entrance, the girls noticed that behind them was a huge fountain water show. Spurts of water were soaring into the sky in synchronized splendour. The streams splashed and squirted, reaching unbelievable heights.

'See that fountain, girls?' Siobhan said. 'That's what my fanny's gonna be like all weekend.'

'SIOBHAN!' Kate laughed.

'Fanny means bum over here, by the way,' Natalie said.

'Well, I think it's time I showed Americans what a fanny really is.'

'God help them,' Chloe laughed.

'Come on, let's check in. My shoes are starting to melt again,' Siobhan said, leading them indoors.

As they walked into the cool, air-conditioned building, Kate was blown away by the size of the lobby. It was gargantuan compared to the hotels back home. The architectural style was so elegant, with several artistic nods to the Italian Renaissance. It was like Michelangelo himself had carved the room from marble.

'Checking in?' the receptionist asked as they approached the front desk.

'Yes,' Kate said. 'We have a room booked under my name. Kate O'Connor.'

'Certainly, let me just check that for you.'

'Just so you know . . .' Chloe butted in. 'I happen to be an influencer back in Ireland. So if there were any room upgrades available . . .'

'I'm afraid that won't be possible.'

'Of course,' Chloe said, mortified.

Siobhan was in stitches laughing at poor Chloe's failed attempt.

'Okay, I see here you've booked a double queen room. Would you like me to charge the card on the booking?'

'No, that's the bride's card. You can put it on mine,' Siobhan said, handing her the credit card.

'But I want to pay for one quarter of the room, girls,' Kate insisted.

'Oh give up, Kate, the bride doesn't pay for the room on her hen party. We're splitting it three ways.'

'I feel bad though. I should have picked a cheaper hotel.'

'Kate, if we're doing Vegas, we might as well do it right,' Natalie said.

'Exactly,' Siobhan said. 'We can always earn more money. We can never earn more time.'

'Ooh, remind me to use that as an Instagram caption,' Chloe said.

'Alright ladies, payment has gone through,' the receptionist said. 'Here are your keycards for room 2169. And by the way, there'll be a complimentary bottle of champagne in the room waiting for you.'

'Because I'm an influencer?' Chloe said, more needy than ever.

'No, because you're a bachelorette party.'

'Oh wow, thank you so much,' Kate said, chuffed.

'Enjoy your stay.'

After a long elevator ride and a walk down a seemingly never-ending corridor, the girls eventually found room 2169. As soon as they opened the door, their jaws hit the floor.

The room was beyond fabulous, with rich colours, opulent furnishings and spectacular views of the fountain below. It seemed even more luxurious than the photos of it they'd seen online, and that was saying something. The two queen beds were huge, and the gorgeous scents of fresh linen and lavender lingered in the cool, conditioned air.

'Oh my God, girls!' Kate said. 'This is even nicer than I thought it would be! Great choice!'

'You're the one who chose it,' Siobhan laughed.

'Oh right, yes,' Kate said. 'So Chloe and I will take this bed and Siobhan and Natalie, you can take that one.'

'Why do I have to share with Siobhan?' Natalie complained. 'I'll probably catch something off her!'

'You'll be fine. Even chlamydia has standards,' Siobhan teased as she opened the bathroom door. 'OH MY GOD!'

'WHAT?' Kate shouted in to her.

'We have a fucking bidet!' she said, ecstatic. 'Girls, my fanny's gonna be sparklin'!'

'There's not enough soap in the world,' Natalie laughed.

'Oh girls, I really needed this trip,' Chloe said, sprawling on the bed. 'It's so nice to get a break from it all.'

'Says the unemployed one.'

'I'm not unemployed. I just believe every woman deserves a six-month holiday, twice a year,' Chloe shrugged.

'Fair.'

'Anyway, working is bad for my skin. I like to surround myself with good vibes.'

'Speaking of which,' Natalie said, 'I should light some sage to cleanse the room of any negative energy. God knows what these four walls have seen.'

'Please don't start with the witchcraft stuff, Nat,' Siobhan sighed. 'You're not a Ravenclaw, you're a thirty-year-old woman who lives with her parents.'

'Yeah, and you told me a moonstone crystal would help heal my acid reflux, but I nearly choked to death!' Chloe said.

'You weren't supposed to SWALLOW it!' Natalie yelled. 'Fine, no sage.'

Kate heard her phone beep and saw that Norman had texted her yet again, despite the fact that it was the middle of the night in Ireland.

Norman: Are you at the hotel yet?

Kate: Yes, it's gorgeous!

Norman: It would want to be with the price of it

Don't open the mini bar. They charge you if you even touch a bottle

Kate: Sure Normie

Go and get some sleep

Text you first thing in morning x

Kate put her phone away and saw the girls immediately heading towards the mini bar.

'Girls, don't open that. Norman just said they can tell if you even touch the liquor,' she said.

'Alright, let's open our complimentary champagne then,' Siobhan said, grabbing the bottle.

'Oh girls, I don't know. I'm still a bit hammered after the—'

But before Kate could finish her sentence, Siobhan had the bottle popped. 'Woohoo,' she said as she filled up the four glasses. 'Oh my God, I have just the thing for this!' Siobhan unzipped the front pouch of her suitcase and took out a bag of plastic penis straws.

'Champagne through a straw?' Natalie asked. 'Really?'

'It's much more efficient,' Siobhan smiled as she placed a penis straw in each of their champagne flutes. 'But the dicks on them are a little small for my liking.'

'Could you not have found paper straws? You know how I feel about plastic ones,' Natalie sulked.

'You wanted me to find paper penis straws? The ones that go soggy after three seconds?'

'They're better for the environment.'

'Well, sorry sunshine, a penis has never gone soft in my mouth and it never will,' Siobhan laughed.

'Girls, let's cheers to a wild weekend in the fabulous Las Vegas,' Chloe said, taking out her phone to take a boomerang of their glasses clinking.

'CHEERS, BITCHES!' Siobhan roared.

Clink.

'Hold on, the boomerang didn't come out right,' Chloe said. 'Let's all cheers again.'

'I'm not doing a million boomerangs every time we have a drink.'

'And Chloe, be careful what you put on your story,' Kate said. 'I don't want Norman to think we're drinking too much.'

'Fine! As much as it kills me not to be seen, I'll make a private story just for us,' Chloe agreed. 'What Norman doesn't know can't hurt him.'

'Exactly,' Siobhan said. 'Alright, let's start getting ready!'

'Ready for what?' Kate said.

'For Omnia. The taxi guy said it's the best nightclub in Vegas.'

'I know, that's why I have Omnia down for tomorrow night on the itinerary,' Kate smiled.

'Tomorrow is Sunday; nightclubs are shite on Sundays. All the rides will be there tonight. So down your drinks and let's get dolled up.'

'But we had cocktails in the airport and champagne on the flight and more champagne now. I think we should hit the hay and try and beat the jetlag. It can hit you like a ton of bricks if you don't get into a normal sleep cycle.'

'Kate, we're not going to bed at 7 p.m. like a bunch of nuns on a pilgrimage. We're in Sin City! And I may or may not have booked us a little surprise. Now, everyone put on a slutty outfit and get ready for our first night of debauchery!'

'I just want to shower off my tan before we go out,' Chloe said.

'Chloe, we don't have time. Just shower it off when we get back.'

'Okay. I'm not too orange though, am I? It's developing a lot faster than my normal tan.'

'As long as you don't run into Willy Wonka, you'll be fine,' Natalie joked.

Kate felt a tad anxious about this new plan. The itinerary had them getting an early night so that they would be fresh as daisies the next morning. And what was this surprise Siobhan had secretly arranged? Kate hated surprises. She had so much planned for the following day and the thought of doing everything hungover did not appeal to her one bit.

'I don't know, girls,' she panicked. 'We'll be dying tomorrow if we keep drinking. And I have so much planned for us on the itin—'

'The itinerary. Yes, we heard you the first thousand times. And it's getting a little old,' Siobhan said.

'Oh, well, sorry for wanting to see the Grand Canyon.'

'Kate, you can see my vagina any time you want!'

'Come on, Kate,' Chloe said. 'Nobody looks back on their life and remembers the nights they got plenty of sleep.'

Kate was trying with every fibre of her being to go with the flow, but it was almost killing her. She had planned for them to go to Omnia tomorrow, not tonight. This sudden turn of events threw everything up in the air. But she knew she couldn't exactly force the girls to go to bed. They were all tipsy and ready to party. She was just terrified of the hangover ruining the following morning.

'Tell you what, Kate,' Siobhan said. 'Two drinks and home by ten. Deal?'

'Okay,' Kate finally conceded. 'Deal.'

Chapter 7

Omnia

About an hour later, the girls were dolled up to the nines and Siobhan, Chloe and Natalie were ready to paint the town red. Kate, however, was hoping to paint the town more of a gentle shade of beige. She was already fairly hammered from the hours of drinking and she didn't think she had much fuel left in her.

She wished the girls would show some more appreciation for the itinerary she had spent months putting together. They really should have been in bed by now so they could enjoy the rest of the trip, jetlag-free. She once again told herself to go with the flow, but it was just so damn difficult for her. It was *her* hen party, however, and she couldn't exactly go to bed while the girls went out. A bachelorette party didn't make much sense without a bride-to-be.

The girls sashayed through the Bellagio, following the signs towards Caesar's Palace. They had truly pulled out all the stops for their debut on the Strip. Chloe was wearing a gorgeous blue bodycon dress with a pair of five-inch nude heels. Natalie wore a black jumpsuit with a criss-cross back, a pair of black Doc Martens and an onyx crystal around her neck. And Siobhan had on a red pleather co-ord that left very little to the imagination; just how she liked it. Around her neck was a dangly shot glass necklace that read 'Designated Drunk' and, under her arm, she was carrying an inflatable male sex doll who was comically well-endowed.

Kate, on the other hand, was a vision of pure class in a stunning white sheath dress and veil, although her cowboy boots and penis tiara gave a unique twist to her otherwise elegant look. Together with their bachelorette sashes, the girls certainly looked the part. They strutted through the Bellagio, turning heads as they made their cinematic entrance.

'Is it just me or are we walking in slow motion?' Chloe said.

'No, we're just very, very drunk,' Natalie said.

'I feel fine,' Siobhan shrugged, still relatively sober. 'And I look even finer.'

'You literally look like the devil in that red pleather.'

'That's the point. And why are you wearing a jumpsuit? It's going to be impossible for someone to get in your pants!'

'It's good to play hard to get.'

'I prefer to get them hard,' Siobhan smirked.

'Good Lord,' Natalie laughed.

'Norman, which way is Omnia?' Siobhan said, referring to the inflatable man on her arm.

'Oh, his name is Norman, is it?' Kate laughed. 'I still can't believe you spent an hour blowing him up.'

'You're just mad that I blew your fiancé.'

The girls continued walking towards Caesar's Palace and were mesmerized by the hundreds of screens illuminating the casino floor. Natalie couldn't help but notice that there was no natural light whatsoever.

'Wait, why are there no windows?' she said, looking around.

'It's so you become disorientated and lose track of time,' Kate said, having learned about it when researching the trip.

'There are no clocks either. It's how they keep people gambling non-stop.'

Natalie looked around at the hundreds of gamblers sitting at slot machines, completely absorbed in a game that was rigged against them. 'Jesus, I didn't realize we were on a journey into the dark heart of late capitalism,' she said.

'Nat, no man is going to buy you a drink if you keep saying things like that,' Chloe said.

'Good thing I like girls too,' Natalie said. 'They're actually capable of critical thinking.'

'Well, I am definitely here for the men. I'm ready to take Vegas by the balls,' Siobhan said, looking around like a hawk.

'By the time you're done, they'll probably name a new STI after you,' Chloe joked.

'Siobhanorrhea?' Natalie suggested.

'Oh, that's good. Remind me to trademark that!' Siobhan said with pride.

ॐ

When the girls arrived at Omnia, they immediately noticed there was a queue a mile long that appeared to consist entirely of men. But Siobhan bypassed the entire line and walked straight up to check in.

'Siobhan, there's a line!' Kate said.

'Not for us,' she said before turning to the bouncer. 'Hi there, I have a booth booked under Siobhan Murphy.'

'No problem. I just need to see some ID,' the bouncer said.

'Of course,' Siobhan said, taking out her driver's licence.

'Perfect. Follow me.'

'Aren't you going to ask for *my* ID?' Natalie asked, offended. She was the youngest of the group, after all.

'No, I'm good.'

'I'm literally Gen Z!'

'Nurse, she's out again,' Siobhan said, slagging her. 'Come on, Grandma, let's get you back to bed.'

After they all got their stamps, the girls followed the bouncer towards the main club floor. But the term 'club' didn't even do it justice.

Omnia was on a whole other level, a surreal symphony of sights, sounds and sensations.

It felt more like the Colosseum than a club. That's when Kate realized they were in Caesar's Palace, and its aesthetic was based on that of Rome's. It literally *was* a Colosseum. The difference was, people came here to dance instead of watch battles – although Siobhan was surely on the look-out for some gladiators. Under the shimmering lights, bodies swirled in rhythmic ecstasy as the sultry scent of perfume and sweat mingled with the sweet taste of cocktails. The music was blasting at full volume and the bass was like a bullet in Kate's chest every time it hit.

'Holy Mary mother of God,' she said, in pure shock. 'This club is bigger than the entire city of Dublin!'

'Now, aren't you glad we decided to come out?' Siobhan said.

They followed the bouncer upstairs to the seating areas overlooking the main stage. From up there, they had the perfect view of the dance floor and the stage below. There was a DJ on the decks and thousands of sweaty people on the dance floor. As much as Kate liked to dance, she was glad she was up high and not down in the Colosseum pit. It looked a little too intense for her.

'Here you are, ladies,' the bouncer said. 'Booth number twenty-two is all yours.'

'I put in a special request that our drinks be here on arrival,' Siobhan said, seeing the table was empty.

'The waitress will be right up with that,' he said. 'Enjoy your night.'

The girls stepped into their VIP booth and were absolutely shocked at how fabulous it was. But Kate was riddled with guilt. She knew a booth like this wasn't cheap.

'Siobhan, this is too much,' she said. 'How did you even organize this?'

'Nothing is too much for my girls,' Siobhan smiled. 'And I found a Vegas promoter on Instagram and negotiated a discount.'

'How did you get the dis—'

'Don't ever ask me what I did for that discount,' Siobhan said, only half-joking. She threw the inflatable doll on the couch and began scanning the room for men. She was immediately impressed with the talent. 'Jesus, girls, the lads here are so fucking hot.'

'Define hot,' Natalie said, unimpressed.

'Oh come on, Nat, look at the muscles on some of these lads!'

'Ew, I hate muscles on a guy.'

'Really?' Kate said. 'Sometimes I wish Norman would hit the gym now and again.'

'I thought he was perfect?' Chloe said, raising an eyebrow.

'He is . . . but a good, strong frame never hurts.'

Natalie grabbed the inflatable sex doll off the couch. 'Are you telling me *this* isn't the perfect male body?'

'I would have blown him some more.'

'KATE, you dirty bitch!' Chloe laughed.

'Oh my God, I didn't mean it like that!' Kate said, mortified.

'I was encouraging you. It's good to see you finally loosening up.'

A cocktail waitress came up to their booth, holding a large

ice bucket. 'Here you are, ladies,' she said. 'Your special drink request.'

'Aww, you ordered champagne too?' Kate said, chuffed. Although, she was so tipsy she didn't know if she could handle another glass.

'Not exactly . . .' Siobhan said, with a devious smirk.

When the waitress placed the ice bucket down on the table, Kate almost lost her life in shock.

It was not champagne at all.

It was so much worse.

Because sitting in the bucket of ice were four large cans of Four Loko.

'Surprise!' Siobhan announced.

'NO, NO, NO, NO, NO,' Kate said, in shock. She refused to even entertain the idea. Four Loko was a recipe for disaster. Every single time they had drunk it in the past, they had completely blacked out with no clue of what had happened the night before.

There was no way in hell Kate was drinking it.

'She means yes,' Siobhan said to the waitress, who then headed back towards the bar.

'Absolutely not! Drinking that stuff is asking for trouble. It always sends us over the edge!'

'Well, yeah, that's where all the fun is.'

'It's literally a blackout in a bottle!'

'That's not true,' Siobhan said. 'It's in a can.'

'Girls, I really don't feel comfortable doing this.' Kate panicked. 'I promised Norman I wouldn't do anything crazy, and this is the very definition of crazy. We were supposed to be in bed by now so we could wake up fresh in the morning and do everything on the itinerary!'

'THAT'S IT,' Siobhan said, at her wits' end. 'Kate, it's time for an intervention!'

'An intervention where you're forcing me to drink?'

'Exactly! The old Kate would be having the time of her life in a VIP booth in Vegas, drinking Four Lokos with her best friends. Instead, you're worried about what your fiancé might think, even though he's thousands of miles away. Norman has turned you into a boring shell of your fabulous self. Well, I know the real you is still in there somewhere, and I won't rest until she's brought back to life. You might be obsessed with planning, Kate, but as maid of honour, it's my job to ensure you have the night of your life. Because you forgot to schedule one tiny little thing on your itinerary, Kate. Having some actual fun.'

Kate had never been confronted like this before.

She knew she could be a bit of a control freak at times, but she never realized she was such a bore. When had this happened? When had she become so obsessed with planning? Had Norman truly made her boring? She got more enjoyment out of planning an event than she did the event itself. She was always living in the future, excited for fun times to come. But there was fun to be had right here in the present, if she could just learn to live in the moment.

The way she had on their J-1 summer in New York.

Maybe it was time for the new Kate to meet the old Kate. Wasn't the whole purpose of a bachelorette party for a woman to let loose before the big day? This could be her last chance to be her wildest self, without any consequences. It was quite literally now or never.

What was the worst that could happen?

'Give me the fucking can,' Kate smiled.

'WOOHOO!!!' the girls screamed.

They each grabbed their favourite flavour of their signature drink. Kate took Electric Lemonade. Siobhan took Black

Cherry. Chloe took Blue Razz-berry and Natalie took Sour Apple.

'The Four Lokos are back, baby!' Siobhan said, as they clinked their cans together and started sipping.

'Back with a bang!' Kate said. 'And Norman doesn't need to know!'

'Well, in that case, our blow-up friend here is no longer named Norman,' Natalie said. 'What should his new name be?'

'Well, with that big inflated dick, he looks like a Trevor to me,' Siobhan said.

'Siobhan!' Chloe said, shooting her a look. 'We're not allowed to say the T-word, remember?'

'No, it's okay,' Kate said. 'I actually like the idea of calling him Trevor. Because I have a few things I want to say to that prick!'

'Okay, I'm literally obsessed with the new Kate!' Natalie said.

'Not the new Kate, this is the REAL Kate! She's back for the weekend. And Trevor Rush, I have a bone to pick with you!' Kate said, turning to confront the inflatable sex doll.

'YAAAASSSS,' the girls cheered her on.

Kate began to address the doll as if she was speaking to Trevor directly. She was fairly plastered at this stage, and she was ready to tell it like it was. She had repressed her feelings for Trevor for too long and they were finally bubbling to the surface.

It was time to let it all out.

'Listen here, you,' Kate began, pointing at him dramatically. 'You and I could have had it all. We were perfect for each other until you decided to be a slimy snake in the grass and cheat on me three months after I left. I was going to come back to you as soon as I finished my degree so we could make music together like we always planned. But I guess one year is just too long for a man to be loyal. And it wouldn't have hurt so much seeing you kiss that woman if you didn't give me that stupid locket. A locket I can't seem to throw away, no matter how hard I try. If you had just told me you were a fuckboy from day one, I would have been fine with it. But you had to go and pretend you were some romantic dream, knowing damn well I would fall in love with you. I believed all of your lies while you were making a fool of me behind my back. Telling me I was beautiful, telling me I was talented, telling me you loved me. I wonder how many other women fell for your act. You promised me you would never hurt me and I was dumb enough to believe you. Well, guess what, Trevor? I don't even care any more. I'm erasing you from my life story. You are no longer welcome in my thoughts. So cheers to me finally forgetting you ever existed!'

'WOOHOO!' the girls applauded.

'How do you feel?' Chloe asked.

'Like I'm finally free of Trevor Rush,' Kate smiled as she held her head up high. 'Bottoms up, bitches!'

The girls all clinked their drinks one last time before throwing back their entire cans of Four Loko. Kate almost choked as she finished the drink in one go.

'Jesus, I forgot how strong this stuff is,' she winced.

'It literally tastes like ass,' Siobhan said. 'Let's order some more!'

'You girls doing okay over here?' the waitress said, as she passed by them.

'Actually, would you mind taking our photo?' Chloe said. 'Girls, we all have a can of Four Loko – we can recreate our first ever photo together!'

'Chloe, that's brilliant!' Kate said, thrilled by the idea. She reached into her handbag and took out her Polaroid camera. 'Here you go. Flash is on.'

The waitress took the camera and the girls all got into the same poses as the photo from nine years before. 'Alright, say Vegas!'

'VEGAS!' the girls said as the camera captured the moment for ever. The Polaroid immediately began to print, and Kate just knew it would be perfect for her hen party scrap book.

'Thank you so much,' Kate said, taking the camera and the photo from the waitress.

'By the way,' Siobhan said to her. 'A guy told us about something called a champagne shower. How does that work exactly?'

'So, in between DJ sets, you can go up on stage and have the new DJ pop a bottle of champagne all over you,' the waitress said. 'There's normally a fee but because you already paid for a booth, I can comp the shower for the bride.'

'Now *that's* what I call a bridal shower!' Siobhan said. 'She'll take it!'

'Oh I don't know, girls,' Kate panicked. She had hoped the girls had forgotten about that idea. 'It could ruin my dress and hair. I'll be a mess.'

'Say yes to the mess, Kate,' Natalie said, egging her on.

'Please Kate, you have to!' Chloe begged.

Kate felt her anxiety begin to creep back in. She really didn't like the idea of champagne being sprayed all over her, but she had already promised the girls that the real Kate was back. She couldn't exactly go back on her word now. And she had made the decision to at least try and live in the moment.

Fuck it.

'Okay, I'll do it!' she conceded.

'Cool,' the waitress said. 'What's your name? The MC will call you up when it's time.'

'Soon-to-be Kate Cox, visiting from Ireland.'

'Okay, perfect.' The waitress began to speak into her headset. 'Hey Dave, I have a last-minute champagne shower request. Yeah, it's for bride-to-be Kate Cox from Ireland. You got that? After this song? Cool, I'll let her know.'

'It's probably too last minute, isn't it?' Kate said, still secretly hoping to get out of it.

'No, you got in just in time. The MC is coming on right after this song. Make sure you're ready,' the waitress said before walking away.

'Oh God,' Kate said, getting flustered. 'I've no time to prepare! I have no idea what to expect.'

'I'm guessing they're going to shower you in champagne. Just a hunch,' Natalie said, sarcastically.

'I'll take a video from here. It'll be such a funny memory to have!' Chloe said, taking out her phone.

'Speaking of which,' Kate said, looking down at the developed Polaroid in her hand. It was just like the one from nine years ago, and she absolutely adored it. 'Our photo is fab, girls!'

'I swear we get hotter every year,' Siobhan said, confident as ever.

The club MC suddenly swaggered onto the stage holding a microphone. 'MAKE SOME NOISE FOR DJ HARD-CORE!' he screamed.

The crowd began to roar.

'We got another one of the sickest DJs coming up for y'all. But first, what's it time for?' the MC shouted into the mic.

'CHAMPAGNE SHOWERS!' the entire crowd shouted back.

'Now, we got a crazy chick from IRELAND out here cele-brating her BACHELORETTE PARTY, is that right?' the MC said, looking into the crowd.

'Oh Jesus, girls, this is so embarrassing!' Kate said, mortified.

'SHE'S OVER HERE!' Siobhan shouted down to the MC as she flailed her arms over the balcony.

A spotlight came on and shone directly into Kate's eyes, practically blinding her.

'People of Omnia, make some noise for the soon-to-be MRS KATE COX!'

The crowd began to roar again.

'GET UP THERE, SKANK!' Siobhan insisted.

Kate felt like a deer in headlights. She hated all the attention. But there was no getting out of it now. There were literally thousands of people cheering for her. As she walked down the stairs, she felt the Four Loko hit her like a ton of bricks. The room was spinning and her vision was blurring. She wasn't sure if she was even going to make it to the stage.

When she got to the lower level, Kate felt like Bambi on ice. She walked up to the stage as the crowd screamed for her. You'd swear she was after winning an Oscar with the volume of the supporting screams. A part of her did like the adulation. She only wished they were applauding her for something other than getting drenched in champagne.

She arrived on stage and stood beside the MC.

'Kate, are you ready for your CHAMPAGNE SHOWER?' the MC yelled.

'Bring it on,' Kate said awkwardly into the mic. Her voice lacked any semblance of charisma and she cringed when she heard her own words reverberate around the massive room.

'I think you can do a little BETTER than that, Kate!' the MC said, signalling the crowd to cheer.

'BRING IT ON!!!' Kate shouted, this time with vigour.

'That's more like it! Omnia, are you ready for our next DJ?' he shouted.

The crowd began to scream even louder than they had for Kate.

'I SAID, ARE YOU READY FOR ONE OF VEGAS'S BIGGEST DJS?!' the MC roared again.

The crowd went berserk. It was enough to burst one's eardrums, but Kate just stood there smiling.

'Omnia, are you ready to . . . FEEL THE RUSH?'

Kate felt time come to a standstill.

She looked up at the girls. Their eyes were like bullets.

Surely it was just a coincidence.

It had to be.

'Then make some noise for the one and only TREVOR RUSH!'

Kate looked back at the girls once again. Their hands were covering their mouths in pure shock.

It wasn't a coincidence. It was a catastrophe.

A dramatic EDM remix of 'Toxic' by Britney Spears began blasting through the speakers. The track had an epic string arrangement and pulsing beat that made it sound like the music used in action movie trailers. Yet, Kate felt she was currently starring in her own personal horror film. A wild light show of technicolour lasers illuminated the room as fog began to fill the stage. Kate tried to breathe but she was engulfed in a cloud of smoke. She was breathless.

That's when she saw a shadowy figure rise up from beneath the stage.

He was posing with one hand in the air and shaking a bottle of champagne in the other. The crowd was screaming for him. They knew who he was.

The platform seemed to be rising up in slow motion and Kate had no idea what to do. She felt herself transition from drunk to hammered. The Four Loko was warping her perception of reality. This couldn't really be happening. It had to be a fever dream. Some kind of alcohol-induced hallucination.

It was a nightmare. It had to be a nightmare. She had to wake up!

The platform finally rose up fully and the fog cleared between them. She was in his direct line of sight. Standing right in front of her before a crowd of thousands.

The man she had first loved.

The man who broke her heart.

The one and only.

Trevor Fucking Rush.

'KATE?' Trevor said as he locked eyes with her.

The champagne popped of its own accord.

And that was the last thing Kate would ever remember from that fateful night.

Chapter 8

The Morning After

Kate awoke to the sound of a drum pounding against her skull.

She tried to open her eyes but immediately felt a cruel sunlight scorch her corneas. She tried to lick her lips but her mouth felt like it had spent forty days and nights in the neighbouring Nevada desert. The smell of alcohol and sweat attacked her nostrils with unforgiving force.

What the hell had happened?

Kate tried to raise her eyelids once again, this time more gradually. When she finally got them fully open, she realized she wasn't in her hotel room. The bed she was in was twice as big as the one she remembered from check-in, and the room was easily five times the size. She was still in last night's white dress but her sash was gone. She looked around in complete and utter confusion. The drum in her head seemed to be getting louder and her mouth was somehow getting drier.

It was easily the worst hangover of Kate's life.

She had never experienced 'the fear' quite like this. She had absolutely no recollection of how she ended up here. Her memory was shattered into elusive fragments. Something about Omnia. The sound of champagne popping. And, for some reason, the name Trevor Rush. But that didn't make any sense.

Kate turned to her right to try and survey her surroundings. In the bed beside her was a large inflatable sex doll.

Of course! That was it.

That's why Trevor Rush's name was in her mind. She remembered confronting the inflatable man and feeling afterwards that she was finally free from Trevor after nine years.

Phew. That was one mystery solved.

But what had happened after that? And where the hell was she? Whose bed was she in? Sweet Jesus, had she gone home with someone? She suddenly felt like throwing up, but it was just a dry heave. It seemed like there were no solids in her stomach that were going to rise.

She needed answers. Fast.

Kate began searching frantically for her phone, her only lifeline in this situation. She eventually found it inside her handbag in the corner of the room, thankfully without any kind of damage. She had drunkenly broken a few phone screens over the years but, by some miracle, this wasn't one of those instances. When she looked at her screen, she was horrified at what she saw.

43 missed calls. All from Norman.

Dozens of texts too. She could see the three most recent ones on her home screen.

Norman: Kate, I've been calling for hours!!! WHERE ARE YOU?

What is going on, why won't you answer me??? I'm worried sick!!!!

KATE PLEASE ANSWER YOUR PHONE!!!!

Kate felt completely smothered. She had promised Norman she would text him every hour to check in, and as she looked at the time, she realized she had ignored him for almost twelve hours. She knew she had to call him back, but she needed to stop her head from spinning first.

One thing at a time.

She looked in the mirror and barely recognized the hot mess staring back at her. Her foundation was destroyed, her lipstick smudged, and her auburn hair looked like it had been backcombed with a toilet brush.

It was clear just by looking at herself that it had been a rough night, even by Vegas standards.

But what had happened?

The girls.

The girls would have the answers.

She needed to find them.

Kate opened the bedroom door and was immediately blown away by what she saw. She was in some kind of penthouse suite. It was easily the most luxurious room Kate had ever seen, let alone spent a night in. It looked like it cost at least $10,000 a night.

There was just one problem.

The room was completely trashed. It looked like a bomb had gone off in the middle of it and the debris of the night before was everywhere. Glasses were smashed, furniture was upside down and the putrid stench of alcohol seeped through the air.

'Hello?' Kate said softly. But the room was so huge that her whisper bounced off the walls and echoed throughout the suite.

Natalie suddenly popped her head up from where she'd been passed out on the couch. 'Kate?' she groaned as she sat up. 'Is that you?' She was a complete mess too. But Natalie seemed to have it worse than Kate. By the looks of things, her hangover was going to last a few weeks.

Because Natalie had no eyebrows.

Shaved or burned off, Kate couldn't tell.

But, either way, they were gone.

'Oh my God, Natalie. Are you okay?' Kate said.

'Where the hell are we?' Natalie asked, trying to open her eyes.

Kate decided not to tell her about her eyebrows, or lack thereof. Best to let her wake up first. 'I have no idea, Nat,' she said. 'And where are the rest of the girls?'

A sudden noise came from under a large pile of party debris. Siobhan appeared from underneath it, like a zombie rising from the dead.

'HELP!' she groaned as she began flailing around. 'HELLLPPP!'

'Siobhan, what's wrong?' Kate said, running over to her.

'I can't move my arms!'

Sweet Jesus, was Siobhan paralysed? Would she ever use her arms again? But when she rolled over, Kate could see why Siobhan couldn't move them.

She was in handcuffs.

'Siobhan, you're in handcuffs!' Kate said, horrified. 'Oh my God, did you get arrested last night?'

'That's what I was about to ask you!' Siobhan said, every bit as clueless as Kate. 'Help me up!'

Kate helped Siobhan get on her feet. As soon as she stood up straight, she looked directly at Natalie.

'NAT! YOUR EYEBROWS!' Siobhan said, laughing hysterically.

'What about my eyebrows?' When her fingers touched her bare brow ridge, however, Natalie knew exactly what was wrong. 'Oh no, this can't be happening!' she cried as she stormed towards the bathroom. But as she was running, she tripped over something that let out a large grunt.

'Ow!' Chloe said, waking up on the floor.

Natalie went flying over her and the two fell to the ground.

Kate couldn't quite believe her eyes when she saw what Chloe looked like. 'CHLOE, YOUR SKIN!' she gasped.

'What's wrong with my skin?' Chloe said. But when she looked at her arms she got her answer.

She was completely and utterly orange. The brightest shade of tangerine she had ever been in her life – and for Chloe, that was really saying something.

'Oh my God,' Chloe cried as she got off the floor. 'The tan developed too much!'

'You look like you slept in a pack of Cheetos!' Natalie said.

'Well, at least I have eyebrows!'

'No, no, no,' Natalie said, remembering her own situation. She ran into the bathroom, and all the girls could hear was a loud continuous scream for about five seconds.

Siobhan was in stitches laughing. 'I can't breathe,' she wheezed.

'WHICH ONE OF YOU SHAVED MY EYEBROWS?' Natalie said, storming back in.

'Don't look at me,' Siobhan said. 'My hands are tied!'

'Girls, my back is burning,' Chloe said. 'It feels like it's on fire.'

'The tan is probably burning from being on so long,' Natalie said. 'Your skin looks like orange peel.'

'No, it feels worse than that. It's my lower back.'

'Show us,' Kate said.

Chloe lifted up the back of her dress and the girls all gasped in horror. On her lower back was a massive tattoo that read 'Live, Laugh, Love' in terrible calligraphy.

'What the hell is it?' Chloe cried.

'It's not that bad,' Kate said, trying to cushion the blow.

'YES IT IS!' Siobhan said, dying laughing. 'You have a tramp stamp that says Live, Laugh, Love.'

'I'm not stupid, Siobhan,' Chloe said, convinced she was winding her up.

'For once, she's telling the truth,' Natalie winced.

Chloe looked like her life was flashing before her eyes. She walked towards a mirror on the wall and turned to look at her lower back. As soon as she saw it, she let out an almighty scream.

'Who the hell let me get a tattoo?' she screeched. 'I HATE TATTOOS!'

'Chloe, I think your tramp stamp looks good!' Natalie said.

'DON'T CALL IT A TRAMP STAMP!'

'Fine . . . your whore's watermark then.'

'Oh my God, girls, my stomach is sore from the laughing,' Siobhan said. But when she looked down, she realized the pain was specifically coming from her navel. To her shock, she saw her belly button was pierced and had a little dangly jewel hanging from it.

'No way!' Natalie roared laughing.

'WHERE THE HELL DID I GET MY BELLY BUTTON PIERCED?' Siobhan snapped.

'Claire's, maybe?' Chloe suggested.

'Belly button piercings haven't been in fashion for YEARS!'

'Maybe they'll make a comeback and you'll be ahead of the curve,' Kate said, trying to make her feel better.

'Oh my God,' Natalie said, looking at her phone. 'I just checked my bank account. It's practically empty. I'm broke!'

'I told you to start letting men buy you drinks,' Siobhan shrugged.

The girls all looked at each other with no clue what to say.

Natalie, with an empty bank account and not an eyebrow

to her name. Siobhan, in handcuffs with a belly button piercing. And Chloe, with bright orange skin and the world's worst tattoo.

The next question was obvious.

'Girls, what the hell happened last night?' Kate said, in disbelief.

'Yeah, this is the worst case of hangxiety I've ever had,' Natalie said. 'Where even are we? This isn't our room.'

'Maybe Chloe managed to get us an upgrade,' Siobhan laughed.

'I don't know why you're laughing, Siobhan!' Chloe snapped. 'You're in handcuffs! You could be a wanted criminal!'

'And God knows how many men you slept with!' Natalie added.

'Shit, I never thought about that,' Siobhan panicked. 'Where's my handbag? I'm supposed to take the pill at 8 a.m. every day!'

'Your bag's here on the couch,' Kate said, grabbing it.

'Siobhan, why are you on the pill? I thought you had the coil?' Chloe asked.

'The coil is only 99 per cent effective. Do you really want there to be a 1 per cent chance of me becoming a mother?'

'Good point.'

Kate opened Siobhan's bag and began rooting around. 'I don't see a pill box. Just a Miss Piggy Pez dispenser.'

'That's it! Hand it over to me!'

'You keep your contraceptive pills in a Pez dispenser?' Natalie said, shocked.

'It's easy to carry around. Kate, put one in my mouth, quick! I've heard horror stories about girls who missed a day and got pregnant.'

Kate popped a pill out and put it in Siobhan's mouth. She swallowed it whole in one gulp.

'Don't you need some water?' Kate asked.

'Do you honestly think Siobhan has a gag reflex?' Natalie said, rolling her eyes.

Kate began to look around the room, searching for some idea of what happened the night before. She felt her stomach drop when she looked down at the floor. There were pieces of pink paper and glitter everywhere.

Her itinerary.

It was ripped into pieces. Her perfect plan, torn to shreds.

She walked over to where it lay and cradled what was left of it in her arms. 'Which one of you did this?' she said, fury in her eyes.

'Kate, none of us can remember anything,' Chloe said, still fanning her back to cool it down.

'Maybe we were spiked!' Natalie said. 'Oh my God, what if we've been trafficked? What if they want to harvest our organs? I've seen documentaries about this where people wake up without a kidney or a liver!'

'I don't think our livers are worth much on the black market after last night,' Siobhan laughed.

'Girls, this is a complete trainwreck!' Kate sighed. 'But we can figure this out. We've blacked out together before. This is just like the J-1 days. All we have to do is start stitching together what happened.'

'The last thing I remember is going to Omnia,' Siobhan said.

'I remember being in a booth and taking a Polaroid,' Chloe added.

'Kate look, on the floor. There's a Polaroid,' Natalie said, pointing at it. 'It might give us an idea of what happened!'

Kate picked it up. It was the photo of the girls holding their cans of Four Loko in the VIP booth at Omnia. She vaguely remembered the waitress bringing them to the table and Siobhan being the one who ordered them.

'Well, girls, at least we know we weren't spiked. We literally drank a liquid blackout!' she snapped.

'Then we need to find more photos from *after* we blacked out,' Natalie said.

'There's one over there by the bar!' Chloe said.

Kate rushed over to the suite's bar, which appeared to be drunk dry from the night before. On the counter was a photo of the girls sitting in a vintage pink convertible. 'Okay, I have no memory of this,' she said, holding it up to the girls.

'Where was it taken?' Chloe asked.

Kate scanned the photo for clues but couldn't see anything. 'Hmm, I don't know. Can anyone remember where this was?'

'No idea. Chloe probably saw a pink convertible and wanted a Barbie moment,' Siobhan deduced.

'Very possible,' Chloe agreed.

'Okay, everyone keep looking!' Kate said. She walked down one of the suite's hallways in search of some inkling of what had happened the night before. The room was still spinning. She could barely walk with dizziness. Christ, was she still drunk?

She suddenly saw another Polaroid right in front of the penthouse door. She bent down and picked it up, hoping to find some more info.

But when Kate turned the photo around, she was thunderstruck with shock.

It was so much worse than anything she could have ever imagined.

In the photo, there was a man dressed as Elvis with a sign above him that said 'The Little White Wedding Chapel'. Kate was standing in front of Elvis, holding her hand out as the man she hated more than anyone in the world was slipping a gold ring on her finger.

It was only then that Kate noticed it.

The gold ring was still on her finger. She held her hand up in horror as her brain realized what her gut already knew.

It was a wedding ring.

She felt her stomach drop. She had all of the information in front of her, but she couldn't quite connect the dots. Fragments of the night that she couldn't seem to piece together. She knew what she was seeing but her mind wouldn't let her believe it. She *refused* to believe it.

But then, she saw him.

The penthouse door swung open and there he was.

His sleek black hair, his tanned Italian American skin and his piercing brown eyes that were currently staring right into her soul.

'Honey, I'm home,' Trevor Rush smirked.

Chapter 9

Bad to Worse

'AAAGGGHHH!' Kate screamed in abject horror.

She did a full one-eighty and ran around the corner towards the girls. This couldn't be happening. She did NOT just see Trevor Rush standing in that doorway. Maybe she was still drunk? Or lucid dreaming?

'Kate, what's wrong?' Natalie said as she dashed towards them.

'In . . . in the hall . . . there's . . .'

'You look like you've seen a ghost,' Chloe said.

But as Trevor walked around the corner and into the room, they saw why she was so distraught. Kate *had* seen a ghost. The ghost of summer's past was standing right in front of them.

'So The Four Lokos have finally woken up, I see,' Trevor laughed. He was holding a box of doughnuts and four coffees.

Kate tried to catch her breath. She didn't have asthma but she suddenly felt like she needed an inhaler. 'Trevor . . .' she finally said. 'What the hell is going on?'

'What do you mean?'

'Why is there a picture of us in a tacky Vegas wedding chapel?'

'Hold on, you don't remember?' Trevor asked, seeming genuinely surprised.

'Remember what?' Kate asked, desperate for answers. But she knew what answer was coming.

A playful grin danced across Trevor's face. 'Our wedding, silly.'

'Our WHAT?'

'That's right, wifey. This is the honeymoon suite,' Trevor said. 'We got hitched last night.'

Kate wanted the ground to open up and swallow her. There was no possible way it could be true. She was Kate O'Connor. And Kate O'Connor was NOT the type of girl who would get drunkenly married in Vegas. Especially not to the one man she hated more than anyone else in the world!

'No, no, no, no, no,' Kate said, hyperventilating. 'This isn't happening. This is some kind of joke. Of course! You and the girls planned some hen party prank. There's a hidden camera somewhere, isn't there?'

'Kate, this isn't a prank,' Natalie said.

'Nice try, girls. You all planned it very well. Making me drink the Four Loko, getting Trevor involved, even the honeymoon suite, now that was a nice touch . . .'

'Kate, we're not pranking you!' Chloe snapped.

'They're telling the truth,' Trevor said. 'Last night you told me you still loved me and you asked me to marry you.'

'No way, that did not happen!' Kate said. She tried to take the wedding ring off her finger, but it was stuck.

'Oh, it happened alright. You got down on one knee and everything,' Trevor laughed.

'I don't believe it. I don't believe any of this. There's no way in hell we got married!'

'You might want to check your phones then. I think some of you put our wedding on your Instagram story.'

Kate nearly died on the spot.

Her drunken Vegas wedding? On Instagram?

'You girls get up to speed while I go take a leak. Doughnuts are fresh – help yourselves,' Trevor said before turning around and heading towards the bathroom.

Siobhan walked towards the coffee table to grab a doughnut but remembered her arms were restrained. 'Could someone put a doughnut in my mouth?' she asked.

'SIOBHAN!' Kate snapped. 'FOCUS!'

'Right! The crisis!'

'Everyone check their stories. Oh God, Norman follows you all on Instagram. That must be why I have forty-three missed calls. He saw me getting married,' Kate cried. Her life was potentially over. Or at least the life she knew.

The girls immediately began to look through the Instagram stories to see what had happened. Kate looked at her account to see her story was blank. 'Nothing on mine, thank God,' she said, beyond relieved.

'Mine just has an infographic about saving the turtles,' Natalie said.

'My story is empty too,' Siobhan said.

'Oh my God, there's stuff on my story!' Chloe cried.

'Show me!' Kate yelled. She needed to do a serious damage assessment. She needed to know how much of her life was salvageable.

The girls all leaned over Chloe's shoulder and began watching her Instagram story. The first video was of the moment Kate went on stage for her champagne shower. Trevor was rising up from under the stage as Kate's body was frozen with shock. Finally, when the platform was fully raised, the two of them locked eyes.

'Oh sweet Jesus,' Kate said, terrified of what was about to happen next. 'I think I remember this!'

On the screen, Trevor was staring at Kate in disbelief. The

bottle popped from its own internal pressure. Kate stood there on stage for a minute, speechless.

'Turn around and run, you idiot!' Kate said to her drunken self on the screen.

But she did not obey. Kate began to walk towards Trevor until they were finally face to face, with barely a few inches between them. Then, out of nowhere, Kate raised her arm and slapped Trevor right across the face. The Omnia crowd gasped, unsure if it was part of the act or not.

'See?' Kate said, looking up from the phone. 'I didn't marry him, I slapped him!'

But on the screen it seemed as if some kind of switch flipped in Kate's mind. Instead of charging off the stage like she should have, Kate grabbed Trevor and began kissing him with unbridled passion. And Trevor began kissing her back with nine years' worth of pent-up desire. The crowd went wild for their dramatic kiss.

Kate felt herself go scarlet as she watched. 'That's not me! There's no way that's me!' She continued to stare in shock at her drunken-self devouring Trevor on the Omnia stage. It was as if she was deprived of air and his mouth was her only oxygen supply. It was so utterly uncharacteristic of her usual self that watching it felt like an out-of-body experience. Surely any second now she would push him away and storm off.

But she just kept kissing him. And the crowd kept cheering.

'Oh my God!!! Chloe, delete this right now!' Kate begged. 'Jesus, can you check if Norman has seen it?'

'Don't worry, it's just on my private story. Only the four of us can see it,' Chloe explained.

Kate let out an almighty sigh of relief.

Norman hadn't seen it. That meant less damage control. There was a chance she could get out of this shitstorm alive.

The girls watched the rest of Chloe's private story, which

consisted of them dancing behind the DJ deck with Trevor on stage, drinking at several different bars and taking a pit stop at a tattoo and piercing parlour. Siobhan was getting her belly button pierced in one story and Chloe was getting inked in another. Natalie then grabbed one of the parlour's electric shavers and started eviscerating her eyebrows.

'Jesus, girls, this is a whole other level of drunk,' Siobhan laughed at the screen. 'Even for us.'

But the next story was far worse than the rest combined, at least for Kate. To her horror, she was getting down on one knee to propose to Trevor.

'No, this cannot be real. There's no way I did this,' she gasped. But the evidence was right in front of her. On the screen, she was asking Trevor to marry her.

He had been telling the truth.

Suddenly, they were all inside the Little White Wedding Chapel of Las Vegas. The narrow chamber had cheap white pews, fake stained-glass windows and plastic vases filled with artificial flowers. Kate and Trevor were standing in front of an Elvis impersonator, just as she had seen in the Polaroid.

'Do you, sexy momma Kate O'Connor, take Trevor Rush to be your lawfully wedded husband?' Elvis said, in a terribly impersonated accent.

'Abso-fucking-lutely!' Kate yelled on the screen.

She immediately cringed at herself. This was a feeling far beyond embarrassment. It was like she had unlocked some new emotion reserved for only the most mortifying of situations.

Trevor waltzed back into the room with a calm, relaxed swagger, as if nothing was wrong. He stood in his stylish black suit with his perfectly groomed hair, completely untroubled by the events of the night before.

'So wifey . . . are you all brought up to speed?' he said, his lips curling into a smirk.

'Are you finding this funny? You married me while I was blackout drunk!' Kate said, furious. 'Oh God, did we have sex? Oh sweet holy Jesus, please tell me we didn't sleep together!'

'Of course we didn't have sex. You were drunk. You kept begging and begging but I kept saying no,' Trevor smiled.

'I would NEVER beg a man for sex! I'd sooner take my grave.'

Trevor took out his phone and opened a video. 'Alright, here you go,' he said, pressing play.

Kate was on the screen totally hammered and slurring her words. In the video she was ripping up the itinerary. The itinerary she had spent months working on.

She was the one who tore it to shreds.

'I'm finally freeeeee!' she yelled on the phone screen.

'Alright, Mrs Rush, it's time to sleep,' Trevor's voice said from behind the phone camera.

'Pleeeease, Trevor, I need that dick,' Kate begged in the video.

'You're drunk, Mrs Rush. You're going straight to bed. Alone.'

'Trevor, please. I want to FEEL THE RUSH!'

The girls couldn't hold in the laughter.

'Zip it, you three!' Kate snapped at them as she looked away from the video. 'Trevor, turn it off!'

'You see?' Trevor said, putting his phone away. 'We didn't have sex. Hello? Haven't you ever heard of informed consent? I would never have sex with someone who was drunk.'

'Oh, so you just decided to marry me instead?' Kate said, raising an eyebrow.

'Hey, you proposed to me. I just said yes,' Trevor shrugged.

'Wait a minute,' Natalie said. 'If you two didn't have sex,

that means the marriage wasn't consummated. It can be rendered null and void!'

'Are you saying there's a way out of this mess?' Kate asked.

'Yeah – if you don't consummate a marriage or if you get married by mistake, you can get an annulment instead of a divorce. It basically means the marriage never happened,' Natalie explained.

'Then that's exactly what we're going to do,' Kate said. She suddenly realized she had no idea how annulments work. 'So what do we do exactly?'

'Maybe go back to the wedding chapel. They might be able to nullify the marriage there and then.'

'Nullify the marriage?' Trevor said, surprised. 'Last night you said you've been in love with me for the past nine years.'

'I never said that!'

'I have a video of that too.'

'Well . . . I was drunk and I didn't mean it!'

'Drunk words are sober thoughts, darling,' Trevor winked.

'Nope. My *real* wedding is in five days' time, so this one needs to be erased from existence. Girls, I'll be back soon,' Kate said, determined to fix the unholy mess she was in. 'Trevor and I have an annulment to sign!'

Chapter 10

The Annulment

'TAXI!' Kate yelled, standing in front of the Bellagio driveway.

She was beyond furious. Not only had her itinerary been derailed, but her entire life was also on the brink of collapse. She was due to marry Norman in five days and here she was, married to her toxic ex after a drunken night of debauchery that she had zero recollection of.

How had she let herself get so crazy? It was completely out of character. These kinds of things simply didn't happen to Kate, at least not any more. A part of her still felt like this was a nightmare that she would wake up from any minute, but she had to accept the reality of the situation if she had any hope of fixing it.

'We don't need a taxi,' Trevor said, in his calm, smug demeanour. 'My driver is here.'

A black Mercedes Benz pulled up and Trevor opened the door, signalling for Kate to get in. She let out a grunt of frustration as she got into the back seat.

'How are the newlyweds?' Trevor's driver said.

'Don't call us that,' Kate said, unimpressed. 'Take us to the Little White Wedding Chapel.'

'Renewing your vows already?'

'Actually, Lorenzo, my wife wants an annulment. Can you believe that?' Trevor said.

'Of course I want an annulment,' Kate snapped. 'You married me while I was blackout drunk!'

'I was just doing what you asked, wifey.'

'Do not call me that!' Kate snapped.

'Okay . . . Freckles,' Trevor said, knowing exactly what he was doing.

Kate felt like screaming until her lungs gave out. It was the nickname he had given her that summer. The nickname she despised more than anything. 'Don't even think about calling me that either!'

'Well, it's one or the other,' Trevor smiled.

Kate wasn't sure which one she hated more. She couldn't stand to be called wifey but on the other hand, Freckles drew attention to her biggest insecurity. It was a nickname she had spent so many years trying to forget, and she wasn't about to let it be resurrected.

'Fine,' she said. 'Wifey will do.'

'Freckles it is,' he said, a wicked grin dancing onto his face.

Rookie mistake. She should have seen it coming. Christ, he was infuriating.

'Look at you two,' Lorenzo said, looking back. 'You're like an old married couple already.'

'Could you keep your eyes on the road please!' Kate said. 'How much longer until we get there?'

'Are you in some kind of hurry?' Trevor asked, knowing well the question would drive her insane.

'YES, I'M IN A HURRY!'

'Fitting, considering your new name is Mrs Rush.'

'That is NOT my name because we are NOT really married. My *actual* wedding is in five days!'

'Two weddings in less than a week. That's gotta be some kind of record. We should call the *Guinness Book of*—'

'We'll be doing no such thing! In a few minutes, this marriage will be erased from history just like it was erased from my memory!' Kate said, folding her arms.

৪৩

When they finally arrived at the Little White Wedding Chapel, Kate flung the car door open and gunned it towards the chapel. The building itself was blindingly white against the clear cerulean sky. It was like she had just arrived at the pearly gates of heaven, except she was currently living in a hellscape of her worst nightmares. In the driveway, she instantly recognized the bubblegum-pink convertible from the Polaroid. This was definitely the place. She pulled open the front door, practically ripping it off its hinges and saw an elderly man at the front desk, half asleep.

'EXCUSE ME!' Kate yelled, ringing the desk bell to wake him up.

The man jumped up, startled by the sudden intrusion. 'My God, woman, that's no way to wake up an old man!' he said.

'Trust me, I had a far worse wake-up call this morning,' she said. 'Do you recognize me?'

The old man put on his glasses and squinted at Kate's face. 'Of course! The Irish beauty from last night! Mazel tov!' he said.

'Vinnie!' Trevor said warmly as he walked in.

'Trevor! So great to see you!' he replied.

'You two know each other?' Kate asked.

'Honey, of course we know him. This is Vinnie, our officiant from last night!' Trevor explained.

'*You* were the Elvis impersonator?' Kate said.

'He's not just any old Elvis impersonator, darling. He's the best in the business!'

101

'*Thank you very much*,' Vinnie said, putting on his Elvis accent. 'The two of you are just in time. Your wedding merchandise is here.' He turned around and headed into the back room.

'I'm sorry? Our what?' Kate said, horrified.

Vinnie came back in from the storeroom carrying a gargantuan cardboard box that he could barely lift. He slammed it on the counter and began taking out an onslaught of tacky wedding memorabilia.

'Okay, let's see, we've got your wedding album, your wedding video, your wedding keychains, your wedding snow globes, your wedding tote bags, your wedding fridge magnets, your . . .' Vinnie went on.

'Please stop talking,' Kate said, distraught at the mountain of merch. She was trying to erase this mistake, yet it seemed to be plastered on every possible object with a printable surface.

'Ah, this one is my favourite. Your wedding T-shirts that say #TeamTrevor,' Vinnie said, holding up the clothing.

'There is no way I ordered that. Or any of this!' Kate said. Surely she didn't.

'Well, the T-shirt was your friend's idea. She was wearing a sash that said Maid of Dishonour.'

'Siobhan,' Kate muttered. She made a mental note to murder her later. 'Look . . . Vinnie. There's been a big misunderstanding. I don't want any of this crap.'

'You have got to be kidding me,' Vinnie said. 'You were the one demanding I print your wedding photo on every single piece of wedding merchandise I have!'

'He's right, Freckles. I tried to tell you we didn't need any of this stuff to express our love. But you said you never wanted to forget the happiest day of your life,' Trevor explained.

'The happiest day of my life is going to be my *actual* wedding next Friday!' Kate said, adamantly. 'There's no way in hell I wanted any of this junk!'

'I can show you the CCTV footage if you want,' Vinnie shrugged.

Kate had no intention of watching that footage. She'd seen enough cringe-worthy videos of herself in a drunken state. How the hell had she lost control like that? Even as a lightweight with a track record of embarrassing herself while drunk, she had never lost herself *this* badly before.

But she had to remain optimistic. Norman hadn't seen what had happened. And what he didn't know couldn't hurt him. All she needed to do was sign an annulment, and last night would never have happened. One signature from Trevor and this nightmare would be over. It was time to get the show back on the road so she could return home and marry Norman.

'Vinnie . . .' she said calmly, trying to get on his good side. 'You see, I was very, very drunk last night and I woke up this morning with no recollection of what happened. Naturally, I'm very eager to move on and put this entire ordeal behind me. So thank you very much for all this merchandise but the only thing I really need is an annulment.'

'An annulment? You want to annul your marriage to this guy? Are you crazy? He's Prince Fucking Charming!'

'Well, I have no interest in being Cinderella. All I want is to sign an annulment and never see this man again!'

'Yeesh, this chick really doesn't know who you are,' Vinnie said as he shook his head. 'Well, first things first, there's the bill for all this merchandise. You ordered it, you gotta pay for it.'

'I'll pick up the tab, Vinnie. Put it on my card,' Trevor said. He reached into his wallet and took out an American Express Black Card. Kate had only ever heard of this mythical object in rap songs. It was supposedly the only card in existence with no limit. She never thought she'd see one in real life.

'Total is $1,350,' Vinnie said.

'Dear God, that is a complete rip-off!' Kate said.

'You can't put a price on memories,' Vinnie smiled.

'Except you literally did just put a price on it.'

'Ignore her, Vinnie – she'll be glad of the merch one day,' Trevor said, swiping his card.

'Okay, so now that the merch has been paid for, will you please TELL ME HOW TO ANNUL THIS MARRIAGE!' she roared, slamming her hands on the counter.

'Yikes. Irish redheads, always such firecrackers,' Vinnie winced.

'NOW!'

'Alright, alright. Well, getting an annulment depends on a few things. Firstly, was the marriage consummated?' Vinnie said, giving Trevor a cheeky wink.

'Absolutely not!' Kate said, folding her arms.

'But not for lack of trying on her part,' Trevor said. 'Am I right, Vinnie?'

'Very right,' Vinnie recalled. 'I couldn't keep her off you during the ceremony. She was like a cat in heat!'

'And now she hates my guts. Mixed messages, right?'

'Eh, excuse me! I'm standing right here!' Kate said, throwing her arms in the air. 'You may think this is all one big joke, but this is my life you're messing with. I have 200 people coming to my wedding in Ireland on Friday!'

'Need any merch?' Vinnie said, pushing his luck. 'We ship interna—'

'Enough about the merch, Vinnie!' Kate snapped. 'Now, shut up and talk!'

'I see what you mean about those mixed messages,' Vinnie said to Trevor.

'Tell me how to annul this marriage or so help me God . . .'

'Alright, alright, jeez. Well, sometimes annulments can be complicated. But no consummation makes it all easier. You can file for an uncontested annulment,' Vinnie said, taking out a stack of papers and putting them down on the counter. 'With an uncontested annulment, you both need to be in agreement that the marriage should never have happened. You just give the reason why the marriage is voidable and then you both sign that neither party will contest the annulment in court. If you go down that route, you won't even need to appear in front of a judge.'

'That sounds perfect,' Kate said, seeing some light at the end of the tunnel. 'How long does it take to be approved?'

'I can handle everything if you give me power of attorney. I can submit it to the judge on your behalf. It's all done online now. I scan the papers and submit them to the courthouse. All going well, the judge gives it their stamp of approval tomorrow morning and BOOM, you're unmarried. The marriage never happened.'

Kate felt as if a crushing weight had been lifted off her chest. In a few hours, this drunken mistake would cease to exist, with no record of it ever having happened. Talk about a miracle. She had mixed feelings about giving Vinnie power of attorney, but what choice did she have? There was no time to research how to scan and submit the papers herself. She needed this nightmare to end now.

'Give me a pen,' she said.

Vinnie reached into the box of merch and took out a pen that had a photo of Kate and Trevor kissing on it. Kate rolled her eyes and began to flick through the papers.

'Okay, let's see . . . power of attorney . . . *signed*,' she said, writing her name.

Trevor stood there in silence as she completed each section.

Next up was 'Reason the marriage is voidable'. There was an option that read 'One or more parties were not of sound mind at the time of wedding ceremony and have since regained their sanity'.

'Yep, that's the one,' Kate said, ticking the box. There was a part of her that loved filling out the form. She was a sucker for any kind of paperwork.

'No children, *check*. No property to divide, *check*. No debts to divide, *check*,' she said, flying through the papers. 'Affidavit . . . *signed*.'

She got to the final page and saw two places for signatures. She signed the annulment – *Kate O'Connor* – and the form was practically complete.

It was just missing one thing.

Trevor Rush's signature.

'Okay, your turn,' Kate said, handing Trevor the pen.

His face appeared stoic. His body didn't move. He looked at the image of them kissing on the pen and then looked back at Kate.

'No,' he said, a crooked smile creeping onto his lips.

'Excuse me?' Kate said, certain she had misheard.

'I'm not going to sign this.'

'I'm sorry, WHAT?'

'Thanks for the merch, Vinnie,' Trevor said, picking up the box and turning to leave.

'My pleasure!' Vinnie shouted after him.

Kate looked around in disbelief. Had Trevor just *refused* to sign the annulment?

'Can he do that?' Kate asked Vinnie, in shock.

'He just did,' Vinnie shrugged.

Kate grabbed the papers and chased after Trevor. He was not getting away with this. When she flung the door open once again, she saw him putting the box of merch in the boot of the Mercedes.

'Who do you think you are?' Kate said, storming up to him.

'Oh, I know who I am, Freckles. It's *you* who's having some kind of identity crisis,' Trevor said.

'What the hell is that supposed to mean?'

'So last night, we finally meet again after nine years, and you start kissing me on stage. Then just a few hours later you tell me you're not in love with your fiancé because you never stopped loving me. Then you get down on one knee to propose, and one hour later we're hitched. Then you wake up and say it was all a mistake? Sorry, Freckles. I'm not buying it.'

'I was drunk!' Kate roared.

'Drunk in love,' Trevor winked.

'You can't do this! I have a wedding in five days!'

'So I'm supposed to just let you go home and spend the rest of your life unhappy with Nigel?'

'It's NORMAN!'

'Sorry, he's just so forgettable.'

'No, he's not!'

'Well, you were quick to forget about him last night.'

'Trevor, I'm literally begging you to sign that annulment.'

He looked her up and down, revelling in the moment.

'You call that begging?' he smiled. 'I think you can beg a lot better than that, Freckles.'

Kate was blind with anger. She was so hungover that her brain couldn't quite process the situation. Not only had Trevor Rush married her, but now he was refusing to release her from the marriage?

'This has to be some kind of joke!' Kate said, still stunned. 'Are you honestly refusing to sign the papers?'

'Yep,' Trevor said, slamming the boot. 'I can't let you go home and marry someone else when you're clearly in love with *me*.'

'I most certainly am NOT in love with you!'

'Okay then,' Trevor said, a devious glint twinkling in his eye. 'Prove it.'

'How?' She knew from his face he had some nefarious idea.

'I'll sign the annulment. Under one condition.'

'What condition?' she asked, terrified of the answer.

'You have to go on three dates with me,' Trevor said with relish.

'That's three conditions!'

'Those are the terms.'

Kate had no words. Was this actually happening?

'This . . . this is beyond ridiculous!' she said. 'Are you trying to ruin my life?'

Trevor's lips twisted into a devilish smirk. 'I see it more as giving you what you deserve.'

'Oh, so that's what this is? Some kind of revenge plot for me dumping you nine years ago?'

'Something like that,' he laughed.

'Trevor, I'm due to fly home tomorrow!'

'Yeah, you won't be making that flight. You'd better call what's-his-name and tell him you need two extra days in Vegas. One date tonight, one on Monday and one on Tuesday. Then, if you still want to ruin your life, I'll fly you and the girls home first-class on Wednesday morning.'

'My wedding is on FRIDAY!' Kate shrieked. 'You can't just hold me hostage here!'

'Can't I?' he said, knowing well that he could. 'Three dates. That's it. Then you're free.'

Kate was in a state of shock. Her hangover had gone from bad to worse to somehow even worse again. He had no right to keep her in Vegas. Her wedding was on top of her. She needed to get home on schedule to make all the final arrangements. She saw right through his motives. Forcing her on three dates as retribution for being dumped. Yet, even for him, this was toxic.

But what choice did she have? Trevor held all the cards. And he wasn't bluffing.

'So three dates and we're done?' she said.

'Yes,' he agreed. 'That is, if you can get through the three dates without admitting you're in love with me.'

'Well, you're wasting your time because there is ZERO chance of me ever saying that!'

'This should be easy for you then. But I think by the end of the third date, you'll be begging me *not* to sign that annulment,' he said with his infamous smirk. 'Come on, get in the car.'

'Does the car ride back count as our first date?' Kate said.

'No.'

'Then I'll walk, thanks.'

'Not happening. It's over an hour's walk to the Bellagio and this area can be sketchy. You're my wife now, Freckles. And it's my job to keep you safe.'

'I don't need a man to protect me, thank you very much.'

'Get in the car before I put you in the car,' Trevor said, deadly serious.

Who did Trevor think he was? She wasn't his property! If she wanted to walk, she had every right to. But then again, it was 40 degrees Celsius, and walking for an hour in her dehydrated state could possibly kill her.

'Fine,' Kate conceded. 'But I'm not obligated to speak to you on the way back.' She wanted to prove she still had some power over the situation, even if she didn't.

Kate got into the car and Lorenzo drove them back to the Bellagio. She remained scornfully silent for the drive.

About halfway there, Trevor took out his phone to make a call. 'Charlie, it's me,' he said. 'I have a favour. Could you move my set at Omnia from Monday to Tuesday? I know it's last minute, but I'll be on my honeymoon for the next few days. Remember that Irish girl, Kate? We got hitched last night. Yeah, turns out she never stopped loving me.'

'THAT IS A LIE!' Kate snapped, breaking her vow of silence.

'I thought you weren't talking to me?' Trevor teased before turning back to his call. 'Oh Charlie, don't be mad. I didn't have time to invite you to the wedding, it all happened so fast. Tell you what, why don't you swing by Omnia on Tuesday and meet my beautiful bride? But keep your hands off her, you horndog! I know what you're like. Ciao.'

'Who do you think you are telling half of Vegas we're married?' Kate said, furious.

'Relax, it's just my manager, Charlie. And Lorenzo won't tell anyone either, will you, Lorenzo?'

'My lips are sealed, Mr. Rush,' Lorenzo said from the driver's seat.

'That reminds me. I'm not talking to you,' Kate said, resealing her lips.

When the car finally pulled up outside the Bellagio, Kate flung the door open.

'Not so fast, Freckles,' Trevor said. 'I'll be waiting here for you at 8 p.m. tonight. Prepare for the best date of your life.'

Kate got out of the car and turned around to him. 'Well, prepare for the worst date of yours,' she said as she slammed the door in his face.

Chapter 11

New Plan

Kate was livid.

She felt completely flustered, both physically and emotionally. Somehow, she had gone from the frying pan to the fire and then from the fire to the furnace. She was sizzling with rage in a hot flash of fury. She needed to cool down before she overheated. She walked through the Bellagio Casino, allowing herself to take a brief second to enjoy the air-conditioned air. She could get out of this. She just needed a plan.

Kate always had a plan.

But Trevor had made it impossible for her to navigate this situation. He had all the power, and she had no choice but to play by his rules. No amount of crisis management experience could have prepared her for this.

It was a control freak's worst nightmare.

Kate heard her phone ping and discovered several messages from the girls waiting for her.

The Four Lokos

Natalie: kate we're at the bellagio buffet btw

Chloe: Siobhan is trying to earn her money back on the food lol

Siobhan: Damn right I am, it was $54!!!

I'm not leaving until I'm in a food coma

Natalie: i bought fake eyebrows

chloe is putting them on me now

Chloe: Did Trevor sign the annulment?

Kate: There's been a development . . .

Chloe: Oh?

Kate: I'll explain everything in person

Siobhan: We already paid for your buffet pass. Don't let the bastards charge you twice!

Kate: I'll be there soon x

Natalie: hopefully there's some food left when you get here

Siobhan: Bitch lol

Kate knew she needed to debrief the girls on the latest development as soon as possible. But first things first.

She needed to call Norman.

Her heart was in her mouth as her finger hovered over his name in her contacts list. He was going to have a conniption, that much she knew. But how on earth was she going to tell him that she had to extend her hen party for a few more days? He had been irked enough by her going for just two nights. He would surely be distraught.

She called his number and walked towards a quiet corner in the lobby, or at least quiet by Vegas standards. It was time to face the music. She couldn't keep him waiting any longer.

'KATE!' Norman answered. 'WHERE THE HELL HAVE YOU BEEN?'

Just as she had expected. Distraught.

'Normie, I'm so sorry,' she said, trying to calm him down. 'I had no signal, but I promise you there's nothing to worry about.'

'Nothing to worry about?' Norman yelled. 'I thought you were dead! I was just about to call the police!'

'I know, I know. We ended up having a wilder night than expected. But everything is fine!' She was trying to convince herself just as much as she was trying to convince him. Everything was the opposite of fine. But she had to keep it together. The train was on fire, but it hadn't yet derailed.

'Kate, that's not really much of an explanation. I've been up the walls all day and you're telling me everything is fine!'

'We just had a lot to drink, and the casinos don't have any windows or clocks so we lost track of time. It's actually very unethical how they do that.'

'Don't blame the casinos, Kate. It's obvious whose fault it is. I knew those girls would try and get you drunk. All they want is to see you make a fool of yourself,' Norman said. His tone hadn't calmed down at all and Kate was running out of things to say.

'Norman, will you accept my apology?' she said. Surely he couldn't keep whining after that.

He let out a sigh, although it actually sounded more like a growl. 'Fine, it's fine,' he eventually said. 'I know I care too much. But at least you'll be home tomorrow and things will be back to normal.'

Kate knew what she had to say next, but she couldn't get the words out. There was an awkward silence, and she knew she had to say it. 'There's . . . one more thing.'

'What do you mean one more thing?' Norman said.

'Well . . . we're going to be staying in Vegas a little longer than expected.'

'WHAT?'

'Just until Wednesday!'

'WEDNESDAY?' he shrieked. 'The wedding is on Friday! Kate, what the hell is going on? There's something you're not telling me!'

Norman was right, of course, but she couldn't exactly tell him the truth. She needed an excuse. And fast. But the Capricorn in her hated lying. It had to be a white lie. Something that didn't seem too far-fetched.

'Well . . . you're never going to believe this, but Chloe told the Bellagio that she's an influencer and they gave us two extra nights completely free of charge,' Kate said. She hoped to God it sounded believable.

'Chloe isn't an influencer!'

Busted.

But it was too late to go back on the lie now. She had to double down.

'Well, I know that, but the girl at the check-in desk believed her. She's going to tag them in her posts in exchange for the two nights. It's an incredible opportunity and Chloe really needs this.'

'Great, the girls can stay on and you can come home to finish planning our wedding!'

'Normie, it's my hen party. Chloe got the room for me, not for her. I can't insult her by going home! It would really hurt her feelings.'

'And what about *my* feelings? Don't you care about me at all?'

'Of course I care about you, Normie!'

'And what am I supposed to do? Plan the rest of the wedding myself?'

'Norman, you know I have 95 per cent of the planning done. And I can do the final 5 per cent from here! It's not a big deal.'

'Don't downplay this situation, Kate. You're being incredibly selfish!'

Kate was a lot of things but selfish was not one of them. On the contrary, she always put others first. She always put Norman first. 'That's a hurtful thing to say.'

'Well, I'm sorry you feel that way,' Norman said.

Kate hated when he said that. It was such an un-apology. Saying sorry while deflecting all the blame. Talk about the ultimate cop-out. But she had to bite her tongue. She needed him on her side.

'Normie,' she said, sweetly. 'The girls are over the moon about the extra nights. I can't let them down. After Friday, none of this will matter. We'll be spending the rest of our lives together. Can we please just focus on that?'

Silence.

'Okay, okay, fine!' Norman finally agreed.

'Thank you. Now, I'm going to join the girls for breakfast. I love you and I'll talk to you soon.'

'Right. But don't forget to text me every hour like you

promised. And next time I call, make sure you answer. My blood pressure is already through the roof after today.'

'I will Norman, I promise. Chat to you soon.'

Kate hung up and let the air out of her lungs. Her lie hadn't been great, but Norman had bought it. That was all that mattered. She just had to get through the three dates with Trevor so he would sign the annulment. Once that was done, she could put this insane ordeal behind her and live happily ever after with Norman.

But now it was time to tell the girls the tea.

ॐ

Kate followed the signs and headed into the Bellagio buffet. She spotted the girls in an instant. It was impossible to miss them, frankly. They were the three most hungover people in the room and maybe even in all of Vegas. They were all having a massive breakfast to try and counterbalance the alcohol from the night before.

'So you're telling me this isn't butter?' Chloe was saying.

'I know, can you believe it?' Siobhan said.

'KATE!' Natalie shouted, as soon as she saw her.

'Hi, girls,' Kate said, sitting down beside them.

The girls were a sight to behold. Siobhan was still in handcuffs, although the chain in the middle had been broken so she was no longer restrained. Chloe was still bright orange and holding an ice pack on her back to soothe the burning from her Live, Laugh, Love tattoo. And Natalie suddenly had two incredibly bushy fake eyebrows to cover her lack thereof.

'Nat, take those eyebrows off,' Kate said, horrified. 'You look like a registered sex offender.'

'That's the problem, Kate!' Natalie said, trying to pull them off her face. 'Chloe stuck them on with SUPERGLUE!'

'The label on the bottle didn't say superglue!' Chloe said, defending herself. 'It said potent adhesive!'

'ALSO KNOWN AS SUPERGLUE!'

'Oh, well, sorry I'm not a woman in STEM, Nat!'

'Jesus, Nat. Should we take you to the hospital?' Kate asked, concerned.

'The hospital? We're in America, Kate. A trip to the ER is thousands of dollars without insurance! I could barely afford breakfast!' Natalie said.

'So you're stuck with them,' Kate said. 'Just like I'm stuck with Trevor.'

'What do you mean? I thought you were going to get an annulment?' Chloe said.

'Actually girls, things have gone from bad to worse. And we have to spend two extra nights in Vegas.'

'Ohhhh noooo!' Siobhan said, sarcastically.

'Wait, I'm confused,' Chloe said. 'Why are we staying an extra two nights?'

'Because Trevor is refusing to sign the annulment until I go on three dates with him,' Kate said.

'You're joking?' Natalie said. 'He can't do that! Can he?'

'Apparently he can. I need his signature to have the marriage erased. And now he's using it as an opportunity to ruin my life! All over again!' Kate said, hopelessly.

'Wow, that's big Scorpio energy. They love creating toxic situations.'

'Well . . . is it really the worst thing in the world?' Siobhan asked.

'Yes, Siobhan, it *literally* is the worst thing in the world. And I hold *you* personally responsible,' Kate snapped.

'Hold on a minute,' Siobhan said, defensively. 'I'm not the guilty one here.'

'Says the woman who woke up in handcuffs.'

117

'We were all hammered and we all made mistakes. But each of us have to own our shit.'

'You said two drinks and home by ten!'

'Pretty sure I said ten drinks and home by two.'

'Classic Siobhan. Lies, lies and more lies,' Kate said.

'I'm not a liar! I just have an open relationship with the truth,' Siobhan shrugged.

'I should have never let you talk me into going out!'

'How is this my fault? I was the designated drunk! And it's not like I held a gun to your head and made you propose to Trevor!'

'You were definitely egging me on. The Elvis impersonator told me you requested T-shirts that said #TeamTrevor!'

'Do they come in large?' Siobhan asked, eager to wear one.

'You probably dared me to shave off my eyebrows too,' Natalie said, giving her a dirty look.

'Oh, cry me a river, Nat. You never take any personal responsibility for your actions.'

'That's my parents' fault!'

'Look, I'm sorry for ordering the Four Loko, okay? But I won't be blamed for anything else. I just wanted us to relive the J-1 days. Sorry for living!' Siobhan said, throwing her arms in the air.

'I knew this was going to happen,' Natalie sighed.

'You knew I was going to get blackout drunk on my hen party and wake up married to my fuckboy ex-boyfriend?' Kate asked, raising an eyebrow.

'Well . . . no. But Mercury went into retrograde last night. We were doomed from the start.'

'So weird how your onyx crystal necklace didn't stop this from happening,' Chloe said, sarcastically.

'Yeah . . . I knew I should have worn obsidian.'

'Focus, girls,' Kate said. 'We have to navigate this shitstorm together. I need all hands on deck!'

'I can go on the three dates in your place if you'd like,' Siobhan suggested. 'I'm willing to take one for the team. And by taking one I do mean Trevor's massive—'

'We know what you mean,' Kate interrupted, unamused.

'I think there's something romantic about the whole thing,' Chloe said.

'No, there's not! He married me while I was drunk!'

'But don't you think it's romantic that he didn't have sex with you while you were drunk?'

'Wow, the bar is really on the floor for men, huh?' Natalie said.

'Well, I wouldn't mind waking up married to a famous DJ. Just saying.'

'We don't even know that he's famous,' Kate said.

'Actually, we do. I did some research while you were gone,' Chloe said, opening his now-unblocked Instagram profile on her phone. 'He has two million followers, and he's verified.'

Kate took the phone and scrolled through Trevor's profile. Like the girls, she had blocked him nine years ago, so she had missed his meteoric rise to fame. His photos had hundreds of thousands of likes and mainly consisted of him holding champagne at massive parties surrounded by stunning, scantily clad women. Nightclubs, yachts, skyscrapers: everywhere Trevor went, the party seemed to follow. Underneath each post was a seemingly endless stream of Insta models commenting fire emojis, to which he would respond with cheeky, flirtatious winky faces. As if Kate's stomach wasn't churned enough.

'I'm going to get sick,' she said in disgust. 'He's literally everything I hate in a man!'

'Yeah – rich, handsome, successful, famous . . . all such turn-offs,' Chloe said, sarcastically.

'That's what *you* see, Chloe. What I see is a vain, flashy, egotistical prick.'

'And it looks like he's a fan of the powder,' Natalie said.

'Really?' Kate said, horrified. 'How can you tell?'

'See that key-shaped necklace he's wearing?' Natalie said, pointing at one of the photos. 'People only wear those so they can do bumps of cocaine off them.'

Kate squinted at the necklace on the screen and saw that Natalie was right. 'Jesus Christ, I literally married an excessive, coke-fuelled megalomaniac!' she said, handing the phone back. 'I knew he was a fuckboy, girls. And it's going to take a lot more than a blue tick on Instagram to change my opinion of him.'

'Speak for yourself. I'd let a man choke me if he was verified,' Chloe said.

'So that's two for Team Trevor,' Siobhan smirked. 'Do those T-shirts come in child sizes?'

'I'm not that small, Siobhan!'

'Chloe, please tell me you're not on Trevor's side,' Kate said.

'Well . . . no. But while we're here, do you think you could ask him to give me a shoutout? It could be my big break.'

'I'm not asking Trevor for anything! I don't want to owe him a single thing,' Kate said, firmly.

'Well, you do sort of owe him answers,' Natalie said. 'You dumped him nine years ago without any explanation and then blocked him on everything. He's bound to have questions.'

'Well, he's not getting any answers from me. Jesus, I can't believe I married the worst man in the world when I have the perfect fiancé back home.'

'Define perfect,' Natalie muttered under her breath.

'And I'm the one who proposed! I can't think of anything more embarrassing!'

'We've all embarrassed ourselves while drunk,' Siobhan said. 'Remember Chloe got hit by that parked car?'

'For the millionth time, I twisted my ankle and fell on the bonnet!' Chloe snapped.

'I'm riddled with guilt, girls,' Kate said, putting her face in her palms. 'Poor Norman calling me all night while I was marrying my ex! I'm literally the worst person in the world!'

'Hey! Don't take my title away from me,' Siobhan said. 'And you're not the worst person, you're the best person I know.'

'Yeah, Kate. People are more than just their worst mistake,' Chloe said in an oddly profound way.

'Wow, Chloe. That was actually very poetic,' Kate said.

'Wait, what did I say again?'

'Chloe, if you had brains, you'd be dangerous,' Natalie laughed.

'So you all really think I'm not a bad person?' Kate asked.

'Of course not!' Natalie said. 'Think of it like your *Reputation* era. You're having a baddie moment but that doesn't make you bad.'

The Taylor Swift reference made complete sense to Kate.

'Yeah, you're right,' she said. 'This doesn't define me as a person. I can put last night behind me and go back to being me. And enter my *Lover* era with Norman!'

'Flop era,' Siobhan coughed.

'We will have no Tay Tay slander in this circle!' Kate insisted. 'I just have to sit through these stupid dates and get the annulment signed so I can marry the man I'm supposed to be with.'

'Did you call Norman yet?' Chloe said.

'Yes. And if he ever asks, Chloe got us two extra nights for free because she's an influencer,' Kate explained.

Siobhan immediately burst out laughing. 'Kate, of all the lies in the world you could have told, you chose the most unbelievable one possible?'

'Give her a break, Siobhan. Capricorns can't lie to save their life,' Natalie laughed.

'It doesn't matter, because Norman believed it. But in all seriousness, girls, Norman can never find out what really happened.'

'Agreed,' Siobhan, Natalie and Chloe said in unison.

'We can survive this, girls, I know we can. I just need some kind of strategy for getting through these three dates. Some kind of plan,' Kate said, rattling her brain.

'Because planning has worked so well already,' Siobhan said, rolling her eyes.

'But what if there's a way to make Trevor want to sign the annulment before the third date? Like, how can I get rid of him sooner?'

'I have an idea!' Natalie said, as if a lightbulb just went on in her mind. 'Give him the ick!'

'Nat, that's brilliant!' Kate said. 'What are some icks that girls can do?'

'Well, whenever I want to annoy a man, I usually say something like "Why can't the government just print more money?"'

'Oh, that's good! What else?'

'Try and use the term "birthday week",' Chloe suggested. 'Last time I said that on a date, the guy got a nosebleed.'

'Yes! Give me more!'

'Order chicken nuggets on the date! And eat them very loudly,' Siobhan said.

'Okay girls, this is all gold. Trevor Rush is about to go on the worst date of his life. He'll be dying to sign the annulment by the end of it and he'll forget about his stupid plan to ruin my life!'

Kate felt as if she had regained a sense of power. Trevor had put her in a precarious situation but she wouldn't go down without a fight. If he was hell-bent on torturing her with his toxic scheme, she would just torture him right back. She would become the world's worst wife. And, with a bit of luck, this fever dream could end sooner rather than later.

Trevor had no idea what was about to hit him.

'Okay, well, I don't know about you skinny bitches but I need a third round of breakfast,' Siobhan said, getting up.

'Siobhan, you've already tasted everything they have!' Chloe said.

'Excuse you, I paid $54 for this buffet and I intend to make it worth my while!'

'Thanks for buying me breakfast by the way, girls,' Kate said. She was grateful the girls had covered the cost, although she wasn't even sure if she was capable of eating after everything that had happened.

'Consider it your wedding present.'

'For which wedding?' Chloe laughed.

'Too soon,' Kate said, unimpressed.

'This place is such a rip-off though,' Natalie said. 'I'm just going to have a deep breath for dinner.'

'Just eat your eight meals of the day now, instead of later,' Siobhan suggested.

'That's a good idea actually! Will you bring a plate down for me?'

'Or you could come down off Brokebitch Mountain and get it yourself?'

'I can't go up there with these eyebrows. I literally look like Ratatouille!'

'That's not true, Nat,' Chloe said.

'Aw, really, Chloe?'

'Yeah, the rat's name is Remy. Ratatouille is the dish he makes. So you look like Remy, not Ratatouille.'

'Well, with that tan, you look like Donald Trump's illegitimate daughter, Tramp!'

'Okay, that was a decent burn,' Chloe laughed.

'Thank you,' Natalie said, proudly. 'Siobhan, will you please get me more food?'

'Ugh, fine, what do you want?'

'I think they're serving lunch now,' Natalie said, looking over at the buffet. 'Could you put together a Caesar salad for me? But instead of lettuce, could you put in kale? And instead of cheese, could you add in some tofu? And instead of bacon, could you add in . . .' Natalie went on.

'How about I just bring you a regular Caesar salad with a dildo on the side?'

'Why the hell would you do that?'

'Well, that way if you don't like the salad, you can go fuck yourself,' Siobhan smiled before strolling in the direction of the buffet.

Chapter 12

The First Date

That evening, Kate was getting ready for her first date with Trevor.

She had showered away the hangover, or at least the worst of it, and her general feeling of malaise was finally starting to fade. They had moved from the honeymoon suite back to their normal double queen room. Even though the suite was superior in every way, Kate had woken up in that room one time too many. Plus, it was trashed to an unliveable standard. Thankfully the room, and all the damages, had been put on Trevor's black card.

Kate had brushed her teeth, blow-dried her auburn hair into her usual wavy style and applied a tiny bit of makeup. She had even managed to get the wedding ring off her finger with some soap and water. Now, she just needed to get Trevor Rush out of her life, once and for all. With the time difference, Norman would be asleep, so she could focus on the task at hand without worrying about texting him. Three dates and she was free, she reminded herself.

She could do this.

'Kate, what the hell!' Natalie said when Kate walked out of the bathroom.

'What?' Kate asked, confused.

'You look lovely! What happened to giving Trevor the ick?'

'Nat's right,' Siobhan said. 'You put in way too much effort.'

'I wouldn't call brushing my teeth and washing my hair *effort*,' Kate said. 'What am I supposed to do?'

'Bad breath is a huge ick,' Chloe suggested. 'We need to find some raw garlic for you to eat.'

'I'm not spending the entire night with the taste of raw garlic in my mouth! Think of something else.'

'Can you queef on demand?' Siobhan asked.

'Obviously not!'

'Amateur.'

'Girls, I know this is very funny to you all, but does anyone have any *real* ideas?' Kate sighed.

'I do,' Chloe said, taking out some lipstick. 'Smile!' Kate opened her mouth slightly and Chloe put a dab of lipstick onto her teeth. 'There, that should do it.'

'I still think she looks too good,' Natalie said.

'Don't worry, girls,' Kate reassured them. 'It's my actions that are really going to give Trevor the ick. I'm going to be the worst wife in history. After this date, he won't be able to get rid of me fast enough.'

The girls left the room and accompanied Kate to the front entrance of the hotel where she was due to meet Trevor. On the way there, Siobhan was struck by a good-looking man in the elevator.

'Getting off?' Siobhan asked when the door opened.

'The night is young,' the mysterious stranger said.

Siobhan smirked and the girls got into the elevator with him.

'Going down?' he asked.

'The night is young,' Siobhan winked at him.

Kate laughed to herself. It was clear Siobhan's plans for the evening were already taken care of.

The girls walked through the lobby and out the front door of the hotel.

'Ah, nothing like a little fresh air,' Siobhan said as she lit up a cigarette.

'I still can't believe you bought a pack of those,' Kate said, unimpressed. As the Mam of the group, she hated the idea of Siobhan paying money to poison herself.

'It's not my fault I'm orally fixated. And cigarettes don't count when you're on holiday, everyone knows that,' Siobhan shrugged. 'Oh look, there's the Italian stallion now.'

Kate looked ahead to see Trevor leaning against his black Mercedes town car in an expensive-looking suit with a black velvet blazer.

'Ugh,' Kate said. 'Even the way he leans is arrogant.'

'Wait, I just had an idea!' Siobhan said. 'Take a drag of my cigarette!'

'Siobhan, you know I hate smoking!'

'Yeah, but maybe Trevor will hate it too. Smoking is an ick for some people!'

Kate took the cigarette in her hands. She had never touched one in her life and had never planned to. But if it could repulse Trevor, it was worth a shot. But as soon as Kate inhaled, she started to cough uncontrollably.

'Didn't peg you for a smoker, Freckles,' Trevor said, walking over to them.

'Ahem,' Kate said, trying to clear her throat and catch her breath. 'Mmhmm, I love smoking. I smoke like three packs a day.'

'Well, it's good to see you're still the worst liar in history. That'll make things easy.'

Great, she had just smoked a cigarette for nothing. And the horrible taste was still lingering in her mouth. She felt like getting sick. Just when her hangover was fading, she felt completely nauseous once again.

'Nice to see The Four Lokos, as always,' Trevor said to the girls.

'They want me home by eleven,' Kate snapped.

'Ladies. Giving the new bride a curfew?'

'Well, maybe midnight is more reasonable,' Siobhan said.

Kate gave her an elbow in the back.

'Midnight it is. Don't worry ladies, she's in good hands,' Trevor said, opening the car door for her. 'Now, Mrs Rush, if you'd like to accompany me.'

'Not my name,' Kate insisted as she got into the car.

Trevor closed the door behind her and turned back to the girls. 'Oh ladies, by the way, I put together some gift bags for you from the wedding.' He opened the boot and handed them each a small pink bag.

Kate could see he was giving them something and she wasn't one bit impressed. The girls peeked into their bags and immediately burst out laughing. Kate knew it was most likely some of the merch from the wedding. She tried to open the car door from the inside but it wouldn't budge. Trevor had put the child lock on to keep her inside.

'DO NOT OPEN THOSE BAGS!' Kate yelled as she banged on the window.

But it was no use. The girls couldn't hear her, and they were already walking away with their little goodie bags full of merch. Those bags had enough embarrassing materials to mortify Kate for the rest of her life. There was no way she would let them bring them back to Ireland. She couldn't have any evidence of her marriage to Trevor lying around.

'Okay then,' Trevor said as he got into the car beside her. 'Are you ready to begin our honeymoon?'

'This is NOT our honeymoon!' Kate snapped.

'Two newlyweds on a romantic holiday? Sounds like a honeymoon to me.'

'Well, I'm not in the honeymood.'

'Not yet . . .'

'Believe whatever you want,' Kate said with a fake smile, making sure the lipstick on her teeth was visible.

'You have a little something on your teeth . . .'

'Oh my God,' Kate said, pretending she didn't know. She took out a napkin from her bag and began to wipe it away. 'This happens to me every time I wear lipstick! You must think I'm so ugly.'

'You couldn't be ugly even if you tried, Freckles,' he smiled.

Damn. Giving Trevor the ick was going to be harder than she expected.

No matter. She still had plenty of icks up her sleeve.

Lorenzo started the car and they drove towards some unknown destination. On the journey, Kate began fidgeting as she tried to relax into her seat. But her stomach was still turning from the cigarette and she couldn't get comfortable.

'Am I making you nervous?' Trevor asked.

'Nervous? No. Nauseous? Yes,' Kate replied.

'Pretty sure that's from smoking your first cigarette. Those things will kill you, you know?'

'Yeah it's funny, ever since I became your wife, I've had this strange desire to die.'

'Till death do us part, darling.'

'The sooner the better.'

'Where's your wedding ring by the way?' Trevor said, noticing its absence.

'I got it off with some soap. And I'm going to get through whatever torture you have planned for me on these stupid dates,' Kate said, folding her arms.

'You think travelling the world is torture?'

'What the hell are you talking about? I can't travel the world! My wedding is next week!'

'Relax, Freckles. I know you're on a bit of a tight schedule. But nine years ago I promised you I'd show you the world one day. Or have you forgotten that too?'

Kate hadn't forgotten the promise Trevor had made. He used to say the two of them would travel the world making love and making music. But time had proven his words to be completely hollow.

'No, I remember your empty promises, don't worry,' she said, unamused.

'Nothing empty about them,' Trevor said. 'Vegas is home to the finest replicas of the world's greatest monuments. So for our three dates, we're going to be travelling the world right here on the Strip.'

'Or you could go and just send me a postcard?' Kate suggested.

'Nah, wouldn't be the same without Mrs Rush by my side.'

'I told you not to call me that.'

'Sorry, Freckles.'

'Good God, you're literally the most annoying man I've ever met!'

'If your husband doesn't drive you insane, is he really your husband?' Trevor winked.

'Are we there yet?' Kate asked the driver.

Chapter 13

London

When they eventually arrived at their destination, Trevor opened Kate's child-locked door and released her from the car. When she got out, she saw a massive Ferris wheel before her. She knew from her hen party research that it was called the High Roller and it was part of the LINQ Hotel and Casino. It looked incredibly similar to the London Eye, albeit much bigger. She had planned for herself and the girls to go on it as part of her itinerary.

The itinerary that had been ripped to pieces.

'Stop number one on our honeymoon trip around the world,' Trevor said. 'London.'

'I don't actually know if the LINQ is entirely based on London,' Kate said.

'Well, we're surrounded by fish and chip shops, there's a red telephone booth over there and, oh look, the London Eye. That's close enough for me.'

'I've actually been on the real London Eye in London, so this knockoff doesn't impress me,' Kate said, sticking up her nose.

'Well, this is going to be a far more *intimate* experience.'

'Just keep your hands where I can see them, please.'

When they arrived at the entrance door, Trevor walked right past the queue and straight to the top.

'Eh, hello! There's a line,' Kate said, always one for

following protocol. The Capricorn in her couldn't condone queue-skipping.

'We're having a different experience than the tourists,' he said. Trevor turned to speak to the hostess at the front desk who appeared to be in charge of checking people in. 'Hi there, I have a special reservation for Mr and Mrs Rush.'

At this point, Trevor was just trying to find any excuse to remind Kate she was married to him. It was driving her insane, but she refused to show it.

That was exactly what he wanted.

'Mr Rush, of course! Welcome to the High Roller!' the hostess said. She was visibly starstruck and practically smitten. The woman looked Kate up and down as if she was trying to figure out what was so special about her. 'Is this Mrs Rush? I didn't see anything about your wedding on Instagram.'

'We're keeping it low key until she tells her fiancé.'

'Oh . . .' the hostess said, clearly confused.

'You have amazing eyes by the way,' Trevor said, shamelessly flirting with her.

'Wow . . . thank you,' the hostess blushed.

Kate was fuming, although she wasn't entirely sure why. What did she care, after all? Now was the perfect chance to show Trevor how unbothered she was. 'I can cover your shift if you'd like to take my place?' she said to the hostess.

'Um . . .'

'You'll have to forgive my wife,' Trevor said. 'She isn't used to being treated properly.'

'Aw, I have a cocker spaniel at home who's exactly the same!'

'Em, can I maybe *not* be compared to a dog please?' Kate said, in disbelief.

'Apologies, Mrs Rush,' the hostess said awkwardly. 'Well, your customized carriage is ready. Right this way.'

The hostess led them up a ramp and their carriage approached them. On the outside, it looked just like any other Ferris wheel carriage. But when the door opened, Kate couldn't quite believe her eyes.

Inside was an ornately decorated table and two baroque chairs, ready for an extravagant candlelit dinner.

'Dear Lord, what is this?' Kate said, in shock at the sheer opulence of it. The other carriages were essentially just glass spheres with a metal railing. But this one was decorated like a five-star restaurant, with a bottle of champagne chilling over ice.

'It's the first date of our honeymoon, silly.'

'Well, Mr and Mrs Rush, enjoy the champagne,' the hostess said. 'Your entrees will be served when you loop back around.'

'Thank you,' Trevor said, stepping into the carriage. He pulled out a chair and gestured for his wife to sit down.

Kate was still in pure awe of the decor. She got into the carriage and took a seat at the lavish table. She couldn't help but wonder if this was an experience any rich person could book or if it was something only he could pull off. She had a feeling it was the latter.

'Champagne?' Trevor said, holding up the bottle.

'As long as it's not a champagne shower. I'm still traumatized from the last one.'

'Maybe this will rejig your memory. You might get a flashback of falling in love with me last night.'

'I wouldn't count on it.'

Trevor popped the bottle and filled up both their glasses. 'A toast,' he said. 'To lovers finding their way back to each other.'

'How about . . . to fixing mistakes?' Kate said, raising her glass.

'To the best mistake of your life,' Trevor said, raising his glass. He took a sip before she could reply, ensuring he got the last word.

Kate felt as if steam was about to come out of her ears, but she reminded herself to relax as she took a sip of champagne. She didn't want to argue with him all night. She just wanted to get through it. But he made it so hard for her to maintain her composure. He was completely and utterly infuriating.

The most enraging thing about him, however, was the fact that he was just as annoyingly handsome as he was nine years ago. Better looking even. He had become the best version of himself, much as she hated to admit it. The Trevor she had known was a deadbeat slacker type. The Trevor she was looking at now was a Renaissance man with the world at his fingertips.

And yet, nine years ago, she had believed in him. He had something other people simply didn't. A rare quality that was impossible to describe. Back then, anyone would have seen a bum going nowhere. But not Kate. She always knew he was destined for greatness. And as she looked at him now, she knew she had been right.

The problem was, after he had broken her heart, Kate didn't want him to succeed. She wanted karma to punish him for cheating on her. The second she had seen that gorgeous woman going into his apartment, she had hated him. It was so hard to wish a person well when they destroyed your self-esteem. She had built him up and told him he would make it.

But when you build a man up, they will often find a way to break you down.

She had to keep her eyes on the prize.

The annulment.

That was all she needed. And she was going to get it.

'So, what do you think?' Trevor said, gesturing to the carriage.

'I actually have vertigo and I need to get off,' Kate lied.

'Nice try, Freckles. Don't you remember our first date in New York that summer?' he asked.

'How could I forget? You took me to Hooters,' Kate said, unimpressed.

'Oh come on, you know I go there for the wings, not the breasts,' he laughed. 'But that was our second date, not our first. Our first date was at Coney Island.'

'Oh yeah, we went on the—'

'—Wonder Wheel,' he said, finishing her sentence.

Dammit. He was right. It was their first official date. They had gone around all the fun fair rides and played all the carnival games. He had even won her a teddy bear on one of those Strongman punching machines. God, she was embarrassingly smitten after that one. Towards the end of the night, they had kissed with uncontrollable passion on the Wonder Wheel, overlooking the serenity of the moon-drenched Atlantic Ocean. It had been one of the best nights of her life. Everything seemed so simple with Trevor back then. Life seemed to be ripe with possibility.

No.

She knew exactly what he was doing. Trying to seduce her with nostalgia. Making her melt in memory. But that was the problem with cheaters. All the memories become for ever tainted by their infidelity. Sure, those tender moments were beautiful at the time but they were now tarnished by unknowns. Had he been texting other women while on his cute dates with Kate? Whenever he had bought her lavenders, was it just guilt for having others on the side? How many women had been in his bed that summer when Kate thought it was a sacred temple reserved for their love alone? That was the worst part about being cheated on that people rarely talked about. Every sweet moment was soured by treachery.

Trevor Rush wasn't being nearly as smooth as he thought he was. If memory was his strategy, it certainly wouldn't work.

'That was a long time ago and I'd like to change the subject,' Kate said, stubborn as a bull.

'Alright then,' Trevor said. 'Back to last night.'

'I don't want to talk about drunk Kate's embarrassing actions either.'

'You mean the *real* Kate?'

'No, I mean the drunk mess who didn't know her arse from her elbow and was in no position to be getting married. So, whatever I told you last night, please disregard it.'

'What about the part where you told me you were still in love with me?' Trevor said, cocking an eyebrow.

'That was clearly the Four Loko talking! I didn't mean a word of it,' Kate said, holding her head up high.

'Maybe not consciously,' Trevor said. 'Sometimes alcohol can give people the confidence they lack when they're sober. I think your true self came out last night after years of repression.'

'Wow, how enlightening. Did you win your psychology degree in a slot machine?'

'No, it was one of those claw grabby machines, actually.'

Kate couldn't help but laugh. 'Are you always this annoying?'

'No, sometimes I'm more annoying,' Trevor smirked.

'Stop giving me that smirk!'

'What smirk?' he smirked.

'*That* smirk! You do it like every few minutes. It's driving me mad!'

'Because you're madly in love.'

'With Norman maybe.'

'You're only in love with Norman *maybe*?'

'Ugh, you're the king of only hearing what you want to hear, you know that?'

'Aw, you think I'm a king?' Trevor said.

'You're anything but. Frankly, I don't know how you convinced all of Vegas you're some brilliant DJ.'

'I seem to recall you being very impressed with my DJ skills in The Emerald Underground that summer,' Trevor said. He leaned back and sipped his champagne in anticipation of her reply. He gave her another piercing look, once again penetrating her soul. She always felt so naked when he looked at her like that. His gaze had an unmatched intensity and he knew it. He was turning up the heat in an attempt to make her squirm.

Classic Scorpio move. They loved to let things linger.

His tactics were working too. She was officially tongue-tied.

'Well . . . I'm not a twenty-one-year-old party girl any more. I've matured,' Kate said, in a holier-than-thou tone.

'Wow, what's the view like up there in your ivory tower?'

'Oh please. You're the one who's on top of the world.'

By now their carriage was at the very top of the Ferris wheel, poised high above the electric hum of the city as the sun surrendered to the night. Kate looked around at the spectacular view of the Vegas skyline, taking in the entire Strip with all its famous hotels and casinos. The neon lights pulsed wildly, painting the canvas of darkness with vibrant prisms of colour.

It was stunning.

'The view's not bad from the top of the world, I suppose,' Trevor said, looking around.

'So how does a Vegas DJ end up with an Amex Black Card anyway? Your remixes can't be *that* good.'

Trevor laughed. 'You're technically right. I invest most of my money from my Omnia residency in stocks. It's the only way to ensure your money grows with the economy.'

Kate suddenly remembered one of Natalie's ick suggestions. 'I don't really understand the economy,' she said, feigning stupidity. 'Like, why can't the government just print more money?'

'Because that would cause hyperinflation.'

'Is that bad?'

'You're a clever girl, Freckles,' Trevor said. 'What do you think?'

'I think the only thing that's been hyperinflated is that ego of yours. Because nobody in Ireland has ever even heard of you. I guess you're not as famous as you think,' Kate said, trying to take him down a peg or two.

'Well, I haven't gone global just yet. If I'm being honest, Vegas can be a prison for a DJ.'

'It seems to be a very comfortable prison. Fancy suits, your own chauffeur, women swooning over you. Not to mention your two million followers.'

'Oh, have you been stalking me, Mrs Rush?' he said, raising an eyebrow. 'Your obsession with me is worse than I thought!'

'I am NOT obsessed with you.'

'Sorry, I meant infatuated . . .'

'Try infuriated,' Kate said, smugly. 'And it was Chloe who stalked you, not me. She would do anything for a shoutout from someone like you. But I'm not so easily impressed.'

'I see . . .' Trevor smiled. 'Well, yes I have two million followers, but they're mostly from here in Nevada. My goal is to go international. Once you get to that level, you can live anywhere really. The world is your oyster.'

'You've certainly held on to your ambition anyway.'

'Well, someone once told me I was the greatest DJ in the world and I guess I believed them.'

'Oh really?' she laughed. 'Who told you that?'

'You did, Kate.'

It was the first time he hadn't called her some aggravating nickname. He was right too. She had told him that. And she'd meant it. Whenever he would DJ at a club, she would always be there hyping him up. She was his groupie back when he was a nobody. Even on the nights he was playing to empty dive bars, she was there, cheering him on. He really did have a gift. His talent was one of the reasons she fell in love with him. She even remembered the exact moment she had fallen.

The night they had first met.

Kate and the girls were finishing their shift at Scallywag's and considering whether to go out. They were all shattered after work, but something told Kate the night was only just beginning. They all went to their favourite nightclub, The Emerald Underground, when Trevor was about to begin his DJ set. Their eyes locked the moment she set foot on the dance floor, and she felt the beat reverberate throughout her entire body. He played his own remix of Taylor Swift's 'How You Get the Girl' and, well, he got the girl.

The rest was history.

Ancient history.

'With your delusions of grandeur, your dream was destined to come true. Fake it till ya make it right?' Kate said.

'True. Although there was nothing fake about our passionate kiss on stage last night,' Trevor winked, a seductive sparkle in his eye.

Kate suddenly realized her face was going red. Why the hell was he making her blush? He didn't have that kind of power over her any more. There was absolutely no reason for her body to send a rush of blood to her cheeks. Embarrassment, that's what it was. She was merely cringing from pure and utter mortification. She needed to shift the attention away from herself.

'That's not up for discussion,' Kate said, eager to pivot the conversation. 'So what exactly is stopping you from going international? I don't see anything in your way.'

'Well, right now I just do remixes and mashups in my live shows. But to go international, a DJ needs to create something new. Something people have never heard before. Think about all the famous DJs you've heard of. They all have original hits.'

'So just write an original song then,' Kate shrugged. She suddenly realized she was doing it again. She was building him up. She was believing in him. Why was she being his cheerleader? This was the man who tore out her heart and crushed it into a million pieces. She couldn't let herself forget that.

'You sound just like my manager, Charlie,' Trevor laughed. 'But I can't write music, so I have nothing new to share. That's the Vegas curse. Without a new sound, you're stuck here. Remixing for eternity in the ninth circle of Sin City.'

'Oh my God, you're so dramatic,' Kate laughed. 'You could easily write a song. Just turn your melodramatic words into lyrics.'

'Nah, song writing was always *your* gift.'

'Maybe a million years ago.'

Trevor's face suddenly went a shade paler, as if he had just gotten news of a death. 'You don't write music any more?' he said.

'God no. I have a real job now.'

'You don't think making music is a *real* job?'

'Well, yeah, maybe for a lucky few. But it's obviously not realistic for everyone. I'm an event planner now. I get to plan some really cool music festivals in Ireland. And I always plan them to perfection, by the way. Some call me the best in the business,' she bragged.

'So you do all the planning behind the scenes for people to perform their music to thousands of people?'

'Exactly. But don't even think about asking me for a festival gig. As soon as these three dates are over, we're done.'

'That's not what I was going to say. I was going to ask you if it hurts.'

'If what hurts?'

'Helping other people live *your* dream.'

Kate began to laugh. 'My dream at twenty-one is very different to my dream at thirty.'

'So what's the dream now?'

'A nice quiet life with a nice secure job and a nice, charming husband.'

Trevor began to snore in an ostentatiously loud manner.

'Excuse me?' Kate snapped.

'Oh, sorry,' he said, pretending to just wake up. 'I must have fallen asleep.'

'You know if you keep being a prick, I'm going to give you your own champagne shower and destroy that fancy suit of yours,' Kate said.

'But then I'd have to strip down. Sorry, Freckles, but I don't get naked on the first date. Maybe the second.'

'Dear Lord, you're insufferable,' Kate said, massaging her temples.

'I never thought in a million years you, of all people, would want a normal life. You're not a normal person.'

'Yes I am! I'm the most normal person ever!'

'So you don't think you're special?' Trevor asked.

'I don't think I'm above anyone, no.'

'That's not what I asked. I was referring to your voice. You think you have a normal singing voice?'

'There's nothing remarkable about it,' she shrugged.

'Wow, that fiancé of yours has really done a number on you,' Trevor winced.

'And what exactly do you mean by that?'

'Well, the Kate I remember was the best singer I'd ever heard. But it seems at some point in the past nine years, someone convinced her otherwise.'

'Reality convinced me otherwise. I released a . . .' Kate realized she had said too much. She had no intention of telling Trevor she had released a song, especially considering it was about him. And especially considering it was a complete flop. If she was the talented singer he thought she was, why had her debut single crashed and burned? The answer was obvious.

'You released a song?' Trevor asked.

'No.'

'You just said . . .'

'Music wasn't my destiny. End of story. Can we change the subject please?' Kate said in a clearly irked tone.

'Okay . . . so back to last night . . .' Trevor pried.

'Dear Lord,' she sighed. She hated him bringing up her mortifying night, but she also couldn't handle him finding out about her failed music career. 'Fine, what about last night?'

'Even though the alcohol turned you into your truest, most honest self, there was one thing you didn't tell me.'

'And what's that?'

'Hmm, let's see . . . how about why you dumped me via text nine years ago and blocked me before I even had the chance to reply?' Trevor said, his tone suddenly becoming incredibly serious.

There it was.

The million-dollar question.

But Kate had no plans to answer it. At least not fully. She couldn't have *that* conversation. *That* conversation was the reason she disappeared. She couldn't confront Trevor about his affair then and she couldn't do it now. She probably never would. She knew she wouldn't get through that conversation without crying. And there was no way in a million years Kate was going to let Trevor see her cry. She didn't want him to know the profound effect he once had on her.

She had spent a long time stitching herself back up after what Trevor had done. She couldn't forget those nights of crying herself to sleep listening to 'Wildest Dreams', 'I Knew You Were Trouble' and 'Teardrops on my Guitar'. That was the legacy of her feelings for him. Emotional devastation. She couldn't even enjoy those songs any more because they made her think of him. Some betrayals can be forgiven, but ruining Taylor Swift songs for a person was an unforgivable offence. The wound had finally healed, and she wasn't about to let Trevor Rush re-open the scar.

Not after all the progress she had made.

And she didn't owe Trevor an explanation anyway. He knew he had cheated on her. He just didn't know that she knew. It was obvious that he was going to dump her after meeting that gorgeous woman. He was just annoyed she had beaten him to the punch. He loved having the last word, but Kate hadn't given him the chance. She refused to tell him why she blocked him. It would only lead to more drama.

She had to keep things simple.

'Oh, did I block you?' Kate said, playing dumb.

'Nice try, Freckles. You know you completely cut me out of your life. In the blink of an eye, I was ditched. For no reason.'

'HA! You think I didn't have a reason?'

'Then let's hear it! Tell me the reason,' he said, his voice laced with urgency.

It was clear by his tone that he was dying for the answer to this question. She could see it in his eyes too. It was like a mystery he desperately needed to solve. A puzzle piece that had been lost to time, preventing the full picture from being completed. He genuinely had no idea why Kate had broken up with him nine years ago, and it was apparently driving him mad. Now it was Kate's turn to smirk.

Finally, some leverage.

'I'll tell you the reason if you sign the annulment tonight,' she said.

'Oh really now?' Trevor said, leaning back in his chair. 'Seems like a fair deal to me.'

'Sorry, Freckles, I'm not cutting our honeymoon short for anything. At least, not until sober Kate admits she's still in love with me.'

'Those words will never leave my lips!'

'We'll see . . .' he said, coyly. 'But there's one thing you can't deny no matter how hard you try.'

'What's that?'

'We still have our spark,' he winked.

The carriage arrived at the bottom of the carousel and the door opened.

'Now Mr Rush, the beef wellington for yourself,' the hostess said, placing a plate in front of him. 'And the same for yourself, Mrs Rush.'

Kate had to admit that the food looked amazing. She had been too sick to eat breakfast at the buffet and she was absolutely famished. But she suddenly thought of a way to infuriate Trevor.

'Oh, I can't eat this . . . I'm a vegetarian,' Kate lied.

'No problem, Mrs Rush, a vegetarian dish was prepared just in case. The tofu tartare.' The lady put the dish down in front of Kate. It looked horrific. She couldn't eat a rectangle of raw tofu. She was starving.

'Give me the damn beef,' Kate caved.

Trevor's face bore a victorious smile as the hostess swapped the dishes once again.

'I believe I also ordered some gnocchi to share?' Trevor asked.

'Yes, Mr Rush, here you are,' the hostess said, placing it down on the table between them.

'Perfect, thank you.'

'Enjoy your meal,' the hostess said, before closing the door to the carriage again.

'Pretending to be vegetarian, darling?' Trevor laughed. 'So predictable.'

'Oh shut up,' Kate said, letting out a faint laugh. She relaxed into her chair and tried to focus on the delicious meal before her. One more loop around wouldn't kill her.

'Is the food up to your standards, Mrs Rush?'

'It's not bad,' she conceded. 'Although it would have been nice if you had let me order for myself.'

'I had to order it in advance. What would you have wanted?'

'I was going to order chicken nuggets.'

'Well, they serve chicken nuggets at the Hooters across the street if . . .'

'This is *fine*,' Kate snapped. She was slightly annoyed that her chicken nugget ick hadn't worked out, but when she saw the delicious food in front of her, she quickly forgot about it. Gnocchi was her favourite food in the entire world, although she never ordered it. Norman always pronounced it 'ganoo-chy' and it drove her insane. 'The food does look good, I'll give you that much. Gnocchi is actually my favourite food.'

'I know.'

'Eh . . . how would you know that?'

'You told me that summer.'

'You remember my favourite food from nine years ago?'

'Yeah, remember we went to that Italian restaurant in Queens? You said it was the nicest thing you ever tasted.'

'Yes! I totally forgot about that place. And I kept asking for breadsticks and the waiter had to cut me off!' Kate laughed.

'To be fair you had him running around like a headless chicken,' Trevor smiled.

'Oh God, that was . . .' Kate almost forgot herself. She was about to say that was a great night. And to be fair, it was. But strolling down memory lane with Trevor wouldn't lead anywhere good. 'Where the hell did this food come from, anyway?' she asked.

'You guessed it. Hell.'

'Sorry?'

'Hell's Kitchen is across the street. I had them run it over here for us,' Trevor said.

Kate was in shock. She had tried to reserve a table at Hell's Kitchen for her and the girls but they didn't have availability for months. And yet Trevor was important enough for them to run food to him wherever he wanted? It had always been on her bucket list to eat there and now she was finally getting to.

'Well, I suppose it would be rude of me not to at least taste it then,' Kate said, picking up her knife and fork.

Thank God she hadn't ordered the chicken nuggets.

Chapter 14

Thrill Ride

Kate spent the rest of the Ferris wheel ride evading Trevor's personal questions and trying to make herself seem as boring and undesirable as possible. Unfortunately, however, Trevor saw right through Kate's game and acted completely unbothered by her sabotage attempts. Her plan to give him the ick was proving more difficult than she anticipated.

After finishing their main course, and the champagne, it was time for Kate to head back. As they got out of the carriage, Trevor winked at the hostess and handed her a hundred-dollar bill as a tip. Although Kate didn't appreciate the shameless wink, she did feel a trifle of admiration for his small act of kindness. Norman didn't believe in tipping, and she often found herself secretly handing a tip to service people behind his back. Having worked as a waitress herself, she knew it could really make a person's day, and she liked to send that kind of positive energy into the universe. But Trevor didn't need to know that she admired his gesture.

It was time to wrap things up.

'Alrighty, that's date one over and done with,' Kate said. She was eager to make it seem like a purely transactional outing.

'The date isn't over yet, darling,' Trevor said, walking in the direction of the Strip.

'Excuse me?'

'You didn't think I'd make it that easy, did you?'

'It's almost eleven. The girls want me back!' Kate said, frustrated.

'I'm pretty sure Siobhan said midnight would be fine. Your glass slippers should last another hour, Cinderella.'

'We had a plan, Trevor. We need to stick to it!'

'What is it with you and plans these days? We never planned anything back when we were together. Everything we did was spontaneous.'

'Spontaneous is just another word for reckless.'

'And reckless is just another word for fun,' Trevor said. 'Don't you remember all our reckless nights together that summer? Like when we snuck into Riverside Park and had sex in the middle of the skater halfpipe?'

'Oh my God, yes! And remember when that security guard caught us?' Kate said, mortified.

'Yeah, but he had been watching us for like ten minutes first.'

'We must have put on a good show,' Kate laughed. She knew she was letting her guard down again and she quickly regained her composure. 'Well, those are things people do when they're twenty-one. If we behaved like that now, we'd be considered lunatics.'

'I'd rather be happy and crazy than sad and sane.'

Lorenzo pulled up in the Mercedes Benz and Trevor opened the door for Kate.

'Where on earth are we going now?' Kate asked as she got in.

'You'll see,' Trevor smiled.

After about a five-minute drive down the Strip, they pulled up at the New York-New York Hotel & Casino. She knew what he was doing. First, the Ferris wheel to remind her of their first date, and now the New York-themed casino to remind her of their summer of passion together.

She could see right through his strategy.

'And what's in here, exactly?' Kate said as she got out of the car.

'You're very impatient, you know that?'

'I just don't like surprises.' Kate suddenly thought of Chloe's ick suggestion and it was the perfect time to use it. 'Unless the surprise is on my birthday week,' she said.

'Your . . . birthday week?' Trevor said, raising an eyebrow.

'Well, yes. Twenty-four hours isn't enough to celebrate your birth. I need an entire week in January every year, all about me!'

'That's the dumbest thing I've ever heard.'

'Oh . . . is that a dealbreaker for you? I understand if . . .'

'You don't need a birthday week. A woman like you should have a birthday month! Thirty-one days of non-stop celebration.'

So much for Chloe's suggestion.

Why was it so hard to sicken him? She was officially out of ideas.

They walked towards the back of the New York-New York Casino and rode an escalator up to the second floor. At the top, Kate realized that they were in some kind of arcade, and she was not amused. It seemed rather juvenile to her.

'Video games?' she said, unimpressed. 'Really?'

'Nope. We're getting the real thing,' Trevor said, pointing to a large neon sign.

Kate's stomach dropped when she saw the sign read 'The Big Apple Coaster'.

'No, no, no, no, no!' Kate said, putting her foot down. 'There is no way I'm getting on a rollercoaster!'

'Oh yes you are,' he said. 'It's part of our date.'

'Absolutely not!'

'Is that like your catchphrase or something?'

'Only around you!'

'And yet at our wedding you said abso-fucking-lutely.'

'Because I was absolutely hammered!' Kate said. 'I refuse to get on that thing. I downright refuse!'

'Let's not forget who's calling the shots here,' Trevor laughed. 'If you don't agree, I don't sign the annulment.'

'Okay well, now you're just being cruel. I hate roller-coasters!'

'I seem to remember us riding all the rollercoasters in Coney Island.'

'That was when I was a twenty-one-year-old lunatic. I actually care about my safety now. I'm sick just thinking about it!' Kate said. She was already sweating buckets. 'What if it derails?'

'What if it doesn't?'

As they approached the ride, Kate saw a sign that read 'Hours of Operation 11a.m.–8p.m.'. Finally, a bit of good luck.

'Ha! It's not even open. They close at eight,' she said smugly.

'They close at eight for the public. But I called in advance and told them Trevor Rush wanted to ride at 11.15 p.m.'

Ugh! How was he always one step ahead of her?

'Trevor, I'm literally afraid of heights! I'm gonna get sick!' she cried. 'Anything else but this!'

'Okay, how about a kiss?' he suggested, with a cheeky smile.

'Now you're *really* trying to make me sick,' Kate scoffed.

'You know what I think? I think you'd prefer a nice little choo choo train.'

'Yes! That sounds perfect!'

'A slow little train with a straight, fixed track going at a predictable speed with no twists or turns.'

'Absolutely! Let's go on that.'

'But what you really *need* is a thrill ride that makes you feel alive,' Trevor said.

Kate was starting to see the point he was trying to make. It was a rather basic allegory, to say the least.

'Wow, let me guess, Norman is the choo choo train? Very poetic,' Kate said, sarcastically. 'There's a lot to be said for safety and predictability, you know?'

'But when the chips are down, you know what you really want to ride,' he winked.

'You're disgusting.'

'Mr Rush, you're very welcome,' an usher said in front of the coaster. 'Big fan.'

'Thank you – means a lot. Appreciate you having us so late.'

'Our pleasure. You can head on up to the waiting area and the car will be up in just a minute. You'll be in the front row, as requested.'

'FRONT ROW?' Kate screamed. 'Are you insane?'

Why was Trevor so hell bent on torturing her? It was downright sadistic making her face her fears like this.

'Don't be nervous,' Trevor said, leading her up to the waiting area.

'Oh, that's a great help, thanks for that. Don't be nervous. Okay, my nerves have suddenly gone. Give me a break,' Kate said, rolling her eyes.

'Is rolling your eyes your new favourite hobby?'

'Only whenever you open your mouth. It's like a muscle reflex.'

'Reminds me of all those nights I used to make your eyes roll to the back of your head.'

'Maybe I was just faking it,' Kate said, stubborn as ever.

She was lying, of course, but she certainly wasn't going to admit that. Trevor's ego was big enough without knowing how good he was in bed. Although he more than likely knew. Even when he was twenty-two he was a stallion, his stamina unmatched. He always knew how to be rough and gentle at the same time. She never once had to fake it with him. They always finished together, something she knew was incredibly rare. But that kind of sex wasn't sustainable. It was the kind of sex you have during a summer abroad, not the rest of your life.

'If you were faking it, you would have won an Oscar by now,' Trevor laughed.

'I agree. My fake orgasms are incredibly convincing,' Kate bragged.

'Well, you must get a lot of practice with Nelson.'

'It's NORMAN!'

'So you admit you fake it with Norman?'

Kate could practically feel the capillaries in her face bursting with temper. He was giving her rosacea with rage. He had no right to comment on her sex life. But what annoyed her the most was that what he was saying wasn't completely untrue. Norman didn't always get her there. But she had convinced herself that sex was about the journey, not the destination. Just because you don't reach the summit of a mountain doesn't mean you can't still enjoy the hike. Right?

'Norman is a wizard of the sexual arts,' Kate lied.

'Now *I'm* going to get sick.' Trevor gagged at her turn of phrase.

'Jealousy is so unbecoming in a man,' Kate said, appearing unbothered.

The rollercoaster car began to pull up towards them and Kate felt her stomach drop in fear.

'Trevor, please don't make me do this. What if we die? Have you never seen that movie where the rollercoaster comes off the tracks?' Kate panicked.

'Oh yeah – they used this exact coaster to film it.'

'WHAT?'

'That was a joke, darling,' Trevor smiled.

'This is not the time for jokes! I'm risking my life here!'

'Life is all about risks, Freckles,' he said. 'Ladies first.'

Kate sat down in the front seat of the rollercoaster, on the verge of wetting herself. Trevor pulled the black restraint down over her head, locking her in.

'Oh God, I'm going to have a panic attack,' she moaned. She hated the feeling of being locked in. She had no control whatsoever. It was quite literally her idea of hell.

The ride operator came by and double-checked their harness restraints were clicked in properly.

'Are you ready to feel the rush?' Trevor said.

'I'd rather experience thrush than the rush!'

The car began to move.

'Oh sweet Jesus!' Kate cried.

'Hold my hand, darling.'

'I wouldn't hold your hand if my life depended on it!'

The car began to ascend upwards, seemingly out of Sin City and into the heavens.

'Please Lord, if you can hear me, I know I haven't been to mass in a while, but I promise if you get me through this, I will go every single Sunday for the rest of my life. I'll even become one of those people who hand out the communion!' Kate prayed.

They arrived at the top of the steep incline and the car stopped just before it was about to drop. For a brief moment Kate took in the beauty of the city from above. It was dazzling. Even though she couldn't see the stars in the sky, she didn't need to. Every lightbulb in the city looked like a beautiful diamond sparkling in the night. But then . . .

The drop.

Kate let out a massive scream as the car went straight down at ninety miles per hour. She felt her soul leave her body and she grabbed on to Trevor's hand for dear life.

But as the coaster flew forwards, Kate's mind raced backwards nine years. She suddenly remembered the first time she had gotten into Trevor's red Mustang. The thing was a complete death trap, a rusted old banger in every sense of the word. But she had learned to love the danger; the rush fuelled by gasoline and adrenaline. She would sit there in the passenger seat with the wind in her hair, drunk on the sheer recklessness of it all. Speeding through the streets of Brooklyn, pushing the limits and breaking the rules. He would take her hand and tell her she was his ride or die. She felt like she could have gone anywhere with him in that red Mustang. There were no wrong turns when she was by his side.

The rollercoaster car went flying sideways, catapulting Kate back into the present moment.

She was being flung from left to right and didn't dare let go of Trevor's hand for fear of being thrown off the car. He gripped her hand tightly in order to tell her one thing.

She was going to be alright.

He had her.

And for some inexplicable reason, she believed him.

Then she saw the loop approach. She let out a screech as she gripped Trevor's hand tighter than before. She felt the blood rush to her head as she was suspended upside down. It wasn't as bad as she had expected, however, and after a few more twists and turns, Kate began to get used to the sensation. The adrenaline was becoming almost euphoric. She started to enjoy the brief seconds of zero gravity.

After a few more twists and turns, the car went into a dark tunnel and the ride began to slow.

It was over.

She had survived.

'How do you feel?' Trevor asked.

'Oh my God, I thought I was going to die,' Kate laughed.

'But you didn't, see?'

'My heart is going ninety!' Kate said, trying to catch her breath. She suddenly realized she was still gripping Trevor's hand even though the ride was over. She quickly pulled away in the hopes he wouldn't mention it. She knew, of course, that he would.

'Alright, folks, you can exit to your right,' the usher said.

The barricades lifted and they got out of the car. When she put her feet on the platform, she realized her legs were like jelly.

'Oh my God, I'm so dizzy.'

'Here, take my hand,' Trevor said.

'No, thank you,' Kate said, pulling away.

'That's funny, you were squeezing it pretty tight a minute ago.'

'That's because I thought I was about to die. Don't read too much into it.'

'Kinda reminds me of those wild nights in my Mustang,' he said.

Had he read her mind? That was exactly where her thoughts had gone to on the coaster as well. He always had a knack for reading people though. Her thoughts, her body language – he could always read her like a book.

'I suppose,' she said, playing it aloof.

'Except now you're my bride or die,' Trevor smirked.

'I'll choose the die option.'

They walked off the platform and were immediately met

with a counter selling photos of the ride. The usher pressed some buttons and suddenly their photo appeared on screen.

'Wow,' Trevor said, seeing Kate's expression in the picture. Her mouth was being blown open by the wind and she had a look of pure and utter shock. Her auburn hair was blowing in every direction and she looked like a madwoman. It was easily the worst photo Kate had ever seen of herself and she wanted it deleted immediately.

'Dear Lord,' she said, horrified at the image on the screen. 'It's a wonder I didn't swallow any flies!'

'Looks like you really felt the rush,' Trevor laughed.

'I felt no such thing.'

'Hmm . . . well in that case I'll have to plan even more thrill rides for date number two.'

'OKAY, FINE!' Kate snapped. 'I felt a rush. Not *the* rush. *A* rush. Are you happy now?'

'Very.'

'Oh, so torturing me makes you happy?'

'A little,' Trevor said, turning back to the photo again. 'But if it was such torture, why are you smiling?'

'That's not a smile, the wind was forcing my mouth open!'

'Wow, you will go to extreme lengths just to prove you're not having a good time. Wouldn't it be easier to just admit you're in love with me?'

'I AM NOT IN LOVE WITH YOU!'

'So much passion when you say that. Where do you think all that energy is coming from?' Trevor said, winding her up.

'I'm not playing this childish game. I did the stupid Ferris wheel and I did the stupid rollercoaster. Now, it's almost midnight and I'd like to go home. Don't make me call my Fairy Godmother.'

'Okay. I don't think I could take Siobhan in a fight anyway,' Trevor laughed.

Kate suddenly felt a knot form in her stomach.

Uh oh.

'What is it?' Trevor asked, seeing her face go pale.

'I think I'm gonna . . .'

But it was already too late.

The hangover mixed with the stomach-churning coaster had been too much for Kate's body to handle. Before she had a chance to stop it, she was already getting sick all over Trevor's black velvet blazer.

'Oh my God,' Kate said, mortified. 'I am so, so sorry,'

'Don't worry, darling.'

'No seriously, Trevor, this is so embarrassing. I completely understand if you find me disgustingly unattractive and want to cancel the rest of our dates.'

'Don't be embarrassed, Freckles,' he said. 'In sickness and in health, remember?'

'Ugh, you're impossible,' Kate sighed. Even though she hadn't gotten sick on purpose, she had at least hoped it would have given Trevor the ick. 'I am sorry for the suit though. I'll pay to have it cleaned.'

'Don't be silly. I'll just buy a new one.'

'It looks like it cost five grand!'

'Ten actually,' he said. 'But it was worth it.'

'Seeing me scream on a rollercoaster was worth ten grand?'

'No,' Trevor said. 'But getting to hold your hand was.'

Ugh, why did he have to say things like that? He had no right to be this charming. But then again, he had always been that way. In Kate's experience, men usually said the wrong thing. But Trevor always said the right thing at the right time. His words were strategic, calculated. Never a mumble, nor a stutter. Everything he said had meaning, intention. There was weight to his words. It was one of the reasons she fell in love with him in the first place.

But history was not about to repeat itself.

'Okay, fun's over,' she said. 'Take me back to my hotel.'

'One last thing,' Trevor said. He turned back towards the usher at the photo counter. 'We'll take a copy of our photo please. The biggest print you have.'

'Unbelievable,' Kate said, infuriated.

When they arrived back at the Bellagio just before midnight, Kate got out of the car and turned to say goodbye. Her first instinct was to thank him, which made absolutely no sense whatsoever. Why were women conditioned to always be polite? She was literally on this date against her will, for heaven's sake.

'One down, two to go,' she said to him, making it clear she was only there as part of their deal.

'Our date will begin a little earlier tomorrow. I'll be waiting here for you at 7 p.m. Don't be late.'

'I've never been late for anything in my life! In fact, I'm always fifteen minutes early for everything,' she bragged.

'Great. That's fifteen minutes longer on our date. See you then, darling,' he winked.

She wanted to scream.

Trevor was way too good at pushing her buttons. But she was eager for the date to end so she let it go. She gave him a fake smile and closed the car door.

Kate got in the elevator and headed up to see if the girls were in the room. There was a good possibility they were painting the town red, but she was excited to give them all the tea.

When Kate opened the door, however, she was infuriated by what she saw.

The girls were all dancing around the room and the goodie bags Trevor had given them lay empty on the ground. Siobhan was wearing a large #TeamTrevor T-shirt, Chloe was drinking out of a massive cup with Kate's drunken wedding photo on it and Natalie was wearing two wedding keychains as earrings. It was obvious the three of them were drunk, and Kate saw that the minibar had been raided. It would undoubtedly cost a small fortune.

They had literally done everything she told them not to do.

'Really?' Kate said with a disapproving glare.

'Busted,' the girls said, without a leg to stand on.

Chapter 15

Wet Republic

The following morning, the girls were walking through the MGM Grand Hotel, on their way to Wet Republic, the biggest pool party in Vegas.

Kate hadn't told the girls anything about her date with Trevor. She had been withholding on purpose, due to them drinking out of the mini bar and dressing up in her wedding memorabilia. She'd been silent on the taxi ride over even as they demanded to hear every single detail from the night before.

As they walked through the casino, Kate took out her phone to text Norman. She needed to prevent him from worrying. If he worried, he would get suspicious.

Kate: Hey Normie, just checking in

Everything fine here x

Norman: The hotel called the house asking about final numbers for the wedding

If you even care

Kate: Of course I care, Normie! Can you tell them there are 200 people confirmed?

Norman: I thought you were handling all this?

Kate: I am. Tell them to call my mobile instead of the landline if they have any questions

Norman: Alright. Text me again in an hour so I know you're safe

Kate: I will Normie, chat soon x

She put her phone away and took a deep breath. She had to keep the show on the road, but Norman was going to have to meet her halfway. She had finalized a couple of last-minute wedding details via email that morning and she had things mostly under control. Apart from already being married, that is. The most important item on her list was getting the annulment signed.

Nothing could distract her from that.

'Kate, we're sorry for wearing the wedding merch. Please stop being mad at us. We just want to know how the date went,' Chloe begged.

Kate hated being mad at them. Perhaps she had given them the silent treatment long enough.

'Fine,' she said, finally giving in. 'But there really isn't that much to tell. He took me on the High Roller Ferris wheel, where we had dinner from Hell's Kitchen, and then he forced me to go on a stupid rollercoaster.'

'That's literally so romantic!' Chloe squeaked.

'It wasn't romantic when I got sick all over him.'

'Stop! Really?' Natalie asked.

'Yep. It was mortifying.'

'But you were trying to give him the ick. What's a bigger ick than someone vomiting all over you?'

'Too bad it didn't work. He said me destroying his ten-thousand-dollar suit was worth it because he got to hold my hand,' Kate sighed.

'Jesus, you should ask him how much a hand job is worth,' Siobhan said, her mind in the gutter as always.

'OMG, Kate, you held his hand? That's so sweet,' Chloe said.

'Oh, knock it off. There is no deeper meaning to the hand-holding,' Kate insisted. 'Anyway, enough about my night. What did the three of you get up to? Before you all raided the minibar.'

'Which we're very sorry about,' Chloe said again. 'Natalie and I went to the spa. I had to get a deep scrub in order to get all my tan off.'

'Well, it's nice to see you looking as pasty as the rest of us for once,' Kate laughed.

'And on the way back from the spa, we saw the ugliest dress in the entire world, and we thought it would be perfect for you!'

'Wow, with friends like you, who needs enemies?'

'NO!' Natalie said. 'She meant it would be perfect for your date tonight with Trevor. He'll think you have absolutely no sense of style. Once he sees it, *he'll* be the one throwing up.'

'Okay, well that makes more sense. Actually pretty genius, girls, thanks!' Kate said. 'What else did you get up to?'

'That's kinda it. Just the spa, shopping and then we had Five Guys.'

'Yum. What about you, Siobhan?'

Siobhan finished taking a large gulp from a can of Red Bull she had laced with vodka. 'I had five guys too.'

'Ugh, I'm so jealous. I love their burgers.'

'Oh honey, I'm not talking about burgers,' Siobhan smirked.

'Please tell me you're joking!' Natalie said.

'Of course I'm joking. Jesus, girls, my fanny's not a clown car.'

'Well . . .'

'But I did ride that lad from the lift.'

'Was he any good?' Kate asked.

'Disasterclass,' Siobhan whined. 'He tried going down on me but he had no idea what he was doing. I swear he was playing Bop It Extreme down there. And not in a good way.'

'You know you don't have to sleep with every Tom, Dick and Harry you meet, right?' Natalie said.

'Am I detecting a smidge of judgement from Gen Z?'

'No, I'm just saying maybe you're trying to find something symbolic during sex that's been inside you all along.'

'Oh, pack it up, Freud. Sometimes a penis is just a penis.'

'I don't think that's the correct quote . . .'

'But after my disappointing lay, I saw a sign for the Chippendales male strip show,' Siobhan said. 'Aaaaand I bought us four tickets.'

'Oh my God, Siobhan! That was one of the things on my original itinerary!' Kate said, thrilled.

'Yeah, I feel kinda bad for your plan going out the window.'

'So you *do* have a heart?'

'Let's not jump to conclusions,' Siobhan laughed. 'The show is on tonight at eleven at the Rio All-Suite Hotel & Casino. Hopefully your husband lets you out early for good behaviour.'

'I'll make sure he does,' Kate said, confidently. 'Sorry I was mad earlier, girls. My life has just been turned upside down and I'm all over the place.'

'Kate, if anyone can get through this, it's you,' Natalie said. 'Trevor Rush has met his match.'

The girls arrived at the entrance to Wet Republic and took out their purses to pay the cover charge.

'Don't worry, ladies,' the bouncer said. 'The three of you can go in free.'

'There are actually four of us,' Kate said, confused.

'Your gentleman friend will have to pay the $250 cover,' the bouncer said, pointing at Natalie.

'GENTLEMAN?' Natalie snapped. 'I'M A WOMAN!'

The bouncer looked Natalie up and down, focusing on her pixie cut, unshaved legs and the fake bushy eyebrows that were still glued to her head. 'I'm afraid I'll need to see some ID.'

'This is ridiculous!' Natalie said, rooting around her bag for her purse.

'I thought you wanted to be ID'd?' Siobhan said, wheezing laughing.

'THERE,' Natalie said, handing over her card.

The bouncer looked at the photo and then looked at her once again. 'You should really do something about those eyebrows,' he said, handing it back to her.

'Or maybe you shouldn't assume a person's gender based on their eyebrows! And why is there different pricing for men and women? It should be equal for everyone!'

'Nat, you can be a feminist *after* we get in,' Siobhan whispered.

'Look, lady, you can either pay the $250 or go in for free. But decide quick, you're holding up the line,' the bouncer said.

Natalie realized this wasn't the hill to die on. Especially considering she didn't have $250 to her name. 'Free is fine,' she conceded.

The bouncer opened the gate and let the four girls in. As

soon as they entered, they were blown away by the place. The pool was massive, and it was absolutely packed with the most attractive people they had ever seen. The girls suddenly felt insecure being at what looked like a model agency's private pool party. All the girls, except Siobhan, of course.

'Now this is the kind of vitamin D I've been looking for,' she said, gawking all the men in Speedos. 'And the sun's out too!'

'Aren't you intimidated?' Chloe said. 'Everyone here looks like a rockstar or a supermodel.'

'Yeah, and I'm a rockstar caught in a supermodel's body. It's perfect for me.'

'I feel tiny without my heels. What if people laugh at my tattoo? And I'm so pale compared to everyone.'

'Well, at least you don't look like an Oompa Loompa any more,' Natalie said.

'You're in no position to be pass-remarkable with those eyebrows, Nat.'

'Or those hairy legs,' Siobhan winced. 'A razor wouldn't go astray.'

'Oh, well sorry I don't conform to every patriarchal beauty standard,' Natalie said, defensively. 'You all know I hate the male gaze.'

'Nat, that's really homophobic!' Chloe said, innocently.

'The male *gaze*, not the male *gays*.'

'Well, the male gays would tell you to shave too. Just saying. I got waxed within an inch of my life before this holiday. I feel like a sexy dolphin.'

'Same, I got the Bermuda Triangle bikini wax before we left,' Siobhan bragged.

'That explains all the lost seamen,' Natalie joked.

Siobhan started howling laughing. 'Okay bitch, that was a good one!'

'Come on, let's find a bed for our bags,' Kate said.

The girls walked along the pool until they found an empty sunbed. The place was packed so there was only one available, but it was enough space for them to put their bags down and get ready in the shade. Kate wore a cute green string bikini, Chloe donned a fifties-style polka-dot tankini that gave her a vintage pin-up look, Natalie put on a jet-black swimsuit and Siobhan wore a cheeky red bandeau.

'Okay girls, who else needs some sun cream?' Kate asked.

'I'm okay, thanks,' Chloe said.

'Chloe, it's still 40 degrees. You're going to burn.'

'Well, I currently have the complexion of a milk bottle, and seeing as my fake tan is gone, I want the real thing.'

'You could always just learn to love yourself the way you are?' Siobhan suggested.

'Don't be ridiculous,' Chloe said. 'Look at me, I could easily lose half a stone. I'm going on a major diet when we get home.'

'Last time I went on a diet I lost fourteen . . .'

'FOURTEEN POUNDS?' Chloe said, desperate to know the secret.

'No, fourteen days of happiness.'

'Well, it's not that hard to lose weight. You just eat 1,200 calories a day.'

'And how many at night?'

'None. That's it.'

'Then count me out,' Siobhan said. 'Trust me, girls, the only weight a woman needs to lose is the weight of other people's opinions.'

'Where was that energy when you saw my body hair?' Natalie asked, raising a fake eyebrow.

'I'm only thinking of your safety, Nat. If you cross your legs, you'll start a fire!'

'She's right, Nat,' Chloe said. 'Your vagina could really use a woman's touch.'

'Yeah, tell me about it,' Natalie sighed.

'Last chance for sun cream, everyone,' Kate said holding up the bottle.

'We're fine, Mam,' Chloe said.

'Okay, but don't come crying to me if you burn,' Kate said, putting the cream away.

Kate, Natalie and Chloe got into the pool slowly after finding an empty space. It was quite a decent spot, with a good view of the DJ deck. The music was pumping, but they could still have a conversation without shouting. The fresh air felt great compared to the smoky interior of the casinos, although the faint scents of chlorine and beer lingered.

'Where's Siobhan?' Kate asked, realizing she wasn't with them all of a sudden.

'CANNONBALL!' Siobhan roared from afar.

The next thing the girls heard was a momentous splash followed by a wave of water whacking them in the face.

'Jesus, Siobhan,' Chloe said, realizing her hair was now soaked. 'My hair is destroyed!'

'Aww, did you get wet at Wet Republic?' Siobhan teased.

'Should we get some drinks?' Natalie suggested.

'In a minute. First, Kate needs to tell us more about last night,' Chloe pried. 'Come on, Kate, spill some more tea!'

'Chloe, we're not here to spill the tea, we're here to make the most of our hen party in America.'

'But America was founded on spilling tea!'

'That's surprisingly accurate, actually,' Kate laughed.

'How did Trevor make you feel? What was it like being with him again? Did you get the flutters?'

'Chloe, Trevor Rush is the last person who'd give me heart flutters.'

'I didn't mean *heart* flutters,' Chloe pried. 'I meant the *other* kind of flutters.'

'I don't even know what you're talking about,' Kate said, innocently.

'God, she's green,' Siobhan laughed. 'Was your fanny throbbin' or not, Kate?'

'SIOBHAN!'

'Well?'

'Of course not!' Kate snapped. 'That's not even a thing!'

'Oh yes it is!' Natalie said. 'Happens to me all the time reading fanfic.'

'Well, I guess it doesn't happen to everyone,' Kate shrugged.

Truth be told, Kate knew exactly what the girls were talking about. But it had been a very long time since she had experienced such a sensation. Nine years, to be specific. Of course Trevor used to give her the flutters. When she would be in his Mustang and he'd put his hand on her thigh, when they would lock eyes as he was DJing, when he was playing a strongman game to win her a teddy bear. But he had certainly not given her any kind of flutters on their date the night before. Even though he was the one in complete control, he didn't have *that* kind of power over her any more.

It used to worry her slightly that Norman didn't give her that feeling. But she had convinced herself that the flutters were a kind of intoxication that ought to be avoided. Nothing good ever came from intoxication; the hen party was a testament to that. Her future with Norman was logical and rational, based on shared values. Not primitive desires and hedonistic lust.

'They say if a man doesn't give you a heartbeat down there then he's not the one,' Natalie said.

'Literally no one says that!' Kate snapped.

'Jesus, if I was on a date with Trevor, I'd be like Thumper from Bambi,' Chloe said.

'I'd be like fucking Jumanji,' Siobhan said, howling laughing.

'I can't with you two,' Kate laughed as she shook her head.

'Did he tell you where he's taking you for date number two?' Natalie asked.

'No, he's keeping me in suspense. But remember that summer when he used to say he would show me the world one day? Apparently for our so-called 'honeymoon', he's bringing me to all the monument replicas so we can travel the world here in Vegas.'

'That's so thoughtful!' Chloe said.

'Yeah, he's putting in a lot of effort,' Siobhan added.

'I can't believe he's fooled you both with the Prince Charming act,' Kate said. 'It's no wonder he's bringing me to monument replicas. Because he's a replica himself. He may look like the real thing, girls, but trust me, Trevor Rush is a complete and utter fake. I fell for his charms before and look where it got me.'

'But maybe he's changed,' Chloe said.

'Oh please. A snake only sheds its skin to become a bigger snake. He was even flirting with the hostess on the Ferris wheel! Trust me, Trevor Rush won't be fooling me with his flashy tricks. Besides, all he really wants is to ruin my life. This is all some elaborate revenge plot.'

'Are you sure?'

'Positive,' Kate said. 'He told me so himself.'

'Did he ask why you blocked him nine years ago?' Natalie asked.

'Of course he did. In fact, he was desperately trying to find out why. You should have seen his face. But I'm not telling him a damn thing.'

'That's heartbreaking!'

'Oh come on, Nat, don't tell me you're Team Trevor too? What happened to hating men?'

'My opinions on men remain the same. But you dumped and blocked Trevor without telling him what he did wrong. It must have driven him insane! It's like locking someone in prison without giving them a trial.'

'He was hardly in prison. If anything, it probably gave him the freedom to sleep with even more women. He didn't have to go behind my back any more. Defend Trevor all you want, but I won't be lured in by his lies. He doesn't actually care about me. He's just trying to win this toxic game we're playing. But he's not going to,' Kate said, sure of herself.

'There must have been at least one good thing about the date,' Chloe said.

'Well . . . he pronounced gnocchi correctly.'

'Fuck, that's hot.'

'But enough about my disastrous life,' Kate said, eager to move on. 'Is anyone catching your eye?'

'Well, Natalie's catching everyone's eye with those brows. They think there's a predator on the loose,' Siobhan laughed.

'You're the one literally wearing broken handcuffs!' Natalie snapped. 'But no, I won't be able to get to know anyone here. It's too crowded. This place is a pansexual's nightmare.'

'Oh give it a rest, Nat. I'm getting tired of listening to Queer and Loathing in Las Vegas.'

'But don't you think it's sleazy that women get in for free and men pay? It's like we're animals in a zoo.'

'Even still, you have to put yourself out there,' Kate said. 'What about that guy?' She pointed to a man on the other side of the pool who was looking in Natalie's direction.

'No, he's too tall,' Natalie said, unimpressed.

'He's six foot three, that's like the hottest height ever!' Chloe said.

'Chloe, look at him. If he was any longer, he'd be late. I'm not having sex with a beanstalk!'

'Well, pick someone else then!'

'There's a girl over there who looks cool,' Natalie said. 'The one with the undercut.'

'So go talk to her!' Kate said, trying to encourage her.

'Oh God no, I get way too nervous talking to women.'

'You're talking to us.'

'That's different. I don't find any of you attractive.'

'Bitch,' Siobhan said, pretending to be offended.

'You know what I mean! Look, I'm not going to meet anyone here. Let's not forget I have two hairy caterpillars on my face!'

'We couldn't forget even if we tried.'

'Chloe, what about you?' Kate asked, ready to be her wing-woman. 'Anyone?'

'Nah. I had a look on Tinder earlier and the line-up is terrible.'

'What is this? Coochella?' Siobhan laughed.

'No matches at all?' Kate said.

'I got one match. But I texted him and he left me on read,' Chloe sighed.

'No, Chloe, he didn't leave you on read. You're just so hot, you left him speechless,' Kate said, trying to reframe the situation in a positive light.

'Yeah . . . maybe you're right,' Chloe said. 'I'm over it anyway. If I see one more photo of a man holding a fish, I'm gonna get sick. Why the hell do they do that?'

'It's their caveman minds,' Natalie chimed in. 'They're trying to show they can provide for you.'

'Well, they're providing me with the ick,' Chloe winced.

'Speaking of which, did you try any of our icks on Trevor last night?'

'None of them worked, girls,' Kate sighed. 'Any new ideas?'

'Maybe try flirting with other guys while you're around him. Men hate that,' Siobhan said.

'Yeah, also men seem to have a big problem with astrology,' Natalie said. 'Say your signs aren't compatible or something.'

'Oh, chew with your mouth open! Everyone finds that disgusting,' Chloe added.

'All brilliant, girls. Thank you!' Kate said, taking mental notes of them all. She would have to pull out all the stops for date number two. She needed to be an even worse wife than she had been the night before. Challenge accepted. 'By the way, Chloe, there's a guy over there checking you out. And he's not holding a fish.'

'Where?' Chloe said, certain she had found true love.

'Right over there!' Kate pointed to a guy, but he was completely unremarkable. He didn't have a single distinguishable feature.

'Ugh, no. He looks like an early draft of a human being. And he has a tattoo.'

'So do you!' Siobhan said, reminding her of the Live, Laugh, Love tramp stamp.

'That was an accident! And it will be removed as soon as we get home!' Chloe snapped. The man saw that Chloe was looking at him and began to approach her. His two friends followed him. 'Oh God, he's coming over!'

'And he's bringing his friends,' Siobhan said, ogling them as they approached.

'They're not even good looking, Siobhan!'

'Relax, I'm just going to flirt with them for some free drinks.'

'You've done worse for less,' Natalie shrugged.

'What are you ladies up to?' the first guy asked.

'No good,' Siobhan smiled.

'Oh, I like the sound of that,' he smiled as he turned and looked into Chloe's eyes. 'Can I ask you a question?'

'Um . . . sure.'

'Did it hurt?'

'Aww,' Chloe blushed. 'When I fell from heaven?'

'No, when you got that tattoo. It looks infected,' he winced.

'I'M SURE IT'S FINE!'

'If you say so,' the guy said. 'I'm Tomas by the way.'

'Chloe,' she sighed.

'Kate.'

'I'm Natalie. My pronouns are she/her.'

'I'm Siobhan. My pronouns are she/whore,' she smirked.

'Oh, now we're talking,' Tomas laughed. 'These are my bros, Richard and Harrison.'

'Hey,' Richard said.

'Pleasure to meet you all,' Harrison said.

'The pleasure's all yours,' Natalie said with a fake smile.

'WAIT A MINUTE!' Siobhan said. 'Your names are Tomas, Richard and Harrison?'

'Yeah . . .'

'As in Tom, Dick and Harry?' Siobhan laughed.

'Dear Lord,' Natalie said, rolling her eyes.

'Oh shit, we never thought of that,' the guys laughed. 'You girls are actually pretty funny. To be honest, from over there, you all looked very unapproachable.'

'And yet . . . here you are,' Natalie muttered.

'How long are you in Vegas for? Because we're throwing a massive fourth of July party. You girls should come!' Tomas said.

'Maybe,' Chloe said. She wasn't overly fond of these three

guys, but she was very fond of parties. 'You never know, we might be free. When's this fourth of July party on exactly?'

'Um . . . it's on the fourth of July,' Tomas said, confused.

'Jesus, Chloe. One hundred million sperm and you were the quickest?' Siobhan laughed.

'I meant which day! We might be able to go!'

'Eh, Chloe,' Kate said. 'That's this Friday. I think we'll be a little busy.'

'With what?'

'MY WEDDING!'

'Oh, right.'

'Aww, that's a shame,' Harrison said. 'You girls would have loved the party. We have a huge beer pong competition. First prize is a date with me.'

'What's second prize? Two dates with you?' Natalie asked.

'Oh shit, that's a good idea!' Harrison said, missing the joke.

'So what's good to drink around here?' Siobhan asked. At this point, she was ready to get the free drinks and ditch them.

'Well, we're drinking Irish car bombs,' Tomas said.

'That's actually really offensive,' Natalie said.

'Nat, I'm trying to score us some free drinks here,' Siobhan whispered to her.

'I'd rather die of thirst.'

'Don't mind her,' Siobhan said. 'What's the difference between three dicks and a joke?'

'What?' the guys asked.

'Natalie can't take a joke.'

The guys erupted in laughter. 'Buuuuurn,' Harrison said.

'How you gonna clapback to that?' Tomas asked.

Natalie cleared her throat. 'Well, Siobhan's given the clap back to a lot of people. If dicks could fly, her mouth would be an airport.'

The guys were in hysterics at this stage.

'When the hell did women become so funny?' Richard wheezed.

'Don't act so surprised,' Natalie said. She was trying to bite her tongue, but they were making it impossible.

'You know what I mean. You never hear women making jokes.'

'Give your mother some credit. After all, she made you,' Natalie smiled.

The joke went over Richard's balding head.

'But seriously, boys, we're parched,' Siobhan said. 'Is there, like, a cocktail menu or something?'

'Hmm, I don't know. But we were talking to some girls last night and they ordered something called an angel shot,' Harrison said.

'An angel shot? What's that?' Siobhan said, unfamiliar with it.

'I don't know, but every girl we talked to last night seemed to order one,' Harrison said. 'Then we got kicked out for partying too hard.'

'Yeah, no club can handle us,' Tomas bragged.

'Well, if everyone is drinking angel shots, they must be good. Why don't you guys go buy us a round?' Siobhan pried.

'Or how about the four of you come back to our room for some fun?' Richard suggested.

'No,' Natalie said.

'No what?'

'No is a full sentence.'

'Oh come on, girls like you always say no when they want to say yes.'

'Let me be as clear as possible,' Natalie said, having reached her threshold for arrogance. 'I'd rather have sex with a sandpaper dildo.'

'Pfft, fine. You're ugly anyway,' Richard said snidely.

'So you can't even pull an ugly girl? That's embarrassing,' Natalie said, giving it right back to him.

'What about you?' Richard said to Siobhan.

'Sorry boys, even though I have a reputation for sleeping with every Tom, Dick and Harry, once you insult my friends, it's an automatic no from me.'

'Aww, thanks, Siobhan,' Natalie said, surprised by her loyalty.

'Chicks before dicks,' Siobhan shrugged.

'Fine – you look like a beached whale anyway,' Tomas said.

Siobhan immediately burst out laughing. 'Too bad your harpoon isn't big enough to give me the Moby Dicking I need.'

'Screw you.'

'You'd like to, I'm sure. But if you can't even get a girl wet at a pool party, it might be time to work on your game.'

The girls erupted in laughter as Tom, Dick and Harry walked away with their tails between their legs.

'Nice one, Siobhan,' Kate laughed. 'I don't know where some men get the audacity.'

'Oh, to have the confidence of a mediocre straight man,' Natalie said.

'Honestly.'

'And isn't it funny how men find women hilarious until we tell them we don't want to sleep with them?'

'Come on,' Siobhan said. 'We can get our own drinks!'

'Will you bring them down to us? I don't want to lose our spot,' Chloe said.

'Ugh, fine.'

'Chloe, you're looking a little red. Maybe we should go to the shade,' Kate said.

'No way, we have such a good spot here!'

'Nat, come and help me carry the drinks,' Siobhan said.

Siobhan and Natalie got out and headed towards the bar.

'Those guys were such Neanderthals,' Natalie said as they walked. 'Are you starting to see why I hate men?'

'Oh lighten up, they're not all like that. There are good men to be found in every corner of the earth.'

'Too bad the earth is round,' Natalie sighed. She looked ahead and saw the tiki bar was surrounded with people. 'Oh God, the bar is packed. This is going to take for ever.'

'I've got this.' Siobhan was never one for queues and was determined to get served immediately. 'Sorry there, coming through, pardon me,' she said as she barged her way to the front. 'Excuse me, do you do angel shots?'

The female bartender's face suddenly appeared very solemn. 'Did you ask for an angel shot?' she replied.

'Yes. I need four of them,' Siobhan said.

'FOUR ANGEL SHOTS?' the bartender said, shocked.

'Yes, and I need them immediately,' Siobhan said, eager to get served.

'Don't worry, I understand exactly what you are saying,' the bartender said, pressing a red button on the bar.

'Oh wow, there's a button just for angel shots?' Siobhan asked, impressed.

'We take this kind of thing very seriously.'

'Wow, the service here is great!'

'Ma'am, is that the person? The one with the eyebrows?' the bartender asked, pointing at Natalie.

'Oh yeah. That's one of the people the angel shot is for,' Siobhan explained.

The bartender began to make a hand signal to two security guards who were approaching Natalie.

'What are they doing?' Siobhan asked.

'Do not worry. Everything is under control.'

The two security guards began to surround Natalie in a threatening way. 'Sir, please come with us,' one guard said.

'SIR?' Natalie said, offended. 'Could you please NOT misgender me!'

'You need to calm down and cooperate,' the other guard said.

'What the hell is going on?' Siobhan asked the bartender.

'You're safe now. Security is going to take care of the threat,' she said.

'The threat? What threat? I just ordered an angel shot,' Siobhan said, confused.

'Didn't you see the flyers in the women's bathroom?'

'No.'

The bartender opened a drawer and took out a flyer that read: 'Are you being sexually harassed? Order an angel shot and we'll call security.'

'Oh my God, there's been a misunderstanding,' Siobhan said, in horror.

But before Siobhan could explain, Natalie was making a break for it in order to escape the security guards.

'WE HAVE A RUNNER!' one guard roared as he took out his Taser gun. He fired it right into Natalie's neck as she was running away, and she was immediately struck with 10,000 volts of electricity.

Everyone around gasped as they saw her being zapped.

'She's going to kill me for this,' Siobhan said to herself.

Chapter 16

The Second Date

'I'm going to kill you for this!' Natalie yelled, banging on the bathroom door.

'It was a misunderstanding!' Siobhan said from inside the locked hotel room bathroom. She had barricaded the door to shield herself from Natalie's wrath.

'Come on, Nat, she didn't know you would get Tasered,' Kate said, trying to calm her down. 'And I need to use the bathroom before my date with Trevor, so open up, Siobhan.'

Siobhan unlocked the door and crept out cautiously. Kate went in behind her, carrying the ugly dress the girls had bought her.

'I'll never forgive you for this, Siobhan!' Natalie said, pointing to the bruise on her neck. 'I could have this scar for the rest of my life!'

'Oh please, I've had hickeys bigger than that,' Siobhan said, downplaying it.

'You're dead to me. I'm never speaking to you again!'

'Nat, it was an honest mistake! How was I supposed to know an angel shot was a secret code for calling security?'

'You should have done something *before* they Tasered me!'

'It all happened so fast. I was just as shocked as you were!' Siobhan said. She suddenly realized what she had said and burst out laughing.

'Ugh, you're such a dick, Siobhan!'

'Well, you know what they say . . . you are what you eat.'

'At least you don't look like a lobster, Nat. I'm burnt to a crisp!' Chloe said. Her decision not to wear sunblock in the Nevada heat had proved unwise, and now she was red raw on her face, back, chest and neck. She was desperately trying to fan herself down in an attempt to cool her skin.

'It's almost like you should have worn sun cream in the desert,' Natalie said, sarcastically.

'Oh, well, sorry I'm not a weatherologist, Nat!' Chloe yelled as she opened a tiny bottle of liquor from the minibar.

'Give me some of that!'

'No, this is my emotional support vodka. Get your own!'

'It's the last bottle! Give some to me or I'll unfollow you on Instagram,' Natalie threatened.

'You wouldn't dare!'

'Wouldn't I?'

'Fine, I'll unfollow you too. All you do is post social justice infographics anyway,' Chloe huffed.

'Yeah, because I'm an activist.'

'Who's never even been to a protest. You're a slacktivist.'

'It's not my fault I live in the middle of nowhere and my parents won't drive me to one!' Natalie sulked.

'The lady doth protest too little methinks,' Siobhan laughed.

'As if either of you two go to protests!'

'We were literally at the women's march at the start of the year!' Chloe said, adamantly.

'Chloe, that wasn't the women's march. It was the January sale at Zara!'

'Well, we were women . . . and we marched!'

'I can't with you.'

'Come on, Chloe, give Nat a break,' Siobhan said. 'The first thirty years of childhood are always the hardest.'

'I'm going to SCREAM!' Natalie said, on the verge of spiralling.

'Girls, enough bickering,' Kate said, walking out of the hotel room bathroom. She had put on the dress the girls had bought her and it was hideous, to say the least. It had a brown base with terrible floral patterns that didn't connect in any coherent way. It was extremely hard on the eyes. 'Well?'

'It's perfect,' Chloe said. 'And by perfect I mean the worst thing I've ever seen in my life.'

'Are you sure it's not *too* ugly?' Kate asked. She felt rather conflicted about the dress. She prided herself on having good fashion sense. Sure, she couldn't afford designer brands like Chloe, but she always looked chic. This dress, on the other hand, made it seem like she had no taste whatsoever.

'The whole point is that it's too ugly. It's supposed to give him the ick,' Chloe said.

'Unless you *don't* want to give him the ick?' Siobhan pried.

'OF COURSE I DO!' Kate snapped, unexpectedly.

'Touchy.'

'Sorry, I'm just a little tense,' Kate said. 'A date with Trevor is a battle of wits, and he always seems to get one up on me. But once I get through tonight, I'll just be one date away from being free.'

'Free from fun, free from excitement, free from laughter . . .'

'Okay, that's quite enough,' Kate said, blocking them out. 'Chloe, put some aloe vera gel on that sunburn once every hour. Natalie, massage some Sudocrem into that bruise to calm it down. And Siobhan . . . take some penicillin. The chances of you having not caught something by now are minimal.'

'At the very least I have herpes from that pool.'

'Or the pool has herpes from you,' Natalie muttered.

'I'll meet you all at the Rio for Chippendales at eleven,' Kate said. She was incredibly excited about the male strip show. Once the itinerary had been torn up and Trevor had hijacked the holiday, she feared she wouldn't get to do any of the things she originally planned. But Siobhan buying the tickets meant a lot to her. And it made her feel like she still had some semblance of control. 'Also, I was thinking we could hike the Grand Canyon tomorrow morning? It was on the itinerary.'

'The one you tore up?' Siobhan laughed.

'Yes, Siobhan, the one I tore up. But lucky for you all I have it committed to memory.'

'Yeah . . . lucky us.'

'Okay, girls, I'm off,' Kate said, heading towards the door. 'Try not to kill each other while I'm gone.'

'No promises,' Natalie yelled as Kate left the room.

ॐ

As soon as Kate left the Bellagio, she immediately spotted Trevor waiting for her. He was wearing a suit once again, except this time, the top two buttons of his white shirt were open, shamelessly showing off his cocaine key necklace.

That wasn't the most striking difference, however. Because Trevor wasn't by his usual town car. He was leaning against a yellow Lamborghini Huracán.

'You rented a Lamborghini for our date?' Kate said.

'It's not rented,' he smirked.

Although Kate knew what Trevor was doing, this was *not* the way to impress her. She didn't care for cars, and it was clearly just a tacky display of wealth. Sure, there were plenty of people who would fall at the feet of a man in a Lamborghini, but Kate was not one of them. She had no interest in ostentatious objects of desire. Norman would never show up in a Lamborghini. He wouldn't need to resort to such tasteless tactics because he had nothing to prove. If Trevor had really wanted to give her a pang, he would have pulled up in his old red Mustang from that summer. If Kate ended up in a Mustang with Trevor, all bets may well have been off.

Trevor looked her up and down and couldn't hide his disapproval. 'That's an . . . interesting dress,' he said with a grimace.

'Oh, thank you,' Kate bragged. 'It's so my style, right? I couldn't wait to put it on!'

'You'd look a lot better with it *off*,' he winked.

'Well, that's a sight you *won't* be seeing. Are we really driving in this thing?' she said, referring to the super car. 'This looks even worse for the environment than that stupid Hummer limo.'

'Hummer limo?'

'Yeah. A pink one the girls tried to rent at the airport. But some of us actually care about the planet.'

'Speaking of the girls, aren't they coming to send you off this time?'

'They're slightly incapacitated at the moment. And they might be on the verge of killing each other. But we're going to see a show at eleven, so I need to be returned by then. Don't argue, the tickets are already booked.'

'Your wish is my command, darling.'

'Okay, then I wish you'd sign the annulment.'

'You only get one wish per night, Freckles. And you shall be returned home safely by eleven.'

Trevor opened the passenger door of the Lamborghini and Kate got in. It was incredibly luxurious inside, with leather seats and tinted windows.

'So, what do you think?' he asked as he sat in beside her.

'A little flashy for my taste,' Kate said, not amused. 'If you ask me, any man who buys a car like this is obviously over-compensating for something.'

'Well, we both know that's not true, Freckles,' Trevor smirked.

Ugh, he was right too. Trevor certainly didn't need this car as an extension of anything. But nevertheless, the car screamed 'Look how successful I am', not 'Look how happy I am'.

'Still, anyone who spends this much on a car is missing something in their life,' she said, unamused. 'I would have been more impressed if you showed up in the Mustang.'

'Sadly, the Mustang broke down on the road several years ago.'

'The perfect metaphor for our love,' Kate said, making a face at him.

'We can go and buy a new one right now, if you'd prefer?'

'Just start the car already!'

Kate's phone suddenly began ringing violently in her bag. She pulled it out and was horrified by the name she saw on the screen.

It was Norman.

He was video calling her. What was she supposed to do? She couldn't answer a video call from inside her ex's Lamborghini. But if she didn't answer it, Norman would be worried sick. She was supposed to text him ages ago, but with the drama of Natalie getting Tasered, she had completely forgotten.

'Oh God, it's Norman. I forgot to text him earlier,' she panicked.

'You sure do forget him a lot,' Trevor said, smugly.

'I have to take this. Do not make a sound!'

'My lips are sealed,' he said, pretending to zip his mouth closed.

Kate took a deep breath and answered the call on voice only. Video was not an option.

'Hi, Normie!' she said, in a friendly tone.

'KATE!' Norman said, irked once again. 'Why is it so hard to text me every hour like you promised?'

'Normie, I'm so sorry. We've just been so busy, and it's so late in Ireland so I thought you'd be asleep.'

'How am I supposed to sleep when you have me worried sick? Turn your video on, I want to see you.'

'Um . . . I can't right now,' she said.

'Kate, what the hell is going on?'

She needed a lie. 'Nothing is going on. We've just been doing so much on the itinerary. We saw the . . . the, uh . . . the Grand Canyon earlier and . . . there was literally no signal out there so I couldn't text.'

'Well, I know for a fact that's a lie because I saw your location on my phone and you were at a pool party earlier!' Norman whined.

Busted.

'Well . . . we had a slight change of plans.'

'Kate, I know there's something you're not telling me. You never break from an itinerary. Who even *are* you any more? Because you're certainly not the woman I proposed to.'

'Norman, that's a very hurtful thing to say.'

'Well, I'm sorry you feel that way, Kate, but you're behaving like a lunatic and I have every right to be worried!'

'There's no need to worry, Normie. It must be the middle of the night there. Go and get some sleep.'

'Not until you tell me why you're acting so strange.'

Trevor started the car and revved up the Lamborghini's engine. It was obnoxiously loud.

'What was that noise?' Norman said. 'It sounds like you're in a sports car!'

'Norman, you have nothing to—'

Trevor grabbed the phone out of Kate's hand.

'Don't you dare!' she whispered.

'Norman, your wife has been taken,' Trevor said, in a scary deep voice.

'OH MY GOD! WHAT?' Norman cried. 'KATE, ARE YOU OKAY?'

Kate grabbed the phone back out of Trevor's hand. 'I'm going to kill you!' she whispered, digging him with her elbow.

'HELLO?' Norman squealed.

'Norman, I'm so sorry, that was a joke.'

'WHO WAS THAT?'

'It was . . . Siobhan! She's been smoking and her voice is all hoarse,' Kate lied.

'That was a horrible joke! Put Siobhan on the phone right now!'

Busted again. She felt the smothering feeling come over her once more. She needed this call to end as soon as possible.

'Norman, I can't hear you!' Kate yelled. 'I'm going through a tunnel!'

'A TUNNEL?'

'You're breaking up . . . there's nothing to worry about. Love you and chat tomorrow!' Kate made a crackling noise into the phone to pretend the call had cut off.

He was gone. She could breathe again.

'Trouble in paradise?' Trevor said, knowing damn well *he* was the trouble.

'That was not funny! Norman could have had a heart attack!'

'Well, that would've solved both our problems,' he laughed.

'He sounded very whiny on the phone. And did I hear him say he was tracking you?'

'He's not tracking me. He can just see my location in real time so he knows I'm safe,' Kate defended him.

'So . . . tracking then?'

'Well, at least he cares about my safety, unlike you, putting me on rollercoasters!'

'The Kate I remember always loved a little danger. She would always choose freedom over safety. I can't believe you became such a people-pleaser.'

There was that term again. Siobhan had used it to describe her as well. There was some truth to it, Kate supposed. She did put the needs of others before her own, after all. But how was that a bad thing exactly? Wasn't being selfless supposed to be a positive quality? Making other people happy made her happy. Of course, Trevor saw it as a character flaw. He was the personification of moral degradation.

'A people-pleaser is just another term for a pleasing person,' she said, trying to rephrase it into a compliment.

'But still . . . sometimes you have to put yourself first. Otherwise, you might end up married to a dentist.'

'He's a dental surgeon and last time I checked, his desk says *Doctor* Norman Cox.'

'I bet he's the tenth dentist in all those commercials who finds something to complain about. Nine out of ten dentists prefer Colgate. Except Norman.'

'Is this date over yet?' Kate sighed.

ॐ

They drove for another couple of minutes before Trevor pulled up at their destination. Kate looked out the window to see where he had taken her.

The Venetian Hotel & Casino.

'We're here already?' Kate said. 'We literally could have walked!'

'I was afraid your legs would still be like jelly from holding my hand last night.'

'That was from the rollercoaster! And if there's another thrill ride on this date, Trevor, I swear . . .'

'Don't worry, this date is more relaxed,' Trevor said. 'And for this section of our honeymoon around the world, I'm taking you back to my homeland.'

'Brooklyn?' Kate said, raising an eyebrow.

'No . . . Italy. My grandparents were originally from Venice. We're going to ride along the Venice canal on a gondola.'

Kate secretly liked the idea. Like the High Roller, this had also been on her itinerary for the girls to do before it was torn to pieces. A part of her was happy she was still getting to do some of the touristy bucket-list stuff. She was a sucker for lists, after all.

'Okay, let's get it over with then,' Kate said, getting out of the car.

They got out and Trevor tossed his keys to the Venetian valet.

'Oh my God! Trevor Rush,' the valet said. 'I'm a HUGE fan!'

Ugh, this was all Kate needed. Another person falling at Trevor's feet and inflating his ego even more. Why did every single person in Vegas know who he was? Sure, he was famous. But he wasn't like famous-famous. It's not like he was on late-night talk shows or Hollywood blockbusters.

Kate suddenly thought of an opportunity. Siobhan had said that openly flirting with another man in front of your date was a major ick. This valet was the perfect target.

'You're a huge fan indeed,' Kate said, approaching him. 'Look at those muscles!'

The skinny valet looked at his spaghetti noodle arms. 'Oh . . . thank you. I started lifting about a month ago. But I haven't made much progress,' he blushed.

'You look like *that* after just one month? Dear God, your genetics must be insane. And that jawline! What's your name? Let me guess . . . Adonis?'

'Oh no,' the valet laughed. 'It's Patrick.'

'Even sexier,' Kate said, putting her hand on his bicep. 'I love a good Irish name!'

'Are you done?' Trevor asked, folding his arms.

'Oh sorry, Trevor,' Kate said. 'I just can't resist a sexy Irish man.'

'Miss, I hope this isn't inappropriate but . . . could I ask you for something?' Patrick asked, awkwardly.

'Let me guess . . .' Kate swooned. 'You want my number?'

'Oh no! I was going to ask if you'd take a photo of me and Trevor Rush.'

Kate saw red. Trevor smirked in victory as her attempt to make him jealous blew up in her face.

Talk about a plan backfiring.

'Sure, no problem,' Kate smiled while secretly grinding her teeth. She refused to show how annoyed she was. She took the boy's phone and Trevor put his arm around him. She snapped a picture and handed back the phone.

'Maybe we should get one with the Lamborghini in the background actually,' Trevor said, knowing full well it would infuriate her.

'Great idea!' Patrick said.

'Last time I checked I wasn't your personal photographer. Now come on!' Kate said as she stormed off.

Trevor caught up and began to walk beside her. 'Trying

to make me jealous, Freckles? You should know better,' he teased.

'Oh shut up!' Kate said, charging towards the canal.

'Anyway, I have no reason to be jealous. You're already my wife.'

'Well, you should be very jealous of Norman because I'll be *his* wife in four days!'

'We'll see about that . . .' Trevor grinned, cocky as ever.

Chapter 17

Venice

When they arrived at the Venice canals, Trevor paid the gondola operator and they both hopped on board.

There was a stunning antipasti board waiting for them with a delectable selection of meats, cheeses, breads and even some strawberries.

'Grazie, Giovanni,' Trevor said as he sat down next to Kate.

Trevor and the gondolier began to speak to each other in Italian, and Kate had no idea what they were saying. She had tried to learn Italian on Duolingo, but she'd found the owl mascot slightly intimidating and never continued. She even had a recurring nightmare where the owl was standing below her bed like a sleep paralysis demon.

The gondola stirred to life as they began their serpentine circuit of the canal.

It was a truly beautiful scene to be fair, Kate couldn't help but think to herself. The surrounding building walls were decorated like old Venetian houses and the water was the most gorgeous shade of turquoise she'd ever seen. Though it was scorching, a gentle breeze swept across the canal, a sweet lullaby that made her feel surprisingly tranquil. There was even a faint smell of lavender threading through the air. At first, she was confused by the scent, but then she looked down to see a vase of her favourite flowers perched alongside the antipasti board.

'Lavender . . .' she said, touching their fragrant leaves.

'Your favourite, right?'

Kate couldn't quite believe Trevor remembered. It was almost a decade ago, after all. First her favourite food and now her favourite flowers? But she reminded herself that he was trying to use memory to manipulate her.

'What is this?' she said. 'Some kind of way of arousing my senses?'

'Why?' Trevor said with a cheeky smile. 'Is it working?'

'Absolutely not!'

'Could have fooled me. So are you ready to tell me why you disappeared nine years ago?'

'Are we really back to this?' Kate said. 'And I'm pretty sure I told you why back then.'

'Oh, you mean the Dear John message you sent me on my birthday via Instagram? The one where you said we were just a summer fling?'

'That's all we were.'

'Oh please,' Trevor laughed. 'As if we hadn't planned an entire life together. Don't you think dumping someone on their birthday is rather cruel?'

'So is refusing to sign an annulment until a person goes on three dates with you.'

'I know, that's why I'm enjoying it so much,' Trevor winked. 'But rest assured, Freckles, I will find out why you *really* dumped me.'

Kate didn't bother responding. The less she said the better. She was not having that conversation, no matter how much he tried to have it. She did find it incredibly interesting, however, that he was so desperate to discover the answer. It was like he had this unknown affliction and only she had the remedy. But she had no intention of giving it to him. If these dates were a way of him torturing her, she could torture him right back by being withholding.

'So, let me ask you a different question,' he continued. 'Was there a specific moment when you stopped being you and became someone else?'

'Said the man who literally went from a deadbeat bum to a famous Vegas DJ.'

'Yes, but that was always my dream. I stayed true to myself. That's the secret to success, you know? As soon as you try to be something you're not, you're destined to fail.'

'Is this TED Talk over yet?' Kate said, making a face at him.

'I'm serious. Was there a moment when you woke up and decided to hate having fun?'

'If you think I'm that boring, you can replace me with any fun-loving woman of your choice. All you have to do is sign the annulment and you're free of me.'

'Nice try, Freckles,' Trevor smiled. 'I know the fun Kate is still in there . . . somewhere.'

Kate sighed and picked up a strawberry from the antipasti board. She remembered the mental note she made to chew with her mouth open so as to give Trevor the ick. She put it in her mouth and began to chew like one of those iPad toddlers, making as much noise with her mouth as she possibly could.

'That's quite a mouth you have there,' Trevor said.

'Oh sorry, I'm such a loud chewer,' she said. 'Terrible habit, I know.'

'Well, if you keep chewing like that, I'll have to kiss you in order to make you stop,' he said, locking eyes with her.

Stalemate.

'Fine,' Kate said, tossing the strawberries aside. 'The ones in Ireland are better anyway.'

'Can't wait to taste them,' Trevor said. 'We should plan a time for me to finally meet your family.'

'You're not coming anywhere near my family!' Kate said. 'My parents are very much Team Norman!'

'That's because they think there's only one team.'

'There *is* only one team, because I'm already taken!'

'Taken for granted,' Trevor said, smugly.

Kate felt like she had been struck by a bolt of anger. Not because Trevor was wrong. On the contrary, she feared he might actually be right.

When Norman began courting Kate, he was the romantic gentleman she had been searching for. He used to take her on cute dates and always made her feel special. But once they had been together for a while, these small but important gestures slowly began to disappear. She sometimes felt that once Norman knew she was his, he became complacent.

Romance, it seemed, was like sand in an hourglass, slowly running out over time. Their relationship had gone from romantic candlelit dinners to Chinese takeaways on the couch. She was a fan of creature comforts, of course, but she often found herself wishing Norman would suggest something exciting for them both. It was like he had idealized her in the beginning but slowly devalued her over time.

Kate had confronted him about the way she was feeling, but Norman reassured her she was imagining things. He loved her, he said, and the idea that he took her for granted was all in her head. Then, out of nowhere, he proposed. The hourglass of romance had been flipped and the sands of love were bound to flow once more. At the time, she was thrilled.

But then he failed to present an engagement ring.

It almost killed her. But she feigned a smile and hoped the lack of a diamond would be overshadowed by an abundance of other romantic gestures. Sadly, however, it wasn't.

It made her think about what Natalie had said on the plane, about men only being romantic as a means to an end. She wondered if men saw romantic gestures as a purely transactional exchange. Are they only romantic up until they *have* you? Do they buy you flowers because they love you, or because it might increase the chances of sex? She didn't necessarily have the answer, but Norman definitely only put in a fraction of the effort he used to.

She loved the courting stage, the little gestures that made her feel appreciated, desired. For Kate, romance was an end in itself. Yet, it seemed she had gotten used to the bare minimum. And somehow, Trevor seemed to know it. He always seemed to know everything.

'Norman makes me feel very appreciated actually,' Kate said, trying to convince herself as much as Trevor. 'That's exactly why he's my fiancé.'

'And yet . . . you're not wearing an engagement ring,' Trevor pried, with a cheeky grin.

Hitting a nerve was one thing. Now it seemed he was trying to set her entire central nervous system on fire with rage.

'Norman and I don't need a diamond to prove something,' Kate said, pretending she wasn't annoyed. 'Anyway, engagement rings were just a marketing ploy that De Beers came up with to upsell diamonds in the forties. It's just one big scam.'

'And let me guess. It was Norman who told you this?' Trevor asked, knowing the answer.

'Well, yes . . . but it's true! Look it up. It's all just clever marketing.'

'Maybe. But deep down, isn't there a tiny part of you that still would have liked one?'

'Nope,' Kate said, adamantly. She was lying, of course.

'Oh come on. Women love all that engagement drama,' Trevor said.

'Men always say women love drama, but men are actually way more dramatic,' Kate said. 'Have you ever seen a man with a common cold?'

'I have to disagree. Men hate drama.'

'HA!' Kate laughed. 'You've obviously never opened a history book.'

'Okay, fair point,' Trevor laughed. 'But you're forgetting the slogan that De Beers used when they were selling diamonds.'

'And what's that?'

'A diamond is for ever,' he smiled. 'They're beautiful and unbreakable. It's not about getting men to cough up money. It's the perfect symbol of true love. That's my only regret from our wedding the other night. It's a shame I wasn't able to give you my grandmother's ring.'

'Why your grandmother's ring?' Kate asked, curious.

'It's been in my family for generations. It's practically priceless.'

'Well, I'm sure that someday, you'll get to give it to some lucky girl who actually wants an engagement ring.'

'Nah – it was stolen. Sold for a fortune, I'm sure.'

'Good thing you have all the money in the world to buy your future fiancée any ring she wants.'

'You see, that's the problem. Success is a double-edged sword. You can never know if someone actually loves you or the money. It's lonely at the top.'

'Aww, the rich and famous playboy with the Lamborghini has feelings,' Kate said, pouting her lips.

'You think I'm a playboy?' Trevor laughed.

'Actually no. I think the term *fuckboy* is more appropriate.'

'Is that so?'

'Well, just look at you. You're a successful Vegas DJ with

two million followers. You probably sleep with a different woman every night.'

Trevor began to laugh once again. 'You think I sleep with 365 women a year?'

'For all I know, yes,' Kate shrugged.

'I didn't know I was such a stud. You honestly think I'm the most attractive man in the world?'

'That is NOT what I said!'

'Well, for your information, I don't sleep around.'

'You honestly expect me to believe that? The women here practically throw themselves at you. And I've seen your Instagram feed.'

'Naturally, when I came to Vegas first, I had some fun. But looking back, I was just trying to fill some kind of void, like I was trying to find a missing piece of myself. There are some amazing women in Vegas but they all have the same flaw.'

'And what's that?'

'They're not you.'

Kate's heart suddenly felt like it was beating out of her chest. It began to thump so loud that she could feel her pulse in every part of her body. *Every* part! This couldn't be happening. Surely she wasn't getting the 'flutters', as Chloe called them. This kind of thing didn't happen to Kate. Or, at least, it hadn't happened in nine years.

His words seemed so incredibly sincere for some reason. For a moment she saw the tender side to Trevor, the vulnerability she used to adore. She felt as if she had just gotten a glimpse of the real Trevor underneath the success. Somewhere behind the mask was the man she had fallen in love with.

No.

She refused to be fooled. He was too good with words, that was the problem. He always knew the right thing to say. For all she knew, he said the same thing to every other girl he was ever with. He probably had a list of romantic lines in his head ready to use at any given moment. It was all part of his toxic scheme. She had to get a grip on herself.

The flutters were not welcome on this date.

'Sorry, but I'm not buying the playboy-with-a-heart-of-gold act,' Kate said, nipping his romantic gesture in the bud. 'No amount of Ferris wheels or gondola rides are going to woo me. Frankly, I liked you better when you were broke.'

'That's what makes you so unique,' Trevor said. 'The girl who doesn't want a diamond deserves the biggest one of all.'

'That would be a good song lyric,' Kate said, putting a melody together in her head.

Trevor's eyes lit up with admiration. 'Well, look at the little songwriter coming out of her shell,' he said.

'Oh for God's sake, can't I say anything without you steering the conversation? It's like you're constantly one step—'

'Ahead?' Trevor smiled.

'Stop finishing my—'

'Sentences?'

Kate started rubbing her temples in frustration. 'Are you trying to give me a hernia with rage?' she asked.

'Don't you think you were a little quick to give up music?'

'I didn't give up, I *grew* up.'

'Tell me more. Yesterday you let slip something about a song . . .'

Kate knew he would bring it up. She hadn't technically told him about the song, she had only almost said it. She hated the idea of telling Trevor about her gigantic failure. But it was no use now. She knew he wouldn't let it go. Maybe she could tell him the bare minimum as a way of getting him to drop it.

'Fine . . . long story short . . .'

'I want the long version.'

'You're lucky you're getting any version at all!'

198

'Fine, fine.'

'After college, I tried the whole independent musician thing, but it was hopeless. I couldn't get any gigs whatsoever. People wanted covers of songs but I only ever wanted to play my own stuff. I figured I'd put myself out there and build an audience for my music. So I released an original song. Guess how many streams it got?'

'With your voice, surely millions,' Trevor said.

'Not even 1,000,' Kate sighed. 'And those streams were just from Siobhan, Nat and Chloe. So your image of me as this great singer-songwriter is completely in your head. It's a version of me that never even existed in the first place.'

'Oh, it existed. You just needed time to develop your craft. That's exactly what we were doing that summer. You were writing songs and I was mixing beats. It felt like the beginning of something special. We could have been an amazing duo.'

'Oh please, we never even finished a single track!'

'That's because we were always too busy having—'

'I know what we were busy doing!' Kate said, cutting him off. She couldn't think about her sex with Trevor that summer. And yet, suddenly she was having a flashback to those hot days in his apartment. Making music and making love. Although they spent way too many hours focusing on the latter.

'I think we could have been the next Sonny and Cher.'

'Well, Sonny cheated on Cher, so I guess we have that in common,' Kate said.

Trevor's eyes narrowed in confusion. 'What's that supposed to mean?'

Kate realized she had said too much. She didn't want him to know that she knew about him cheating. It would lead to a million more questions that would ultimately lead Kate to tears. And that was not happening.

'Look, we never would have worked as a duo, Trevor. And you made it on your own which only proves I would have held you back. So let's just leave it at that,' Kate said, eager to change the subject.

'You know, Freckles, something I've learned is that if you have a voice in your head that tells you you're not good enough, somebody put that voice there,' Trevor said. 'My guess is Norman.'

'Oh please, Norman is a great man.'

'What does he think of your music?' Trevor asked.

'Well . . . he's not a big music fan in general,' Kate defended him.

'He doesn't like music? That doesn't strike you as a red flag?'

'Like you can talk. You have more red flags than a golf course!'

'Name one.'

'Well, for starters, you're wearing a cocaine key necklace,' Kate said.

Trevor looked down at his necklace and smiled. 'Wow, you really have me all figured out, don't you, Freckles?'

'I most certainly do,' Kate said, smugly.

'But you still haven't answered my question. What does Norman think of your music?'

'He encouraged me to get a job where I could actually apply my skills. And it was good advice, because now I have a great career in event planning. What point are you even trying to prove here?'

'My point is that loving someone who doesn't believe in you is like a bird loving its cage.'

'Norman isn't my cage,' Kate scoffed.

'Isn't he? Seems to me like you're settling down in a nice

little birdcage because you think you're at the age to lay some eggs, and you'd rather play it safe than learn to fly.'

'Give me a break,' Kate laughed. 'At least I'm not a peacock. Showing off with expensive suits and overpriced sports cars.'

'Well, I'll never forget the first time I heard you sing. Do you remember?'

'Oh God, that karaoke bar, yes! I sang . . .'

'Taylor Swift's "Love Story",' Trevor said. 'As soon as you started singing, I got goosebumps.'

'Whatever goosebumps you got came from Taylor's genius lyrics, not my singing,' Kate said, putting herself down as usual.

'Let's put it to the test,' Trevor said. 'There should be a karaoke bar around here somewhere.'

'ABSOLUTELY NOT!' Kate said. 'Norman would kill me!'

'Norman would kill you?'

'Yeah, I started singing at one of his work events while I was drunk and I made a show of him. I was a hot mess apparently. My karaoke days are officially over.'

'You don't hear that?'

'Hear what?'

'You just proved my point. Norman's the reason you stopped singing.'

'No he's not! If anything, he's the one who picked me up when I was down! And I'm perfectly content with the way my life turned out.'

'Content isn't the same as happy,' Trevor said, looking deep into her eyes. It was like he was reaching into her soul, desperately trying to rescue her.

But Kate wasn't some helpless damsel in distress. She was a grown woman.

'It is once you turn thirty,' she said. 'And after thirty, the chances of becoming a famous artist are slim to none.'

'I don't know about that. Bram Stoker didn't start writing *Dracula* until he was fifty. And Dracula didn't start killing people until he was dead,' Trevor joked.

'How inspiring,' Kate laughed. 'This TED Talk keeps getting better and better.'

'I'm just saying, maybe you threw in the towel a little early. If I didn't keep pushing myself, I wouldn't have gotten to where I am today. If I'm being honest, I owe a lot of my success to you.'

'Oh please.'

'I mean it. Behind every great man is a greater woman.'

'And in front of every woman is a man stealing her spotlight,' Kate said, gritting her teeth.

'I would never steal your spotlight, Kate,' he said, looking straight into her eyes with his piercing gaze. 'All I want is to see you shine.'

Shit.

The flutters were back.

Whenever he called her Kate, he seemed so sincere. But she had to remind herself that it was all an act. It genuinely meant a lot that he acknowledged her role in his success, however. She was the first person to ever hype him up, to tell him he was good enough. But then again, all his success had come after she left New York. She couldn't really take any credit.

'Well, I appreciate what you're trying to say, but it's not entirely true. You made it without me, Trevor.'

'No, Kate, I made it *because* of you. Nothing motivates a man like a broken heart.'

She had broken *his* heart?

Now that was rich.

He had finally said the wrong thing and she was able to get

a grip of herself once again. The flutters were officially gone. He cheated on her and somehow *he* was the victim? She felt like calling him out on his bullshit, but she had to retain her poise and remain aloof.

She needed that signature.

'Well, everything worked out for the both of us in the end,' she shrugged.

'Still, you have a beautiful voice. It's a shame the world will never hear it.'

'If nobody listens then it doesn't make any difference.'

'I just wish your dreams were bigger than your excuses. If the right person listens, that's all that matters,' Trevor said.

Kate was sick of talking in circles about a stupid pipe dream she had a million years ago. He knew her failed singing career was a sensitive subject but he refused to let it go. Just one of his many attempts at torturing her, she supposed. And whenever people brought up her music, all she could think about was that internet troll's hate comment:

Another delusional hack going absolutely nowhere.

Who could blame her for not wanting to discuss it to death?

'Can we please talk about something a little more interesting?' she said, desperate to change the subject.

'Okay, back to Norman . . .'

'Nope! He is also not up for discussion. It's bad enough that you've jeopardized my life with him. You're literally a homewrecker!'

'It's not homewrecking if it's an obvious upgrade. It's home renovation,' Trevor teased.

'Oh please, he's a doctor who makes six figures.'

'Six figures. How cute.'

'It's more than enough.'

'More than enough to buy you a ring.'

'Okay, that's it!' Kate said. 'I'm not going to let you have some stupid dick-measuring contest with Norman.'

'No, I imagine that's something you definitely wouldn't want to happen,' Trevor said, a triumphant smirk tugging at his lips.

That was the final straw.

Everything with Trevor was a battle of wits and she was officially at her wits' end.

'Excuse me, sir? Steer us back to shore please,' Kate said to the gondolier.

'He only speaks Italian,' Trevor explained. 'Guess you're stuck here.'

Kate rattled her brain for some Italian phrases she had learned on Duolingo. But her mind was completely blank.

'Fine, I'll steer us myself,' she said, getting up. She grabbed the paddle off the gondolier and began trying to steer the boat.

'Get down from there,' Trevor said.

'No!' she replied, like a stubborn child.

'You're up shit creek without a paddle.'

'I have a paddle, thank you very much!'

'You're going to regret it if you don't start behaving.'

'I doubt that!' Kate said, determined to prove she could turn the gondola around.

'Stop being such a brat.'

'Make me!'

'With pleasure,' Trevor said. He stood up and tried to grab her.

'No!' Kate said, turning around too quickly. Before she knew it, she had accidentally whacked Trevor with the paddle and sent him flying off the boat and into the water.

'OH MY GOD!' Kate shouted as Trevor splashed in.

Trevor came back up from beneath the water. Thankfully, it wasn't deep. 'Now you're really being a brat, aren't you?'

'I'm so sorry, it was an accident!'

'Are you hell bent on destroying every suit I own?'

'Here, take my hand,' Kate said, trying to help him up.

'I already took your hand, wifey. Remember?' Trevor joked.

'Oh shut up and climb aboard.'

Trevor reached up and grabbed Kate's hand. He gripped it firmly but for some strange reason, he did not get up on the boat. That's when Kate saw the mischievous look on his face.

'Don't even think about it,' she said, sternly.

'I told you you'd regret it, darling,' he said with a twisted grin.

In one swift motion, Trevor pulled Kate off the boat and directly into the water beside him. She began to shriek as she came up for air.

'HOW DARE YOU!' Kate yelled. 'We're both destroyed!'

'This reminds me of when we went skinny-dipping in the Lake at Central Park,' Trevor laughed.

'I have no recollection of that,' Kate lied.

'Ah yes, your selective memory problem.'

'That's not the problem. You are! And forgetting you is the solution.'

'How's that been working out for ya?' Trevor winked.

Kate tried to think of a snappy comeback but she couldn't find the right thing to say.

'Come on, darling, use your words,' he said, knowing it would annoy her even further.

'I'm speechless with anger!'

'Well, another stunt like that and I'll make it four dates, instead of three.'

'You're bluffing!' she said.

'Try me.'

Kate couldn't risk it. She needed that annulment. He had

all the power. She had to keep her eyes on the prize. This was all a game. And she needed to win, even if it meant playing by his rules.

'So, are you ready to behave?'

'Fine,' she said in defeat.

'Good girl.'

Chapter 18

Italian Style

As they walked towards the main entrance of The Venetian, Kate was still trying to squeeze the remaining water out of her ugly floral dress. Thankfully, the sizzling Vegas heat had almost dried her hair out, but her dress remained slightly damp.

'I still can't believe you pulled me in,' Kate said.

'I still can't believe you *pushed* me in,' Trevor replied.

'That was an accident. Just like marrying you was an accident!'

'Accidentally on purpose.'

'This isn't funny, Trevor. I'm soaking wet because of you!'

'Mrs Rush, behave! It's only our second date.'

'Ugh, you're worse than Siobhan for making everything sexual.'

'Nobody's worse than Siobhan for making everything sexual.'

'Good point,' Kate said, accidentally smiling.

'Was that a smile, Freckles?'

Another rookie mistake on her part. Winning this game meant keeping her guard up at all times. She was a woman on a mission, she reminded herself.

'It was a grimace at best,' Kate said, correcting herself.

'I'll take it,' Trevor said. 'Anyway, we better get you a new dress.'

'It's starting to dry out. I'm sure it'll be fine eventually.'

'That dress will never be fine,' Trevor said, looking at the horrific floral patterns. 'You need a dress that's worthy of your beauty.'

'Oh give me a break, I'm like a seven on a good day.'

'There you go, running yourself into the ground again. I thought you would have gotten over your ugly duckling syndrome by now.'

'Great, more psychoanalysis from the Vegas DJ,' Kate said, throwing her eyes up to heaven.

'You don't believe in self-love?' Trevor asked.

'Well, loving myself would be a lot easier if you didn't keep highlighting my flaws.'

'I've literally never done that,' Trevor said, confused.

'Oh please, you call me Freckles like every ten seconds!'

'Don't tell me you're still insecure about your freckles after all these years?'

'I just don't like any attention being drawn to them.'

'Women never cease to amaze me,' Trevor laughed.

'Be very careful what you say next,' Kate said. He was on thin ice as it was, without making sweeping generalizations.

'Women still don't realize that what makes them unique is also what makes them beautiful.'

His statement was surprisingly inoffensive. And on top of that, there was some truth in it.

For as long as she could remember, her self-esteem had conditions. It was either 'I'll love myself when I lose five pounds' or 'I'll love myself when I get these freckles lasered off'. Self-love was always something she would achieve in the future based on reaching a certain goal. But when she actually achieved the goal, there was always another thing to fix down the line.

Confidence, it seemed, was an oasis in the desert, a mirage

always so near yet so far. She knew how dysfunctional that sounded, especially from a feminist perspective. After all, every time a woman hates herself, the patriarchy wins. She hated herself for not loving herself. It was a self-defeating cycle that she feared would never be broken.

'Well, women are given unrealistic beauty standards from the moment they're born,' she explained. 'If you don't fit the mould, society makes sure you know it.'

Trevor stopped and looked Kate dead in the eye. 'How the hell can't you see that your freckles are the most beautiful thing about you?'

Shit.

The flutters were back.

But it was time to close the shutters.

'Hasn't saying "your flaws are beautiful" become a bit of a cliché?' she said, refusing to be wooed.

'Except they're not a flaw,' he laughed. 'When I call you that nickname, I'm trying to compliment you.'

'And yet you always manage to make my blood boil.'

'So what, you want your skin to have the same complexion all over?'

'That's the dream.'

'Your dream is to be a sky without stars?'

'Oh my God, you're the most dramatic man in the world,' Kate laughed.

'Let me guess – you always compliment other women's freckles?'

'Well, yeah, they look gorgeous on *other* women.'

'But they only look ugly on *you*?'

'Well . . . I . . .' she stuttered. When he said it like that it really brought her self-esteem issues into full focus.

'Word of advice, Freckles,' Trevor said. 'You can't hate yourself into loving yourself.'

It was an oddly profound thing to say, delivered with a kind of conviction only he was capable of. But she didn't feel like discussing it any further. She didn't like the way he was holding a mirror up to her. But then again, wasn't that just further proof that she didn't love her reflection?

৪৩

Trevor led Kate through the Venetian to a fabulous little shopping area. It had its own Venice canal, just like the one outside, and the roof was painted like a stunning blue sky. For a brief moment, Kate forgot she was indoors.

As she looked around the designer stores, Kate felt like a fish out of water. Sure, there were designer brands in Ireland but Kate could never afford them. She used to window-shop from time to time, but whenever Norman was with her, he would always say designer clothes were a rip-off. He was right, she supposed, but was there anything wrong with day-dreaming about it? Everyone has the right to fantasize.

'Is Versace okay?' Trevor asked.

'Excuse me?'

'For your new dress. They also have Gucci, Armani, Prada . . .'

'Trevor, that's not exactly within my budget,' she said. 'Let's just find a souvenir shop with something cheap.'

'Freckles, haven't you figured out yet that you're not the one calling the shots?' Trevor asked. 'I'm the one with all the power.'

'But . . .'

'My wife should be dressed in designer, and that's non-negotiable. So I'll ask you once again. Is Versace okay?'

'Alright,' Kate agreed, apprehensively.

Trevor walked ahead towards the boutique and Kate followed behind him. When they got to the store window, she looked up in awe at a dress being displayed on a mannequin. It was beyond anything Kate had ever seen before. It was a blue velvet gown with a plunge neckline and a thigh split. It was elegant yet bold, the epitome of glamour and sophistication. It was the kind of haute couture one only ever sees at the Met Gala. A work of art, in every respect.

'Wow,' she said as she stared at it.

'Oh so you *do* have good taste . . .' Trevor teased. 'Come on.'

They walked into the store and were greeted by a beautiful stylist with cheekbones for days.

'Mr Rush, you're very welcome,' the stylist said, looking him up and down. She was clearly another one of his fans.

'Hi there. My wife and I had a little boating accident,' Trevor said. 'We'll be needing some new clothes.'

'But the cheapest thing you have,' Kate insisted.

'Ignore her. She's a rescue.'

'Excuse me?'

'You have amazing cheekbones, by the way,' Trevor said to the stylist.

Kate was raging, but she had to admit he had a point. The stylist should have been modelling the clothes, not merely selling them. She looked like one of those women in Trevor's Instagram photos. Perfect face, perfect body – perfect everything, really. But the cheek of him to compliment her while Kate was standing right there. Even though it was clearly just an attempt to annoy her, she hated that it was working. Then again, why did she care?

'Thank you, Mr Rush,' the stylist said. 'Quite a compliment coming from you.'

'My wife will take the dress in the window, and I'll take something similar to what I'm currently wearing.'

'Wonderful. I'll take your wife to the fitting room and my colleague will take you to the men's section. Mrs Rush, right this way.'

Before Kate could object she was already being whisked off to the women's fitting rooms. She was in love with the dress from the window, but she was terrified to learn the price. The stylist grabbed one of the dresses off the rail and opened the fitting room for Kate. 'Let me know if the size is okay,' she smiled before closing the door.

Kate braced herself as she turned over the price tag.

$4,500.

She nearly collapsed with shock. But at the same time, she shouldn't have been surprised. The dress was a work of art. And art wasn't cheap.

She wanted it more than she had ever wanted an item of clothing, but she felt so guilty about the price. It was more expensive than her wedding dress, for crying out loud. But it truly was divine. And if Trevor really wanted her to have it, then she didn't exactly have a choice. Maybe this could be one little out-of-character indulgence she could allow herself to enjoy. She could even take it home to Ireland. Norman didn't need to know who bought it for her. Or how expensive it was.

She took off her soggy floral dress and began to unzip its fabulous replacement. But just as she was about to slip it on, her phone began to ring in her handbag again. Surely Norman wasn't calling again so soon. She needed him to give her some space while she tried to get her life back on track.

Kate took out her phone. It was worse than Norman.

It was her mother.

'Shit!' Kate said.

'Everything alright in there?' the stylist asked.

'Yes, I just have to take a phone call!'

'No problem – I'll circle back.'

Kate took a deep breath before answering the call. Several years prior, she had made the mistake of showing her mother how to do video calls. She was regretting it more than ever now. 'Hi, Mam!' she said, pretending as if nothing was wrong.

'Kate O'Connor, I'm not one bit impressed with your behaviour!' Margaret said. Her face was way too close to the screen and all Kate could see were her chapped, pursed lips.

'Mam, hold the camera further away from your face,' she instructed.

Margaret pulled the phone back to reveal the entirety of her sharp face. She had a scornful look that Kate knew all too well. She was about to give one of her lectures.

'Kate!' Margaret said. 'Where in God's name are your clothes?'

'They're on the ground beside me, I'm just changing,' Kate said. She didn't need to mention she was changing in Versace. 'What's the matter, Mam? It must be the middle of the night back home.'

'It certainly is the middle of the night, Kate. And I've just been woken up by a very disturbing call from Norman. He said that you've extended your hen party by two days and you're behaving like a lunatic!'

'Chloe got us two extra nights for free because she's an influencer. I couldn't say no.'

'And if Chloe influenced you to jump off a bridge, would you do it?' Margaret asked.

'No, Mam, I obviously wouldn't.'

'Oh, so you *do* have a bit of common sense left? So why did Norman tell me you're behaving like a completely different person? He's worried sick!'

'I'm still me, Mam. Women are allowed to blow off some steam on their hen party. It's not the end of the world.'

'It might be. Norman is up the walls with nerves. He said he was looking at plane tickets to go to Vegas and bring you home.'

'HE CANNOT COME TO VEGAS!' Kate panicked.

'Well, he said something about you being in a sports car and a strange voice saying you'd been taken. He thinks you've been human trafficked!'

'Mam, look at me. Does it look like I've been human trafficked?'

'Well, you're in a tiny little room, wearing only your bra and knickers and your hair looks soaking wet. So yes, Kate, it *does* look like you've been human trafficked actually.'

'I just fell into a canal . . .'

'A CANAL?'

'A very shallow canal, Mam! I got a bit wet so I'm in a changing room now putting on a new dress.'

'Great, you'll have pneumonia before the wedding. If there's even going to be a wedding!' Margaret snapped.

'Of course there'll be a wedding, Mam. Will you please call Norman back and tell him not to come to Vegas? He's overreacting.'

'Is he, Kate? Because it seems to me like you've forgotten who you are. I don't know what's going on over there but I'm your mother and I know when something is off.'

Margaret always knew when Kate was lying. But she couldn't find out about her drunkenly marrying Trevor Rush. Margaret had always told Kate that he was a lowlife, a ruffian who didn't deserve her. She always said that Trevor was completely wrong for her. He wasn't 'good people', as she put it. Which wasn't particularly fair, considering she never even met Trevor.

But wasn't she right to a certain degree?

Margaret was there through all the tears after Kate caught Trevor cheating. She knew the devastating effect he'd had on her. Those sleepless nights listening to Taylor Swift heartbreak songs had seemed never-ending at the time. But Kate had risen above it. She couldn't revert to those days.

One cannot heal backwards.

Trevor was a cheater and Norman was loyal. That was all there was to it. But the only way to get away from Trevor and back to Norman was to power through these dates. Once they were over, she could go back to normality and pretend this never happened.

'Mam, I promise I have everything under control. You just have to trust me,' Kate said.

'Fine. I'll tell Norman I spoke to you. But mark my words, if you do anything to jeopardize this marriage, I'll be found dead of shame. And your poor father is worried sick too. You know full well stress can cause cancer to come back!' Margaret said.

There was a knock on the fitting room door. 'Mrs Rush,' the stylist said. 'Do you need more time?'

Shit.

'I'll be out in just a minute!' Kate said, in a fluster.

'Kate . . .' Margaret said, suspiciously. 'Did that woman call you Mrs Rush?'

'No! She was talking to someone else!'

'So why did you respond?'

Kate felt the smothering feeling engulf her once again. She felt completely caught out. 'She's . . . she's telling me to rush because someone else needs the fitting room.'

'But she—'

'I have to go, Mam! Tell Norman everything is fine! See you Friday!'

Kate hung up and caught her breath once again.

She felt unbearable pressure from Norman and Margaret. There was nothing she hated more than when they teamed up against her, which was something that happened quite often. They needed to give her some space and let her get this annulment. Calling her and panicking wasn't going to help the situation. She had been very nearly caught out in the lie about who Mrs Rush was, but at least Trevor hadn't barged into the video call. That would have been a whole new level of disaster. But the smothering feeling was easing. She just had to keep it together until this nightmare was over.

Kate looked down at the price tag once again.

$4,500 was far too much to spend on a dress, no matter how much she would have loved it. She couldn't let Trevor pay that much. Sure, the dress was a work of art, but she wasn't the type of girl who wore works of art. That was for the runway models, celebrities, taste-makers. It's not like she was going to be invited to the Met Gala any time soon. Her mother was right.

She had to remember who she was.

'Excuse me,' Kate said, opening the dressing room door.

'Yes, Mrs Rush?' the stylist said, coming over.

'Yeah, so this isn't really in my price range. Do you have anything for around $400?'

'You mean like a belt?'

'Well . . . no,' Kate said. She couldn't exactly wear a belt on its own. 'I'll just take your cheapest dress. Sorry to be a pain.'

The stylist gave Kate a strange look. 'Mmhmm, I'll be right back,' she said.

After a minute or two, she returned with a silver bodycon dress.

It was perfect. Simple yet elegant.

And only $999.

Still not in Kate's price range, but at least she wouldn't feel as guilty for wearing it.

She slipped it on and put her own heels back on, which matched the dress surprisingly well. She walked out of the dressing room and saw Trevor standing in a fancy new suit, waiting for her. He looked both impressed and disappointed at the same time.

'Well, what do you think?' Kate asked, giving him a twirl.

'It's nice,' he said. 'But it's not the one you wanted.'

'The other one was very flashy. I'm a simple girl, I like simple dresses.'

'Hmm . . .'

'This is perfect for me, honestly.'

'Well, it's certainly an improvement from earlier anyway,' Trevor said. 'Miss, could you take off the labels and scan them for us? We'd like to keep these clothes on for the rest of the evening.'

'Sure,' she said as she removed the label from Kate's dress. 'And what should I do with the dress she wore in?'

'Burn it,' Trevor said, deadly serious.

'Hey!' Kate said. 'I love that dress!'

'Well darling, it most certainly does not love you.'

Chapter 19

Lady Luck

After swiping his Amex Black Card to pay for their new clothes, Trevor led Kate out of the store and back through the Venice-inspired indoor canal walk.

'Now, isn't that better than walking around in wet clothes?' he asked.

'I suppose,' Kate said. 'You're causing havoc back home by the way. My mother called in a complete panic.'

'Why?'

'WHY? Let's see, how about because my wedding is on Friday and you're holding me hostage in Vegas, after practically kidnapping me?'

'Oh my God, and you call *me* dramatic?' Trevor laughed.

'I'm serious!' Kate said. 'My mother is worried sick. She's afraid the wedding isn't going to happen on Friday.'

'Why don't you call her back and tell her you already had the perfect wedding?'

'Don't even joke about that. She would die of heart failure! She is not a Trevor Rush fan, trust me,' Kate said.

'She will be.'

'And what do *your* family have to say about our drunken Vegas wedding?'

'They're overjoyed. Although they are upset they didn't get to come to the ceremony. But I assured them we'll have a proper Italian wedding in a Catholic church by the end of the year.'

'We will do no such thing! The only church wedding I'll be having will be at the Church of the Sacred Heart in Donnybrook. And you will NOT be the groom!'

'I don't know, I think we should do a bigger wedding down the line. Invite all our family and friends. My manager, Charlie, is dying to meet you too.'

'Why's that?'

'Probably to try and steal you off me. It's happened before. Maybe it's not such a good idea actually. I don't want you getting stolen out from under me.'

'Except I'm not *under* you and I never will be!' Kate said, rather sternly.

'You're being a brat again, Freckles,' Trevor said.

'No, I'm not!'

'So you're going to behave?'

'Absolutely not.'

'Shame. Looks like you'll be missing your show at eleven then . . .'

Kate was infuriated. But she had to play ball once again. 'Sorry, dear,' she said, in an overly fake and submissive tone.

'That's better. So, are you ready for the second part of the date?'

'Which is?'

'The roulette table,' Trevor said, leading her into the casino section of the Venetian.

'Gambling? Really?'

'What's wrong with a little gambling?'

'Hmm, let's see. How about the fact that it's just one big scam? The house always wins.'

'Not always. I have something most people don't.'

'And what might that be?'

'Luck.'

'HA!' Kate said, laughing in his face.

'You don't believe in luck?'

'Well, I know some people experience luck. Like being in the right place at the right time. But it's not like some force in the universe.'

'I disagree. Think about it. You just happen to have your bachelorette party in Vegas, where I just happen to be a resident DJ, and you just happen to order a champagne shower as my set begins? Either you planned the whole thing, or it's Lady Luck bringing us together.'

'I didn't plan this! Are you insane? This has been the most reckless situation of my entire life.'

'You say reckless . . . I say lucky,' Trevor said. 'Don't you believe in manifesting?'

'Well . . . yes. But that's completely different.'

'No, it's not. You manifest something and hope the universe gives you a lucky break. Maybe that's why you're here.'

'What's that supposed to mean?'

'Like, maybe you were manifesting a big dick,' Trevor smirked.

'Oh, well I certainly got that,' she laughed, referring to his personality.

'Be careful what you wish for,' he winked. 'Do you honestly expect me to believe you haven't thought about me once over the past nine years?'

It was a downright brazen question to ask. And Kate had no intention of revealing the answer. Of course she had thought of him. Every single day for nine years straight. But they were not fond thoughts. They were thoughts of pain and betrayal.

She often found herself lying awake in bed, creating imaginary scenarios about Trevor in her head. Like how she would have done things differently. She fantasized about what her life would have been like if she never gave him the chance to break her heart in the first place. But that also raised a deeper question.

Was it better to have been hurt by love than to have never loved at all?

She still didn't quite have the answer to that one.

The question seemed particularly relevant to bad boys like Trevor. They were like a drug. Euphoric, intoxicating, enrapturing. They had the power to give you the greatest high of your life. But drugs can be addictive and dangerous. The comedown is always inevitable. And the higher one climbs, the further one falls. Trevor had shown Kate how to feel alive but he had ruined her life in the process.

Nine years later, she knew better.

'Oh I've thought about you alright, Trevor. But trust me, they were not kind thoughts. And it certainly wasn't manifesting,' Kate said.

'I have this theory about manifesting – would you like to hear it?'

'Nope.'

'Well, I'll tell you anyway. So, people mostly associate manifesting with positive affirmations and dream fulfilment. But I think it works both ways. For example, if you spend every single day thinking you're going to crash your car then you'll probably end up crashing your car. So no matter what you manifest, good or bad, the universe will conspire to provide it.'

'Your point being?' Kate asked.

'Your thoughts of me may not have been fond, but you sent a clear message to the universe every time you thought about me. And the message was that you and I had unfinished business. Our story wasn't over,' Trevor said, sure of himself.

Was he right? Had her daily dwelling on Trevor brought this terrible situation to fruition? Had she conjured him accidentally, like a demon being summoned from hell?

No.

She refused to let Trevor imply that she was somehow responsible for this whole mess. He had created this toxic situation. Not her.

'Is your arse ever jealous of all the shit that comes out your mouth?' Kate asked.

'You have to admit our meeting was meant to be. The universe is clearly shipping us.'

'Well, I'd like to return to sender,' Kate said. She suddenly thought of an ick suggestion from Natalie. And it was a good one too. 'Your theory is nonsense because the universe would never bring a Scorpio and a Capricorn together.'

'Oh, give me a break,' Trevor said, unamused. 'All that star sign stuff is completely made up.'

'Said the biggest Scorpio in the history of Scorpios.'

'I can't even tell if you're being serious. You believe it's okay to judge an entire person based on the month they were born? It's basically space racism.'

'All I know is that I'm an earth sign and you're a water sign. Not compatible in the slightest.'

'Seems to me like earth needs water in order to grow. The only way to bloom is to let yourself get drenched,' Trevor smirked.

Why in God's name was she having palpitations? She was trying to give him the ick, for Christ's sake!

'Deserts seem to survive just fine without water,' she said, stubbornly.

'Even deserts need a good downpour. And when it rains . . . it pours,' he whispered into her ear.

Not the flutters. Not now.

This was NOT the time.

'Out of curiosity, what type of sign is Norman?' Trevor asked.

'He's a Leo, which makes him a fire sign,' Kate bragged.

'Perfect. Water extinguishes fire.'

'This isn't some game of rock, paper, scissors!' Kate said, blowing a fuse. Yet another failed ick attempt, sabotaged by Trevor. 'Fine, forget astrology. But your theory is still wrong.'

'Nine years of thinking about each other, and we end up married in Vegas? I'm telling you, Lady Luck is lurking around here somewhere.'

'Well, you might have gotten lucky with your career but you won't be getting lucky with me,' she said. 'You're just a fly in the ointment of my life.'

'Another good song lyric. You're on a roll, Freckles!'

'Dear Lord,' she sighed. He literally had a comeback to everything she said.

As they walked through the casino, Kate became hyper-aware of all the noise in her ear. She could hear the clinking of coins being released from slot machines, the shuffling of cards, the rolling of dice, the occasional cheer of someone winning and the frequent groan of people losing. The smell wasn't great either. Her nostrils were being assaulted by the scent of indoor smoking and binge drinking. But finally, they arrived at a classier section of the gambling floor where more traditional games were being played. It felt more like a casino one would find in Monte Carlo.

'Alright, here we are,' Trevor said. 'Let's play some roulette.'

'How about Russian Roulette instead?' Kate suggested. 'You play, I'll watch.'

'And leave my beautiful wife a widow? No, you'd never recover.'

'Well, technically I'd inherit all your money so I could dry my tears with hundred-dollar bills.'

'Tell you what. You can keep whatever we win and put it towards your sham marriage with Nolan.'

'WITH NORMAN!'

'So you admit it's a sham marriage?'

'It most certainly is NOT!'

'Sorry, what's the politer term? Oh yes, a marriage of convenience.'

'Well, that must make ours a marriage of inconvenience, considering I couldn't see straight during the ceremony!'

'Or maybe it was the first time you were seeing straight in years.'

'You always have an answer for everything,' Kate sighed. 'Can we at least play a game I know how to play?'

'Okay, how about Spin the Bottle?'

'There are only two of us!'

'Exactly,' Trevor winked.

'How about Hide and Seek? I'll hide and you go seek professional help,' Kate said, giving it right back to him. Her comebacks were improving slightly.

'You're getting quicker, Freckles,' he smiled, as if he was proud of her. 'Roulette is easy. I'll show you how to play.'

They found a spot at one of the larger roulette tables and Trevor took out a $50 bill. 'Deal us in, my friend,' he said to the baby-faced dealer.

'Certainly, Mr Rush,' the dealer said. Yet another person who instantly recognized him.

The dealer took the cash and handed them back one chip worth the same amount.

'So how do we play exactly?' Kate asked.

'It's simple. The ball spins and you have to predict where it'll land. You can make easier predictions, like if it'll be red or black or an odd or even number. Or you can guess specific numbers. The more specific the prediction, the bigger the pay-out. Make sense?' Trevor explained.

'Alright,' Kate said. 'Let's start with a prediction on odd.'

'Fifty dollars on odd,' Trevor said. The dealer placed the chip.

The wheel began to spin and the little white ball bounced around. Kate had to admit that the suspense was a little thrilling. When it eventually stopped, she saw it landed on thirty-five.

'Black thirty-five,' the dealer said.

'We won!' Kate said. 'How much did we win?'

'We doubled our investment. So now we have $100.'

'Oh, I like this,' Kate said.

'Famous last words,' Trevor laughed. 'What's your next prediction?'

'Put one chip on red and the other on even,' Kate said.

'You heard the lady,' Trevor said to the dealer.

The wheel began to spin again and Kate felt a sense of excitement. It was easy to see how one would become addicted to a high like this. After a few agonizing seconds, the ball finally stopped.

'Red, eighteen,' the dealer said.

'OH MY GOD!' Kate said. 'We won twice!'

'We sure did. Now you have $200. Want to take the money and run?' Trevor asked.

'No!' Kate said. 'I'm just getting warmed up!'

'So what's next? You can also bet on groups of numbers that are next to each other by the way.'

'Okay, let's say the first twelve,' Kate said. 'Two of the chips only. We'll keep the other two.'

The dealer spun the wheel once again. Kate's heart was in her mouth.

'Red five,' the dealer said.

'YES!' Kate shouted. 'How much did I win that time?'

'You tripled your stake. You have $300 plus the $100 you didn't gamble,' Trevor explained.

'Okay, I want to bet on a group of six numbers. Four-hundred dollars on twenty-eight to thirty-three,' Kate said to the dealer.

'Risky,' Trevor winced. 'That's all your chips.'

'I have a feeling.'

The dealer put her chips down and spun the wheel. Kate was on the edge of her seat. The suspense was as excruciating as it was exhilarating. She held her breath in anticipation.

The wheel stopped.

'Red thirty,' the dealer said.

'AAAHHHHH,' Kate screamed.

'It's her first time in Vegas,' Trevor said to the dealer.

'Well, she seems to be a natural,' the dealer said.

'How much do I have now?' Kate asked, excited.

'You now have $2,400,' Trevor said.

'WHAT!' Kate said, blown away. She had just won a whole month's net salary with the spin of a wheel. The idea was insane to her.

'So what's the next big move?'

'I have this weird feeling about black thirteen,' Kate said.

'Thirteen. Unlucky for some.'

'I know. But I keep picturing it for some reason.'

'Well then, follow your instincts,' Trevor said, encouraging her.

'What's the pay-out if you only bet on one number?' Kate asked the dealer.

'Thirty-five times your bet, madam,' the dealer said.

'Sweet Jesus! And what happens if I'm wrong?'

'Then the house wins.'

Kate was torn. She had just won $2,400, which was a fairly significant win. But she could potentially multiply that by thirty-five! Yet, the number thirteen was infamously unlucky. Risking it all on such a number would be lunacy. Then again, thirteen was Taylor Swift's lucky number.

She felt a pit in her stomach. She was terrified of getting egg on her face after her winning streak. It was better to walk away with what she had.

'No, dealer. I'd like to cash out please,' Kate said.

'Are you sure?' Trevor asked. 'You said you had a feeling about thirteen.'

'Yeah but I'm very superstitious and thirteen is the riskiest number ever. The hotels here don't even have a thirteenth floor, for God's sake. It would be crazy to bet $2,400 on it.'

'It's your call,' Trevor shrugged.

Kate didn't want to lose it all. She wanted to sicken Trevor by spending her winnings on something for Norman. If she lost it all now, it would be mortifying.

'I've made up my mind,' she said. 'You need to know when to walk away, right? I never even dreamed of winning $2,400 in Vegas.'

'But maybe you need to learn to dream a little bigger.'

'We'll cash out, dealer, thank you,' Kate said, sure of her decision.

The dealer handed them their chips and spun the wheel for the other guests at the table.

'Let's see what we missed out on,' Trevor said.

The wheel continued to spin and for once, Kate prayed she would be wrong. After a few painful seconds, it came to a stop.

'Black thirteen,' the dealer said.

Kate felt like she had just been hit by a bus. It was one of the biggest gunks of her life.

'Well, would you look at that,' Trevor said. 'Black thirteen.'

'Oh shut up, Trevor,' Kate said, furious. 'There's no need to rub salt in the wound.'

'That's not what I'm doing. I just think you should have followed your instincts, that's all.'

'No rational person would have gambled $2,400 on the number thirteen.'

'And yet . . . if you had, you would have walked away with—'

'I don't want to know the amount!' Kate interrupted him. 'I played it safe and I don't regret my decision.' She did, of course, regret it terribly.

'Alright. But playing it safe will only get you so far in life. If your gut tells you to take the risk, you probably should,' Trevor explained. 'Do you want to play again?'

'No, that's enough gambling for me, thank you very much,' Kate said, collecting her chips and leaving the table.

'So what are you going to buy Norman with your winnings? A new heart monitor for when he finds out his fiancée is married, maybe?' Trevor teased as they strolled.

'I'm thinking a nice watch actually, not that it's any of your business.'

'A watch is a terrible idea.'

'Why?'

'You know I have no time for Norman.'

'Hilarious,' Kate said, rolling her eyes.

'Why would you spend all that money to buy him a watch when he won't even buy you a ring?' Trevor said, raising his eyebrow.

Kate couldn't think of a comeback. Trevor did have a point, after all.

'Well . . . maybe I could spend some of the money on myself,' she said.

'As you should.'

'Wait, that was *your* money I was gambling,' Kate realized. 'You should at least take half the chips. As payment for the dress.'

'Don't be silly. It's only money. Consider it an investment.'

'In what?'

'In you,' Trevor smiled. '$2,400 could get you some decent studio time. You could record some new music.'

'Wow, you're really not going to let this go, are you?' Kate laughed.

'It's just an idea,' he shrugged. 'After all, you invested in me nine years ago.'

'I never gave you any money.'

'Even still. You told me to put it all on black thirteen when the world told me not to. Before I met you, I used to be embarrassed to tell people I dreamt of being a DJ. People used to laugh in my face. But not you. You made it all seem possible. If I had listened to society instead of you, I wouldn't be where I am today. Who knows, maybe I can return the favour someday. Maybe I can be the person who makes it all seem possible,' Trevor said with a sincere smile.

There it was again. A rare glimpse of the vulnerable man beneath the shell. His tone was tender. Genuine, even. The mask had slipped and his authentic self was momentarily exposed.

It reminded her of the way he used to speak when they lay in bed together that summer. They would lie there, with naked bodies and naked souls, talking about their hopes and dreams. They used to get so lost in one another. She used to forget where she ended and he began. One of the reasons she fell for him was because he wasn't afraid to lay himself bare.

He let her in.

Beneath the mask. Beneath the covers.

Kate suddenly realized she was thinking about her and Trevor lying naked in bed together. Jesus, what was wrong with her? She needed to rein it in.

'Well, I appreciate you saying that,' Kate said, regaining her focus. 'But I'm an optimist. It's important to value what you have instead of longing for what you don't.'

'But doesn't a part of you wonder *what if*?'

'Yeah like, *what if* you weren't such a dickhead?' she teased him.

'Or *what if* you didn't settle for what's-his-name?'

'You think I'm settling for Norman?' Kate laughed. 'He ticks every box on my list. He's literally the full package.'

'And yet he still can't make you feel the way I do,' Trevor said with confidence.

'You mean annoyed? Irritated? Enraged?'

'The word I would use is flustered,' Trevor said, a twisted smirk painted on his face. 'After all these years, I still know how to push your buttons. Get you all hot and bothered.'

'Oh please, Norman has ten times your sex appeal.'

'So what did he do to make you fall in love with him?'

'It was effortless.'

'So he put in no effort?'

'That's NOT what I said!' Kate snapped. 'It was effortlessly romantic. I went in to have my wisdom teeth removed and afterwards, he asked for my number. It was the perfect meet cute.'

'Ahh, so *that's* how he made you fall for him . . .' Trevor said. 'He removed all your wisdom. It finally makes sense.'

'Oh shut up! He's extremely sexy!'

'So Norman the dentist really does it for you, does he?'

'Yep. Every single time.'

'Too bad you'll always have a sweet tooth for me,' he winked.

'Okay, that's enough,' Kate said. 'It's time to cash out of this conversation.'

They walked up to a cashier and Kate handed in her chips in exchange for cash. She felt so bizarre collecting the $2,400. She had never held that amount of money in her hand before. It felt like monopoly money, not a real currency she could actually buy things with. A part of her felt guilty for having it. But Trevor wouldn't let her give it to him, so she put it in her handbag. It would help her pay for some of the wedding expenses.

'Alright,' she said, turning back to Trevor. 'It's almost eleven, so I have to go meet the girls for Chippendales. And don't even think about saying you have another surprise planned, because we had a deal.'

'You never told me Chippendales was the show you're going to,' Trevor said, unimpressed. 'I don't know if I approve, Mrs Rush.'

'Too bad. It's my bachelorette party and a male stripper is a rite of passage.'

'But you're not a bachelorette any more. You're a married woman.'

'Don't tell me you're jealous, Mr Rush? I thought you didn't get jealous?'

'No. But Marcus, the choreographer, is a very good friend of mine and he said it can get pretty raunchy,' Trevor warned.

'Great. The raunchier the better,' Kate said, trying to annoy him.

'Alright,' Trevor said. 'Just don't say I didn't warn you.'

Chapter 20

Striptease

Trevor drove Kate to the Rio All-Suite Hotel and Casino where she had arranged to meet the girls for the strip show.

As she sat in the passenger seat of the obnoxious super-car, she took out her phone to text Norman. The fact that he had called her mother meant he must have been up the walls with worry. She understood that he was just being caring, but on the other hand, she hated when he teamed up with Margaret. They always claimed to have her best interests in mind, but sometimes she wondered how true that was.

Giving up her dream of music, for example, was a by-product of their 'advice'. As infuriating as Trevor was being in bringing up her biggest failure, she was beginning to question things. If she had had someone who encouraged her to follow her dream instead of forsaking it, would things have worked out differently for her?

As she began texting Norman, she felt the smothering feeling come over her once again. She knew she should message him and say that everything was fine and that he didn't need to worry, but she remembered that with the time difference it was still in the wee hours of the night in Ireland. She didn't want to disturb his sleep. That would be inconsiderate, wouldn't it? Kate put her phone back in her handbag and felt the smothering feeling fade away.

When they arrived at the Rio, Trevor handed the Lamborghini over to the valet and they walked through the casino, following the signs for Chippendales. They knew they were in the right place when they saw the massive posters of half-naked men with bodies of gods.

'KATE!' the girls screamed when they saw her and Trevor approach.

'Here she is, ladies,' Trevor said. 'Safe and sound.'

'Thank you for bringing her back to us early,' Chloe said.

'Although if you want more time with the Italian Stallion, we don't mind, Kate,' Siobhan said.

'Is that what you girls call me?' Trevor smirked.

'No, it's not!' Kate said. 'Siobhan just likes embarrassing me.'

'We'd better go in, girls – the show is starting soon,' Natalie said.

'See you later, ladies. Behave yourselves,' Trevor winked.

'Never,' Siobhan winked back.

Kate was so excited to be back with the girls. But she had to do a double take when she looked at Natalie. She had a completely new hairstyle. Her pixie cut had been styled into a fringe, covering her fake eyebrows.

'NAT!' Kate said. 'Your hair! It's gorgeous! Why the change?'

'Well, you know how earlier I was upset about getting Tasered and I was on the verge of spiralling into depression?' Natalie said.

'Yes . . .'

'Well, I decided to get BANGS instead!'

'I love it! Honestly, I was afraid you girls were going to kill each other while I was gone.'

'Women aren't allowed to fight when one of them gets bangs,' Siobhan said.

'Yeah, that's like Feminism 101,' Chloe added.

'Plus, now you can't see the fake eyebrows. It's win-win!' Natalie smiled.

'Stunning!' Kate said, relieved the girls were all back on good terms. 'Chloe, how's the sunburn?'

'How'd you think?' Chloe said, gesturing to her red skin. 'I look like a LOBSTER!'

'I'd say you look more like Mr Crabs,' Siobhan laughed.

'You're the expert on crabs, Siobhan. Your vagina is like the Great Barrier Queef!'

'Oh good burn, Chloe. Ten out of ten!'

Kate laughed to herself. The gang was back to its usual dynamic. Ruthlessly roasting each other in the most original of ways. 'Come on,' she said. 'Let's go get our seats!'

The girls showed the bouncer their tickets and headed straight into the venue. There was a large stage surrounded by lots of different tables, with booths on the back wall. Siobhan had booked front-row seats, and they sat down at the table that said 'Kate's Bachelorette Party' on a reservation sign. Kate wasn't really that into the idea of male strippers, but it was part of the Vegas bachelorette party experience. Plus, she found the venue quite nice, and a lot classier than she had expected it to be.

'You got me front row seats, Siobhan?' Kate said, chuffed. 'That's so thoughtful.'

'I did it for me, not you. I want the ball sweat to hit us right in the face.'

'I should have packed a poncho,' Natalie sighed.

'Oh, Kate – put this on,' Chloe said. She reached into her handbag and took out a small veil for Kate to wear.

'Aww, thanks Chloe,' she said, putting it on. 'It's nice to remember that we're on a hen party. And thanks again for the tickets, Siobhan.'

'My pleasure,' Siobhan smiled. 'Quite literally. I might actually have an orgasm.'

'How was the second date with Trevor?' Chloe said. 'SPILL!'

'Well . . . it wasn't *that* unbearable, I suppose,' Kate admitted.

'Wait, where's the ugly dress we bought you?' Natalie said, confused.

'Yeah, and is that Versace you're wearing? It looks like their Spring/Summer collection,' Chloe said. She always had a keen eye for anything designer.

'Yeah . . . Trevor took me on the gondola boats over at the Venetian. But I knocked him into the water by accident and then he pulled me in after him. Then he took me to buy a designer dress, even though I told him any old dress would be fine. And to make matters worse, my mother called and had a conniption about us staying here for longer.'

'Oh God, I can only imagine what Margaret said. She's a real piece of work,' Siobhan said.

'Apparently Norman was so worried he was thinking about coming to Vegas to bring me home!'

'Did you tell him that flying on a plane costs money?' Natalie laughed. 'That should stop him.'

'Kate, get back to the date already,' Chloe demanded, slapping her leg for more gossip.

'Right, sorry! Well, that's kinda it actually. After he bought me the dress, he took me to play some roulette. I had a bit of a winning streak, actually. I won $2,400.'

'You're joking?' Siobhan said. 'That means we actually have money for the strippers!'

'I'm not throwing my money at naked men!' Kate said. 'I actually feel bad for winning it. Maybe I should give it to charity.'

'Oh pack it up, Mother Teresa. We need cash to make it rain on the dancers!'

'Not a chance.'

'I have some pennies in my purse,' Chloe said. 'We could always make it hail?'

'I'm sure these men are well paid. Probably a dollar for every 77 cents a female stripper makes,' Natalie whined.

'Nat, we can go to a female strip club for your hen party and redistribute all the wealth you want. But it's Kate's night,' Siobhan said.

'Fine.'

'Kate, spill more about the date,' Chloe said.

'I literally just told you everything,' Kate shrugged.

'Jesus, will you stop being such a closed book? What did he say? How did you feel? Give us something to work with!'

'He said something that really annoyed me actually. He said that I manifested this entire situation by thinking about him for the last nine years. Can you believe the cheek of him?'

'But what if he's right? Sometimes you can manifest your biggest fears!'

'There's no way that's true.'

'Let's put it to the test,' Siobhan said. 'Oh noooo, sexy hot strippers with chiselled abs giving me a lapdance. I'm soooo scared! Shiver me timbers!'

'Wait, does that mean the two of you discussed the past?' Natalie asked. 'Did you get any kind of closure?'

'I'm not doing this for closure, I'm doing this for an annulment,' Kate said, reminding herself of her mission. 'I need to stay detached from him. He's trying to woo me with memories, and money but it's not going to work. I have a man at home who wouldn't hurt me in a million years. And that is something money can't buy.'

'OH SHIT!' Natalie said, out of nowhere.

'What's wrong?'

'I just realized I'm supposed to be at work tomorrow! I only booked today off!' Natalie panicked. She took out her phone and began frantically typing an email to her boss. 'Greg is going to kill me. And he already tried to fire me before!'

'Why? What did you do?' Kate asked.

'He said I wasn't getting my work done on time. But in my defence, I thought EOD meant End of December!'

'Chloe moment,' Siobhan muttered.

'Will someone proofread my email before I send it? I'm dyslexic.'

'Sure,' Siobhan said, grabbing the phone. 'Hmm . . . no, this is all wrong. You email like a woman.'

'What's that supposed to mean?'

'You're so polite and apologetic. Can I make some changes?'

'Okay fine but show me them first.'

'Dear Greg,' Siobhan began to type. 'I hope this email finds you dead.'

'GIVE ME THAT!' Natalie said, snatching the phone back.

'Chloe, did your Tinder match reply to you yet?' Kate asked.

'Let me check again,' Chloe said, reaching into her handbag for her phone. 'But I don't care either way because I am so done with men letting my messages marinate for days as if they're God's gift when they literally do nothing but harm to the world.'

'Wow, Chloe in her feminist era,' Natalie said. 'I'm obsessed.'

'Never mind, he texted back!' Chloe said, looking at her phone with pure excitement.

'So close,' Natalie sighed.

A topless male waiter suddenly approached the girls' table. Siobhan nearly fell off her chair when she saw him. 'Sweet merciful divine,' she said.

'Can I get you girls some drinks before the show begins?' the waiter asked as he approached them.

'Oh right,' Kate said, picking up the cocktail menu. 'Emm . . . I'll go with the "Penis Colada".'

'Great choice,' the waiter said.

'I'll have a "Screaming Orgasm",' Natalie said.

'First time for everything,' Siobhan muttered.

'I'll have the "Leg Spreader",' Chloe said.

'And I'll have the "Meet me after the show and blow my back out until I have scoliosis".'

'I don't think that's on the menu, miss,' the waiter said, confused.

'Oh, you meant a drink?' Siobhan said, coyly. 'Just a "Porn Star Martini" then.'

'Coming right up, ladies,' the waiter said.

'Oh, and buy yourself a cocktail on me. Something with pineapple in it,' Siobhan winked.

'I certainly will,' the waiter winked back before heading to the bar.

'Why pineapple?' Natalie asked.

'I'll tell you when you're older,' Siobhan smirked.

'I'm actually quite excited, girls,' Kate said. It was the first time in ages that she felt like she was on her hen party again. 'This show has great reviews.'

'Only you would look up stripper reviews,' Chloe laughed.

'They're more than just strippers. It's an entire show they put on. They're artists.'

'Well, I've always been a patron of the arts,' Siobhan said, putting on a posh accent. 'I hope there's a lot of crowd inter-action. I like a very . . . immersive experience.'

'Someone tie her to the chair before she slides off it,' Natalie said, shaking her head.

'Nat, please. Leave the bondage to the performers.'

'What are you and Trevor doing for the final date?' Chloe asked.

'No idea. Hopefully it's quick so I can get him to sign the papers and get the hell out of my life. Touch wood.' Kate looked around for something wooden to touch but couldn't see anything. The table and chairs were metal. 'Crap, there's no wood to touch.'

'Where's Trevor when you need him,' Siobhan laughed.

'Not that kind of wood!'

'Isn't there a part of you that's secretly enjoying the dates?' Chloe asked.

'Nope.'

'Oh come on, Kate. You have to admit he's an absolute ride,' Siobhan said.

'But he's *too* good looking. You don't marry a man like Trevor.'

'And yet . . . you did.'

'By mistake! Yes, he's ridiculously handsome, six foot three and completely ripped, but that's all surface level. There's nothing underneath. He's all style, no substance,' Kate shrugged. 'Nat, back me up here.'

'Sorry, Kate,' Natalie said. 'Even I have to admit he's pretty hot . . . for a man.'

'Nothing beats eight inches of personality,' Siobhan smirked.

'Girls, we all know that if a man says eight inches, it never actually is. You give them an inch, they take a mile! And for the record, size isn't everything,' Kate said.

'And yet I've never seen a woman buy a two-inch vibrator.'

'Siobhan's right. Every time I've seen Trevor on this trip, I can't help but stare at his crotch,' Chloe admitted.

'Chloe!' Kate gasped.

'I swear it looked at me first!'

'And in those pants he wears? It's like the battle of the bulge,' Siobhan said. 'I bet he has to use Dropbox just to send a dick pic.'

'He must have been so good in bed that summer,' Chloe said.

'Of course he was, but that's a very specific kind of sex. That's crazy-summer-abroad-when-you're-still-in-college sex. That's not the kind of sex you have for the rest of your life. You can't have mind-blowing sex every night of the week.'

'Why not?' Siobhan said, confused.

'Because it's just not realistic. And for the record, girls, Norman is the perfect size down there.'

'That's what I tell guys when I'm trying not to offend them,' Chloe said.

'Well, not every girl wants a guy who uses Magnums, okay?'

'I KNEW IT!' Siobhan said. 'I KNEW HE USED MAGNUMS!'

The waiter returned with their tray of drinks and set them down on the table. The cocktails looked fabulous – exactly what Kate needed after an evening of tit-for-tat with Trevor.

'These look unreal,' Chloe said. 'Wait, let me get a pic before we drink them. Will you take one for us?'

'Sure,' the waiter said, taking the phone.

The girls all bunched together holding their drinks and smiled for the camera. The waiter handed the phone back to Chloe who was immediately unhappy with how she looked in the photo. 'I don't really like that one. Could you take another?' she asked.

'Ignore her,' Natalie said to the waiter. 'She's a Leo.'

'It's okay,' he laughed. 'So am I.'

'And I can't wait to hear you roar,' Siobhan flirted as she paid for the drinks.

'Thank you, ladies. The show is about to begin.'

The lights dimmed and the girls relaxed into their front row seats for their first ever male stripper show.

'Ladies . . . are you ready to get hot?' a man said as he appeared on stage. He appeared to be the host of the show.

'WOOHOOO!' everyone yelled.

'Are you ready to get sweaty?'

'YEEESSSSS.'

'Then get ready for CHIPPENDALES!'

The stage was suddenly swarming with a dozen of the hottest men the girls had ever seen. They all wore suits and made their entrance in a synchronized formation.

Siobhan was in her element. 'Oh sweet Jesus, they're even hotter than I imagined!' she said.

The men froze in position on the stage and for a split second, you could hear a pin drop as the crowd waited with bated breath to see what was about to happen. Then, in one swift moment, all of the men ripped their suits off exposing their chiselled abs and bulging pecs.

'I think my coil just fell out,' Siobhan said.

'Siobhan!' Kate laughed.

'The dam has burst! I repeat, the dam has burst!'

The men began to dance in sync to the music that was playing. Once their first routine was finished, they re-appeared in police uniforms shining flashlights into the crowd.

'Do we have any naughty brides here tonight?' the host said.

'Officers, we have a bride over here!' Chloe shouted at them.

'Girls, stop! I don't want a lap dance!' Kate said, taking off her veil.

'Give me that,' Siobhan said, snatching the veil and putting it on herself. 'OOOHHH BOYSSSSSS!'

Two of the dancers walked over and began to grind up against Siobhan. The girls cheered him on.

'Woohoo!' Kate said.

'Slay, I guess!' Natalie shrugged.

'This proves that Trevor was right,' Chloe said. 'Manifesting works!'

'I don't manifest,' Siobhan said as she licked one of the dancer's abs. 'I manipulate.'

The song changed and the strippers went back to the stage. 'Aw, I wanted the handcuffs,' Siobhan sighed.

'You just got out of handcuffs!' Kate laughed.

As the show went on, the men began to dance to a variety of different themes, the stand-out ones being firefighters, construction workers and cowboys. After about an hour, Kate assumed they had gone through every theme and the show was soon to wrap up.

But then the host appeared on stage one last time.

'Ladies, our show is almost coming to a climax!' he said.

'SAME!' Siobhan roared.

'But first . . . I believe we have a very special bride here this evening,' the host said. 'Make some noise for Kate from Ireland everybody!'

The crowd began to cheer, and Kate immediately went pure scarlet. 'What is going on?' she said to the girls, utterly confused.

'I didn't book anything special,' Siobhan said, just as perplexed.

'Make your way to the stage, Kate!' the host instructed.

'Girls, I'm going to kill you!' Kate said as she got up from her seat. She walked awkwardly onto the stage and the host greeted her.

'Kate, is it true that you're here on your bachelorette party all the way from Ireland?' he asked.

'Yes,' Kate said, awkwardly into the mic.

'And you're engaged to a dentist back home, is that right?'

'Ehh . . . yes.'

'Well then lay back and let us make your ultimate dentist fantasy come true.'

Behind her, four strippers started wheeling a medical chair out onto the stage. There was no way she was about to get a lap dance in front of all these people! She was going to murder the girls for this stunt.

'Oh no . . . I'm . . .' Kate began. But before she knew it she was being tipped back on the dentist chair and the strippers were tying her down with silk rope. At first, she wanted to object but she remembered she was a bride on a hen party at a male stripper show. What did she expect?

'Kate, are you ready for a very raunchy lap dance from Norman the dentist?'

That's when the penny dropped. There was only one person who could be behind this, and she was now powerless to stop him.

The speakers came alive as '. . . Ready For It' by Taylor Swift began to play on full blast.

'MAKE SOME NOISE FOR TREVOR RUSH,' the host roared.

Trevor walked out on the stage dressed as a 'sexy dentist'. He had a white lab coat on, a pair of geeky glasses and blue surgical gloves. The crowd began to scream with excitement. Most of the women in the audience seemed to recognize him.

Kate tried to get up from the dentist chair but it was no

use. Her wrists and ankles were restrained. She was utterly helpless.

'I think our patient needs an oral exam!' the host shouted into the mic as the crowd went wild.

Siobhan, Natalie and Chloe couldn't help but laugh hysterically. Only Trevor Rush could hijack a male strip show just to prove a point. It was his own unique brand of drama.

Trevor began to dance erotically to the music towards Kate. He started grinding up on the dentist chair as Kate rolled her eyes.

'This better count as our third date,' she said, unimpressed.

'Nope, this is a bonus round, just for you,' Trevor winked. He began to slowly take off his surgical gloves, teasing the crowd who were gagging for more.

'I think our patient has a sweet tooth,' the host said. 'Let's see if she has any cavities that need to be examined!'

Trevor ripped off his lab coat, exposing his naked torso. It was even more defined than Kate remembered. He had obviously spent the last nine years working out consistently. Or perhaps constantly.

He looked like a Greek God!

'Christ on the cross,' Siobhan said, having full palpitations.

Trevor turned back around to Kate and got up on the chair with her. He began to grind his body up against hers, his oil-soaked abs gently grazing her.

'You think this is a turn on?' Kate said.

'I thought you loved dentists?' Trevor said, raising an eyebrow.

'Not currently.'

'Oh that's right, you said the raunchier the better,' Trevor smirked.

'Uh oh,' the host said. 'The dentist has found a cavity. Our patient needs to get DRILLED!'

'Brace yourself,' Trevor winked.

In one swift motion, he ripped off his stripper pants and the crowd let out a massive gasp. His biceps weren't the only muscle that were even bigger than she remembered. In his Speedos, the battle of the bulge was being waged. And the Speedos were losing.

'He's too big for Magnums,' Siobhan said. 'He needs Anacondoms!'

Trevor began to grind on Kate once again but she was determined to look as unimpressed as possible. She kept trying to avert her gaze from his package. Thankfully, she knew she wouldn't be physically turned on in a room full of people watching. And yet, she couldn't help but wonder how she would feel if it were just her and Trevor in a room alone.

But she couldn't even entertain such a thought.

'Still not aroused,' Kate said, adamantly.

'Well, then I guess I was right. Dentists are not sexy,' Trevor said turning to leave. He walked to the front of the stage and took a bow.

'THOR, SHOW US YOUR HAMMER!' Siobhan begged him.

'Give it up for TREVOR RUSH, ladies!' the host shouted.

The crowd went wild for the surprise performance, as expected. Trevor turned around and winked at Kate as he walked backstage.

'And give it up for the wonderful Kate!' the host said as he loosened her restraints. She got off the medical chair and faked a smile for the crowd. She walked back down to the girls, completely scarlet.

'I can't believe he just did that,' Kate said, peeved.

'I know, it should have been me up there,' Siobhan sighed. 'It hurts to see other people living my dream.'

The strippers performed one final synchronized dance and

the show came to a crescendo. Siobhan gave a standing ovation despite her legs being like jelly.

Kate knew that Trevor would be waiting outside to gloat after the show ended. But she was determined to show him that his little stunt had not worked.

'Enjoy the show, ladies?' Trevor smirked as they left the venue.

'We were enjoying it until this arrogant DJ took over the stage and made it all about himself,' Kate said.

'Some say he was the highlight of the show.'

'The jury is still out on that one.'

'It's definitely a hung jury,' Siobhan said, staring down at Trevor's crotch.

'It looked at me again!' Chloe said, putting her hands over her eyes. 'Thumper is thumping!'

'Tell me, Trevor . . .' Siobhan smirked. 'Have you ever played Jumanji?'

'Get it together, girls!' Kate snapped, elbowing them in the side.

'So did I prove my point that dentists aren't a turn on?' Trevor asked.

'Absolutely not.'

'Oh, so I *did* turn you on?'

'That's NOT what I said!'

'Sure seems like it. I thought the dentist chair was a nice touch. Marcus had to bring it out of storage for me. He owed me a favour,' Trevor said, delighted with himself. 'Anyway, ladies, I'd like to invite the three of you to join my wife on our third date tomorrow.'

'Well, if you insist . . .' Siobhan said. 'Where are we going?'

'The Grand Canyon,' Trevor said. 'I heard it was on your original itinerary. Be a shame for you all to miss it.'

'We were actually planning to *hike* the Grand Canyon tomorrow,' Kate said, sticking up her nose. '*Without* you.'

'Hike? No, darling, hiking isn't the way to see it,' Trevor said. 'The view is much better from above.'

'Above?'

'I'll be out front at 3 p.m. tomorrow. Don't keep me waiting,' he winked before walking away.

'Ugh!' Kate said, turning back to the girls. 'I cannot stand that man!'

'Well, I always say if you can't stand a man, you should try sitting on him,' Siobhan said.

'Dear Lord,' Kate laughed. 'Right, girlies, let's head back to the room.'

'You three nuns go on ahead,' Siobhan said, ready to go on the prowl. 'My night is just getting started.'

Chapter 21

Late-night Lurking

Kate woke up in the middle of the night around 3 a.m.

She had the most dreadful dream.

She was standing at the altar, unable to say her vows to Norman. The entire church was looking at her with dagger eyes as she became more and more tongue tied. Then, out of nowhere, her teeth began to fall out, one by one. Her friends and family looked at her in shame as she desperately tried to gather her teeth from the church floor. Then she saw Trevor, standing at the church door with a white light shining behind him. He was the only one who wasn't looking at her in disgust. He had his usual annoying smirk painted across his face.

That's when she woke up.

Kate rolled over in the bed to see the girls sleeping in their beds. Chloe was wearing earplugs and a silk eye mask beside her. Natalie was in the other bed, snoring like a jackhammer and occasionally talking in her sleep.

'Peppa, please let my family go,' Natalie said, sleep-talking.

Siobhan was absent, having decided to wait around after the Chippendales show to meet the cast. She had obviously scored. Kate hoped she was okay, but reminded herself that Siobhan was always in control.

Meanwhile, Kate felt like she had no control whatsoever. Not only was Trevor making her life a living hell but now he was penetrating her dreams too. Wasn't it bad enough that he was torturing her consciously? Did he really have to torment her subconscious as well? But the worst part of it was that the more time she spent with him, the less she hated him.

She feared she was warming to him. He was annoyingly charming and irritatingly handsome. His behaviour was downright ridiculous but there was something charismatic about even his most outrageous actions. Crashing a male strip show just to prove dentists weren't sexy, for example. Where did he get the audacity? It was something only he would do. His behaviour was so quintessentially him. He was so brash, so brazen, so bold.

And yet, she found herself smiling.

He was getting under her skin, the very same way he had nine years ago. It was those sporadic glimpses of the tender man beneath the façade of extravagance. The soft heart underneath the flashy armour. But for all she knew it was part of the act. He could have been feigning vulnerability to make her fall for him. Was it working?

No.

He was just a wordsmith, that was all. He always knew just what to say to get her flustered. Why did he enjoy toying with her so much? And why was she starting to enjoy it? But she couldn't think those forbidden thoughts. She had to remain as cold and distant as possible. She might have been warming to him but she hadn't melted yet. All Kate needed was to remind herself of the fuckboy he really was.

And she knew exactly how to do it.

She leaned over and grabbed her phone from the night-stand. Opening Instagram, she navigated to her blocked list. If anything could remind her of who Trevor Rush really was, it was his Insta feed.

As she scrolled through her blocked list, however, she was surprised by how long it was. She had blocked a significant number of people over the years. But they all deserved it, to be fair. They were mostly strange men asking her for feet pics, girls from secondary school caught up in pyramid schemes and bots telling her she had won competitions she had never even entered. But then at the very bottom of the list, she saw the first person she had ever blocked.

@TrevorRushOfficial

Ugh, the arrogance. Official? He was a DJ, not some A-lister.

His blue tick irritated her. Not because he didn't deserve to be verified but because he used to hate social media. Kate was actually the one who forced him to join Instagram that summer. He said he liked to live in the moment, but she explained that social media could be used as a tool to promote himself and grow a following. She had been right, of course. She always was. But it was frustrating that she had to beg him to join Instagram and now he was verified with two million followers.

Just another example of women building men up and getting torn down in return.

The night they said goodbye was actually the night he finally agreed to join. He conceded that it would be a great way to keep up with each other's lives as they did long distance. Texting internationally was expensive, so it made sense for them to communicate through Instagram. After she took the Polaroid of them in front of the Statue of Liberty, he said he finally had a photo worth posting. He took a picture of the Polaroid with his phone and uploaded it there and then. She still remembered the caption he had written.

To be continued . . .

She had posted a photo of the Polaroid too, of course. It was very *1989* cover energy after all, an aesthetic Kate was obsessed with. But after Trevor had cheated on her, she deleted it, along with every other photo she had posted of him.

Scorched earth.

What else was she supposed to do? After all, he had scorched her heart.

Her finger hovered over the unblock button for a moment. She had sworn she would never unblock him, but she knew she could just block him again immediately after she took a peek. And as soon as she hit the button and opened his profile, Kate found exactly what she was looking for.

Hundreds of photos that epitomized exactly the type of man he was. Trevor on party yachts, surrounded by beautiful models. Trevor on skyscrapers, popping champagne. Trevor in limos, pools, planes, living the hedonistic life of a playboy. By the looks of things, Trevor Rush didn't just go to parties.

Trevor Rush *was* the party.

Her stomach turned when she saw all the women in his comments. She could tell they were all tens by their profile pics alone. They all essentially said the same thing on each of his posts. They were mostly a barrage of fire emojis but some also said, 'See you soon', 'Best DJ in Vegas' or 'Zaddy'. As if that wasn't nauseating enough, she saw that Trevor had replied to some of the comments with cheeky winky faces. Classic him. He loved the attention from these women, and she had no doubt his DMs were just as full as his comments section. She hated the way these women fuelled his ego. Wasn't he vain enough already without endless praise? But then again, he had them all fooled, just as he had fooled her nine years prior.

That's when Kate decided to click on the messages button on his profile to see if their old texts were still there. Surprisingly, after almost a decade of countless Instagram updates, all their conversations were still readable, like a time capsule of their relationship.

But the first messages she saw were the last ones they exchanged.

Trevor: Can't talk, in a meeting

Kate: Trevor,

I've been doing some thinking and I've decided not to come back to New York next summer. My life is here, and what we had was really just a summer fling. We're not right for each other and I think it's best if we go our separate ways.

All the best 👍

That was the moment she had blocked him. It almost killed her to do it, especially considering she saw that he had seen the message and was typing a response. But it was the right thing to do. She couldn't let him have the last word. She was far too proud for that.

Looking back now, though, her message did seem rather cold. They had been madly in love and she had sent him such a stock break-up message. It was as basic as it was ruthless. And that thumbs up emoji was downright brutal, a merciless mic-drop if ever there was one. It was no wonder he was desperate to know her real reasons for dumping him. For a brief moment, she wondered how *he* must have felt.

But that line of thinking was ridiculous. Trevor Rush didn't deserve any sympathy. She was right to have been a savage. He had savagely destroyed her self-esteem, after all, even if he didn't know it. And he would never know it. Admitting to Trevor that he had ruined her represented a kind of victory for a man like him. Heartbreakers must get a thrill from breaking hearts. Why else would they do it? It would have only been a matter of time before he dumped her. And she never would have recovered if she had been cheated on *and* dumped. She was still proud of her decision to have the last word.

Kate suddenly found herself curious as to how he had gotten to where he was today. It was somewhat of a meteoric rise from deadbeat DJ to King of Vegas, after all. Kate knew she should just block him again and go back to sleep, but she couldn't stop herself from looking at his timeline in chronological order. She wanted to see the story of Trevor's success.

From the beginning.

Kate began to scroll quickly through his feed, ignoring most of the posts as she went. Her finger flicked the screen again and again, trying to get to the bottom. But there were a lot of posts. Even more than Chloe, and that was saying a lot. All this from a man who used to hate social media? He certainly adapted quickly. She continued to scroll until finally, she reached the start of his feed.

That's when Kate's breath suddenly hitched.

His very first photo was still the Polaroid of him with her.

He hadn't deleted it.

Kate sat up in the bed, blindsided by what she was seeing. There they were, standing in front of the Statue of Liberty, madly in love. Why the hell hadn't he deleted it? It didn't make any sense. Kate had wiped her Insta clear of Trevor Rush and yet she was still the first photo on his timeline. Her heart was in her mouth as she read the caption.

To be continued . . .

She was having major palpitations. This photo didn't fit the playboy image of Trevor Rush. It was completely off-brand. And yet there it was. On the screen, sending shockwaves through her body. Her flutters had returned with a vengeance. Her mind was desperately trying to despise him, but her body was dancing with desire. It just seemed so romantic that he hadn't deleted the photo. And not romance with an ulterior motive, either. It felt pure. It required a deep dive to find but there it was, for the world to see. Beneath the photos of wealth and extravagance was another glimpse of his true, tender self.

Due to the nature of phone cameras at the time, the quality of the image wasn't great, and so she zoomed in to see the smaller details in the photo.

But then, catastrophe.

Kate accidentally double clicked the photo and LIKED it. Which meant Trevor would get a notification that she had just liked the photo of them as a couple!

She smashed the unlike button and flung her phone to the bottom of the bed. She needed to stay calm. Trevor had lots of followers, which meant lots of likes. Maybe her like would get lost in a barrage of notifications. He probably wouldn't even notice.

But then her phone beeped.

She leaned forward to pick it back up and saw the notification.

@TrevorRushOfficial started following you.

'No, no, no, no, no,' Kate whispered.

Chloe rolled over in her sleep from the noise but thankfully didn't wake up. This couldn't be happening. Trevor would never let her live this down. That's when a message from him appeared.

Trevor: I saw that, Freckles ;)

This was officially a trainwreck. She hadn't a leg to stand on. And she couldn't ignore him. He knew she was online and she had nowhere to hide. She had no choice but to reply.

Kate: I don't know what you're talking about . . .

Trevor: Stalking me at 3 a.m.? Damn, you've got it bad ;)

Kate: Oh shut up, it was an accident!

Trevor: So you unblocked me at 3 a.m., scrolled to the very bottom of my timeline and liked a photo of us as a couple . . . by accident?

Kate: My finger slipped!

Trevor: Just like when I slipped a ring on your finger ;)

Kate: You're impossible!

Why are you even awake?

Trevor: I'm working on a project.

Why are you awake?

Kate: None of your business

Trevor: Dreaming of me, I assume ;)

Kate: Any dream with you in it counts as a nightmare!

Trevor: Sometimes nightmares reveal our deepest desires ;)

Kate: I'm going to sleep!

Trevor: Good girl.

You'll need your rest for the Grand Canyon tomorrow

Oh, and if you block me again, I'll add an extra date to our agreement ;)

Kate: That's not fair!

Trevor: I think it's very fair.

You stalked my timeline. It's time for me to stalk yours

Goodnight Freckles ;)

Kate would have screamed were it not for the girls sleeping soundly.

How had she been so careless? One stupid like and suddenly Trevor had access to her entire Instagram feed. And she was powerless to stop him. If she blocked him again, he would prolong the nightmare she was in. She began to panic about the posts she had on her timeline. Her mind began to race about what Trevor would see.

Oh God, he would see what Norman looked like. He would see everything from their couple pics to their engagement announcement. Perhaps she should go through her photos and archive the ones she didn't want Trevor to see.

No.

She wasn't going to allow Trevor to get her flustered like this. What did she care? She loved Norman and maybe Trevor *should* see him. See what a gentleman looked like – the kind of man who doesn't spend every night drinking champagne and partying with models. The kind of man who doesn't flirt with absolutely everyone. The kind of man who doesn't cheat. Trevor could scroll through all the photos he wanted.

She refused to let it bother her.

Thankfully, she had deleted any posts about her failed music career. At the time, she had tried to promote her song 'Your Scar' as an independent artist. It seemed so easy at the time. Put your music online and get discovered. That happened all the time, didn't it? Turns out it didn't. Without a label behind her, Kate was pretty much singing into the abyss, unheard by any of the right people. But all those posts were gone so she didn't have to worry about Trevor finding them.

Kate decided to continue her stalking, considering he was doing the same. She began to scroll upwards from the past to the present, following the story of how @TrevorRush became @TrevorRushOfficial. From what she gathered, he had continued to play shows in New York after she left. But they seemed larger in scale. They were certainly not the dive bar gigs she had gone to see him in. Slowly but surely, the venues got bigger and bigger and assumedly, his fanbase grew from there. It actually made sense considering his talent. He could turn any event into an unforgettable night with his skills. They used to joke that he could turn a retirement home bingo night into Ibiza with his remixes.

There was a part of her that was happy his talent was recognized. But of course, the other part of her wished his music career crashed and burned, the way hers had. They planned on being a duo but only one of them had succeeded solo. It was a natural feeling, in fairness. After all, does anyone really want to see their cheating ex succeed?

Halfway through Trevor's timeline, Kate got yet another pang, this one far greater than the last. In one of his photos was the woman Kate had seen.

The woman Trevor kissed on the cheek.

The woman he led inside.

The woman he cheated on her with.

She felt a lump in her throat as she looked at the image on the screen. The woman was every bit as stunning as Kate remembered. In the photo, she and Trevor were both laughing candidly at some kind of red carpet event. The woman was surely a model, and they were clearly some kind of power couple. But it was the caption that really tore Kate's heart out of her chest.

Behind every great man is an even greater woman.

The rotten, two-faced, slimy bastard. It was the phrase Trevor used to say to Kate. And suddenly it was the caption for his photo of the woman who he had cheated on her with. There were no words to describe her rage. He had even used that phrase on their date at the Venice canal. It was clearly just some sort of pick-up line he used on everyone.

Had he no shame?

She took a screenshot to show the girls the following morning. They would surely be just as appalled as she was. And to think she was developing a soft spot for him after seeing she was still his first photo. He clearly didn't delete any pictures of women he had slept with. Maybe he wanted women to say, 'Who's she?' as a way of making them jealous. Was there no end to his mind games? Well, she refused to play. She decided she wasn't jealous, not even a single bit.

Kate clicked on the woman in the photo to see if she was tagged. Her profile name came up when she tapped the screen.

@Viola89

Of course her name was Viola. A gorgeous name for a gorgeous woman. And of course she was born in 1989, literally the best year a person could possibly be born in. Kate clicked the tag to open her profile. But she was immediately disappointed.

Private Account. Request to Follow.

30 posts. 1,320 followers. 950 following.

Kate would have given anything to find out who this woman was. But maybe it was for the best that she couldn't see more of her. Kate's self-esteem was fragile enough without her comparing herself to some picture-perfect model. It wouldn't serve any purpose. Considering this was the woman Trevor had cheated on her with, obsessing over her would only re-open the wound she had spent nine years trying to heal. She reminded herself that she was not jealous. Not one bit.

She had a man at home who didn't constantly try to drive her insane. And she realized that, with the time difference, Norman would be awake. It was the perfect time to text.

Kate: Hey Normie, my mother called to say you were worried

I just want you to know that I'm safe and everything is fine

Miss you x

Norman: Spoke with Margaret again

> She agrees that your behaviour is concerning

> We are very worried about your mental state

Kate: There is nothing to worry about Normie

I just need you to trust me x

> **Norman:** You're making it very hard for me to trust you Kate

> Imagine if I had a stag party and extended it by two days and didn't even bother to check in every hour

Kate: I promise everything is under control

I love you and I will see you on Wednesday x

Kate locked her phone and put it back on the nightstand. She had hoped that texting Norman would make her feel better after Trevor's social media mind games. Sadly, she had been mistaken. But even though she felt herself far worse off than she had been before, she remembered that she initially opened Trevor's profile to remind herself how much of a fuckboy he was.

Well, mission accomplished.

Chapter 22

The Third Date

'Come on, it's almost three! We're going to be late!' Chloe said as she waited for the girls to finish getting ready in the hotel room. She was still red raw with sunburn but that wasn't going to stop her missing out on a photo opportunity.

'For once, Chloe is ready first,' Natalie laughed.

'I just don't want to miss it!'

'Chloe, the Grand Canyon is six million years old. It's not going anywhere,' Kate said, as she finished her makeup.

'Well, Trevor said we're seeing it from above and I want to get some good content from the helicopter. We need as much daylight as possible,' Chloe explained.

'I want to see as little daylight as possible. I'm hungover again,' Siobhan groaned as she sprawled on the bed.

'Oh come on, Siobhan, it's going to be a great day.'

'I was having a great day until 10 a.m.'

'What happened at 10 a.m?'

'I woke up.'

'In God knows whose bed,' Natalie said, in a judgemental tone.

'It was the waiter from Chippendales' bed actually,' Siobhan bragged.

'And what was his name?' Natalie asked, knowing she wouldn't have an answer.

'His name? It was a hook-up, not a wedding. I'm not Kate, going around marrying everyone.'

'HEY!' Kate said.

'But maybe you should ease up on the hook-ups, Siobhan. You don't want a venereal disease,' Natalie suggested.

'Jealousy is a disease too, Nat,' Siobhan said, smugly. 'Get well soon.'

'I'm not jealous! I'm just worried!'

'I can't believe *you*, of all people, turned out to be a prude. You literally dressed up as a clitoris last Halloween!'

'That's because I was trying to avoid my ex-boyfriend Mark. I knew that was the only way he wouldn't find me!'

'Be that as it may, you were supposed to get the ride on this holiday and you've made zero effort!'

'Well, not all of us have the stamina to sleep with three guys in three days.'

'Oh give me a break,' Siobhan said. 'Can you imagine if a man pulled three women on a stag party? He'd be given a fucking parade and called a living legend for the rest of his life. What happened to sex-positive feminism?'

'Yeah, but when I said "fuck the patriarchy", I didn't mean fuck the entire patriarchy.'

'Trust me, girls, society will call you a slut no matter what you do in life. So you might as well get the ride.'

'Okay, are we all ready to go?' Chloe said, interrupting them. Her patience had officially run out.

'Yes,' Kate said, finishing putting on her mascara. 'But I just want to say, for the record, that I'm not happy about this. The plan was to *hike* the Grand Canyon.'

'I think your plan went out the window a long time ago, Kate,' Siobhan laughed.

Kate knew there was no point in denying it. Her plan had well and truly gone up in flames. But still, she was excited she was getting to see the Grand Canyon. It would have been nice to have seen it on the ground, but a view from the sky wasn't exactly something to whine about. If anything, it could be better. And, to Trevor's credit, it was nice of him to invite the girls.

But she was still mad at him after what she had seen on Instagram in the middle of the night.

'Nobody be nice to Trevor today by the way,' Kate instructed.

'I could have sworn you were just getting to like him,' Chloe said.

'I almost made the mistake of warming to him. But then I stalked his Instagram last night.'

'Now you're speaking my language! What did you find?'

'Well, his first pic is still the one of me and him. The Polaroid of us in front of the Statue of Liberty. The night we said goodbye.'

'He never deleted it? That's the most romantic thing I've ever heard! I'm literally going to cry!'

'That's what I thought, but then I also found a photo of him with the woman he cheated on me with. Her name is Viola and she's clearly some kind of runway model.'

'Let's see,' Natalie said.

Kate sighed and took out her phone. She opened up the screenshot and showed the girls the pic of her.

'WOW! She's the hottest woman I've ever seen,' Natalie said, practically drooling. 'I'd call her Mommy.'

'Show me,' Chloe said, looking at the picture. 'Holy shit.'

'Can we not rub salt in the wound please?' Kate begged.

'But Kate, you said you're still his first pic. That's gotta mean something. And you're every bit as gorgeous as that Viola woman,' Chloe said.

'Ugh, Viola is such a hot name!' Natalie said, smitten.

'Okay, we get it,' Kate said, snatching the phone away from them. 'I'm Dolly and she's Jolene. She's a million times better than me and I'll never compare.'

'Kate, no one is better than Dolly Parton. She's literally the only thing Americans can agree on.'

'Well, it doesn't matter either way because now I know I made the right decision by leaving him back then. Rule number one, never be someone's number two. Trevor is still very much a fuckboy, so we are not going to be nice to him today. That means no flirting, Siobhan.'

'Oh come on! If he dumps you for me, it'll solve all your problems. I'm just trying to be a good friend!' Siobhan said.

'So selfless,' Kate laughed.

'Right, come on!' Chloe said. 'It's time to go!'

§☺

The girls took the elevator to the ground floor of the Bellagio and walked outside. Trevor was waiting for them, as expected. But when Kate saw what he was leaning against, her jaw dropped to the floor.

Because Trevor was leaning against a pink Hummer limo.

The exact same one the girls had wanted at the airport.

'Now that's what I call a ride,' Siobhan said to the girls. 'And the limo's not bad either.'

'Siobhan, please don't make his ego any bigger,' Kate whispered as they approached him.

'Your carriage awaits, ladies,' Trevor said, gesturing towards the pink beast.

He knew exactly what he was doing. She had stupidly let it slip about the girls wanting the Hummer limo, and now he was getting them on his side by hiring it. Kate should have known he'd pull a stunt like this. After his striptease, he was seemingly willing to do anything just to infuriate her.

'Shall we?' he said, opening the gargantuan door.

The girls were shocked when they sat inside. The interior was something else. Everything was pink. There were pink leather seats, a pink fluffy carpet, a pink TV and a pink bottle of champagne.

'Jesus, it's like fifty shades of pink in here,' Natalie said, looking around.

'Well, I know how much you girls wanted to rent this. And I feel bad for hijacking your bachelorette party,' Trevor said.

'Look who's suddenly grown a conscience,' Kate muttered.

'Fuck me pink, is that a stripper pole?' Siobhan said, seeing a pink cylinder stretching from the roof to the floor.

'It most certainly is,' Trevor said, closing the door behind them. 'Lorenzo, the airfield please.'

Lorenzo started the engine and drove them towards their destination. Trevor pulled a pink bottle out of a bucket of ice and presented it to the girls. 'Pink champagne, ladies?'

'Good Lord,' Kate sighed. Talk about overkill.

'Something the matter, darling?'

'Just seems like a little much, don't you think?'

'Nothing is too much for my wife.'

'Well, I would love some pink champagne, Trevor. I need the hair of the dog,' Siobhan said, still dying from her hangover.

Trevor popped the champagne and filled up Siobhan's, Natalie's and Chloe's glasses. 'And for the bride, perhaps a champagne shower?' he suggested.

'Perhaps not,' she said, putting on a fake smile.

'So, Trevor . . .' Siobhan said as she sipped her drink. 'That was quite a show you put on last night.'

'Well, I've always considered myself an entertainer. I hope my pelvic thrusts weren't too much for you girls.'

'Not at all.'

'Well I, for one, might sue you for whiplash,' Kate said.

'Personally, I like a little whiplash now and then,' Siobhan said, winking at Trevor.

'Oh Siobhan, if only I wasn't married,' Trevor winked, clearly trying to make Kate jealous.

'We can be unmarried right now, darling,' Kate said. 'One signature and you're free.'

'Nice try, Freckles.'

'I do have some feedback on the striptease though, Trevor,' Siobhan went on. 'You really should have taken off the Speedos and done the helicopter. I mean, give the crowd what they want, right?'

'What do you think, Freckles?' Trevor asked, eager to enrage her.

'I think that would have violated several of the Geneva Conventions,' Kate said.

'Hmm . . . well, it's always good to leave them wanting more.'

'Or have them wanting to leave.'

Kate took out her phone to appear unbothered by Trevor's attempts to annoy her. She was due to text Norman anyway.

Kate: Hey Normie, we're on our way to the Grand Canyon now.

Miss you x

Norman didn't respond immediately like he usually did, which Kate found a little odd. But when she looked closer, she saw that the message hadn't delivered yet. He would surely reply as soon as it did.

'Does this beautiful pink dream machine have an AUX cord by any chance?' Siobhan said, taking out her phone.

'Over here,' Natalie said, handing it to her.

Siobhan connected her phone and finally got to use the hen party playlist she had finely crafted. A few seconds later, Shania Twain's 'Man, I Feel Like a Woman' roared through the speakers.

The girls all began to scream with excitement. Even Kate couldn't contain herself.

'YAAASSSS!' Chloe roared.

'This hen party was missing this song, big time,' Natalie said.

'Now, Trevor Rush,' Siobhan said, getting up on the stripper pole. 'Let me show you how a striptease is really done.'

After a few glasses of pink champagne and several different pole-based choreographies by Siobhan, the Hummer limo arrived at the airfield. But when the girls got out of the car, they were surprised by what they saw. They were expecting a helicopter tour of the Grand Canyon, but before their eyes was a small private jet.

'Wait, where's the helicopter?' Kate asked.

'Oh so you *do* want the helicopter?' Trevor said.

'I mean the one that was supposed to give us a tour of the Grand Canyon!'

'I never said we were taking a chopper. We're seeing it by plane.'

'A plane won't even get us close to the ground,' Kate said annoyed. 'We'll barely see a thing!'

'Yeah, I was hoping for some good content,' Chloe said, disappointed.

'I promise it's the best view of the canyon money can buy,'

Trevor said. 'But you'll all have to leave your bags in the limo – there's a weight limit on the plane.'

The girls threw their handbags in the Hummer before climbing up the small plane staircase. When they got into the cabin, they saw three rugged-looking men in suits waiting for them. They were rather strange characters. All three were extremely attractive, there was no doubt about that, but the suits . . . well, they didn't suit them.

'Oh sweet baby Jesus,' Siobhan said, as soon as she saw their guests.

'Ladies, I'd like you to meet Michael, William and Luke. Your dates for this afternoon,' Trevor said.

'I'll take William,' Kate said, spitefully.

'I'm afraid you're stuck with me, Freckles.'

Kate was confused. Why had Trevor brought dates for Siobhan, Natalie and Chloe? It was a bizarre move. And there was something strange about the men, something she couldn't quite put her finger on. But as she looked at the girls' jaws on the floor, she didn't bother to question it. They seemed happy and she genuinely wanted them to enjoy themselves. The hen party was as much for them as it was for her, and even though the itinerary had been derailed, Kate was glad they were still having fun.

'Captain, wheels up in five,' Trevor shouted into the cockpit.

❧

During the flight, the girls were getting to know the three men, individually. Siobhan had gone for Michael because he looked like the strongest of the three. 'So, Michael,' she said, flirtatiously. 'Not to brag but I happen to be a certified member of the mile high club.'

'Oh really?' Michael smiled. 'That makes two of us.'

'Interesting. What do you say we renew our membership?'

Chloe had been drawn to William because his name made him sound like royalty, and she was a sucker for that kind of thing.

'Do you know when the best time will be to take some pics?' Chloe asked, looking out the window.

'Not for a little while. But I can take some photos of you now, if you'd like?' William suggested.

'I . . . I think that's the nicest thing a man has ever said to me,' Chloe said, tears in her eyes.

Natalie ended up with Luke, in the hopes his personality would arouse some interest. But she found herself rather nauseous on the plane.

'Sorry, I'm a very bad flyer,' Natalie said. 'How often do planes crash?'

'Just once,' Luke said.

'Oh God. I need to distract myself. Tell me, Luke . . . what date and time were you born?' Natalie asked, eager to read his birth chart.

'Well . . . I was born on the seventeenth of March. I don't know what time though,' he admitted.

'Oh wow, Pisces is literally my favourite sign. And you were born on St Patrick's Day. And I'm Irish. Please tell me you have an Aries moon. Oh my God, this is so exciting! We actually might be compatible!'

'What was your name again?' Luke asked, terrified.

As Kate looked out the window, she wondered how much longer it would be before she could see the Grand Canyon. She was slightly concerned because the plane was above the clouds and she could barely make out the surface. She feared that when they passed over it, it wouldn't even look like much.

She wished she could have just stuck with the plan and gone hiking through it. That was what most people did. This entire ostentatious plane ride didn't appear to serve much of a purpose apart from Trevor showing off. She didn't care for Lamborghinis and private jets. He should have figured out by now that material things didn't impress her. And yet, the plane seemed rather bare for a private jet. It was far from luxurious, and from the looks of things, it didn't even have a bar.

'Why are we here exactly?' Kate asked him eventually.

'To see the Grand Canyon, of course,' Trevor shrugged.

'Nobody wants to see it by plane. We're way too high up and the windows are tiny. Something about this doesn't feel right.'

'Your instincts are once again razor-sharp, Mrs Rush.'

'So I was right? You're up to something?'

'Maybe.'

'Oh God. I know what it is. These men are strippers from last night, aren't they? I knew they looked weird in those suits. They're naked under those clothes!'

'We're all naked under our clothes, Freckles.'

'Let me guess,' Kate said, unimpressed. 'This is about to turn into some inescapable striptease!'

'I'm afraid it's far worse than that.' Trevor got up out of his seat and began to address the entire group. 'Ladies, if you look out to your right, you'll see that we are approaching the Grand Canyon,' he said.

The girls all went over to the windows and looked down. They could make out the red and orange hue of the rock below them but it didn't exactly blow them away. Chloe began to zoom in for a good picture of the arid, rocky landscape but it was incredibly blurry from their current altitude.

'We can barely see it from up here,' Chloe sighed.

'I'm aware of that,' Trevor said. 'Which is why it's time I revealed my true ulterior motive.'

The girls looked around in confusion.

'What kind of ulterior motive?' Natalie asked.

'You see, Michael, William and Luke aren't actually your dates today,' Trevor smirked. 'They're your skydiving instructors.'

Chapter 23

Falling

Kate felt her life flash before her eyes.

Surely this was some kind of twisted joke. Trevor couldn't honestly expect her to jump out of a moving plane. He was taking his mind games to a whole new level. This wasn't just toying with her, this was downright torture.

'No, no, no, no, no,' Kate said, distraught.

'I think the word you're looking for is *yes*,' Trevor said.

'Absolutely not! This has to be a prank. There isn't even any skydiving equipment around!'

'Actually, there is,' Michael said, opening up a crate that had previously been concealed.

'I knew you'd never get on the plane if you saw all the gear,' Trevor said.

'Wait a minute,' Natalie said as she turned towards Luke. 'So you're just here to be my instructor?'

'Sorry,' Luke shrugged.

'I trusted you!' Natalie snapped. 'Are you even a Pisces?'

'Yes.'

'Hmm, with a Scorpio moon, no doubt!'

'This is not happening!' Kate snapped. 'We have been lured up here under false pretences and I demand to be taken back.'

'Well, our captain is flying north to Utah so unless you're heading up, the only way out is down,' Trevor explained.

'I'll do it,' Chloe said.

Kate shot her a dirty look.

'What? This is really good content!' Chloe said, defensively.

'I'll do it too,' Siobhan said. 'Having Michael strapped behind me doesn't sound like the worst thing in the world.' She threw Michael a flirtatious look which he immediately returned.

'I'll agree to jump too but I want William as my instructor. I could never trust Luke again after his betrayal,' Natalie sulked.

'Okay so it's settled then,' Trevor said. 'Let's all suit up.'

'Excuse me?' Kate said, waving her hand in the air. 'I haven't agreed to any of this!'

'Aww, that's a shame. On the plus side, I hear Utah is lovely this time of year. Make sure to send us a postcard.'

Kate was flustered with fury. She was afraid of heights, and he knew that. Who did Trevor think he was to force her so far out of her comfort zone? It was such a classic him thing to do. Getting on a rollercoaster was one thing, jumping out of a plane was another! But then again, what choice did she have? It was bad enough to be stuck in Vegas three days before her wedding, but being stuck in Utah would be a whole lot worse considering she had no idea where it was.

She reminded herself that this was the final date. This was the last torturous trick Trevor had up his sleeve. If she could get through this, she'd be rid of him.

'FINE!' she conceded.

After spending about twenty minutes getting into their gear and listening to the tutorial, the girls were just about ready to go.

'You're going to be falling at rapid speeds so please try and stay calm while in the air,' Michael instructed. 'And remember what I said about breathing. Nice deep breaths in . . . and out.'

'I'm loving this jumpsuit, to be honest,' Chloe said, looking down at her outfit. 'Wait! Is that why they call it a jumpsuit? Because it's a suit you jump in?'

'I guess so . . .'

'I feel like it's missing something though,' Chloe said, thinking of accessories. 'Can I belt it?'

'No you cannot,' Michael said. 'Now, any volunteers to go first?'

'I will,' Siobhan said. 'If the parachutes don't work, you can all just land on my arse.'

'Aww, that's so noble of you,' Natalie said.

'Siobhan, will you take my phone and record my landing?' Chloe begged.

'Ugh . . . fine,' Siobhan said, taking the phone and zipping it into her jumpsuit pocket.

'Actually, do a live stream on Insta instead of a video. I want my followers to see me landing in real time,' Chloe said.

'Alright, let's go,' Michael said, attaching himself to Siobhan.

'Siobhan getting attached to a man? Has hell frozen over?' Natalie slagged her.

'Yep. And this pig is about to fly,' she laughed.

The plane door opened and the air hit them like a train.

'Oh my God!' Kate said, losing her breath.

'Aww, did I take your breath away?' Trevor said.

'I hate you.'

'Hate's a strong word.'

'Not strong enough.'

Michael and Siobhan approached the open door and they both grabbed the railing.

'Girls, if I die, don't say any bullshit at my funeral about how I was such a good person or how my smile always lit up a room. Tell them I died how I lived. With a man on top of me,' Siobhan said.

Michael let go of the railing and they jumped out of the plane.

'AND BURY ME WITH MY VIBRATOR JUST IN CASE!' Siobhan screamed as she fell thousands of feet.

'WHICH ONE?' Natalie shouted after her.

'Chloe, we're up,' Luke said.

'If Siobhan doesn't get a good angle of me landing, I'll kill her,' Chloe said.

'I hope you survive, Chloe,' Natalie said. 'Luke, I wish I could say the same for you.'

'Well, don't curse him! If he dies, so do I!'

'Fine, I'll hex him *after* you land.'

Luke let go of the railing and the two were suddenly gone.

'Are you ready?' William asked Natalie.

'As I'll ever be,' Natalie sighed.

William let go of the railing and they followed the rest.

'And then there were two,' Trevor said.

'Trevor, I can't do this. I'm going to throw up again,' Kate panicked.

'No, you won't. I promise. You just need to trust me.'

'Absolutely not! You didn't even get me a proper instructor!'

'I have a skydiving licence. I do this once a month. You're in good hands.'

'But why are you doing this? Why are you torturing me?'

'I'm not torturing you. I'm trying to show you how to live,' Trevor said.

'Live? What if we die?' Kate said. Her heart was leaping out of her chest.

'Oh, so you'd rather stay in your comfort zone for the rest of your life, never experiencing anything new?'

'Yes! Exactly!'

'Kate, everything you want in life is on the other side of fear. You have to take a leap of faith every now and then. You have to put it all on black thirteen.'

Kate remembered the feeling she experienced when she saw her number come up. But this was different. The stakes were a lot higher than a game of roulette. She wasn't gambling with money.

She was gambling with her life.

'If it makes you feel any better, the odds of dying in a sky-dive are .000002 per cent,' Trevor said.

'THAT HIGH?' Kate freaked. She gripped the metal railing for dear life.

'Okay, time to go or we'll miss the view.'

'I can't do it, Trevor,' she said, gripping the bar even tighter.

'You have to let go, Kate.'

'No, I don't!'

'I'm going to count down from three,' Trevor said. 'Three . . .'

'Trevor, I really . . .'

'Two . . .'

'I can't do this!'

'ONE!'

Kate closed her eyes. And then, she did the impossible.

She let go.

'AAAHHHHHH!' Kate shrieked as they jumped out of the plane and began to plummet.

She lost her breath immediately and the sensation was horrific. She felt like she was suffocating. It was ten times worse than the feeling she had experienced on the rollercoaster.

'KATE,' Trevor shouted over the sound of the wind. 'JUST BREATHE IN . . .'

Kate tried to calm her nerves and just concentrate on taking a breath. But she felt like she had absolutely no control of the situation whatsoever. Freefalling helplessly? It was hell on earth. But she reminded herself that after a few seconds on the rollercoaster, she began to enjoy the feeling. Maybe the same would happen here. She focused her mind and took a breath in through her nose.

'AND EXHALE,' Trevor said.

Kate let the air out of her lungs and felt like she had taken back control of her breathing. She opened her eyes to see the most stunning view she ever thought possible. The Grand Canyon stretched for miles, its copper majesty winding infinitely into the distance. The jagged contours and rugged gorges were mesmerizing, a masterpiece carved by nature's hands.

It was quite literally breathtaking.

'OH MY GOD,' Kate shouted. 'I'M FLYING!'

'What did I tell ya?' Trevor laughed. 'Best way to see the canyon.'

'It's beautiful,' she said. Her heart felt so full in that moment. Like anything was possible. If she could jump out of a plane, there was nothing she couldn't do.

After a few more seconds of free falling, Trevor pulled the parachute open and they were rattled to a slower speed. She could appreciate the view even more as they came closer to the surface. Beneath her, the Canyon's veins of copper and rust etched serpentine paths across the canvas of the earth, and she knew its beauty could only be fully comprehended from above. It was spectacular in every regard.

'Trevor, this is amazing!' Kate roared.

'You might even say you're . . . feeling the rush,' he teased.

Although Trevor was being as obnoxious as ever, he was right. Kate had never felt anything like this before. It was a feeling of pure liberation. Sure, Trevor had forced her to go on this date and forced her to jump out of a plane, but despite being made to do it against her will, she had never felt more free in her life. Perhaps his push had been exactly what she needed.

ॐ

When Siobhan landed on the ground with Michael, she felt completely exhilarated as well.

'Jesus, that was almost as good as sex,' she said.

'Not bad, huh?' Michael said as he disconnected from her.

'I felt that stiffy against my back by the way,' Siobhan laughed. 'We'll have to see to that later.'

Michael detached from her and she immediately took out Chloe's phone to open Instagram. But the phone was asking for a passcode.

'Oh shit,' Siobhan panicked. Chloe hadn't mentioned anything about a passcode. 'Let's see . . . 1111.' Siobhan punched the code in and the phone unlocked. 'Classic Chloe. Okay, Instagram Live . . . Begin livestream.'

Siobhan began to stream and saw a few people join to watch.

'Hello, Chloe's followers,' Siobhan said. 'We are coming to you live from the Grand Canyon, where Chloe is about to land after her first skydive.' She switched to the back camera and aimed it towards the sky.

A few miles up, Chloe could be seen approaching the landing zone. But something wasn't quite right. A massive wet patch all around her crotch could be seen in crystal-clear high definition, as drops of pee started raining from the sky.

'Uh oh,' Siobhan said. 'Today's forecast. Cloudy with a chance of golden showers!'

Chloe was coming in hot, and she screamed as she and Luke landed on the ground. When she took off her goggles, she looked disturbed by the experience. Urine had soaked through her entire jumpsuit and the pee stretched from her navel to her knees.

'I PISSED MYSELF!' Chloe said, distraught.

She clutched her stomach and it was obvious what was going to happen next. Chloe got sick all over the ground as her followers watched on her live stream. As if the pee wasn't bad enough, she was now covered in puke as well.

'TURN IT OFF!' she screamed at the top of her lungs.

'Over to Ed with sports!' Siobhan said as she ended the live stream.

Natalie landed safely to their left and seemed to enjoy the experience. 'That was actually fun!' she said. But when she took off her goggles, she saw Chloe's wet patch and couldn't stop herself from laughing. 'Oh, Chloe, no!'

'It's not funny! I'm drenched in piss!' Chloe cried.

'That makes two of us,' Luke sighed, having also gotten soaked.

'It's what you deserve, Luke!' Natalie snapped.

Kate and Trevor swung into the landing zone and hit the ground gracefully. 'Oh my God, girls! Is everyone alright?' she shouted over to them.

'Chloe pissed herself,' Siobhan laughed.

'SHUT UP, SIOBHAN!' Chloe screamed.

'Oh, Chloe, are you okay?' Kate asked, concerned.

'I'm humiliated. Siobhan livestreamed the whole thing!'

'Because you begged me to! Jesus, I can't catch a break,' Siobhan sighed.

'Alright, ladies, I say we get some photos over by the canyon,' Trevor said.

'I don't want ANY photos ever again!' Chloe sulked.

'Fair enough,' Trevor laughed. 'But I booked a chopper to take us back and it won't be here for twenty minutes. Might as well see the view.'

The group walked towards the canyon and broke off into their pairs. Although Chloe had peed all over him, Luke stayed with her in fear that Natalie would push him off the cliff.

When Kate arrived at the edge, she was struck by the canyon's magnificence. As she looked down into the chasm below, she realized her fear of heights had suddenly disappeared. It was the way she used to feel beside Trevor on rollercoasters and in the passenger seat of his Mustang.

Fearless.

'Beautiful, isn't it?' Trevor said.

'It really is,' she said, forgetting herself for a brief moment.

'So, I'm getting good at planning these dates, am I?' he smirked.

She turned to look at him.

It was the first time his smirk didn't annoy her and it was the first time in nine years she didn't hate him. She felt her heart beat throughout her body. It could have been the adrenaline still pumping through her veins, but Kate knew that wasn't entirely it. All the things that infuriated her about him were suddenly the things she liked the most. His confidence, his charm, his downright brazenness. It was suddenly so easy to remember why she fell in love with him in the first place.

But, nevertheless, she turned her head away.

She couldn't let the nostalgia of her bubbling emotions blind her. His betrayal had cut too deep. His cheating had irrevocably changed her as a person. The dagger he had unknowingly lodged in her heart was no longer there.

But its scar would always remain.

And seeing him with Viola on Instagram had reminded her of the pain she felt. But that was part and parcel of Trevor's life as a hotshot DJ. Of course he would be seeing beautiful women. Women infinitely more beautiful than Kate.

She couldn't compete with the Violas of the world.

She was a nobody.

A life with Trevor was amazing in theory, but what about in practice? Sleepless nights wondering if he was at a party full of models. Constant anxiety wondering if he was on a yacht with influencers or a skyscraper with Hollywood starlets. She wasn't necessarily a jealous person, but her self-esteem wasn't strong enough to live in Trevor's world. If he had cheated before, he could cheat again. He had the capacity for deception. She would for ever live in fear of another betrayal.

How could she ever trust the man who had broken her heart?

Norman was the only man she had learned to trust after the damage Trevor had done. He was safe. He was secure. Sure, maybe she was settling a little bit but that's what normal people did. There was nothing wrong with a normal life. There was nothing wrong with not wanting to be hurt. It was Trevor who had destroyed her. Norman was there when she felt like an ugly, talentless failure. Even if he didn't fulfil all her emotional needs, there was a lot to be said for loyalty. And no matter what feelings for Trevor came bubbling up, nothing would change what he had done.

She couldn't betray her man for the man who betrayed her.

'Penny for your thoughts?' Trevor said, sensing her contemplation.

'My thoughts are worth far more than that,' she said, returning to their tit-for-tat antics.

'Indeed they are. I'd give every penny I own for a peek inside that head of yours.'

'Well, too bad it's the end of the final date.'

Kate felt an unexpected pang as the words left her mouth. Because she didn't want the date to end. She wanted this moment to last for ever. If she could have stayed here, without any responsibilities or consequences, she would have.

But this wasn't real life. It was a fantasy. Her reality was back home.

'Oh, Freckles,' Trevor smirked. 'The final date is just beginning.'

Chapter 24

Paris

The helicopter brought the girls back to Vegas and landed on a private helipad just east of the Strip.

The sky turned a melancholy pink as the sun set in the distance. For the entire journey, Kate's mind was all over the place. Her feelings for Trevor were bubbling to the surface, but she needed to keep them down. It was like an agonizing heartburn she couldn't get any relief from.

She checked her phone to see that Norman still hadn't replied to her. Was he furious with her? It was unlike him not to text back.

Kate: Are you mad with me Normie?

Please reply x

Siobhan was rather disappointed that the skydiving instructors had organized their own pickup at the canyon, meaning she only got to kiss Michael, nothing more. Natalie, on the other hand, was happy that she would never see Luke again.

The blade stopped spinning and the girls got out to see their pink Hummer limo from earlier waiting for them.

'Where to next?' Siobhan asked, eager to remain part of the third date.

'I'm afraid the next part of the evening is reserved for my

wife and me,' Trevor said. 'But we will be seeing you again later tonight.'

'Are you sure Siobhan can't take my place? She's a lot more fun than me,' Kate said.

'And a lot more . . . experienced,' Siobhan flirted.

'Sorry, ladies, but Freckles and I have a lot to discuss. Lorenzo will take us all back to the Strip and then we'll part ways,' Trevor said, opening the limo door.

The girls got into the limo and Chloe immediately began checking her phone.

'Siobhan, be honest. How many people saw me piss myself?' she panicked.

'Chloe, there were only like fifty people watching. Thank God most of your followers are fake,' Siobhan laughed.

'THEY ARE NOT FAKE!'

'Well either way, it's not the end of the world.'

'It could be the end of my career!'

'Define career,' Natalie muttered.

'Come on, Chloe, I'm sure you're worried about nothing,' Kate said, touching her shoulder.

'Yeah, don't worry, Chloe,' Trevor said, out of nowhere. 'Plus I'll be giving you that shout out, remember? Your career is only beginning.'

'Oh, so you asked Trevor for that shout out, did you?' Kate said, unimpressed.

Chloe had a strange, guilty look on her face. 'Well . . . not exactly,' she said.

'Lorenzo, to the Eiffel Tower please,' Trevor interrupted.

'Certainly, sir,' Lorenzo said, starting the engine.

'Wait, we're going to the Eiffel Tower?' Kate said.

'Yes, for dinner. Just the two of us,' Trevor smiled. 'Sorry, ladies.'

After a short drive, the limo pulled up at the Paris Las

Vegas Hotel & Casino. Kate got out and looked up at the glittering Eiffel Tower. It was only a replica, of course, but it still had a certain magic about it. It appeared like a glimmer of hope against the sad pink sky.

'Lorenzo, drop the girls back to the Bellagio and return the limo,' Trevor said. 'And did you pick up that package?'

'I most certainly did,' Lorenzo said. He reached over to the passenger seat and handed Trevor a large unmarked bag.

'Thank you, Lorenzo.'

Kate waved goodbye to the girls as the limo pulled off. Suddenly it was just the two of them again. And, as guilty as it made her feel, she sort of liked being on her own with him.

'Shall we?' Trevor said, turning to his wife.

'Well, I suppose it won't kill me,' Kate shrugged.

'Wow, you're in a good mood. That's the nicest thing you've said on our entire honeymoon.'

Damn.

She was slipping. She was actually enjoying herself. More than she wanted to.

But she couldn't.

Trevor led Kate into the Paris casino and towards a large old-fashioned elevator. They stepped in and Trevor hit the button for the top-floor viewing deck.

'I thought we were going to the restaurant?' Kate asked.

'We are,' Trevor said, coyly.

The elevator began to rise at an excruciatingly slow pace and Kate realized Trevor was standing incredibly close to her. Close enough for her to feel his breath on her neck. Her heart started pounding throughout her body. She could have cut the sexual tension with a knife.

Was he about to kiss her? Were they about to have a passionate elevator moment?

Christ, did she actually want that?

'Put this on,' he finally said, taking something out of the unmarked bag.

Kate turned around and saw he was holding the blue velvet dress from the Versace window. The dress she had wanted more than anything but not allowed herself to get.

'I told you that was too expensive! And the lift is almost at the top.'

'You have time.'

'Trevor, I . . .'

'Put it on before I make you put it on,' he said, deadly serious.

She felt her legs go like jelly. Their eyes locked and she felt him piercing her soul, the way he always did. But she wasn't about to strip naked in front of him.

Not a chance.

'Fine,' she said. 'Turn around.'

Trevor handed her the garment and turned to face the elevator wall. Taking a deep breath, she slipped out of her old dress, standing vulnerably bare in the limited space between them. She had never experienced flutters like this before. Her entire body was beating like a drum, a primal rhythm that threatened to be her undoing. Dear Lord, why did she want Trevor to turn around? Why was her subconscious betraying her like this?

She needed to get dressed before her urges took hold. She slipped on the velvet gown and pulled it up onto her shoulders in one swift motion. But her back was bare. She still felt naked, exposed to her own yearning. She reached behind, desperate to zip up her dress and extinguish the burgeoning desires igniting within her.

But her arm couldn't reach.

'Trevor . . .' she said, her voice barely a whisper. 'You'll need to zip me up.'

She felt him turn around slowly and approach her. She suddenly got a whiff of his cologne. Dior Sauvage. Why did it have to be *that* fragrance? It was practically a pheromone, and she was borderline feral. Dior had a lot of nerve releasing such a scent. Each note felt like it was specifically crafted to unravel her.

Her palpitations were becoming louder and louder. She was terrified he would hear the drum that was beating just for him. That's when she felt his breath on her neck, once again. Her entire body began to shiver with anticipation. She was quivering for his touch. If he kissed her neck now, she knew she would have no control. She knew she would crave surrender and melt like butter in his arms. She was on the cusp of losing herself.

But then she felt the zipper go up her back.

The motion snapped her back from the precipice, sealing her lustful abyss of desire within the confines of the fabric. Thank God.

She was Kate again.

'Now . . .' he said. 'Finally a dress that's worthy of you.'

'Well . . . thank you,' Kate said, desperately trying not to blush.

She put her €12 Primark dress in her handbag just as the doors opened at the very top of the tower. But something felt strange. The place was empty.

'Where are all the tourists?' Kate asked, confused.

'The viewing deck is privately booked for the next hour,' Trevor said.

'You reserved the Eiffel Tower for me?'

'Don't you think you deserve that?'

Fuck.

This wasn't going to be easy. He was pulling out all the

stops. It would take every fibre of her being to not be seduced. She had to stop herself from melting.

She just had to.

'Good evening, Mr and Mrs Rush,' a waiter said, appearing out of nowhere. 'Apologies for the elevator being so slow. It's quite an old structure.'

'Not a problem. It gave my wife a chance to catch her breath,' Trevor smirked.

Bastard. He knew she was melting. But then again, of course he did.

After all, he was the one turning up the heat.

She had to cool down.

She needed to be the most cold-hearted ice queen imaginable.

'Excellent – your table is right this way,' the waiter said. He led them around the corner to a table for two with the most spectacular view of the Vegas skyline. It was even better than the one on top of the High Roller. The sun had just set, and the neon lights were starting to illuminate the darkness below, like fireflies coming to life. On the viewing deck before them was an art-deco-style table, set for dinner, with a flickering lantern in the middle.

Trevor pulled out a chair and gestured for her to sit.

'The restaurant downstairs would have been fine,' Kate said, taken aback.

'Well, it might be the last date we ever go on. So I wanted it to be special.'

Kate was suddenly reminded of the fact that this would all end soon. It was the moment she had been trying to reach as soon as possible, but now, she didn't seem in such a hurry.

'Champagne?' the waiter said.

'Please,' Trevor said.

The waiter poured them each a glass and disappeared around the corner once again.

'To the end . . .' Trevor said, raising his glass, '. . . or the beginning.'

'What do you mean?' Kate asked.

'Isn't it obvious? I always knew our story was to be continued . . .'

'Like your caption.'

'Of the photo you liked at 3 a.m., yes.'

'By mistake!' Kate said. 'The real question is, why didn't you delete the photo?'

'Why would I delete my favourite photo in the entire world?' Trevor asked.

'Well, it doesn't exactly fit with your playboy image online.'

'Because that's all it is. An image,' he said. 'I had a lot of fun going through your feed by the way. That's quite a grin your fiancé has. Do you need to wear sunglasses every time he smiles?'

'I happen to think his veneers are perfect.'

'It's what's behind the veneers that I'm worried about,' he winced. 'Doesn't matter, anyway. He won't be smiling once you tell him you're in love with me.'

Kate laughed. 'You make everything seem so simple, don't you?'

'Life is simple. If you allow it to be. You allowed it to be nine years ago.'

'I was a different person back then.'

'No, you were *yourself* back then. You became someone else in the past nine years.'

'You're one to talk. Who exactly is the real Trevor Rush? Because your persona online is not the man I knew back then.'

'So it seems we both wear masks. I wonder what we're trying to hide behind them,' he said, his tone intensely profound. 'Although I definitely got a glimpse of the real Kate today when we were flying through the sky.'

'Well, that kind of thing doesn't happen every day,' Kate said.

'You don't think you deserve to fly?' Trevor said, raising an eyebrow.

'Don't tell me we're back to talking about my music?' Kate sighed. 'Lots of people don't get a chance to fly in life. I'm just one of those people.'

'Because you gave up.'

'No, I tried to fly and I fell flat on my face. That's completely different.'

'Your wings needed time to develop.'

'Can we drop this bird metaphor already?' Kate begged. 'I failed, Trevor. It happens all the time. Not everyone gets to be successful.'

'The opposite of success isn't failure. Settling is. People settle for what they think they're worth.'

'Or maybe they're just tired of the pain. It's human nature to not want to get hurt. Sorry to break it to you, but I'm not worth anything.'

'You think you're worthless?'

'Well . . . I didn't say that, exactly.'

'You're not worthless, Kate,' Trevor said. 'You're priceless.'

Christ, he was good.

A few more lines like that and she'd slide right off the seat.

'Can we please stop having this argument again and again?' Kate said, trying to get a hold of herself.

The waiter came over with their appetizers and placed them on the table. 'The calamari rings to share.'

'Thank you,' Trevor said.

'And for your main course, sir, the chef is asking how you would like your steak cooked.'

'Like winning an argument with a woman.'

'Rare it is, sir,' the waiter said. 'And your steak, madam?'

'The thing men expect to hear after doing the bare minimum,' Kate said, smugly.

'Well done it is, madam,' the waiter smiled. 'Bon appétit.'

Kate knew that her joke was far from the truth. Trevor was doing the opposite of the bare minimum. He was going above and beyond what was expected of a person on a date. He had rented her the Eiffel Tower, for Christ's sake! Still, it was the only comeback she could think of, and she couldn't let him know how impressed she was. She couldn't reveal the fact that she was being swooned.

'Look at you getting quicker and quicker,' Trevor said, impressed. 'But well-done steak? Maybe I *should* sign that annulment after all.'

Kate began to laugh again. Ugh, he was being so charming. He was making it damned near impossible for her to keep her eyes on the prize. But she couldn't forget why she was here. 'Well, I have the papers in my handbag, if you'd like to sign now?'

'Nice try, Freckles.'

'Fine,' Kate said. 'Although I still don't know why you want to stay married to me.'

'Maybe I have a thing for redheads.'

'Oh, so that's what I am?' Kate said, raising an eyebrow. 'A fetish?'

'I would use the term . . . fixation.'

'Well, that's an interesting choice of word because it seems like you want to *fix* me.'

Trevor laughed. 'Oh, Freckles. Just when you were getting quick, you go and say something so clueless.'

'Well, am I wrong?'

'I'm not trying to fix you, Kate. I'm trying to show you that you're not broken.'

But Kate *was* broken.

And Trevor was the one who had broken her.

That's what he did. He was a destructive force of nature leaving chaos in his wake. Even now, his storm was causing her life to tear at the seams. The home she shared with Norman was being torn down in her mind, brick by brick. But what kind of a monster would she be if she abandoned Norman? Would her mother ever speak to her again? And if her mother refused to speak to her, how would she still be able to have a relationship with her dad? What if his cancer came back and she couldn't be there for him? The seeds of freedom Trevor was sowing in her mind couldn't be allowed to sprout. She had too many people depending on her back home. She had to think about everyone who would be affected by her actions.

'Why don't you just fixate on someone else?' Kate said. 'I'm sure your DMs are full of those bikini models in your Instagram pics. You could probably have any of them.'

'I have no interest in gold-diggers,' Trevor said.

'Well, how do you know I'm not a gold-digger? Maybe this is all an intricate plan to get your money,' Kate joked.

'Nope. If that were true, you'd be asking for a divorce, not an annulment. With a divorce, you'd get half of everything I own. We didn't sign a prenup. With an annulment, you get nothing.'

'Well, you're starting to make a divorce sound very tempting,' Kate laughed.

'Okay, deal. No annulment. Just a divorce. But in Nevada a divorce takes around four months, which means you'll have to postpone your wedding.'

'So, you're telling me that you'd agree to divorce me, even though it would mean losing half of everything you've built?'

'Yes. In exchange for the four months together.'

'Four months with me is worth half of what you own?'

'No, Kate. Four months with you is worth *everything* I own,' Trevor said, his heart on his sleeve.

Kate felt her heart going ninety. He was saying all the right things. His vulnerable side was showing again, the side of him she couldn't resist. She was still falling.

'You can't just say things like that,' she said, trying to catch herself.

'You're offended that I see your worth?'

'Well, it's a pretty ridiculous thing to say. You're honestly telling me that everything you've built, all your success and fame and fortune, all of that is worth more time with me?'

'Yes.'

'WHY?' Kate cried. 'FOR THE LOVE OF GOD, WHY?'

'Because my success, fame and fortune have always had a very singular purpose. You see, I always knew you'd come back to me. I've been manifesting it every day for the past nine years. And I vowed that when the universe finally brought us back together, I'd be able to give you everything I never could that summer. That has been the driving force behind all my success for the past nine years. Because everything I've built, Kate, I built for you,' Trevor said, looking her dead in the eye.

Fuck.

He meant it. Somehow, she just knew he was telling the truth. He didn't smirk, for once. It was like he was voluntarily pulling down his mask to give her another glimpse of the real him. His true self that she was so primally attracted to. She felt her own mask slipping too. Her people-pleasing persona was crumbling as she realized what *she* desired, not what others desired for her.

But what about his malevolent revenge scheme? Was this a confession of his true motives or a surprise fourth act in his plot to ruin her? 'Hold on,' she said, steadying herself. 'I thought this was all some elaborate revenge plot to ruin my life? You said so yourself!'

'That's not what I said,' he explained. 'I said I was going to give you what you deserve.'

'Which is?'

'The world.'

Fuck. Fuck. Fuck.

Kate was on the cusp of losing control. She suddenly imagined Trevor flinging the table up and grabbing her, there and then. Pushing her against the railing of the Eiffel Tower and kissing her neck. Would she do anything to stop him? Maybe she could kiss him back for just a second. Or maybe two?

Did the five-second rule apply for kissing your ex?

Sweet Jesus, she was all over the place. He was still looking at her, waiting for a response, while she was being seduced by her own intrusive thoughts. She needed to get a grip.

'Trevor, I really don't know why you think I'm so special,' Kate said, regaining her composure. 'I'm a nobody!'

'But you were born to be a somebody. You should be with someone who fuels your fire, not someone who dims your spark.'

'And what am I supposed to do? Cancel the wedding I've spent two years planning?' Kate said.

'Oh, so that's it. It's the planning you're in love with.'

'There are 200 people coming to Donnybrook Church on Friday to see me get married. I can't let them all down. It's going to be the happiest day of my life!'

'You keep saying that. It's *going* to be the happiest day of my life. It's like you're trying to convince yourself.'

'No, because I've planned that it will be!'

'The way you planned your bachelorette party?'

'That would have gone according to plan if you didn't derail the entire thing!'

'And yet it was *you* who tore up the itinerary,' Trevor said. 'I'm just saying, if you want to make God laugh, make plans.'

'Oh, and you're God in this scenario, are you? Well, if you ask me, being a god in Sin City isn't something to brag about. I don't fit into your world. I don't belong here.'

'Neither do I,' he explained. 'I told you about the Vegas curse. I want to get out of here as much as you do. Maybe a nice castle in the Irish countryside. You can choose which one.'

'You really are impossible,' she laughed.

'Impossibly handsome, I know.'

She hated that he was. His stupid face with his stupid smirk was making things so stupidly difficult.

Kate's phone began ringing in her bag.

'The old ball and chain, I'm guessing?' Trevor asked.

She took out her phone and saw that Trevor was right. Norman was calling.

But she didn't want to answer.

And even if she did, there was a chance that Trevor would say something to make Norman worry even more. Plus, she had texted Norman earlier and he hadn't even bothered to reply. She was well within her rights to leave him waiting.

She put her phone on silent and placed it back in her handbag.

'Ignoring Norman's calls? Interesting . . .'

'Don't read too much into it. I just don't want you grabbing the phone and saying something stupid. Last time you made him think I was kidnapped.'

'Or maybe you're planning on running off with me.'

'HA!' Kate laughed. 'And what would that entail? We just drive off into the sunset without a care in the world?'

'Why not?'

'Life isn't a movie, Trevor.'

'No, but it could be a song. We were always supposed to be a duo. You give me the lyrics, I give you the beat,' Trevor said.

As soon as he said it, the flutters came back. He gave her the beat alright, he just didn't realize what kind. Or maybe he did. It was as if he had full control over her circulatory system. Just a few words and he could send pulses wherever he wanted. She was at the mercy of his music. The drum was unyielding, like a prisoner banging on a cell door, begging for release.

But freedom was a fantasy.

'It's a nice idea, Trevor, it really is,' Kate said, crossing her legs. 'But I have a real life waiting for me at home. And I need that annulment to get back to it. It's time for this crazy chapter in my life to come to an end.'

'That's the problem, Kate,' Trevor said. 'I was just a chapter in your book. But you were the title of mine.'

Kate felt her heart split in two.

Did he mean it? He seemed genuine. Whenever he called her Kate instead of some infuriating nickname, it seemed like he was being his truest, most honest self. But how could she know that for sure? That was the trouble with Trevor. After his infidelity, she would never be able to know what was real and what was fake.

What good was the word of a cheater?

'I don't know what to say to that, Trevor,' Kate said. 'You're making this very hard.'

'I'm just trying to stop you from making the biggest mistake of your life.'

'Well, your time has run out. Your plan to make me admit I'm in love with you has failed.'

'Maybe . . . but your plan to give me the ick failed too,' Trevor smirked.

'Wait a minute,' Kate said, gobsmacked. 'You knew I was trying to give you the ick all along?'

'You say that as if it wasn't the most obvious thing in the world. But it was never going to work. You couldn't give me the ick in a million years. Loving someone means accepting them, icks and all. For better or worse, remember?'

'No, I don't remember. That's the whole problem,' Kate laughed. 'Look, Trevor, for what it's worth, a different time, a different place. Maybe things would have worked out.'

Trevor let out a sigh. It seemed like he was finally starting to accept that Kate was going back to Ireland. 'Well . . . we'll always have Paris,' he said, looking up to the tip of the Eiffel Tower.

'And New York,' Kate smiled. 'It really was an amazing summer.'

'But you're ready for the winter of your life, I understand,' Trevor said.

'You're such a dickhead,' Kate laughed as she threw a calamari ring at him.

'Are you proposing to me again, Freckles?'

'You wish.'

'I do,' he smiled. 'But don't worry, I respect your final decision.'

'Wow. That's very mature of—'

'For now,' he interrupted her.

'Good Lord,' she laughed.

'But I promise I will sign the papers after Omnia.'

'After Omnia?'

'I'm performing at 10.30 p.m. I have a private booth reserved for you and the girls.'

'Trevor, we're flying home first thing in the morning . . .'

'I booked you four first-class tickets on the Aer Lingus flight to Dublin at 7 a.m. That's hours away.'

'And how do I know you even really booked our plane tickets home?'

'You don't. I guess you'll just have to trust me,' Trevor said. 'Either way, this date isn't over until midnight, darling.'

'Fine,' she said. 'But as soon as the clock strikes twelve, you're signing those papers.'

'Deal. That should give me enough time.'

'For what?' Kate asked.

Trevor looked at her, his eyes gleaming with determination. 'To convince Cinderella she doesn't belong in the attic.'

Chapter 25

Torn in Two

After their meal, Kate and Trevor went in separate directions.

He headed towards Omnia in Caesar's Palace and Kate went back to the Bellagio to round up the troops. As she walked through the casino, Kate felt more torn than ever.

Had Trevor truly meant all that he said? Had he really built everything for her? It was a romantic thing to say, of course, but how genuine was it? She had believed he was doing all this to torture her, to ruin her life in pursuit of revenge, yet his intentions had been pure all along. Why hadn't he just been honest about his motives from the start?

And would it have killed him to grab her and kiss her?

No, she couldn't think like that.

Christ, she was a hot mess.

She needed her girls.

The Four Lokos

Kate: Where is everyone? X

> **Natalie:** we're at a bar in the bellagio called baccarat

> **Siobhan:** There's a situation with Chloe . . .

> **Chloe:** MY LIFE IS OVER!!!

Kate: OMG, what happened?

> **Natalie:** she's being a drama queen

> **Siobhan:** We'll explain when you get here.

Kate: On my way x

Kate walked through the Bellagio and followed the signs towards Baccarat. She tried to collect her thoughts but her head was in a tizzy. What would she tell the girls? Where would she even begin? She felt like she was losing her mind, but the girls would surely ground her. They always had the best advice. Well, unless that advice involved alcohol.

'KATE, OVER HERE!' Siobhan shouted as Kate walked towards them.

'How'd it go?' Natalie asked. 'Did Trevor sign the annulment?'

'Not yet. He wants us all to go to Omnia to see his set. He booked us a booth,' Kate explained as she took a seat beside them. 'Chloe, what's the situation with you?'

'Oh, how about me being a complete laughing stock on the internet!'

'What happened?'

'Somebody screen-recorded the livestream of me pissing myself and sent it to one of those meme pages. They posted the video and tagged me in it. Look!' Chloe said, handing the phone to Kate.

Kate looked at the screen and saw the video. In it, Chloe

could be seen landing on the ground, covered in her own pee. And then, after a few seconds, she began throwing up in front of the camera. It was the first time Kate had actually seen it. She had still been in the sky when it all went down. She tried with every ounce of her willpower not to laugh but she couldn't help it.

'KATE!' Chloe snapped. 'IT'S NOT FUNNY!'

'Yeah, funny doesn't do it justice. Hilarious is the right word,' Siobhan laughed.

'My life is over! Look at the comments. They're calling me PISS GIRL!'

Kate scrolled through the comments to see what people were saying. They were brutal.

Piss Girl. Piss Face. Miss Piss.

Just some of the many new names Chloe had been christened. Kate looked down at the bottom of the screen and saw the view count.

'Chloe, it has 1.2 million views!' Kate said.

'WHAT? It only had 900K five minutes ago,' Chloe cried as she grabbed the phone back.

'Definitely viral,' Natalie said.

'And the worst part is, now everyone is following me because they tagged me!'

'How many followers do you have now?' Kate asked.

'10.5K.'

'Chloe! This is what you've always wanted. You hit 10K! You're an influencer!'

'I didn't want to be an influencer for PISSING MYSELF!' Chloe screamed.

'Be careful what you manifest, sweetie,' Natalie laughed.

'There's no such thing as bad publicity, Chloe. Enjoy your fifteen minutes of shame. Sorry, fame,' Siobhan said.

'But who screen-recorded it and sent it to the meme page?' Chloe said.

'Probably some randomer.'

'OMG! I bet it was Casper! He probably wanted to get back at me for keying his car! That bastard!'

'Well, at least you've learned your lesson,' Natalie said.

'No, I haven't! I'm going full Beyoncé *Lemonade* on his car as soon as I get home!'

'I'm starting to think you two deserve each other,' Siobhan laughed. 'I can already see the headlines. Piss Girl lemonades all over ex's car.'

'I can't even deal with this right now. Kate, tell us more about Trevor – I need a distraction.'

'Well, there have been a lot of developments,' Kate explained. 'My head is all over the place. I have no idea how I'm feeling.'

'Do you wanna wear my mood ring?' Natalie said, taking it off.

'No, Nat,' Kate sighed. 'Trevor just told me that everything he's built, he built for me. He said he's spent the last nine years hoping I would find my way back to him so he could give me everything he never could back then. And now I'm freaking out because I think he's telling the truth!'

'Jesus,' Natalie said. 'Men will literally build an entire empire instead of going to therapy.'

'OMG! You're his Daisy! You're his green light!' Chloe said, out of nowhere.

'Chloe, *you've* read *The Great Gatsby*?'

'It was a book?'

'Dear Lord,' Natalie sighed. 'But Kate, this is big. Did you tell him that he broke your heart?'

'No.'

'Ugh, Kate, you are such a headwreck!' Siobhan said. 'Why won't you just have an honest conversation with him?'

'I'm afraid! I don't want to relive that experience. I'd probably have a complete meltdown. I don't want him to see me cry!'

'But you're making the same mistake you made nine years ago. You should have confronted him back then, but you ran away instead. Now you have another chance to confront him and you're trying to run away again! I told you on the plane you can't just block people out of your life.'

'Siobhan is right, Kate,' Chloe added. 'You're the smartest of all of us but you have the emotional intelligence of a toddler. When someone hurts you, you tell them why they hurt you. You don't just dump them and block them before they can reply. That's not how you get closure.'

'Okay, okay, I hear you all,' Kate agreed. 'I don't know why I'm so afraid to have that conversation with him. I've spent nine years trying to move on from that moment. I think I'm scared of opening up the scar again because it took so long to heal.'

She was finally facing it. It was terrifying. But necessary.

'But that scar would have healed a lot faster if you got closure back then,' Natalie said. 'Get it now while you can, or you never will.'

'Okay. Thanks, girls,' Kate smiled. 'There's just one teeny tiny problem.'

'What?'

'I'm falling for him all over again!'

'Called it,' Siobhan muttered.

'OMG, KATE! REALLY?' Chloe said, ecstatic. 'I mean, I saw it coming a mile away, but really?'

'On the Eiffel Tower, I wanted him to kiss me. Even though

I wouldn't have kissed him back. Oh God, what is wrong with me? I'm going to hell,' Kate said, bowing her head in shame.

'Kate, don't be silly. We're in Sin City. God doesn't see what happens here. It's a moral blind spot,' Siobhan said, trying to comfort her.

'But what am I supposed to do now? I'm marrying Norman in three days! Everything is planned. I can't let everyone down. I can't ruin the happiest day of my life for someone who cheated on me! That's beyond insane. Falling for Trevor broke me. But Norman put me back together again.'

'You're not Humpty fucking Dumpty, Kate,' Siobhan said.

'I know that, but I also know I wouldn't survive being broken by Trevor Rush twice. I have to listen to my brain telling me to go home and marry Norman.'

'But what's your heart telling you?' Siobhan asked. 'I mean, I don't have one but if I did, I'd listen to it.'

'Yeah, do you think it could work with Trevor?' Natalie said.

'It could have worked if it weren't for him cheating. Like, yes, he's making me feel everything I felt back then. The euphoric high of being his. But what about the way he made me feel when he betrayed me?'

'So you don't think you could ever forgive him?' Chloe asked.

'Even if I did forgive him, how could I ever trust him again? I still carry the scar of his first betrayal. I don't think I'd survive another wound like that. And think about his lifestyle. All the parties with all those half-naked Instagram models. Could any woman trust a man surrounded by so much temptation? I gave Trevor my heart once and he smashed it into a million pieces. I've spent nine years gluing it back together and I'm not going to let him smash it again.'

'Then it looks like you have your answer,' Natalie said.

Kate felt like her choice was clear. There was no place for her in Trevor's life. She belonged back home. 'Okay, here's the plan,' she said.

'Third plan's the charm,' Siobhan said, rolling her eyes.

'We'll go to Omnia and listen to Trevor's set. Then afterwards I'll tell him he broke my heart when I saw him cheating on me with that Viola woman. Once he admits it and hopefully apologizes, I'll be able to get my closure. Then he'll sign the annulment and we can fly back home so I can marry Norman. Sound good?'

'It has a lot of steps; maybe you should make an itinerary,' Siobhan said, sarcastically.

'Very funny, Siobhan,' Kate said, giving her a look. 'Finish your drinks, girls. This crazy ride began in Omnia. And that's where it's going to end.'

Chapter 26

Scene of the Crime

The girls walked from the Bellagio to Omnia, the original scene of the crime. The crime being drinking Four Loko and kissing Trevor on the stage, that is. They saw the usual line outside the club and headed straight to the front.

'Hi there,' Kate said to the bouncer. 'My hus— erm, Trevor Rush booked a booth for us. Under Kate.'

'Ah yes, right this way.'

'Did you almost call Trevor your—' Siobhan asked.

'NOPE!' Kate lied.

The bouncer led the girls to their VIP booth that over-looked the stage. It was even bigger than the one they had last time. It could have easily fit twenty people in it.

'I'm starting to like being friends with Mrs Rush,' Chloe said, seeing the size of the booth.

'Well, don't get used to it. I'm just here to get my closure so we can get out of here. Eyes on the prize.'

'I'd prefer to keep my eyes on the guys,' Siobhan said, scanning the room for her potential last lay.

The MC came on the stage and began to hype up the crowd.

'Party people, make some noise one last time for DJ DEAD-ASS,' he yelled into the mic. The crowd began to roar. Kate figured there were at least three thousand people there, and the sound of them cheering was thunderous.

'Jesus, that's so loud!' Chloe said. 'I can't even hear myself think!'

'So, same as any other day?' Natalie teased.

'WHAT?'

'Never mind.'

'Y'all know what time it is, right?' the MC continued. 'It's time to . . .'

'FEEL THE RUSH,' the crowd screamed.

'I still can't believe that slogan became a thing,' Kate said.

'It's starting to grow on me,' Natalie shrugged.

'Yeah, like a tumour.'

The crowd went crazy for Trevor as he rose up from underneath the stage. They were worshipping him like a god. For a brief moment, Kate felt strangely proud of him. She had told him nine years ago he would make it and he did. Dear Lord, was she proud to be his wife?

No, that would be ridiculous.

'Omnia, make some noise,' Trevor shouted into the mic, electrifying the crowd even more.

'He's one hell of a showman, I'll give him that,' Natalie said.

Trevor looked up at their booth and winked at Kate. She couldn't help but smile back at him. It was the same wink he used to give her when she would watch him perform at dive bars in New York. She felt the euphoric nostalgia flood her brain.

Fuck.

SHE WAS FEELING THE RUSH.

'Girls, I need a drink,' she said, turning back around to them.

'Four Loko?' Siobhan suggested.

'Absolutely not! But I could have some vodka.'

'That's the spirit!' Siobhan said. She waved over at a passing cocktail waitress. 'Excuse me, how much is four vodka and Cokes?'

'Top shelf or well vodka?'

'Just the regular one,' Kate butted in.

'Should be around $200 then.'

'SWEET JESUS! Never mind then, we'll be fine.'

'This booth has a prepaid tab. I can bring you girls whatever you want and there won't be a charge.'

'Twelve top-shelf vodka and Cokes then please,' Siobhan said.

'Ignore her,' Kate said to the waitress. She didn't want to take advantage of Trevor's generosity. 'We'll have four regular ones with Coke.'

'Diet Coke!' Chloe said.

The waitress headed towards the bar and the girls relaxed into their booth. Although the music was loud, Trevor was playing all the bangers, so Kate didn't mind. His remixes and mashups truly were electrifying. It wasn't that kind of trancey house music either. It was proper music you could sing and dance to. He even played plenty of Taylor Swift, knowing how much she and the girls loved her music. She could tell they were Taylor's Versions too. Jesus, if a man playing Taylor's Versions of her songs wasn't flutter-worthy, what was? She was practically taking flight!

But Kate still found herself slightly on edge. She knew the conversation she was going to have with Trevor after his set would be difficult. She was in a ball of sweat just thinking about it.

What would she say? What would he say back? Would it result in a huge fight or a peaceful apology? War or reconciliation?

But Kate wasn't nearly as on edge as Chloe, who was back

to checking her phone every thirty seconds, obsessively reading the comments. Her follower count kept going up and up as more people watched the video. She now had 12.7K followers. Her biggest dream had become her worst nightmare.

'Chloe, you need to unplug,' Kate said. 'You're going to drive yourself insane.'

'Yeah, it's our last night in Vegas – you need to make the most of it. And that guy over there is giving you the eye,' Siobhan said.

'Really? Where?' Chloe said, desperate for some positive attention.

'Him!' Siobhan pointed.

The guy was handsome. Hot, even. Very much Chloe's type. A rough and ready type of man. And he wasn't holding a fish! They hadn't met on an app, either. It was a real-life meet-cute, or at least it was by Chloe's standards. She gave him an inviting look and he began to walk towards the booth.

'OMG, he's coming over!' Chloe panicked. 'I have no idea what to say. What's a good icebreaker?'

'Global warming,' Natalie said, deadpan.

'Just be yourself!' Kate said.

'Oh grow up, Kate!' Chloe said. 'Being yourself is for *after* he becomes your boyfriend!'

'Go over to him – quickly, he's waiting for you to walk over!'

Chloe took a deep breath and went over to meet her admirer. 'Hi,' she said, at the booth entrance.

'Hey, can I ask you a question?' the handsome stranger said.

'Anything,' Chloe said, batting her eyes and pouting her lips.

'Are you Piss Girl?'

Chloe saw red. 'Do you like your kneecaps?'

'Em . . . yes?'

'Then I suggest you run while you still have them!'

The man gave Chloe a confused yet terrified look and scurried away from the booth. She turned around to see the girls in stitches laughing.

'See? My life is over!' Chloe sulked.

'Oh Chloe, it'll pass, don't worry,' Kate said.

'I think you should just embrace it. You were due a re-brand anyway,' Natalie said.

'Re-brand as PISS GIRL?' Chloe snapped.

'At least it's relatable. We've all pissed ourselves before.'

'Not in front of millions of people! My life as an influencer is over!'

'Oh relax, Chloe,' Siobhan said. 'You can always become some rich old man's trophy wife.'

'They don't give out trophies for LAST PLACE!' Chloe yelled. 'My mental health can't handle this. I'm deleting Instagram.' She took out her phone and deleted the app.

'Five euro says she'll be back on it by tomorrow,' Natalie laughed.

Kate felt vibrations coming from her handbag and realized her phone was ringing again. She peeked at the screen and saw that Norman was calling yet again. There were also two texts from him.

Norman: WHERE ARE YOU???

ANSWER YOUR PHONE!!!!

His timing was terrible. She hadn't been able to answer on the Eiffel Tower and she certainly wasn't able to answer in a nightclub this loud. She put her phone back in her bag and pretended she didn't see it. She needed some space to fix the mess she had created. She was so close to the end of this crazy journey and Norman needed to stop bothering her so she could get the annulment signed and return home.

The waitress returned with their drinks and Kate immediately started sipping some vodka. She needed something to calm her nerves. The thought of confronting Trevor about his cheating had her sweating buckets. But it was necessary for her closure.

Eyes on the prize, she told herself once again.

Trevor's voice suddenly echoed through the room. 'Beautiful people of Omnia, make some noise!' he said.

They made plenty of noise alright.

The Colosseum walls were practically shaking.

'I have a little surprise for you all tonight,' he continued. 'This last song is something none of you have ever heard before.'

What the hell was Trevor up to?

'You're about to hear a brand-new Trevor Rush remix of an original song called "Your Scar".'

Kate froze.

No.

There was no way he had her song. She had deleted any links to it from her Insta.

But as soon as Trevor played the first note, she recognized it. It was her song, alright. The song she had written about him.

Yet, it seemed different somehow. Trevor had done something to it. The acoustic guitar was gone and had been replaced by a cinematic EDM-style beat. He had remixed it into a club song. An epic club song at that. She couldn't quite believe what she was hearing.

Used to be the type to wear my heart upon my sleeve
Till you came along and took it from me like a thief

So blind in love, I never would believe
That one day, you would leave

Kate's face went completely red. This song had been a total flop. Why was he torturing her by playing it? Showcasing her biggest failure to thousands of people? It was utterly mortifying.

'Kate, this is your song,' Natalie said.

'I KNOW THAT!'

Siobhan began to dance along. 'It sounds really good!'

'How the hell did Trevor find my song online?' Kate said, looking at the three of them. Only Chloe had a guilty look on her face. 'Chloe?'

'He offered to give me a shout out on Instagram in exchange for the song,' Chloe admitted.

'JUDAS!' Kate snapped. 'You literally made a deal with the devil!'

'That was the old Chloe who wanted followers. I take it all back!'

'But Kate, look,' Natalie said. 'The crowd is going crazy for it!'

Natalie was right. Three thousand people were dancing like there was no tomorrow. Kate looked around in shock as the song went into the pre-chorus.

But don't make a girl a promise you're not willing to keep
You said you were honest but I guess talk is cheap
I thought I was the strongest till you made me feel so weak
Baby . . . 'cause you cut me deep

The redness in Kate's cheeks started to fade. Maybe it wasn't as embarrassing as she thought. Everyone seemed to love it! Trevor had worked his magic and made it into some kind of pop hit. It was infinitely better than the slow acoustic version she had released. That's when the chorus began.

For years now, we've been apart
But babe you left your mark
Time healed my broken heart
But I'll always have your scar
I'll admit that it was hard
Leavin' you in the dark
Time healed my broken heart
But I'll always have your scar
Yeah, I'll always have your scar

The beat dropped and Trevor introduced a new post-chorus melody that had the crowd losing their minds. A laser light show began illumining the room to the beat of the track. It was mesmerizing.

'Kate – everyone is obsessed!' Chloe said.

'I always said this was a banger,' Siobhan said, twerking on the table.

'Omnia, make some noise if you like the song!' Trevor shouted.

The crowd erupted. Their collective roar was practically seismic. They genuinely loved it.

The song went into the bridge and Kate felt goose bumps.

And I know it sounds crazy and I know it sounds mad
But of that scar baby, I'm so glad
I wear it on my heart, just like a badge
'Cause the scar's the last part of you I have

Kate felt tears begin to dampen her eyes. It was the hardest lyric she had ever written. And she meant every word of it. Because even after what Trevor had done, she would always have done everything the same. Her three months with him that summer were worth the scar.

And in that moment, she knew he was The One.

No matter how many times her mind told her to choose Norman, she knew her heart belonged to Trevor.

That was why she had never fully healed.

That was why she had never stopped thinking about him.

That was why she had never thrown away the locket.

Because she always was, and always would, be one thing. *His.*

The chorus played one last time and the crowd went even more berserk than before. It was the first time she had ever considered the possibility that the internet troll's hate comment was wrong. Maybe she wasn't another delusional hack going absolutely nowhere. Maybe she was talented. The crowd were cheering, after all. She couldn't believe their reaction. It was all she had ever wanted. For people to listen to her music. For her voice to be heard. And here they were, dancing to something *she* had created.

But she couldn't have done it without Trevor. His magic had created this.

She had written the lyrics. He had given her the beat.

The heartbeat that brought her back to life.

'OMNIA, DID YOU ENJOY THE NEW SONG?' Trevor roared as the song faded out.

They began to erupt once again.

'Well, we happen to have the singer/songwriter in the audience tonight. My amazing wife, Mrs Kate Rush, everybody!'

A spotlight swung over in Kate's direction and almost blinded her.

Good God, everyone was looking at her.

And they were cheering.

Cheering for her.

'Omnia, that's my set. Make some noise for one of Vegas's

biggest names: DJ Nightcall!' Trevor said before turning and heading backstage.

'Oh my God, girls, that was incredible!' Kate said.

'We know! Now go and tell that to Trevor, you dope!' Siobhan demanded.

'Come backstage with me!' Kate led the girls out of the booth, down the stairs and towards the stage. They waded through the crowd until they finally got to a bouncer blocking a velvet curtain.

'Hi, I'm Trevor Rush's wife,' she said. And she liked saying it. Fuck, she *loved* saying it!

The bouncer let the girls through and they rushed backstage. They ran down a narrow corridor and turned a corner into a large room filled with tech equipment and music gear.

And there he was.

Waiting for her.

'How does it feel to fly, little bird?' Trevor smiled.

'Well . . .' Kate said, pacing towards him coyly. 'What you did was completely outrageous. Brazen, even. Downright unacceptable . . .'

'And?'

'And it was a dream come true,' she smiled.

Trevor looked into her eyes and took a step forward. She knew he was about to kiss her. And she wanted him to. Dear Lord, she wanted him to. Not for one, two or three seconds but for all the seconds until the end of time.

'TREVOR!' a woman's voice yelled from behind them.

Kate turned around and felt the wind being knocked out of her.

Standing before her was the woman Kate had seen going into Trevor's apartment nine years ago. The woman he kissed on the cheek. The woman he led inside. The woman she saw with Trevor on Instagram.

Viola.

'Well, look who it is!' Trevor shouted, his face lighting up as soon as he saw her.

'Trevor, that song was amazing!' she said, running over to him. She leaned in and he kissed her on the cheek. She kissed him back on his.

Kate felt a lump in her throat. The feeling was somehow worse than it was nine years ago. Because she had been made a fool of twice. This woman was obviously still a big part of Trevor's life. Kate could tell from the way his face lit up.

She couldn't stomach it any more. She had to leave. She needed to be anywhere but here.

She never would have guessed the next words that came out of Trevor's mouth.

'Kate, I'd like you to meet my manager, Charlie Viola!' he said.

'YOUR MANAGER?' Kate said, in pure and utter shock.

Charlie was a woman? Viola was her surname? The woman Kate saw going into his apartment was his manager? Was he sleeping with his manager? Her mind was going a mile a minute.

'So, this is *the* Kate?' Charlie said. 'As in, the girl you've been crying over for the past nine years?'

'Charlie loves embarrassing me, in case you haven't noticed,' Trevor laughed.

'Kate, you are absolutely gorgeous!' Charlie said, looking her up and down.

Kate couldn't find the words to answer. 'Oh no . . . you are!' she said, awkwardly.

'What is it about Irish girls? Honestly Trevor, I would have married her if you didn't,' Charlie laughed.

'Easy there, tiger. Kate is straight,' Trevor laughed.

'Well, nobody's perfect,' Charlie shrugged.

Did Kate hear that right? Charlie was a lesbian? Or was she bi perhaps? Or pan? Her head was spinning!

The girls looked at each other as they all silently tried to piece everything together.

'Charlie, this is Kate's bridesmaid, Natalie,' Trevor said. 'She might be more your type.'

Natalie stood there awkwardly in awe of the goddess of a woman.

'Well, hello there, Natalie,' Charlie said, turning to her. She was so confident and so dominant. Somehow handsome and pretty at the same time. It was clear Charlie was a woman who never doubted herself.

'Hi, Mommy,' Natalie blurted out. 'I MEAN CHARLIE! SORRY!'

Siobhan and Chloe began dying laughing.

'Don't worry, I get that a lot,' Charlie laughed. 'Love your style – very spooky chic.'

'I told you it was a thing!' Natalie said to Siobhan.

'Can you all believe these two finally got hitched after all these years?' Charlie said. 'I guess anything really is possible in Vegas.'

'I hit the jackpot, that's for sure,' Trevor smiled.

'Anyway, let's give these two love birds some space. But Kate, is it okay with you if I send your song to my contacts in the music industry? I honestly think it has serious potential.'

'Oh, I don't know . . .'

'She means yes,' Siobhan butted in.

'Okay, great. I'm looking forward to sitting down and discussing what's next for "Your Scar". But we can talk shop next time we meet. Natalie – can I buy you a drink?'

Natalie was so smitten that she couldn't even get a word out. Instead, she just nodded and followed Charlie back to Omnia.

'Have fun!' Trevor yelled after them.

'We'll get out of your hair too,' Siobhan said. 'Come on, Piss Girl, let's go get pissed.'

'I hate you,' Chloe said as she followed Siobhan towards the backstage door.

'Well, that was a surprise,' Trevor said, turning back to Kate.

'You have no idea,' Kate said, still completely blindsided by learning who Charlie was.

'Follow me,' Trevor said.

'To where?'

'It's not midnight for another thirty minutes,' he said. 'And I have one last stop for our final date.'

Chapter 27

The Truth

As they walked along the Vegas Strip towards a mysterious final stop, Kate's mind was in a frenzy.

Suddenly everything had changed. Trevor wasn't the cheater she had spent nine years believing he was. It had all been completely innocent. His manager had simply visited him for his twenty-third birthday with a bottle of wine and he had kissed her on the cheek in a friendly, platonic manner. Kate had jumped to the mother of all conclusions and assumed that their relationship was romantic – when it was anything but!

How could she have been so stupid?

And more importantly, how was she going to tell Trevor that she had dumped and blocked him based on an idiotic misreading of a situation? Her stomach was churning as she tried to find the words.

Trevor's 'infidelity' had left her with an all-encompassing sense of worthlessness. It was even the reason behind her falling for Norman. Her self-esteem was in the gutter when he came along. The fact that he showed her any kind of affection at all made her feel temporarily healed. That was why her personality had changed so dramatically. From a reckless, wild-at-heart party girl to a reserved, organized, control freak. Because Trevor cheating made Kate ask herself a terrible question: 'What did I do wrong?'

That's when she decided to never do anything wrong again.

She would be whatever kind of woman Norman wanted her to be. That way, he would never cheat. She became a malleable shell of her former self so that she would never be hurt again. That was how she had become such a people-pleaser.

But Trevor hadn't hurt her after all. She had sacrificed her very essence based on a complete misunderstanding.

'So did you ever think you'd hear your song being played in one of the biggest nightclubs in the world?' Trevor asked as they strolled.

'Honestly, I'm still not sure that even happened,' Kate said, still in shock.

Her brain was so preoccupied with telling Trevor the truth that she wasn't able to enjoy the moment. She had a lump in her throat the size of a golf ball, and the thought of explaining herself made her want to throw up.

'Well, I hope you don't mind but I took the liberty of uploading it to YouTube.'

'YOU DID WHAT?'

'Relax, I just wanted to give people a chance to go stream it after the club. That's how a lot of people gain a following,' he explained.

'Trevor, I didn't ask you to do that,' Kate panicked. She took out her phone and opened YouTube. 'What's it called on here?'

' "Your Scar" by Kate. Trevor Rush Remix.'

Kate searched the song and it came up immediately. When she clicked on it, she saw it had 1,540 views. It had already outperformed her own acoustic version. But at least it hadn't gone viral or anything. She didn't know if she would be ready for that.

'It has about fifteen hundred views,' Kate said.

'Not bad for the first hour. Once it blows up on YouTube, that'll give Charlie some leverage with record labels. But honestly, she won't even need it. Once they hear your voice, it'll all take off.'

'This all just seems like it's happening too fast.'

'Kate, what are you so afraid of? You have an amazing voice and the world deserves to hear it. What could possibly be so terrible about that?'

'But what if I flop?' she panicked.

'Oh, Freckles,' he laughed. 'What if you fly?'

'I don't know, Trevor – my mind is going a mile a minute.'

She was all over the place since learning who Charlie was. The woman she had hated for nine years was suddenly going to be sending her song to record companies? Kate hated feeling stupid in any situation but she had never experienced this level of regret for an idiotic mistake before.

'Kate, we live in a world where the right person hearing your voice can change your life. Nine years ago, you told me I had what it takes and you were right. But when I tell you that you have what it takes, you don't believe me. It doesn't make sense.'

'I gave up on that dream, Trevor.'

'No, you gave up on yourself. Well, guess what, I never gave up on you, not for one second. We could achieve anything if we stay together. We could travel the world making music.'

Kate felt her phone vibrating in her handbag again. Norman seriously needed to get lost.

'Is that him again? The man you've convinced yourself you love?'

'I do love Norman!'

'But you're not *in* love with him. There's a difference. That summer we shared, Kate, that is what it means to be in love,' Trevor said.

'I wanted that summer to last for ever,' she said, welling up.

'It could have. You're the one who left and never came back.'

Trevor stopped walking and turned to look up. They had arrived at the Vegas replica of the Statue of Liberty. Kate knew what he was doing. Their honeymoon around the world had finally come full circle.

'Trevor . . .'

'This is the way it was supposed to be, Kate. It was always supposed to be continued. You were supposed to come back to New York so we could build a life together. So we could make music together. And then on the seventeenth of November – my birthday by the way – you dumped me. With the coldest of messages that didn't explain anything. And then, when I tried to reply, your profile disappeared. I tried calling but the call wouldn't go through either. I thought I was going crazy, so I tried to get in touch with Siobhan, Natalie and Chloe. But they had all vanished too. And then it hit me. I'd been blocked. On everything. Ditched, in the cruellest way possible. Without you even bothering to tell me why. I didn't know your Irish address so I couldn't even write to you. I had no way of finding out why the love of my life threw me away. Have you any idea how that can break a person?' Trevor said.

'I never meant to break you. I thought you broke me.'

'How? How did I break you?' he said, begging for answers. 'Why did you completely cut me out of your life like I was nothing?'

'You weren't nothing, Trevor. You were my everything!' Kate said, tears in her eyes.

'That's still not a proper answer. I know you wrote "Your Scar" about me. That's why you didn't want me to find it.'

'Of course it's about you!' she admitted.

'But what scar did I give you? I never did anything wrong by you. I always promised I would never hurt you!'

'I know!'

'Then tell me the truth. Because I know our love is real. I know you were meant to come to Vegas. I know we were meant to find each other again. And if you don't feel the same, then why did you kiss me on the Omnia stage?'

'I can't remember why I kissed you!'

'Then let me remind you,' he said.

Trevor took Kate in his arms and kissed her with every part of his soul. She felt herself melt in the clutches of his kiss as she surrendered to her deepest desires. As the flutters took hold and her body pulsed with passion, she suddenly remembered every one of the million reasons she loved him. She knew she belonged in the sanctuary of his embrace.

No matter how hard she tried to hammer Norman's jigsaw piece into place, it would never fit. That missing part of her puzzle was in the shape of Trevor. He was the only man who ever made her feel beautiful. She had never liked the way she looked in the mirror. But she loved how she looked in the reflection of his eyes.

He was her first and final love. Not her *to be continued*.

Her beginning, her middle and her end.

'You can't tell me you didn't feel anything,' he said, pulling back from her.

'I felt everything,' Kate said, the dam holding back her tears about to break.

'Then tell me why you broke my heart. That question has consumed me for nine years. I need to know,' Trevor begged.

This was it.

The moment she was dreading.

What could she possibly say that wouldn't make him hate her? She had finally been honest about how she felt about him. But now she feared the truth would tear them apart.

'Okay, Trevor. You deserve the truth,' she said, taking a

deep breath. 'I'm just afraid that once I tell you, you won't forgive me.'

'What is it?' he asked, desperate for answers.

'After I left that summer, I missed you so much that I booked a plane ticket for November to come and see you. I was going to surprise you for your birthday.'

'You never came to New York that November.'

'Actually, I did. I got on the plane to New York and took a cab to your apartment in Brooklyn. But . . .'

'But?'

'But when I was crossing the street to your building, I saw this gorgeous woman walk in before me. She was one of the most stunning women I've ever seen, and she was holding a bottle of wine. You opened the door and kissed her on the cheek. And then the two of you went inside. When I saw that happen, I felt my heart shatter into a million pieces,' Kate said, barely able to get the words out.

Kate could see Trevor's mind trying to figure it all out. The penny was about to drop.

'Wait, don't tell me it was . . .' he began.

'It was Charlie.'

There was a piercing silence between them, even with the loud uproar of Vegas booming in the background.

Trevor began to step backwards from her, as if she had repelled him away. He began massaging his temples in frustration. 'Please tell me you're joking,' he said.

'I tried calling you, but you didn't answer. And then you sent me a text that said you were in a meeting . . .'

'Because I WAS in a meeting,' Trevor said, anger seeping into his voice.

'I know that now, but at the time it seemed like such a lie. I jumped to the wrong conclusion . . .'

'No Kate, you LEAPT to the wrong conclusion!'

'Up until, like, thirty minutes ago, I thought . . .'

'You thought I cheated on you? The one thing I would NEVER do! That's why you cut me out of your life? Because Charlie brought me a bottle of wine for my birthday and I kissed her on the cheek?'

'I didn't know . . .'

'FIRST of all, she's my manager! And even if she wasn't, she's not attracted to men! And I'm not attracted to her! She's been my manager for the past nine years. I even told you that summer that a manager was interested in signing me!'

'I just assumed Charlie was a man and I never connected the dots!'

'Oh, you just assumed she was a man because she's a manager? That's kinda messed up, Kate.'

'I know, I know! But I had seen her at one of your gigs and the way she was looking at you, it was like she wanted you . . .'

'She wanted to SIGN me! She was scouting that night!'

'But I remember you winking at her.'

'I wink at everyone!'

'The way you kissed her on the cheek made me think . . .'

'We're both Italian, Kate! It's not weird to kiss someone on the cheek. She signed me on my birthday and she brought over a bottle of wine to celebrate! Jesus, I can't believe what I'm hearing,' Trevor said. There was immense pain in his voice.

'I thought it was only a matter of time before you dumped me. That's why I wrote that message. But it was a stupid, stupid mistake . . .' Kate cried.

'And here's a crazy idea, Kate, why didn't you cross the street and just ASK me who she was? Did you ever consider that?'

'I was afraid of what I would see if I went inside.'

'Two sentences, Kate. That's all it would have taken to avoid this. You would have said, "Who is that woman?" and I would have said "This is my manager, Charlie!" Two sentences would have stopped nine years of pain and confusion!'

'Trevor, please . . .' she said, blinded by tears. 'I was so hurt by what I saw that—'

'*You* were hurt? And how do you think I felt to be suddenly dumped and blocked with no explanation? I spent nine years in the dark because you misread a situation!' Trevor said.

Kate was so upset she couldn't articulate the words she desperately wanted to tell him. 'Tell me what to say, Trevor. Tell me how to fix this,' she cried in desperation.

'You already did fix it, Kate. You said "I do" at our wedding three nights ago. And after nine years, the hole in my heart finally went away. But the next morning you woke up and said it was a mistake. So you broke my heart by mistake and you fixed my heart by mistake. And now you're hell-bent on marrying Norman. Another mistake. Might as well make it a trifecta,' he said, now furious.

'Trevor, please . . .'

'You think you can just do whatever you want without thinking about how it might affect others,' Trevor said. He was looking at her like he didn't even recognize her. She suddenly hated her reflection in his eyes. She had never felt uglier in her life. She feared he would never see her in the same way again. She would be tainted by her mistake for ever.

'That's not fair,' she cried.

'Let me just dump and block my long-distance boyfriend and not give him an explanation. It might emotionally cripple him for the rest of his life but who cares?'

'I never meant to hurt you!'

'Of course you didn't. Because nothing is ever your fault, is it? Well, guess what, Kate. This is the last time you're ever

326

going to hurt me. It's officially midnight, Cinderella. And I think it's about time you left the ball.'

'I need to explain—'

'Go home, Kate. Go home to Norman's little cage, and keep believing you're an ugly duckling who doesn't deserve to fly. Because at least when you're locked up there, you can't mess with my head any more. Give me the annulment!' Trevor said.

'Can we please just . . .'

'GIVE IT TO ME!'

With her hands shaking, Kate reached into her handbag and grabbed the papers. Trevor snatched them from her with lightning force. Suddenly she would have given anything for him not to sign those papers. She didn't want to be released from him. She wanted to belong to him for eternity.

'You want rid of me so bad, well here you go!' Trevor said.

He put the papers down on a nearby ledge and took a pen out of his suit jacket.

'Trevor, don't!' Kate cried. 'I'm begging you!'

But it was too late. The ink began to flow as he signed his name.

'There,' he said. 'The annulment is officially signed. You got your wish.'

She felt a sharp pain in her heart. All she wanted was for him to rip up the papers and take her back in his arms. 'This isn't what I want!'

'You don't know what you want, Kate. And I don't think you ever will. Well, here you go, the annulment is signed. Our marriage never happened. I was nothing but loyal to you, Kate. I promised you I'd never hurt you and I meant it. But instead of trusting me, you broke my heart for something I didn't even do. Well congratulations, Kate, you finally found my ick.'

'Trevor, please. I thought you broke my heart,' she said, flooded with tears.

'You broke your own heart, Kate. The so-called "scar" in your song? You gave that to yourself. And by the way, it's nothing compared to the scar you gave me. I'll take the annulment back to Vinnie myself right now. In the morning, a judge will approve it and you can cut me out of your life again,' Trevor said, turning to walk away.

Tears were blinding Kate in a haze of regret. 'Trevor, don't go!'

'Oh, one more thing,' he said, turning back around. 'My key necklace, you know the one you accused me of using for cocaine? It's the key to the locket I gave you nine years ago.' He ripped the necklace off and threw it on the ground.

'I . . .' Kate said, looking down.

'Take it,' Trevor said. 'You've already taken everything else from me. You might as well have this one last thing.'

Flooded by tears, Kate bent down to pick the key off the ground.

When she looked back up, Trevor was already gone. She searched around frantically for him but he had disappeared into a crowd of tourists.

She knew she couldn't leave things like this between them. There was still so much left to say. If she could just have more time to explain. To tell him that she still loved him. That she never stopped loving him, even when she hated him. She hadn't gotten a chance to articulate her feelings properly. Her words had failed her. But then again, what could she possibly say? Did she even deserve his forgiveness? She had punished him so cruelly for something he didn't even do.

Kate couldn't let this be the end. She had to chase after him. She had to win him back.

But that's when she heard her name being called from behind her.

'Kate!' The voice said.

She turned around and got the biggest shock of her life.

'NORMAN?' Kate said as she saw her fiancé standing in front of her with his phone in his hand.

Chapter 28

Bad Timing

'Norman, what the hell are you doing here?' Kate said in complete disbelief.

This couldn't be happening. She felt more smothered than ever as she saw her fiancé standing right in front of her. She could barely breathe.

'What do you mean, what am I doing here? I was worried sick! I've been calling and texting you non-stop. I'm here to take you home,' Norman said.

No.

Not right now.

Not when she was about to chase after Trevor to win him back.

'How did you even find me?' Kate asked, wiping the tears from her eyes.

'I tracked your phone, obviously! I thought you were in danger!'

'I told you not to worry. And I told my mother to tell you not to come to Vegas!'

'Margaret agreed with me that you needed to be brought home!'

'I'm clearly fine, Norman. Everything is fine!' she said, her mascara running down her face.

'Then why were you crying? And why wouldn't you answer the phone? There's something you're not telling me. I'm not stupid, Kate!' Norman said, angrily.

Why did he have to show up now of all times?

There was still time to catch up to Trevor.

But now it seemed impossible.

'Norman, I need a minute to breathe,' Kate said, completely blindsided by the moment. 'I feel smothered.'

'Well, I'm sorry you feel that way, but you didn't leave me with much of a choice, did you?'

'Please just give me a second to catch my breath . . .'

'Catch your breath from what? You've spent the last few days relaxing on your extended hen party in Vegas,' Norman said. 'It's time to go home.'

Kate looked back towards the crowd where Trevor had disappeared, desperately trying to find him. She was completely overwhelmed with emotion, practically bordering on a panic attack.

Finally, she spotted him in the distance. Lorenzo pulled up in the black Mercedes and Trevor got into the back seat without even the slightest hesitation. Not even a glance back in her direction. A moment later, the car was gone, headed in the direction of the Little White Wedding Chapel.

It was over.

Trevor had just shattered her. And Norman was here to pick up the pieces. The glue had come just after the hammer's final blow.

What choice did she have but to follow her fiancé?

Kate turned and looked back at the Statue of Liberty replica one last time. Perhaps her story with Trevor wasn't *to be continued* after all.

It seemed it was the end.

'Alright, Norman,' Kate said, in defeat. 'Let's go.'

༺ོ༻

As they walked towards the Bellagio, Kate realized she had a lot to fill the girls in on. They would need to pack immediately, but Norman couldn't come into the hotel room. Some of her wedding merch was still in there and the girls would undoubtedly let something slip about Trevor.

A plan.

She needed a plan.

Her priority now was to ensure Norman didn't find out anything. If by some miracle she could keep the events of the hen party under wraps, she might just have some semblance of a life. Crisis management mode was officially activated.

She took out her phone and began to type frantically.

The Four Lokos

Kate: EMERGENCY!!!!!

Chloe: OMG what's wrong? x

Siobhan: You kissed Trevor didn't you?

Called it.

Kate: NO GIRLS, THIS IS A REAL EMERGENCY!

NORMAN IS HERE!!!

Natalie: wtfffffff

Chloe: Are you taking the piss?

Siobhan: You'd know Piss Girl lol

Kate: EVERYONE BACK TO THE
ROOM RIGHT NOW!!!

Chloe: Okay, we're on our way!!!

By the time she and Norman arrived at the Bellagio, Kate was in a ball of sweat. It felt like her life was tearing at the seams, but she had to keep it together. As the hotel lobby air conditioning hit her, she took a steadying breath and focused on the task at hand.

'Norman, I need you to stay here while I go and pack with the girls,' Kate said.

'Absolutely not!' Norman said. 'I'm coming up there with you.'

Shit.

She needed a lie. And fast.

'Norman, I didn't want to say this, but Siobhan is having sex in the room right now. So I need to go up there by myself.'

'Jesus, Siobhan is disgusting! This is exactly what I mean when I tell you you're above those girls.'

'She's allowed to have a little fun in Vegas, Norman,' Kate sighed. 'Look, if you come up to the room, it'll only slow the whole thing down. Please just trust me on this.'

'Ugh fine, but I want you all back down here in thirty minutes or I'm asking for the room number at reception and coming up,' Norman said, sitting down awkwardly on one of the lobby couches.

'We'll be down in thirty minutes, don't worry!' Kate said before dashing off. She legged it to the elevator, and took it to her floor. Half an hour was not a lot of time to fill the girls in and pack all their cases.

But she had no choice.

She had almost blown up her life on this trip and now it was time to do some serious damage control. Trevor was gone; Norman was here. She kept repeating it in her mind. She no longer had a husband but she still had a fiancé. Dear Lord, even hearing those words in her mind made her feel like a lunatic.

When she reached the room, Kate flung the hotel room door open and thankfully saw the girls waiting inside.

'Kate, what's going on?' Natalie said as soon as she walked in.

'The shit just hit the fan, that's what's going on. Everyone start packing,' Kate instructed.

'Is Norman really here or was that a joke?' Siobhan said.

'Do I look like I'm joking?' Kate said, pointing at her running mascara and frizzy hair.

'Wait, wait, wait!' Chloe said. 'What happened with Trevor?'

'I don't have time to explain. Norman wants us downstairs in thirty minutes. Please start packing!'

'Kate, take a deep breath and tell us what happened,' Natalie said, putting her hands on Kate's shoulders.

'Trevor signed the annulment,' Kate cried. The tears began to flow again as soon as she said it.

'But I thought things were just about to work out?' Chloe said.

'They were but I ruined everything. I told him the truth. I told him that the woman I saw go into his apartment was Charlie.'

'But Charlie is a lesbian,' Natalie said. 'She told me so herself.'

'I know that now, but I didn't know that back then. He mentioned a manager called Charlie but I just assumed it was a man!'

'That's very problematic, Kate,' Natalie said.

'I know. I'm a monster!'

'But shouldn't everything be okay now? He never cheated, which means he never broke your heart,' Chloe said.

'But I broke his! I told him why I never came back to him and he was furious. He hates me!'

'Kate, you need to chase after him!'

'I was about to. But just as he was walking away, Norman appeared out of nowhere!'

'How did he even find you?'

'He has her chipped, remember?' Natalie said, unimpressed.

'My head is spinning,' Kate said, sitting down on the bed. 'Norman is downstairs waiting to take me home!'

'Jesus, Kate, this is a real clusterfuck,' Siobhan said. 'And not in a good way.'

'We all have to pull together. Here's the plan . . .'

'What number plan are we on now?'

'We're all going to pack and meet Norman downstairs. And we're going to make sure we don't let anything slip about what happened on this hen party. Then we go to the airport, leave Vegas and never come back,' Kate said as she stood up.

'You can't leave if you have unfinished business with Trevor,' Chloe said.

'I've had unfinished business with Trevor for nine years. And he just walked away from me. He got in his town car and went straight to the Little White Wedding Chapel to submit the annulment. So, I would say our business is well and truly finished!'

'Eh, hello!' Natalie said. 'I finally found someone I connect with and we have to leave? Charlie is waiting for me at the bar.'

'I'm sorry, Nat, but we don't have any other choice. Norman is literally in the lobby!'

'I vote to chase after Trevor,' Siobhan said, raising her hand.

'Siobhan, please. He's gone!'

'He's not gone, he's just hurt that you broke his heart over something he didn't even do. He loved you and you disappeared on him without any explanation,' Siobhan said, sympathetically.

'But when I tried to give him an explanation, he looked at me with pure disgust.'

'Yeah, because if you trusted him nine years ago, this never would have happened. He kissed his manager on the cheek and you crucified him for it. I told you that you can't be so extreme, blocking people out of your life without telling them why! It's you, Kate! "You're the problem, it's you!"'

'I am fully aware of that, but when I tried to apologize he grabbed the annulment and signed it. He doesn't want anything to do with me!'

'So is the marriage officially annulled then?' Natalie asked.

'Not yet. It'll be sent to a judge tomorrow and he'll approve it,' Kate explained.

'OR SHE!' Natalie said. 'Women can be judges as well as managers, Kate.'

'Natalie, please don't make me feel worse than I already do.'

'Kate, there's still time to make things right,' Chloe said.

'No, Chloe. Trevor is gone!'

'Oh please, men are never truly gone. They cool off and come back. Here, give me your phone,' Siobhan said, holding her hand out.

'For what?'

'Just give it to me!'

Kate handed Siobhan her phone and she opened Instagram.

'Siobhan, please, what are you doing?' Kate panicked.

'I'm just going to call him on Instagram,' Siobhan said as she looked up his profile. 'Oh . . .'

'Oh?'

'User not found,' Siobhan winced.

'OMG, he blocked you!' Chloe gasped.

'Ouch,' Natalie said under her breath.

'You know what? It's what I deserve,' Kate said, accepting her fate. 'I have nobody but myself to blame. It's a taste of my own medicine and honestly, it makes everything a lot clearer. I cut Trevor out of my life and now he's cutting me out of his. So now my choice is clear. Norman is the man I'm destined to be with.'

'What if—' Chloe began.

'Girls, that's the end of it. I've been dumped by my husband. It's time to marry my fiancé. And I need us all to swear that Norman never finds out about Trevor. We take this to our graves. Understood?'

'Understood,' the girls agreed.

'And you all have to be nice to him. Please don't do anything to make this situation worse.'

'I can't be held responsible for what I say to Norman,' Siobhan said.

'Siobhan, I'm begging you. I need to stop my life from blowing up in my face. Do it for me.'

'Ugh . . . fine! I'll be nice.'

'Okay, now everyone start packing. We need to be out of here in twenty minutes.'

Thirty minutes later, the girls were ready to leave the hotel room. It would have been twenty minutes were it not for the ridiculous amount of clothes Chloe had packed in her three Louis Vuitton suitcases.

'Come on, girls, we're way behind. Everyone out of the room,' Kate said sternly.

'I'm almost done!' Chloe said.

'You brought way too much stuff, Chloe. Twelve pairs of knickers for a weekend is insanity,' Natalie said.

'Well, in her defence, she does have a habit of pissing herself,' Siobhan laughed.

'Shut up, Siobhan!' Chloe snapped.

'Okay, let's go!' Kate said.

The girls wheeled their cases out of the room, with Kate taking Chloe's third one. They got in the elevator and rode it to the ground floor. When it opened, Norman was standing there waiting.

'There you are!' he said, unimpressed. 'I was just about to come up. That was way longer than we agreed!'

'So nice to see you too, Norman,' Siobhan said, sarcastically.

'Sorry, Norman, we were just double-checking everything. We're ready now,' Kate said as they got out of the elevator. 'Natalie, could you go and check out? Everything is already paid for. Just give them these key cards.'

'Ugh, fine,' she agreed, taking the cards.

'As long as it's not Chloe checking out and getting more extra nights added on,' Norman said.

'What?' Chloe said, confused.

'Chloe, you know,' Kate said, elbowing her. 'How you got us the free extra nights?'

'Oh yes . . . of course. Classic me being an influencer,' Chloe nodded along.

'And Siobhan, you picked the wrong time to have sex in the room,' Norman said.

'What?' Siobhan said, confused.

'Siobhan, you know,' Kate said, widening her eyes. 'How you had a man in the room that delayed us packing?'

'Oh yes . . . of course. Classic me being a whore,' Siobhan said, biting her tongue.

Kate was in a fluster. All the lies were catching up with her. It was almost as if Norman was trying to catch her out. She couldn't let him trip her up.

'Kate . . . slight problem,' Natalie said, rushing back over.

'Oh God, what is it?'

'So the room is paid for . . . but the bill for the minibar is $2,196.'

'WHAT?' Norman yelled.

'Girls, I told you all not to drink from the minibar,' Kate cried. But she was in no mood to argue with anyone. She just needed to get the hell out of Vegas. Kate opened her handbag and took out the massive wad of cash she had won in roulette.

'Where the hell did you get that?' Norman said, shocked.

'I won it gambling.'

'YOU WERE GAMBLING?' he snapped.

'Here, Nat, pay with this,' she said, handing her the cash. 'We'll meet you outside.'

Natalie went back to the desk and Kate led the others towards the main door of the Bellagio.

But as they were walking, they heard a man's voice shout at them.

'STOP!' the man's voice said.

Could it have been Trevor? Had he come just in time to stop her from leaving? Why was that all she wanted?

But when they turned around, Kate saw it wasn't Trevor but rather a police officer that was charging towards them.

'DON'T TAKE ANOTHER STEP!' the officer shouted.

'Kate, what the hell is going on now?' Norman panicked.

The police officer walked up to them and grabbed Siobhan. 'I've been looking everywhere for you,' he said, turning her around. 'Ma'am, you're under arrest.'

'Officer, there must be some kind of mistake!' Siobhan said as she was being cuffed. But there was no mistake. She had been arrested on the night they blacked out and the law had seemingly caught up with her.

'Officer,' Kate said. 'Can you tell us what's going on?'

'Your friend here is under arrest for soliciting illegal drugs,' he explained.

'DRUGS?' Siobhan exclaimed. 'I DON'T EVEN DO DRUGS . . . THAT OFTEN!'

'Oh yeah? Then how come three nights ago you asked me where you could purchase crack cocaine?'

'Crack cocaine? That's impossible!'

'Listen, Officer . . . ?' Kate said, trying to find out his name.

'Byrne.'

'Officer Byrne. We had a lot to drink that night and our memory is a little fuzzy,' Kate said. Norman was looking at her with disdain and she was mortified that this was happening. 'Can you at least tell us what she said?'

'She asked me if I had any crack and when I said no, she asked me where the best place to find crack would be,' he said.

'OH MY GOD!' Chloe said.

'Of course!' Siobhan said. 'Officer Byrne, there's been a mix-up. I wasn't looking for crack, I was looking for craic!'

'Excuse me?'

'We're from Ireland. Craic in Ireland means something completely different. Having "the craic" means having a good time. And saying "any craic?" is a way of asking how a person is. Please, it's just one big misunderstanding!'

'Honestly, officer, she's telling the truth!' Kate said.

Officer Byrne looked Siobhan up and down. 'So you asking me if I had any craic was you asking me how I was?'

'YES! Honestly, I was probably chatting you up. I mean, look at you! I've always loved a man in uniform,' Siobhan flirted. Officer Byrne was incredibly handsome with a thick handlebar moustache and a muscular physique.

'Well, there is the issue of you resisting arrest. When I cuffed you, you made a break for it and evaded capture.'

'I was very drunk. I never would have evaded the long arm of the law now that I've seen your biceps up close,' she winked.

'I'm getting married in two days, Office Byrne, and Siobhan is my maid of honour. We're about to board a flight and leave Vegas for good. Is there any way you could let this slide?'

'Hmm . . . very well. But only because my grandfather was Irish,' he said, uncuffing Siobhan.

'Well if you ever visit, you should look me up. If you google "things to do in Ireland", I'm the top result,' Siobhan winked.

'I think you're a bit too much of a troublemaker for me,' Officer Byrne said. 'But you girls have a safe flight home.'

'WAIT!' Siobhan said. 'Can I at least get your number?'

'Yeah . . .' he said as he put on his aviator glasses. 'It's 9-1-1.'

Officer Byrne turned around and just like that, he was gone.

Natalie came over to the girls after paying the minibar tab.

'What the hell was that about?' she said.

'Siobhan got arrested . . . again,' Chloe said.

'AND I MISSED IT?'

'Forget the arrest. I think that man is the love of my life!' Siobhan said, staring at him as he walked away.

'Sweet Jesus,' Norman said, massaging the bridge of his nose.

'Siobhan, you're lucky you're not in jail!' Kate said.

'Plus, I think he just rejected you,' Chloe said.

'I must have him. I can't live without him. I'm going to make it my life's mission to be with him,' Siobhan said.

'Jesus, Libras really can't handle rejection, can they?' Natalie laughed.

'If I streak through the lobby, he'll have to arrest me again, won't he?'

Chloe began to smell Siobhan's neck. 'What is that? Desperation by Calvin Klein?' she joked.

'OKAY, THAT'S IT!' Norman snapped. 'Everyone outside! We're leaving this degenerate hellhole right now!'

Norman marched the girls outside and hailed down a taxi. 'Airport as soon as possible!' he said into the driver's window.

'Sure, no problem,' the taxi driver said. He got out and opened the boot so they could all load in their suitcases.

Once they were all in, the engine started and they took off towards the airport.

Siobhan let out a sigh as she looked back towards the Bellagio. 'The only man I ever loved,' she said, longing for Officer Byrne. 'And I never even got his real number.'

'I never got Charlie's number either,' Natalie sighed.

'Who the hell is Charlie?' Norman asked.

'She's Trev—'

'Charlie is just a girl Nat met at Omnia!' Kate said, shooting her a look. She had almost said she was Trevor's manager, and that would have opened an un-closable can of worms.

'Right! Yes, just some girl,' Natalie said, catching on.

Kate let out a sigh of relief. Was this what her life would be like? Tiptoeing around Norman? Praying he wouldn't find out what had really happened on the hen party?

'Don't worry, Kate. We'll be out of this shithole soon,' Norman said, taking her hand.

But Kate didn't want to take his hand.

All she wanted to do was stay.

Her heart was breaking, but she felt powerless to do anything about it. And it seemed as if the decision had been made for her.

Trevor didn't want her. Norman did.

Perhaps it was as simple as that.

Chapter 29

What Happens in Vegas

'What do you mean you have to tip a taxi driver?' Norman said when they arrived at the airport.

'You have to add 20 per cent to the fare,' Kate whispered. She was embarrassed by how loudly he was speaking. The taxi driver could undoubtedly hear his whining.

'I'm not tipping a driver just for doing his job!' Norman went on.

'I'll pay the tip,' Chloe said, taking out the last of her dollars. 'Here you are, sir.'

'Thank you, ma'am,' the taxi driver replied.

They all got out and grabbed their cases from the boot. As she looked up at the airport doors, Kate felt an unbearable sense of longing. It was a longing for what could be but also for what could have been. She had spent three days trying to get rid of Trevor and now all she wanted was for him to save her. It was supposed to be mission accomplished but it felt like the biggest failure of her life.

She felt a pit open up in her stomach. The girls and Norman were already walking through the airport doors, but she found herself lingering outside. She was desperately searching for something. It was the most embarrassing thing to admit but she couldn't deny it.

She was looking to see if Trevor would magically appear and stop her from boarding the plane.

Talk about a cliché.

Those kinds of things didn't happen in real life, she reminded herself. She knew it was just a Hollywood trope that was completely detached from reality.

But deep down, that was what she wanted.

She suddenly had cold feet about marrying Norman. Her entire dating life since her J-1 had been a search for a man who was the polar opposite of Trevor. A man who would never hurt her.

But after the revelation that Trevor never cheated on her, her entire life had been turned upside down. She had always believed he was a no-good cheater who didn't deserve an explanation, but nothing could have been further from the truth. She had ripped his heart out all because she feared confrontation. She had spent nine years thinking of herself as the victim when in actual fact she was the villain.

'You ready, Kate?' Natalie asked.

Kate realized she was still lingering outside the airport doors. 'Yes, sorry. I'm ready,' she said, snapping out of her daze. She took one last look around, but couldn't find what she was looking for. What she was *longing* for.

So she went inside.

The girls checked in for their flight and got their boarding passes. Trevor had kept his word and there were four first-class tickets to Dublin in each of their names. He could have been spiteful and cancelled the flights. A part of Kate wished he would keep her trapped in Vegas, keep her locked in their marriage. It was such a dysfunctional thought to have, but it was there nonetheless.

Kate realized the fact that he hadn't cancelled their tickets meant one thing and one thing only. He wanted Kate out of Vegas, as far away from him as possible.

Norman was trying to buy a ticket for the same flight and was haggling with a man over the price of a last-minute seat. It gave the girls a few minutes to talk without him hearing them.

'Are you okay, honey?' Chloe said, rubbing Kate's arm.

'Yeah . . . I'll be alright,' Kate said with a sad smile.

'Were you hoping Trevor was going to chase you through the airport?' Natalie asked.

'Of course not.'

'It's okay, Kate, we all have that fantasy,' Chloe said.

'We can wait a few extra minutes out here if you want?' Natalie suggested.

Kate knew there was no point. She didn't deserve a happy ending. 'No, girls,' she said. 'My story with Trevor is over. He doesn't want me.'

'I know exactly how you feel, Kate. Officer Byrne doesn't want me either,' Siobhan said.

'I don't think that's exactly the same . . .'

'But we can't give up hope, Kate. If it's meant to be, they'll fight for us!'

'Of all the insane things that's happened on this holiday, Siobhan falling in love has to be the craziest,' Natalie laughed.

'I've never felt like this before, girls,' Siobhan admitted. 'It's like he makes me horny . . . but in my heart!'

'Back to Kate, please,' Chloe said. 'Are you sure Trevor actually submitted the annulment?'

'Well, I'm pretty sure. But not 100 per cent sure.'

'Maybe you should call and check with the chapel. You know, just in case you accidentally commit bigamy on Friday,' Natalie said.

'I hadn't even thought of that. You're right!' Kate said. 'Will you three distract Norman while I call them?'

'I think he's fairly busy trying to get a cheap plane ticket,' Siobhan said, looking over at him.

Kate took out her phone to google 'The Little White Wedding Chapel' and called the number that popped up.

'Hello,' a man's voice said.

'Hi, is that Vinnie?' Kate asked.

'It sure is. Who's asking?'

'It's Kate from the other day.'

'Who?'

'Trevor Rush's wife,' Kate sighed.

'You mean ex-wife?' Vinnie said.

The words hit her like a ton of bricks.

'Oh,' she said. 'That's actually why I was calling. I was just checking to see if he submitted the annulment.'

'He sure did. About an hour ago. I was surprised, too. Of all the couples I've married, I really thought you two were going to make it,' Vinnie said.

'Did he seem . . . how did he seem?' Kate asked.

'Honestly, he seemed pretty upset. He asked for the annulment to be processed immediately.'

'So . . . it's done then?'

'I already scanned the papers and submitted them online. The judge will approve them first thing in the morning and the marriage will be erased from history.'

'Oh . . . alright.'

'Isn't that what you wanted?'

'Yeah . . . I suppose everything worked out. But Vinnie, if you ever happen to see him again, will you tell him something for me?' Kate asked.

'Sure, what would you like him to know?'

Kate felt the tears rise again. This was it. Potentially the last thing Trevor would ever hear from her, even if it was unlikely Vinnie would pass on the message.

But it was worth a shot.

'Tell him he was right,' Kate said with a quivering lip. 'Tell him I made a huge mistake and I'll regret it for the rest of my life. Tell him that I should have trusted him, instead of assuming the worst-case scenario. I dumped him because I thought he had found someone better and was about to dump me. If my stupid pride hadn't got the better of me, none of this would have happened. I ran away to protect my heart but instead I broke it. And I broke his too, by being a coward. And tell him that even though he hates me, I still love him. I always have and I always will. If I could drink another Four Loko and wake up married to him again, I'd do it in a heartbeat. Tell him that even though I ruined everything, I'll always be his ride or die.'

'I don't have a pen and paper, should I have written that down?' Vinnie asked.

Kate let out a bittersweet laugh. 'No, it's okay, Vinnie. It probably wouldn't have made a difference anyway.'

'Well, if I see him, I'll tell him what you said. My memory isn't what it used to be, but I'll try.'

'Thanks, Vinnie. Take care,' Kate said, hanging up.

She took a breath and tried to calm herself down. She was an emotional wreck, but she couldn't let Norman see her crying. He would ask too many questions.

It was officially done. The annulment was signed, sealed and delivered. The judge would sign it in the morning and the marriage would be erased. She had gotten away with it. She had married her ex on her hen party and somehow was able to go back home and marry her fiancé without him finding out or without committing bigamy. It was a downright miracle. A blessing from above if ever there was one.

And yet, it felt like a curse.

'I got a ticket,' Norman said, coming up behind her. 'But the bastards put me in the back of the plane beside the toilet and charged me $2,000 for it!'

347

'It doesn't matter, Norman.'

'Of course it matters!' He suddenly noticed how puffy her eyes were. 'Were you crying?'

'No, it's just my hay fever,' Kate lied.

'I don't think there's any pollen in—'

'Come on, Norman,' Kate interrupted. 'It's time to go home.'

After an agonizing five-hour wait, the girls boarded the flight and took their seats in first-class. Norman was forced to keep walking to the back of the plane and Kate was beyond relieved she wouldn't have to listen to him sulking for ten hours.

The flight attendant began closing the overhead compartments and instructing people to take their seats. First class was even more luxurious than business class, but it made no difference. Kate wanted to be anywhere but there. It wouldn't be long now before the plane took off.

But as Kate looked out the window, more and more intrusive thoughts began to creep in.

Why the hell did she want Trevor to suddenly appear and beg her to stay? Not that it would require much begging, she'd be gone in a heartbeat. But she was being beyond irrational. What was Trevor going to do? Storm onto the plane? The mere idea was outrageous, especially considering modern airport security measures. He would surely be arrested, if not shot!

But if anyone could do it, it was Trevor Rush.

No.

He was out of time anyway. The cabin door was closed. There was no way he could stop the plane at this stage.

Or was there?

She needed to snap herself out of it. She didn't deserve a Hollywood ending. She deserved a taste of her own medicine.

This feeling was what Trevor experienced nine years ago. Actually, that feeling must have been infinitely worse. To be dumped and blocked by the person you love without rhyme or reason? It was gut-wrenching. And all that time he had spent wondering what he had done wrong, when he hadn't done a single thing to hurt her. He deserved so much better than that.

He deserved so much better than *her*.

She needed to let Trevor go. She had hurt him twice now. The only silver lining was that now he might finally have some closure. He could date any woman he wanted in Vegas. Women infinitely more attractive than her. If holding a torch for Kate had kept him from meeting someone new, maybe extinguishing that torch for good would be a blessing in disguise.

For him, at least.

But the thought of him with someone else turned Kate's stomach. What if she should be the one to run through the airport? Maybe she had done enough damage and maybe she needed to get off the plane and run back to him?

'Ladies and gentlemen, please fasten your seatbelts – we will be departing shortly,' the voice on the intercom said.

Kate felt smothered once again. The massive first-class cabin suddenly felt so claustrophobic. She had no idea what the right thing to do was. Everything she had believed about Trevor had been wrong. He was still the man she fell for all those years ago. Underneath the persona, the vulnerable man she loved was still alive. The mask he put on online was clearly to hide the gaping wound she had given him. Just as she adopted the persona of a perfect, people-pleasing planner to hide the scar she carried. The scar she had unknowingly given herself. But considering they had both once loved each other for their true, bare selves, didn't that mean they were supposed to be together?

She tried to calm herself down and rationalize.

It was too late to get off the flight now anyway. Wasn't it?

Ugh, why did this feel like such a pivotal moment in her life? Maybe she was just drunk on the drama of the situation.

What was she supposed to do? Run to the back of the plane and tell Norman she was still in love with Trevor? Get off the plane and run back to Vegas to find Trevor, only for him to repeat the same harsh words? How could she leave a man who loved her for a man who had just dumped her?

She considered calling off the wedding but all she could hear was her mother's voice in her head saying: 'You'll be back to square one', or 'The clock is ticking'. As much as she hated to admit it, the idea of being alone terrified her. She wasn't brave enough to blow up her life and live in its ruins. After such a chaotic few days, perhaps stability and security was what she needed now more than ever. And wasn't that what Norman had always been?

While Kate was still trying to figure out what to do, the plane began to move.

It seemed as if the decision had been made for her.

'I'm starting to think he's not coming,' Siobhan said, looking out the window.

'I told you already,' Kate sighed. 'Trevor is done with me.'

'Trevor? I was talking about Officer Byrne. It's not always about you, Kate.'

'Siobhan, I think Kate's nine years of history with Trevor trumps your nine seconds with Officer Byrne,' Natalie said.

'Love is love,' Siobhan shrugged.

'How are you feeling, Kate?' Chloe asked.

'Too many emotions to list,' she sighed.

'But you love lists.'

'If you want, I can say there's something wrong with the left phalange?' Natalie suggested.

'No, girls. I don't deserve a happy ending. I'm the bad guy. I punished Trevor for something he didn't do. He has every right to hate me,' Kate said.

'But hate sex can be so hot,' Siobhan sighed.

'It's too late anyway, girls. Vinnie said the annulment is already submitted and will be approved first thing in the morning. It's time for this insane story to come to an end. My chapter with Trevor is closed. And my new chapter with Norman is about to begin,' Kate said.

'I suppose not every chapter can have a climax,' Natalie muttered.

'Girls, from now on we are all Team Norman. I'm marrying him and I need you all to support me. No more mentioning Trevor. We have to go back to never saying his name. I have to forget the past few days. I hope none of you brought any of that stupid merch home. We can't have any evidence of what happened lying around. And please delete any videos from that night.'

'Oh come on, Kate, we won't show anyone. They'll just be for us,' Chloe said.

'So you're okay with me re-watching the video of you pissing yourself?' Kate said, raising an eyebrow.

'Fair point.'

'Seriously, girls. This hen party never happened. We are never to speak of it again, deal?'

'Deal,' the girls replied.

'I used to think it was just a saying. But I finally understand what people mean.'

'What phrase?' Chloe asked.

'What happens in Vegas . . .' Kate said, looking out the window one last time, '. . . stays in Vegas.'

But although the phrase was somewhat relatable, Kate knew it wasn't entirely true in her case. One thing had very much not stayed in Vegas. Something she knew she should have left behind but couldn't. Something the girls didn't even know she had in her possession.

Because after nine long years, Kate finally had the key to Trevor's locket.

Chapter 30

The Locket

On the morning of her wedding, Kate found herself in a hot sweat.

Her Thursday had been stressful, to say the least. She had finalized the seating arrangement, collected her dress, paid the band their deposit, arranged a time for the vintage wedding car to be collected, confirmed the time of the cake delivery, gotten a manicure, arranged for flowers to be delivered to the church, dropped off place cards to the venue, packed an emergency kit for anything that might go wrong and arranged the rings.

But it was now Friday morning and she had spent the entire night tossing and turning in the bed alone. Norman had gone to stay at his family home to keep up with the tradition of the groom not being allowed to see the bride the morning of the wedding. But even after a full sleepless night, she still hadn't written her vows for Norman. She was right back at square one with no idea what she was going to say at the altar. She had gotten up several times during the night and stared at the blank page.

She couldn't think of a thing.

Because when Kate was left alone with her thoughts, she found herself tormented by a longing for Trevor. And the source of that torment was coming from within her closet. The locket was calling out to her, demanding to be opened.

She finally had the key after all these years, but opening it could possibly make her feel infinitely worse than she already did. She had no idea what was inside, and she had to keep it that way.

She had gotten through the whole night without opening it. She could get through the day too. She just had to stay focused. At this point the girls would already be on their way. And an hour later, her mother would be arriving with the photographer. It was time to be the person everyone needed her to be. She knew she was reverting back to her people-pleasing persona but what choice did she have? She couldn't let everyone down. She had to snap into character.

She needed to become the bride.

This was supposed to be the happiest day of her life, for God's sake. No, not supposed to be, Kate tried to convince herself.

It was *going* to be.

She showered, washed and conditioned her hair, shaved her legs and moisturized her body. As she slipped into her bathrobe, however, Kate turned her head towards her walk-in closet. The locket was calling out to her once more. As if she was in some kind of trance, she opened the closet door, like Sleeping Beauty wandering towards the cursed spindle. Against her best judgement, she grabbed her J-1 memory box and brought it to her bed. She whipped off the lid and saw it. Such a small innocent thing, with such destructive emotional power. But as she took the locket in her hand, the doorbell suddenly rang.

The girls were here.

Perfect. That would distract her from self-sabotage. They would help her get into character and become Mrs Cox. She left the locket on the bed and headed down the stairs.

'AAAHHHHH,' the girls screamed when Kate opened the

door. They were already fully made up in their bridesmaids dresses and they all looked stunning. The dresses were a gorgeous shade of lavender. They were all technically the same dress, but each had a unique style. Chloe's was an asymmetrical one-shoulder neckline, Natalie's was a halter neck and Siobhan's, as one might expect, was strapless.

'Girls, you all look gorgeous,' Kate said, letting them in.

'Well, it's our job to make you look even better than the three of us combined,' Chloe said, holding up her makeup bag. She was ready to get to work.

'I can't believe the big day is finally here,' Natalie said.

'Neither can I,' Kate said. 'I feel like I have a million things to do.'

'As if you don't have every single thing planned minute by minute,' Siobhan laughed. 'You probably even have our toilet breaks rostered.'

'Kate, you look a bit tired,' Natalie said. 'Did you sleep okay?'

'Not really. Just so excited,' Kate said, trying to convince herself.

'Don't worry, I can hide the bags under your eyes,' Chloe said.

'My hair is shampooed and conditioned, I just need you to blow-dry and curl it. Then we'll move on to the makeup.'

'Perfect! I'll get set up.'

'My mam will be here in about an hour. She's coming with my cousin, Niall. He's the photographer,' Kate explained.

'A photographer, you say?' Chloe said. 'Is he single?'

'He's twenty-one.'

'Ugh, a foetus,' Chloe said, disappointed.

'I'll set up some nice backdrops for the photos and find the best lighting,' Natalie said.

'And I'll get started on the Prosecco,' Siobhan laughed.

'Nice try, Siobhan – you're getting my dress ready.'

'What do I look like? Your maid?'

'You're literally the bride's maid, yes. Now chop chop!'

After about forty-five minutes, Kate's auburn hair was done to perfection. She wore it half up and half down, with loose curls flowing and the rest clipped up. Her makeup was almost finished too, and she was dying to see the result.

'Kate, you look stunning!' Chloe said, applying the final touches.

'Can I see?'

'Not yet, I'm almost done. You just need some mascara.'

'The dress is ready for you by the way,' Siobhan said. 'But it tore a bit when I tried it on.'

'WHAT?' Kate snapped.

'I'm joking,' Siobhan laughed.

'Girls, please no unnecessary heart attacks today. I'm already stressed enough as it is.'

'I have some areas set up for photos,' Natalie said.

'Lickarse,' Siobhan muttered.

'Honestly, girls, thank you all so much. I don't know what I'd do without you,' Kate smiled.

'I'm honestly shocked we're still alive after the hen party,' Siobhan laughed.

Kate's feathers were immediately ruffled. 'I thought we agreed to never mention the hen party ever again,' she said, unimpressed.

'Oh come on, we can talk about it when it's just us.'

'No, Siobhan, we take it to our grave. What happens in Vegas, stays in Vegas, remember?'

'Tell that to Chloe's tattoo,' Siobhan laughed.

'I'm getting it removed in two weeks. It's costing me two grand!' Chloe sighed. 'But at least my sunburn has calmed down.'

'And at least Nat got those massive fake eyebrows off her face.'

Natalie lifted up her bangs to reveal her new feminine eyebrows. 'I bought proper fake ones for women while my real ones grow back,' she said. 'Too bad Charlie will never see what I look like with real eyebrows. I never even got her number.'

'I know how you feel, Nat,' Siobhan said. 'But even though Officer Byrne doesn't want me, I know one day, he will. And when that day comes, I'll be ready to hang up my whore boots.'

'Well, that's some character development, I suppose,' Natalie laughed.

'And I downloaded Instagram again!' Chloe said, as if it was some kind of breakthrough.

'I thought you were on the verge of a breakdown from everyone calling you Piss Girl?'

'I was. But I'm taking a break from my mental health to focus on social media. I have a following now, and everyone loves a comeback.'

'You should reach out to Pampers for a brand deal,' Siobhan laughed.

'Hey, a win is a win,' Chloe shrugged.

'You see, Kate? It's good to look back and laugh at it all.'

'Okay, but that's enough about the hen party, girls,' Kate insisted. She couldn't let her mind wander to Trevor. She had to stay focused.

'Your mascara is done,' Chloe said, standing back to look at her.

'Can I please see now?'

'Put the dress on first! You need to have that BAM moment where you see yourself.'

'Okay, help me get into it,' Kate said, getting up.

Kate got into the dress and the girls pulled it up on her. It was exquisite, yet simple in its design. It was understated but still elegant enough to make a dramatic entrance. It was her big day after all, and wearing the perfect white dress was integral to that. The girls zipped up the dress and began to pull out the bottom of it, for the full effect.

'Okay, now you can look,' Chloe said.

Kate turned around and was mesmerized by the image in the mirror. She did look like a princess, there was no denying that. The problem was, she didn't feel like one. She felt like a fraud.

It was as if she was playing a role. The Happy Bride. A role she didn't want to be cast in any more, despite waiting her entire life for her curtain call. How could she have planned for this moment since she was a little girl, only for it to turn out completely wrong?

It didn't make any sense.

'Is everything okay, Kate?' Chloe asked, sensing something wasn't quite right.

'Yes . . . of course. Everything is perfect. The hair is perfect. The makeup is perfect. The dress is perfect. How could anything not be okay?'

'So why aren't you smiling?' Natalie asked.

She couldn't hold it back any more.

The dam broke and a river of tears began to flow.

'Oh my God, no, no, no, the makeup!' Chloe panicked.

'Forget the stupid makeup,' Natalie said. 'Kate, tell us what's wrong. We're here.'

'It's just . . . I spent all last night trying to write my vows to Norman and I'm completely blank. I can't think of a single thing to say!' Kate said, panicked.

'Just speak from your heart,' Natalie said. 'The words will just come to you naturally.'

'You really think so?'

'Of course. Anything you say will come off as sweet and sophisticated. You're just too in your head about it,' Chloe explained.

'Yeah . . . yeah, you're right.'

Siobhan was audibly silent.

'Have you something to say, Siobhan?' Kate asked.

'No . . .' Siobhan said, trying to keep her words in. 'I mean . . . if you have nothing nice to say, you shouldn't say anything, right?'

'Oh, spit it out already!' Kate snapped.

'Don't you think going blank on your vows is a sign?'

'A sign of what?'

'Sweet Jesus, you're dense,' Siobhan said. 'A sign that you're not in love with Norman!'

'That's not relevant! It's going to be the happiest day of my life. Everything is planned to perfection!'

'Oh don't start, Bridezilla!'

'I'm allowed to be a Bridezilla, it's my day!'

'Well call me Queen Kong because I've had enough of your bullshit!'

'What bullshit?'

'YOU'RE STILL IN LOVE WITH TREVOR!'

'Don't say his name!'

'He's not fucking Voldemort, Kate!'

'He might look like Voldemort in a few years if he keeps doing coke,' Natalie said.

'Trevor doesn't do coke, Nat! That necklace wasn't a cocaine key, it was the key to the fucking locket and he gave it to me after he signed the annulment and I stupidly brought it home and now I'm losing my mind because I've been up all night trying to stop myself from opening it!' Kate said, all in one breath. She hadn't meant to say all that, it had just come out.

Naturally, the girls were gobsmacked.

'WHAT?' Chloe said.

'Where's the locket?' Siobhan said.

'It's on my bed, but—'

Before Kate could finish her sentence, Siobhan was running up the stairs to the bedroom.

'But girls, what difference will opening it even make? Trevor is gone. He wants nothing to do with me. I should just throw it away and forget about him.'

'But you said it kept you up all night. Are you going to be an insomniac for the rest of your life over a locket?' Natalie asked.

'Well . . . that's a good point.'

'Maybe it's the final part of your closure,' Chloe said. 'Maybe once it's open, you can move on and marry Norman without any loose ends.'

They were making sense. Was she going to be tormented by it for the rest of her life? That would be crazy, wouldn't it? Perhaps even crazier than opening a locket from her ex on her wedding day.

No, she reminded herself, it was Pandora's box. Nothing good could come out of it. It was an atom bomb. Detonating it on her wedding day would be an act of self-annihilation.

'Found it,' Siobhan said, walking down the stairs with the locket in her hand.

'No, girls, we can't open it,' Kate said firmly. 'That's my final decision.'

'Okay, then I'm flushing it down the toilet.'

'WHAT?'

'Well, you either have to open it or flush it. You can't just keep it locked. It'll torture you for ever.'

'Fine, flush it. See if I care,' Kate said, folding her arms. Trevor was the past, Norman was the future, she reminded herself. A locket didn't change that.

Siobhan walked into the downstairs bathroom and held it over the toilet bowl. 'I'M ABOUT TO FLUSH IT!' she shouted out to Kate.

'I DON'T EVEN CARE!'

Then, the sound.

The torturous sound of the toilet flushing and the regret that came with it. It was only then that she realized how much she needed to open it.

'STOP!' Kate roared as she rushed to the bathroom. She went flying in and looked into the toilet bowl that was just about to finish flushing.

'NOOOOOO!' Kate screamed when she saw the bowl was empty. It felt like the biggest mistake she had ever made. She would spend the rest of her life tormented by what was inside that locket.

But when she turned around, she felt the greatest relief of her life.

'I obviously didn't flush it, you stupid bitch,' Siobhan smiled as she dangled the locket in her hand.

'I thought we said NO MORE HEART ATTACKS?'

'Shut up and get the key,' Siobhan laughed.

'Change of heart?' Natalie said as the two walked out of the bathroom.

'Okay girls, here's the plan . . .' Kate began.

'Kate, we love you to bits but if you say the word "plan" one more time, I'm going to knock you out with a box,' Siobhan said, only half joking. 'Now open that fucking locket!'

Kate reached into her handbag and took out the key Trevor had given her, on the necklace he had worn around his neck on their dates.

'So it definitely wasn't a cocaine necklace?' Natalie asked.

'No, Nat, it wasn't,' Kate said, unimpressed. 'You jumped to the total wrong conclusion.'

'Well, that's just the pot calling the kettle black now, isn't it?'

Kate took a deep breath and braced herself for what was about to happen. With the key in one hand and the locket in the other, it was time to end nine years of wondering.

'Moment of truth,' she said.

Kate put the key into the locket's hole and Siobhan made an orgasmic moan.

'Not now, Siobhan, this is serious!'

'Sorry, I hate tense moments!'

Kate collected herself and twisted the key.

The locket opened.

The girls all gasped at once. It was far beyond anything she had ever imagined could have been inside. It quite literally took her breath away.

In her hand was the most stunning, ornate diamond engagement ring Kate had ever seen.

Not just any ring.

'His grandmother's ring,' Kate cried. She took it in her hand and the mascara started flowing.

'Oh my God, makeup emergency. Makeup emergency,' Chloe panicked, running to her bag.

'I'm confused. What does this mean?' Natalie said.

'He gave me this locket at the end of our summer together. He told me that when I came back the following summer, he would give me the key!'

'Which means he was going to ask you to marry him,' Siobhan said, in shock.

'And you never went back to him!' Natalie said. 'Oh my God, now *I'm* going to cry.'

Chloe came rushing over and started to pat the tears off Kate's face. 'Nobody else cry or *I'm* going to start crying!' she demanded.

'I ruined his romantic gesture because I never gave him the chance to propose. If I went back, I would have been able to get a visa and we could have spent the last nine years making music together. I used to think Trevor ruined my life. I ruined it my fucking self!' Kate cried.

'The ring looks like it's worth a fortune!' Siobhan said, looking at it closer.

'It's priceless. It's been in his family for generations. And it's been in my closet for the past nine years,' Kate said, bawling.

'No, no, no, the makeup is falling apart! Could you cry on the inside?' Chloe begged.

'This is a disaster! Why the hell did you make me open it?' Kate yelled.

'Eh, hello? Are you saying we should have flushed a priceless engagement ring down the toilet?' Siobhan said.

'It would have been better to never know what was inside!' Kate said, tears rolling down her face.

'Inside tears, inside tears,' Chloe continued.

'What the hell am I supposed to do now?'

The doorbell rang and the girls were suddenly frozen in shock.

'Shit!' Kate panicked. 'It's my mother and the photographer!'

'You can't take photos looking like this!' Chloe said. 'I need to reapply!'

'What should we tell them?' Siobhan asked.

'My mother will know what's wrong as soon as she sees me!'

'Will I stall them?' Natalie asked, going to the door.

'There's no point,' Kate said, helplessly. 'Open it.'

Natalie opened the door to reveal Kate's stern-faced mother.

Margaret walked inside, proudly wearing a flamboyant yet elegant hat, as was tradition for the mother of the bride. Niall, the photographer, walked in behind her. But when Margaret saw her daughter's puffy eyes and running mascara, she immediately had a conniption.

'Sweet suffering Christ on the cross!' Margaret snapped. 'What in the name of God is going on in here?'

'It's kind of a long story,' Siobhan said.

'Well, we don't exactly have time for a long story, do we?' Margaret said, scathingly. 'Niall, wait in the car.'

Niall scurried back out the front door, half afraid of Margaret.

'Sorry, Mam,' Kate said, brushing away the tears.

'What in God's name has you in such a state?'

'Trevor Rush,' Kate said, holding up the locket and the ring.

Margaret looked at it and immediately figured out what had happened.

'I knew he was somehow involved in all this. I told you from day one that he was a loser who'd never amount to anything!'

'Except he did amount to something, Mam. He made something of himself. Nine years ago he gave me his grandmother's priceless engagement ring. But I never went back to him. I never gave him the chance to propose!' Kate cried.

'Of course you never went back – you saw him cheating on you, for God's sake!'

'But he didn't cheat! It was all just a big misunderstanding,' Kate cried. 'It turns out—'

'I don't want to hear it!' Margaret interrupted. 'Crying about your ex from nine years ago the morning of your wedding? Have you any idea how pathetic you look?'

Siobhan and Natalie looked at each other in shock at Margaret's candour.

'I can't help how I feel, Mam.'

'You've shed enough tears over Trevor Rush. And don't forget who helped you get over him. I was the one who had to listen to you crying every night. Had to listen to you writing silly little songs about a lowlife who never gave a damn about you in the first place. He is completely wrong for you!'

Margaret may have been there through the tears, but she didn't have the full picture. Sure, in many ways, Trevor was Mr Wrong.

But he was the right kind of wrong.

The kind that makes you want to break every rule in the book.

The kind that makes you want to risk everything.

The kind that makes you want to put it all on black thirteen.

Even on your wedding day.

'You don't understand, Mam,' Kate said. 'He's spent nine years heartbroken just like I did! He never stopped loving me!'

'And where is he now, Kate?' Margaret said. 'If he loves you so much, where is he?'

Her mother's words cut deep, as they always did. 'He's . . . he's gone,' Kate admitted.

'Well then, that's the end of it. You are due to marry a doctor in two hours . . .'

'Dentist,' Chloe muttered under her breath.

'. . . a doctor whose family are very good people. You're thirty, Kate. If you mess this up, you'll be back at square one. Well, if you think I'm going to let you throw away your future over some ruffian you met nine years ago, then I have news for you. Your father will be here in the vintage car to take you to the church in one hour. So pull yourself together. This is the happiest day of your life. Now start acting like it.'

'Okay, Mam,' Kate said, kicking into planning mode again. 'You're right.'

'I always am,' Margaret said. 'Give me the ring.'

'What?' Kate said. 'Why?'

'Because there's a ring waiting for you at the church. Hand it over,' Margaret said, holding out her hand.

Kate placed Trevor's ring into her mother's hand and watched her put it into her handbag.

'And your phone.'

'Why my . . .'

'Because I don't want you making a fool of yourself by ringing him. Surely you'll hang on to the last bit of dignity you have left?'

Kate sighed and handed over her phone. It didn't matter. She had no way of contacting Trevor on her phone anyway. He'd blocked her.

'Now, that's all that silliness over,' Margaret said, putting the phone in her handbag. 'Chloe, can you fix my daughter's face for the photos please?'

'Eh . . . yes, I'm on it,' Chloe said, leading Kate to the mirror.

'Good. Natalie, you go fetch Niall from the car. Siobhan, you go make some tea,' Margaret said, proudly adjusting the hat on her head. 'Everything is going according to plan.'

Chapter 31

The Wedding

As Kate sat in the passenger seat of the vintage car on the way to the church, she felt a massive lump in her throat. She had spent the last hour faking a smile for the photos and it had felt like an eternity.

Her dad was driving the cherry red 1965 Ford Mustang, and they would arrive at the church in a matter of minutes. She had planned to have a chauffeur drive them, but Tom had a thing for Mustangs and insisted he drive. She wanted to tell him how she was feeling but it was such an awful thing to unburden onto someone. Especially considering he was looking so forward to walking her down the aisle. He had always said throughout his life that he hoped he would be alive for the rite of passage of giving her away. What if his cancer came back and he never got the chance? She didn't want to rob him of that.

He probably had no clue how terrible she was feeling internally. She certainly looked the part of the bride, after all. Chloe had fixed her makeup and she was back looking pristinely perfect. But inside, Kate was screaming. She still had no clue what to say in her vows. The engagement ring in the locket had been a complete curveball. Why on earth had she been stupid enough to open it?

Ignorance would have been bliss.

But now she knew the truth and there was no going back.

She missed hating Trevor. She wanted to go back to seeing him as the fuckboy who broke her heart. But she was the monster who had broken his. And she had hoarded his grandmother's ring for almost a decade. His grand romantic gesture was literally like something from a Taylor Swift song, and she had completely ruined everything. All those nights crying over him as she listened to 'Wildest Dreams' had been self-inflicted torture that could have been avoided with an honest conversation.

The car pulled up in front of the church and she looked out at the tall building. The videographer was outside, getting a shot of the car pulling up. Niall was there too, getting photos for the wedding album.

Kate felt like getting sick. But perhaps if she could just get through today, the rest of her life would be fine. It might not be a life full of joy but it would be a safe, secure life without pain. That was something, wasn't it?

'Here we are, pet,' her father said as he turned off the engine.

'Yep . . . here we are,' she said. She knew she was supposed to open the door. But she just wanted to drive off anywhere.

Anywhere but here.

'Come on, pet, tell me what's wrong,' Tom said. He was more shrewd than she had given him credit for.

'I'm a bit of an emotional mess if I'm being honest, Dad.'

'Well yeah. I'm old but I'm not stupid. What's wrong?'

'I love Norman, Dad, but I'm not *in* love with him. He's not the one,' she admitted.

'Ah . . . I see. But is there someone you *are* in love with?'

'Yes. But he's gone. He wants nothing to do with me. So it's pointless even feeling like this. Longing for a man who doesn't even want me. It's pathetic.'

'It's never pathetic to admit how you feel, pet,' Tom said.

368

'But you probably shouldn't have waited until the very last minute. Everyone is waiting for you inside.'

'I know,' Kate sighed. 'I can't let everyone down.'

'Well, you shouldn't get married just to please everyone else. Are you absolutely sure the other fella wants nothing to do with ya?'

'Yep. He told me right to my face.'

'Well, maybe that's your answer. I'd hate for you to run to him only for him to turn you away again.'

'That's exactly my fear. I don't think my self-esteem could handle a double rejection.'

'If it makes you feel any better, pet, we all have the one that got away,' Tom said.

'Mam wasn't your first choice?' Kate asked.

'If I'm being honest, no. But we made it work. We both chose to be happy.'

'But how did you put up with her? She's so smothering.'

'Isn't that obvious, pet?' he smiled.

'No.'

'Because she gave me you. How could I not love her for that?' Tom said.

It was a genuine heartfelt sentiment that gave Kate hope for the future. Perhaps this feeling would pass. She had always been taught that love was a choice.

It was time to choose Norman.

'Thanks, Dad,' Kate smiled before giving him a hug. 'We'd better not keep them waiting any longer.'

Kate and her father walked to the church door. She knew people were probably wondering if she had done a runner. It was time to get a grip.

The show had to go on.

Kate got out of the car and saw the girls standing in the church doorway along with the pageboy, Norman's nephew, and the flower girl, Kate's younger cousin. Niall was snapping pics as she walked towards them.

'Ready, Kate?' Chloe asked.

'Last chance if you want me to fake a seizure,' Siobhan offered.

'No, it's okay, girls,' Kate said. 'I'm ready.'

Siobhan opened the church door and began to walk down the aisle with Chloe and Natalie. The pageboy entered next, with the rings on their ceremonial cushion. Then it was time for the flower girl to enter. But her little cousin Suzie was giving her a strange look.

'Why aren't you smiling?' Suzie asked her before she entered the church. Children always asked the most no-nonsense questions.

'Oh,' Kate said, taken aback. 'I just have a lot on my mind.'

'I can't wait for my wedding. I'm going to smile for the whole day.'

It made Kate think about how she had envisioned this moment her entire life. How she had manifested the perfect wedding since she was a little girl. She was wearing an immaculate white dress with her veil resting elegantly upon her wavy auburn hair, just as she had always imagined. Except she wasn't smiling. Her lifelong dream.

Now a nightmare.

'Be careful what you wish for, Suzie,' Kate said.

The flower girl opened the church door and began to walk down the aisle.

Now it was Kate's turn. 'Ready, Dad?' she said, linking arms with her father.

'I'm ready, darling,' he said. 'But are you?'

'As I'll ever be,' Kate said, accepting her fate.

The doors opened and the organ player began playing 'Here Comes the Bride'.

Everyone turned around to see Kate's entrance. Their eyes all widened with joy when they saw how amazing she looked in the dress. She painted a smile on her face and began to walk down the aisle.

At the altar, Kate could see Norman waiting for her. Why the hell was there a part of her that still wanted to turn and run? Now was not the time for ridiculous intrusive thoughts. She needed to get it together. It was too late to do a runner now anyway.

But what the hell was she going to say for her vows? This was her last chance to think of some poetic words before the ceremony began. And her mind was still a complete blank.

Then, before she knew it, she was at the altar and Norman was pulling back her veil. She said a silent prayer that the words would magically come to her when it was her turn to speak.

'Hi,' Norman smiled, when he saw her face.

'Hi,' she said back.

Really? Was that all he had to say to her? Not even, 'You look beautiful?'

Let it go, she told herself. It was her wedding day. There was no need to fester on the small things.

The music stopped and people took their seats as the priest began to speak.

'We are gathered here today in the sight of God to join together Norman Cox and Kate O'Connor in holy matrimony, which is an honourable estate, instituted by God . . .' Father O'Toole began.

His voice was incredibly dull. She had wanted a modern priest who would make things a little more entertaining. Instead, she got one who was doing everything by the book. Literally. He was taking forever to say each word which made every passing second unbearable. He had horrifically bad breath too, and all Kate could smell was the foul odour of gum disease. Suddenly, Elvis didn't seem like such a bad officiant.

'... Marriage should not be entered into unadvisedly or lightly, but reverently and soberly. Into this holy estate, Norman Cox and Kate O'Connor come now to be joined. Therefore, if anyone can show just cause why they may not be lawfully joined together, speak now or for ever hold your peace.'

Kate's heart was in her mouth.

She wanted someone to object. Was Siobhan's fake seizure offer still on the table? She wanted to object to her own wedding, but she was afraid.

Afraid of ruining her own life.

'Wonderful,' Father O'Toole said. 'We will begin with a reading from the Apostle Paul, the first letter to the Corinthians, Chapter 13: Love is patient, love is kind . . .'

Great, a prayer. That gave Kate a few seconds to think of some vows. What did she love about Norman? She needed to make a mental list of some bullet points to guide her.

Why was she completely blanking on everything? Norman literally ticked every box on her list! So why couldn't she name a single point on the list to save her life? All she could think about were the things she loved about Trevor.

But loving Trevor was hopeless.

It wasn't a Corinthians reading she needed.

She needed a Hail Mary.

'. . . through Jesus Christ our Lord, Amen,' Father O'Toole concluded.

'Amen,' everyone replied.

'Oh yes, amen,' Kate said, snapping out of her daze.

'I believe the bride and groom have prepared their own vows, is that right?' Father O'Toole asked.

'Yes,' Norman said, taking a flashcard out of his jacket pocket. He cleared his throat and began to speak. 'Kate, I knew we were perfect for each other the moment we met. You had a toothache, I was a dentist. Need I say more? It certainly doesn't get much more romantic than that. The day I removed your wisdom teeth, I knew you were a keeper. And when I gave you that crown, I knew you'd be my queen. And when we are old together, I will give you a perfect set of veneers to make sure you never stop smiling . . .'

The guests smiled at the words, but Kate immediately cringed. She didn't want to be an old lady with a perfect set of teeth, faking a smile for the rest of her life.

'. . . I can't wait for you to make me the happiest man in the world,' Norman said, wrapping up.

That was a weird thing to say, Kate thought to herself. Was it her job to make him the happiest man in the world? Why not say, 'I can't wait to make you the happiest woman in the world'? Was she overthinking?

Shit.

It was her turn to give her vows. But she didn't have any. And her mind was more blank than ever. All eyes were on her and she couldn't get a word out.

Kate's silence was being noticed. She could hear whispers and coughs in the aisles.

'This is when you tell everyone how much you love me,' Norman joked to the guests, who laughed awkwardly.

'Well . . . I . . .' Kate began to stutter.

Siobhan looked at Natalie and Chloe with wide eyes, but they were helpless. They couldn't speak for her. It was up to Kate to get the words out.

'Eh . . . so . . . sorry, I'm just trying to find the perfect words,' Kate said in a fluster.

'Well, hurry up, you're embarrassing yourself,' Norman whispered.

She felt as if that nightmare she had was becoming a reality. All that was left to happen was for her teeth to start falling out. 'Love . . . love is . . .' Kate waffled. '. . . Well, it's love . . .'

'Kate, get it together. You're making a show of me,' Norman whispered again, louder this time.

It was only then that Kate made her decision.

She couldn't go through with it. A life with Norman wasn't what her heart wanted. She didn't want the life that had been prescribed for her by her mother and society. Even if that meant being alone, it was better than living in another person's version of happily ever after. Kate's days of people pleasing were officially over. But she was about to leave her own wedding early. How on earth was she going to tell Norman and the 200 people watching her?

Her heart was in her mouth.

'Norman, I'm so sorry but I can't mar—' she began.

But before Kate could finish her sentence, she heard the BANG of the church doors swinging open. A gust of wind swept down the aisle, blowing the hat right off Margaret's head. Everyone turned around in shock to see who had caused such an unholy ruckus.

And when Kate turned her head, there he was.

The only man she had ever loved.

The only man she ever would love.

The one and only.

Trevor Fucking Rush.

'STOP THE WEDDING!' Trevor roared, barging in with a piece of paper in his hand.

The crowd gasped as they watched him approach the altar like a madman. Kate almost fainted in disbelief. Surely this wasn't really happening. She looked over at the girls and saw their jaws on the floor.

Had Trevor Rush really just barged into her wedding?

'What is the meaning of this?' Norman said, dumbfounded. 'Who the hell are you?'

'I'm Kate's husband,' Trevor said, arriving at the altar.

'EXCUSE ME?' Norman said, in pure and utter shock.

'Jesus, girls, my fanny's going ninety!' Siobhan whispered.

'Same!' Chloe and Natalie whispered back.

'Our annulment was denied, Freckles,' Trevor said. 'You messed up the paperwork.'

'What?' Kate said, getting her voice back. 'What do you mean?' Kate never messed up paperwork. She loved paperwork!

'The judge rejected our annulment because you signed it incorrectly,' Trevor said, handing her the papers.

'What annulment?' Norman said. 'Somebody tell me what the hell is going on!'

'You almost married a married woman, Norton,' Trevor said

'It's Norman!'

'It's irrelevant,' Trevor said. 'She's married to me, which means you can't legally marry her.'

'Well, I can't marry two people if one of them is already married,' Father O'Toole said.

Kate looked down at the papers and didn't see any problem.

'I don't understand – we filled in all the sections,' she said.

'Yeah, but look at your signature,' Trevor instructed.

Kate looked down to see her signature. *Kate O'Connor.* 'I signed it Kate O'Connor. That's my name.'

'No, it's not. It's Kate Rush. You took my name, Freckles. The judge said the marriage can't be annulled unless your correct legal name is used. So you're going to have to cross out O'Connor and sign it as Kate Rush.'

'What in God's name is he talking about?' Norman screeched.

'Stay out of this, Norbit,' Trevor said.

'IT'S NORMAN!'

'Well, if your fiancée simply signs the annulment with her correct legal name, I can be on my way,' Trevor said, his lips curling into a devious grin. He knew exactly what he was doing.

Trevor Fucking Rush at his finest.

'KATE, WHAT IS THIS BASTARD TALKING ABOUT?' Norman shouted, demanding an explanation.

'He's telling the truth, Norman,' Kate admitted. 'This man is my husband.'

'WHAT? Then sign that fucking paper and get rid of him!'

Kate looked around the church at everyone staring in horror. Her mother in particular had the most unholy grimace she had ever seen. Her dad, however, couldn't help but smile. He nodded his head at her and Kate knew exactly what it meant.

He had just given her away.

'I'll sign the annulment,' Kate said, turning back to Trevor. 'Under one condition . . .'

'What condition?' Trevor replied.

'You have to go on three dates with me,' Kate smirked.

'KATE!' Norman squealed.

'That's three conditions,' Trevor said, raising an eyebrow.

'Those are the terms,' Kate said.

A coy smile painted itself across Trevor's face. 'Well, then I guess I have no choice but to agree,' he said.

'EVERYBODY SHUT UP! WHAT THE HELL IS GOING ON HERE?' Norman cried at the top of his lungs.

Ignoring him, Kate stormed over to her mother and held out her hand. 'Give me the ring.'

'Kate, have you lost your Goddamned mind?' Margaret snapped.

'No, mother. I think I've finally found it,' she said, snatching the bag out of Margaret's hands. She grabbed her phone and slipped Trevor's engagement ring onto her finger where it belonged.

'Yes!' Siobhan said. 'Team Trevor all the way!'

'Kate, you better start fucking explaining yourself!' Norman said.

'Everything he said is true, Norman,' Kate said, walking back over. 'I'm already married. And for the past nine years, I was already engaged. I just didn't know it.'

'Is this some kind of elaborate joke? I made you who you are. Before me you were just another delusional hack going absolutely nowhere!'

Kate felt her entire relationship with Norman flash before her eyes. His words were too specific for it to be a coincidence. *He* was the anonymous troll who had commented on her song. *He* was the one who had caused her to give up on her dream.

'It was you,' Kate said, disgusted. 'You're the one who left that hate comment.'

'It wasn't a hate comment, Kate, it was an *honest* comment. I couldn't let you embarrass yourself with that cringey music!'

'Actually, her song just hit one million streams on YouTube,' Trevor said, a glint of pride in his eyes.

'I don't care if it hits one billion streams!' Norman screamed. 'Kate, are you actually going to throw away what we have for this prick? Are you really that worthless?'

'Call her worthless one more time and I'll knock those veneers clean out of your mouth,' Trevor said, deadly serious.

Norman looked Trevor up and down. 'Not if I knock you out first!' he shot back, lunging forward with a poorly aimed fist.

Trevor was poised and ready, however, side-stepping to avoid the clumsy attack with ease.

Overcommitted and off-balance, Norman tripped over his own feet, falling face-first towards the ground. The crowd held their collective breath as he plummeted, the silence shattered by the splintering of Norman's two front teeth on the hard church floor.

'MY VENEERS!' he cried, clutching his mouth as the chipped porcelain abandoned his smile.

'Hmm . . . that was easier than I thought,' Trevor shrugged.

'How could you do this to me, you bitch?' Norman roared as he desperately tried to pick his teeth up off the floor. 'Are you not even going to apologize?'

'Well, Norman,' Kate said, looking down on him. 'I'm sorry you feel that way.'

'Ready, darling?' Trevor asked, turning to Kate.

'Abso-fucking-lutely.'

Kate took Trevor's hand as they darted out of the church's grand entrance and hopped into their red getaway car. Behind them, the congregation spilled out, in a colourful flurry, Margaret still trying to get her hat back on her head.

Norman emerged from the mass, still cradling his two front teeth in his hand. His roar of outrage was drowned by the Mustang's mighty growl as Trevor ignited the engine with a wicked smirk. Before anyone could stop them, he slammed the accelerator and the two were bolting towards freedom.

'Oh my God,' Kate said, pumping with adrenaline. 'Trevor, how did you even find me?'

'Are you kidding?' he laughed. 'You wouldn't shut up about the Church of the Sacred Heart in Donnybrook. Maybe subconsciously you always wanted me to come and save you.'

'Maybe you're right.'

'I was serious about your song hitting one million streams by the way.'

'You mean *our* song?'

'The first of many, I hope,' Trevor said. 'Charlie said a lot of record labels are interested in hearing more.'

'Then we'll just have to give them more.'

'And Charlie also wants Natalie's phone number,' Trevor laughed.

'That can certainly be arranged,' Kate smiled.

'But you know what this means though, don't you?'

'Back to Vegas?'

'Nope. The Vegas curse is broken. We can go wherever we want.'

'As long as I'm with you, I don't care where we go,' Kate said, her heart full of genuine joy. 'But Trevor, what made you come back?'

'Vinnie called to tell me the annulment was denied. He told me what you said.'

'And I meant every word of it. I love you, Trevor. I always have and I always will.'

'Well, you haven't won me back just yet, Freckles,' he said, playfully. 'You have three dates to make me admit that I'm still in love with you.'

'And that's exactly what I intend to do,' she smiled. 'Get ready for the honeymoon of your dreams.'

Kate felt her phone vibrating like crazy, and she immediately knew why. She opened the group chat to see exactly what she expected.

The Four Lokos

> **Chloe:** Kate, that was iconic!!!

> **Siobhan:** Obsessed!!!

> #TeamTrevor all the way baby!

> **Natalie:** norman who???

> **Siobhan:** My fanny's still throbbin tbh

> **Chloe:** So proud of you Kate!!!

Kate: Thanks girls, I love you all so much!

See you after my honeymoon x

Kate smiled uncontrollably as she closed the group chat and turned to face Trevor.

'So what's the plan, Freckles?' he asked.

'You know what?' Kate smiled as she took the clips out of her hair. 'Why don't we just see what happens?'

'It's nice to finally have you back, Kate.'

Trevor smiled and leaned over to kiss his wife. After nine long years, Kate was finally back in a red Mustang beside her ride or die, with no plan whatsoever.

And she had never felt more free.

But she couldn't help but laugh at the one thing she had always known in her heart and soul ever since she was a little girl.

Because Kate's wedding truly was the happiest day of her life.

Acknowledgements

Firstly, my deepest gratitude goes to my incredible parents, Kathleen and Finian. Thank you for being the most wonderful parents anyone could ever ask for. Without your unwavering support, this book would never have been written.

A massive thank you to my powerhouse agent Marianne Gunn O'Connor who believed in my writing from day one. You have literally changed my life and made my dreams a reality. I cannot thank you enough.

To the dedicated team at MGOC – Vicki Satlow, Patrick Lynch, Dan Bolger and Alison Walsh – thank you for your ongoing hard work and for helping to get *Hitched* to where it is today.

Huge thanks to my sisters Jessica and Lisa, and my cousins Kelly, Mandy and Emma for encouraging me to go for this idea. Your insights into what it's like to be a woman in Vegas were invaluable and had a huge impact on the narrative.

To Francesca Pathak at Pan Macmillan – thank you for believing in *Hitched* from the moment you read it. You are an absolute dream to work with and I know I am incredibly lucky to have someone like you championing me as a new voice in fiction.

Thank you also to Charlotte Tennant for your fantastic attention to detail during the entire editing process. A warm

Acknowledgements

acknowledgment to Christina Webb and Ross Jamieson for their invaluable contributions as well.

And to the broader Pan Mac family – Natasha, Ana, Rosie, Bríd, Cormac, Lara, Kinza, and the many others – your outstanding work is so truly appreciated and I know *Hitched* is in the best of hands.

To all the booksellers who have embraced and promoted my work: thank you for uplifting my voice as an emerging author, it means the absolute world to me.

And finally, to everyone who picks up a copy of *Hitched* – from the bottom of my heart, thank you. I hope reading about Kate's wild hen party brings as much joy to you as writing it did for me.

About the Author

J. F. Murray is an Irish writer based in Gibbstown, a small Gaeltacht area in County Meath. From the age of sixteen, Murray began writing screenplays and directing short films, which led to a Most Original Award at Fresh Film Festival. After graduating from Trinity College, Murray moved to Los Angeles and began working as a digital content specialist. When the Covid pandemic hit in 2020, Murray was determined to use the lockdown as an opportunity to pursue storytelling full-time and fell in love with writing again. Murray has also gained a following on TikTok (@j.f.murray) with a unique brand of comedy sketches.

OUT NOW

FLING

The next one might be closer than you think . . .

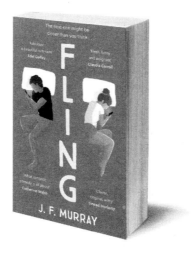

Tara loved Colin at first sight. Colin loved Tara at
first fight. That's when they knew they were
meant for each other.

But after six years, their marriage has started to crumble.
Unable to recapture the spark they once had, it seems
it's all over. Until they meet their 100% match on a
controversial new dating app: Fling . . .

'Clever, original, witty and great insight into marriage
and the problems that come when communication
breaks down' – **Sinéad Moriarty**

Turn the page to read an extract now . . .

Chapter 1

'Let's go home,' said Tara, feeling as if her life had just ended.

To her right, her husband Colin sat rigidly, trying to process the devastating news. Behind his desk, Dr White was explaining that the embryo transfer had been unsuccessful and that their third attempt at IVF had failed.

Time seemed to stand still for Tara in that moment. All she could hear was a strange ringing in her ears, as if a bomb had just been detonated. She couldn't take in what Dr White was saying, just the piercing hum of defeat.

But Tara didn't need to listen to know what was being said. She knew the spiel off by heart at this stage. She had known as soon as she saw the same tired, apologetic expression on Dr White's face that her dream of motherhood would remain just that.

A dream.

'Go home?' Colin said, turning to her. 'We literally just got here.'

'I know you must be disappointed, Tara, but rest assured, there is still hope,' Dr White said unconvincingly, as if reading from a teleprompter.

'I'm sorry, doctor, but I can't do this any more,' Tara said, picking up her handbag. 'I don't mean to be rude but I just really want to go home.'

'Tara, we need to know what our options are,' Colin said, visibly frustrated by Tara's eagerness to leave.

'Colin, we know how this goes. This is the part where we start everything again from scratch. Back to square one.'

'Well, many couples don't have a successful IVF treatment until their fourth or sometimes fifth try. In fact, we had one couple who weren't successful until their eighth round,' Dr White explained.

Tara winced at the thought. She couldn't bear the idea of going through the entire ordeal once more, let alone multiple times. She had retained a glimmer of hope after their first and second attempts failed but there was only so much disappointment she could take. Colin had kept telling her that the third time would be the charm. He had almost convinced her of it. Yet here she was, reliving the worst experience of her life for the third time in a row.

'Doctor, I think it's time we accepted that I'm not meant to be a mother,' Tara said with a heavy heart.

'Tara, stop that kind of talk,' Colin said.

'Oh come on, Colin, I'm almost thirty-seven. My eggs are basically tumbleweeds at this point.'

Dr White almost laughed, but Colin shot him a look of disapproval.

'Tara, it's only our third attempt. Come on, the fourth time's the charm!'

'You say that about every attempt, Colin. In a few years, you'll be saying the fifteenth time lucky. We've spent thirty grand on this already. We need to stop throwing good money after bad,' Tara said, still eyeing the door to leave. She felt smothered.

'Well, maybe they have a loyalty card programme or something,' Colin said, giving Dr White a hopeful glance.

'Oh yeah, Colin, we'll just get a stamp on our way out and

our next one will be free. We're talking about my eggs, not a cup of coffee,' Tara said, rolling her eyes. 'They don't care about our loyalty anyway. They sold us all of those stupid add-ons that made absolutely no difference.'

'Well, you did opt for the Premium Package,' Dr White explained.

'Yeah, and what do we have to show for it? I mean, for ten grand a pop, you could have thrown in a feckin' tote bag. Or a top that says "I tried IVF and all I got was this lousy T-shirt",' Tara said, frustrated.

'Tara, this is serious,' Colin said, mortified.

Tara knew she was being ridiculous. But she also knew if she didn't laugh, she would cry. And Tara was done crying. She had been through this rigmarole enough times to see how farcical it all was. She had every right to make jokes because that's exactly what the whole ordeal felt like.

One big joke.

'I completely understand your frustration, Tara,' Dr White said. 'But you can't make an omelette without breaking a few eggs.'

'Well, I'm sorry, doctor, but I ordered my eggs fertilized, not scrambled,' Tara said, standing up. 'Now, I'm sorry but I really just want to go home.' Tara turned and walked out of the room, her mind fully made up. Colin sighed and sluggishly got up off his chair.

'I'm sure she'll come around eventually,' Dr White said to Colin.

'You clearly don't know my wife,' Colin said, as he followed Tara to the car.

On the drive back, Tara was trying to process the news in silence. She didn't want to talk about it, she just wanted to go home. As she leaned against the window, twirling her ash-blonde hair, she noticed the sky was endlessly blue, teeming with pastel perfection. It annoyed her. Of course the sky would be clear on the one day she wanted rain. She wanted the sky to weep because she had no tears left. At least if there was a cloud, she could tell herself something about silver linings.

After the first IVF treatment didn't take, Tara was an emotional wreck. Even though she had never actually got pregnant, Tara mourned the many million possibilities that would never come to be. The second failed attempt was similar, but those tears were from anger, not despair. This time felt different, however. She didn't feel sad or angry. In fact, she didn't feel anything. It was like there was a void in her chest, an overwhelming emptiness. She suddenly found herself questioning her entire belief system. Tara's world view was complex at times, but if there was one belief that anchored her entire philosophy, it was her belief in destiny.

Tara truly believed there was a path for everyone and that one's life was predetermined by fate. She refused to accept the scientific theory that life was just random chaos. In her opinion, such a world view made life completely meaningless. After all, the universe had begun with chaos yet somehow formed spontaneous order. That was all the proof she needed that there was some force out there greater than her. Her father Paddy Fitzsimons had been a devout Catholic up until he passed away, and her mother Shannon was a renowned psychic healer by trade. Tara was therefore an unusual mix of religious and spiritual. She believed in a higher power but she saw it more as energy flowing rather than a bearded man in the sky. She knew she didn't have all the answers but she believed in belief. Whether one chose to call it fate, God's plan, kismet, predestination or destiny, it all came back to what her mother always told her.

Everything happens for a reason.

But what was the reason for this? Why was the universe preventing her dream from coming true? There was only one reason Tara could think of. The universe was quite clearly telling her that being a mother was not her destiny and she had no choice but to listen. It was a difficult pill to swallow but Tara knew denying it wouldn't get her anywhere. Trying IVF a fourth time would only be swimming against the currents of fate. She couldn't put herself through the ordeal again. But even though she had told Colin from day one that she would only try three times, she knew he wouldn't accept her decision.

Her mind began to reach backwards, to the night she first met Colin. She was a student at Trinity College Dublin at the time, but she always returned home to Galway to work weekends at O'Malley's pub. One fateful November night, a young man walked into O'Malley's while she was working and ordered a pint of Guinness. She expected to see a much older man, but when she turned around, there he was.

The man of her dreams.

Stupidly handsome, short brown hair, and ocean eyes deep enough to drown in.

That was the first time Tara experienced what she considered to be synchronicity, a strange gut feeling, like a mix of déjà vu and women's intuition. She had butterflies in her stomach, goosebumps along her arms and a tingle on the back of her neck. She felt like she had tuned into the universe's hidden frequency and was suddenly connected to the deeper vibrations of life. It was her spiritual compass that let her know she was on destiny's right path. Like she was with the right person in the right place at the right time.

She fell for Colin there and then. By the time his Guinness had settled, she was already his. 'Of all the pubs in all the towns in all of Ireland, you had to walk into mine,' she had told him. Against all rationality, she had thrown caution to the wind and got on the back of his motorcycle to Nimmo's Pier. When he kissed her in the shimmering moonlight, she began to melt in his arms and lost herself in sweet consensual surrender. She had snuck him into her bedroom later that night. Even though they had just met, she was ready to give herself to him completely, the way she would for the rest of her life. Her feelings weren't logical at the time, but when Tara got her gut feeling, she knew it was fate whispering that she was on the right track.

But Tara had never once got her gut feeling during the entire IVF process. She knew in her soul it wasn't meant to be. And even though Tara's dream of being a mother was over, she knew she would pick herself back up and find a new dream. The entire experience of constant failure had sucked the life out of her. She needed a dream that brought her endless joy, not endless disappointment. It was time to turn the page on failure and begin a new chapter of infinite possibility.